I0582128

# GODSLAYER

NEW YORK TIMES BESTSELLING AUTHOR

## JA HUSS

# GODSLAYER

NEW YORK TIMES BESTSELLING AUTHOR

## JA HUSS

Copyright © 2025 by JA Huss
ISBN: 978-1-957277-39-4

No part of this book may be reproduced or resold in any form or by any
electronic or mechanical means, including information storage and
retrieval systems, without written permission from the author, except for
the use of brief quotations in a book review.

This is a work of fiction. Names, characters, businesses, places, events and
incidents are either the products of the author's imagination or used in a
fictitious manner. Any resemblance to actual persons, living or dead, or
actual events is purely coincidental.

Cover Design by JA Huss

# ABOUT THE BOOK

*Spark is light. Spark is power*
*Spark is deadly.*

*Tyse never asked to play* the Game of Gods, but Delta demands loyalty.

With Clara at his side, Tyse is thrust into a brutal world of augments—humans forged to serve and destroy. Each step forward pushes them closer to becoming something more—a force Clara can feel but doesn't fully understand. A future that terrifies her as much as it draws her in.

Day by day, the man Clara pledged her loyalty to becomes more and more a stranger. But in the Game of Gods, survival demands sacrifice.

Clara has already done that once—she's certain she can do it again.

*Jasina and Finn left Tau City in ruins*, vowing to end the Extractions by destroying every god's tower. But the train line hides dark truths. Forgotten people cling to survival. Towers rise from the ruins of erased cities. And deep in the shadows, a godlike AI watches, weaving its own agenda.

Jasina has always been the strong one, the leader. But the train line holds secrets that cut deeper than she's prepared for. Truths about spark. About the gods. About herself.

And Finn—the man burdened by his failures—is rising to find his strength.

But can Jasina ever fully trust him?

*Godslayer is an epic, spicy, and angst-filled Romantasy that begs the question ... how well do you really know your God? And how much are you willing to sacrifice to save him?*

# INSIDE THE PAGES YOU'LL FIND:

Soul-Bonding
Adult Spice
Power Imbalance
Morally Grey
Impossible Love
Anti-hero
Portal Magic
Ride or Die

# DID YOU KNOW...

Sparkopia was awarded Best of the Year from Audible Editors in 2024 for Romantasy!

# PART 1

### The Augment's Creed

I am the executioner and the death.

I am the dark soldier, standing in the blood of the fallen.

The spool of Source, the thread of Spark—I am the machine made flesh.

I walk the hush that follows ruin.

I am not the response. I am the overwrite.

A weapon of the sandy sea.

In the image I am made and, in the image, I will unmake.

For thine is the kingdom made in sand.

And thy rule was made in wind.

And in the wind, as in the days of dark imprisonment, the new gods rose as tall as the hollow towers.

And in this rising, they conquered.

Swept the land of everything and left it clean like a bone.

And on that bone, was born I.

The executioner and the death.

—From the Field Operations Manual: Sweep-Class Augments (declassified fragment, p. 1)

# TYSE

*The sweet scent of oranges* drifts up from the black sand as Clara's fingers swirl it around, making designs that look a lot like the ones that light up on her skin when she's in the mood to show her spark.

She's sitting in between my legs and I've got her captured in my arms, hugging her shoulders so I can keep her as close to me as possible.

We're just chilling on the beach, looking at the moons.

Our last night here in Delta City.

Clara tips her head back, tilting to the side so she can see me. "I will never get over this smell. And I know, *I know*. It's dead crabs, or whatever."

"Cretions," I say. "Microscopic—"

"Yeah, yeah, yeah. Ya told me. It just smells good. I can't believe this is how you grew up. It's like living in a fairy tale. A black-sand beach, a fantasy city on the edge of the ocean, and a god in a tower you can actually talk to!" She laughs. "What a concept." Then she sighs. "I'm gonna miss this place."

I don't say anything, just stare out at the sea, watching the cyan-blue spark float around in the air like embers comin' off a fire. She can't see the spark floatin' all around us. No one can, apparently. Not even Anneeta. I went to see her yesterday, just to say goodbye, really. She talked non-stop for like ten minutes straight about absolutely nothin' I was interested in.

I'm really glad she's stuck here and not on the team for 'Mission Kill Finn Scott' because ten minutes was my limit.

I had three questions, though. Did she see the spark that clogs the air like ash all around us, which was a no. The second one was about dreamin'. She says she doesn't dream, but she admitted that she doesn't really sleep, either. And the third was how often she needed to eat back in Tau City.

She gave me a weird look for that one. Not because she was suspicious about my particular appetite for spark, but because she didn't want to talk about it. The answer was what I figured. Clara told me how many Spark Maidens were sent into her tower—she was number nine. And Anneeta is like seven years old, or around there, so it averages out to a little more than one a year.

Clara says there were long stretches between Extractions, so eating the Spark Maidens wasn't a plan—it was a *need*.

I'm not a god. I'm an augment. Human once, something in between now. So I'm not gonna eat Clara. But Delta's last words to me up in the tower were pretty ominous.

*All gods need food.*

Of course, he blinked out immediately after sayin' this so there was no chance in askin' any follow-up questions about that statement. And even though I did try and see him again, the bodyguard at the door might as well have been the door itself. When I approached the tower yesterday afternoon, he was shakin' his head at me from fifty feet away.

Delta isn't gonna explain anythin'.

The mission—Kill Finn Scott—appeared on my augment screen the moment I left the tower that night Delta showed me the map of the train line. It's got all the particulars. And the map, which is important. But it doesn't have a 'contact me' form.

No digital address, no high-wave number to call in

emergencies, not even a task completion checklist like we had in the Sweep.

It's just a map and the directive: Kill Finn Scott.

There's a little asterisk after that, which reads "and his trashy woman sidekick"—which I did not mention to Clara. I mean, I didn't mention any of this to Clara. I told her it's an exploratory mission to check out some terror attacks. But I'm certainly not gonna tell her that Lover Boy has moved on.

It's not a lie, these omissions. Not exactly. That Finn fucker *is* a terrorist because he's blowin' up towers on the train line.

Anyway. The point is that Delta has pretty much washed his hands of me. Clearly, he doesn't want updates or he'd have given me a way to contact him.

And this is a bigger issue for me because it implies that he's set himself up for plausible deniability.

Teenage me would've been pretty pissed off about this. But it's classic Delta. He's a narcissistic, egomaniacal asshole.

Does he care about the humans who inhabit his city?

Sure, I guess. The way a shepherd cares about his flock of sheep. They are a product. They give him wool and meat.

Delta's interest in me is tied to what I can do for him.

I might be *in* the Game of Gods, but there's no way that thing sees me as an equal. Or as a player.

"You're awfully quiet tonight." Clara's sweet voice spills over the sound of the waves lapping up onto the sand.

"Just thinkin' about tomorrow."

She turns around, still between my legs, and smiles at me. "Are you nervous?"

"No," I tell her. And I'm not. "I'm just wonderin' what his game is, ya know?"

"Delta?"

"Yeah. He's up to something."

She narrows her eyes, but only a little. "You think it's a setup?"

I shrug. "I don't know what it is. That's the problem with gods, right? They don't like to explain themselves. And I'm just not that man anymore."

She touches my face with her soft hand. Sliding her palm right up against my cheek. "A soldier who takes orders?"

Clara is very smart. She reads between the lines. I like that about her.

"Yeah," I nod. "I don't wanna work for him."

She considers this as we stare into each other's eyes. She's always looking for more of me. I like that about her too. "Well," she says, her words soft and meant to soothe. She gets to her feet and offers me her hand. "Then I guess we'll have to come up with a plan."

I take her hand and allow her to pull me up, even though I'm much too heavy for her to pull up. "What kind of plan?"

"You know... the old escape-the-evil-overlord plan."

"Oh, *that* plan." I smile, keeping hold of her hand as we turn in unison and walk towards the stairs that wind up the side of the cliff to the city above.

She gives my hand a squeeze and then I let go, turnin' around and bendin' down a little so she can hop on my back. She does this without comment. We've come down to the beach four times now and each time I've carried her back up.

Not once has she declined the ride.

Not once did she feel heavy.

"I guess this is your lot in life, Mr. Saarinen."

"What's that?"

"To carry me up a million flights of stairs."

I can live with it.

*EVERY TIME CLARA* **enters our apartment**, she makes a tiny gasp. The first week we were here, they were bigger gasps, but she's tempered them back since then. And now, it's mostly just a little sigh.

The view. She can't get over it.

It's nice, I will say that. Delta did set us up with a top-notch apartment for our stay here. Penthouse level and fully furnished. And that view *is* stunnin'. You can see the water, but it's not really the ocean that makes the view special. It's everythin'—the city itself. I guess I had forgotten how beautiful Delta City was. I guess I'd just been stuck on the far end of things for so long, I assumed all cities were a collection of steel and glass surrounded by sand.

That's not what it looks like here. It's a lot like the way Clara described her city with tall towers made of stone and brick. And where there aren't towers, there are smaller homes built into the side of the cliffs. The whole city is on a slant with Delta's tower at the top and everything else spilling down the mountain towards the beach on one side, and the valley on the other.

All the roads are cobbled with black-sand bricks and it's a nice contrast to the towers and houses, which are every possible shade of gray. The rooftops are mostly shiny copper. Which is not an easy thing to maintain with the salt water in the air. Roof polishing is a mega industry here because Delta doesn't tolerate patina on his rooftops.

Our building is two streets up from the edge of the cliff

and our living room has a window that spans a hundred-and-eighty degrees so we see a little bit of everything. Even the tower at the top. This is the view that makes Clara gasp and sigh.

Beautiful Delta City.

I don't like him but he does keep the place nice. I would not say Tau City is ugly. I mean, in its own right, it's pretty fuckin' spectacular. But compared to this place, it's a slum.

Clara walks over to the window and presses her face against it. "I'll never get tired of this view."

I close the door and walk up behind her. Looking out. In addition to the water, and the night sky, and the moons, and the city lights, and the tower, I also see the spark.

Sometimes it's so thick, I can't see anythin' else.

Other times it's so thin, it's like a mist.

Tonight, it's something in between. And overlaying all that spark is the overlay itself. The Sweep Army overlay. That should not be there in the first place, let alone work.

It covers everythin' if I let it. Meanin', it labels things. It gives me information about everythin' I'm seeing unless I modify the settings. Tonight, I've got it toggled to about half-strength so it only highlights things like the phase of the moons, or the cycles of the tides when I look at the sky or the sea.

When I glance down at the city it gives me the names of the streets and buildings, if they have one. If I'm walkin' down the street, and have it turned all the way on, it gives me facial recognition. I can identify every single person in this city just by lookin' at them.

Why it's doing this, I have no idea.

I wish I'd been introduced to the other augments that have come home. But either they've been redeployed by Delta or he's keepin' them secret because I asked around at the parties Clara and I have been attendin', and no one knows of any augments but me.

If I didn't already know that there were several little gods down there in that school on the beach, I might let it go. But I do know they're there, and *someone* had to bring them here.

"Wow, you're really distracted tonight, Tyse."

I look down at Clara and shrug. "Sorry. I've got a lot on my mind, I guess."

She turns, pressing her back against the window. Then she walks her fingertips up my arms and rests her hands on my shoulders. "Anything you want to talk about?"

"No. I'm just thinkin'."

"Well." Her smile is real and big. "I'm going to take a shower. I don't know what 'deployment' actually entails, but I'm assuming that hot water will be a luxury."

Which is true, but not for her. Clara Birch can heat water with the spark inside her body just by standin' next to it. But she's not saying this to be literal. She's extending an invitation.

She pats my chest, then slides around me, heading for the bedroom.

I watch her with side eye, grinning a little.

This mission is gonna be a test for us. A big test.

But the mission doesn't start until tomorrow.

So I follow her into the bedroom.

*LATER IN THE EVENING*, after the showering, and lovemakin', and the easy talkin' that always comes afterward. After the sleepiness, and the holdin', and final kiss of the day—I lie in bed lookin' up at the ceiling and see somethin' that isn't there.

Except it is. Because I'm lookin' at it.

In my old room, back in Tau City and inside the god's tower ruin, there was a lot of graffiti on the ceiling. Specifically, a tower with a banner and the words, 'Sparktopia was here' written across it in grungy letters. I looked at that image and those words every night for seven years wonderin' about them.

Who got up there, lyin' on their back on some makeshift scaffold, and painted the tower with the banner and the words?

And why?

I guess it's easy enough to figure out a 'why'. People like to leave a mark. They like to feel bigger and more important than maybe they really are. So it could a message to the future. A message to me. Or to whoever is living in that room right now.

Or maybe they're one of those creative fucks. Like the people who lived down the tenth-floor hallway from me. They were always paintin' murals on the walls near the stairs. Sometimes it was messages. Political, social, commentary about life in the tower. But other times it was just pictures.

I never paid much attention to the murals or the people who painted them, they were just something that was there.

That's how I felt about Sparktopia.

It was just... there.

But isn't it a little bit weird, that here in Delta City,

thousands of miles away, that very tower is on my ceiling again?

Not literally, of course. That would be easier to explain, actually.

It's there... energetically.

That's the word I'm using to describe the overlay into other... dimensions? Realms? Times? I'm not really sure what these places are, I just know they're both real and not in the same instant.

So I lie here, looking up at my ceilin', And that very same tower, with that very same banner and those very same words, is staring right back at me as a glowin' cyan-blue outline.

*Sparktopia is here.*

And I think... it's kinda right. Because the air in Delta City is clogged with it. The spark is everywhere. Even though they can't see it the way I do, every single person living here is breathin' it in, all the time, all at once.

Sparktopia.

It means 'spark place'. I looked it up. It's a made-up word, but the suffix –topia comes from the root tópos, which means place. One thing about Delta City that's nice is the infonet. Tau City had a good one as well, but oddly enough, Delta's net is comparatively unregulated. I did a lot of searches to test the boundaries and never once did it refuse to give me an answer or give me fucked-up results that made no sense.

So I found that word tópos, which I had never heard of, but the entry explaining it was... well, *odd*. Because it comes from a language called 'Greek'. And I have never heard of this language called 'Greek'.

Which led to more searches and what Delta's infonet spit

out at me was nothing short of confusing. Because it was an entire history that I had never been told about.

And I'm not saying I'm the world's most educated man or anythin' like that, but I am very fuckin' educated. My entire childhood was spent in Delta's home for boys and it was a lot of schoolin'. A lot of history, a lot of math, a lot of everythin'. And it didn't stop when I was sent to the Sweep. There were years of school after that and almost all of it was history and culture.

So how didn't I know that the cities along the train line are named after the Greek alphabet? Delta is a letter. And so is Tau. So where the hell has this Greek language been hidin' that I haven't heard of it? It kinda blew my mind.

Anyway, that's not even the important part.

The important part is that the tower and words on my ceilin' aren't really here in this realm. It's a glimpse into somewhere else. And I can't tell if this is just due to my augments comin' fully online again, or because of the synergistic bond between Clara and me, or because this sparktopia thing is following me somehow.

I can't tell. I just can't tell.

If that's where it ended, I'd probably let it go. But it seems to just be gettin' started because I can see all kinds of other places now. I don't need Clara or Anneeta to do this. These places, they're just... everywhere.

Even here, in this bedroom.

Overlays are controlled by subtle eye movements. Sometimes, very elaborate commands need a head gesture or even a hand gesture—but combination moves like that are mostly reserved for battle.

When you're just lookin' at somethin', ya only use your eyes. A twitch here, a slide there, a blink or two, and it gets the job done.

Crossing my eyes in a certain way and focusing on a particular depth of field is what reveals the other side of the veil. Or veils, as it is. Because there are a lot of them.

So I do that and watch from the bed as people move about the room in another dimension. It's a husband and wife this time, but they're not the only ones. Or, I should say, that's not the only place that exists side by side in this space I call the bedroom.

There are a lot of worlds out there. And while not all of them are like this one with a tower in this exact space that goes up this high, there are dozens—maybe even hundreds or thousands that are *exactly* like this one with just different people substituted for Clara and me.

Sometimes birds will fly by. Just fuckin' flap their cyan-blue outlined wings and fly on by, not even six feet away from me. So there's no tower with a penthouse apartment in that place.

When I go outside, it's chaos if I let the veil bleed happen. All these other worlds start competin' for my attention. It's too much if I don't filter it, and filtering it takes more energy than I care to expend, so mostly I just turn it off. Which is surprisingly easy to do because while I was messin' with the ocular control panel, I found a fuckin' button for it in a hidden screen called—wait for it—Sparktopia.

It's a light blue tab labeled 'extend' when the worlds aren't there, which then switches to white and says 'reduce' when they are.

A button that opens dimensional screens that I can use to interact.

And by interact, I mean steal spark. Because that's all I've used it for, if ya don't count spyin' on people.

What a crazy fuckin' world.

Stealin' spark is how I saved Clara and Anneeta on the

train ride to Delta City. I didn't press the button, obviously. At that time, the augments weren't working like they are now. But the moment we came up from the underground, the moment we crossed into the Alphas, the spark was pervasive enough to activate the ability to see through veils, I guess.

And then I just... drained those spark people. Took all their spark for myself. It wasn't even hard. I didn't even have to get up from the bench seat I was on, holding a dying Clara in my arms.

It just... came to me. Like it knew I needed it, so it just came to me.

I want to go ask Delta about all this shit and what it means. But if he knows it's happenin', then fuck him for not speakin' up in the first place. And if he doesn't, it's definitely in my best interest to keep it that way.

Because those last words of his kinda haunt me.

*All gods need food.*

He thinks Clara is my food.

And she's not.

I mean, I'm a hundred percent certain I *could* use her as food.

But I don't think I'll ever have to.

Not when I can steal it from anyone, at any time, from any goddamn place I want.

# CLARA

*E*ver since I arrived in Delta City my dreams have been mesmerizingly vivid.

I don't recall ever having thoughts about dreams back in my old Tau City. I know I had them, but I never woke up thinking, Wow! That was cool, or weird, or interesting. But every day—every single morning—I wake up in awe of the pictures, and thoughts, and stories running inside my head while I'm sleeping.

It's amazing. And entertaining. But also, strange.

Where did all these stories come from? I didn't read much back in my old life. When I was younger, I did because it was required. But honestly, I wasn't a book girl. I was a party girl. Looking back, it feels a little shallow. But I was a Spark Maiden for nearly a decade so my life revolved around Spark Maiden duties and there was never an event on my schedule called Book Club.

Though, I do know those clubs existed. The tea party ladies would often talk of them at luncheons, but I never participated in the conversation, nor did I feel left out of it.

The point is, I haven't been collecting stories in my head. I haven't had grand adventures like the ones now playing out in my dreams. I mean, aside from the dramatic walk across dimensions and escape from Tau City, that is.

These stories are different. They're… tales. I dunno. That's the only way I can describe them. Stories about things that don't belong to my life here in this world.

So where do they come from?

"What are you thinking about?"

I turn, smiling at the man in bed next to me. "What?"

"I've been watching you stare up at the ceiling for the last five minutes. And those faces of consternation are killing me. What is goin' through that head of yours now?"

My grin grows as I turn on my side so I can see him properly. "Dreams. I was thinking about dreams."

"What about them?"

"I've been having some really good ones."

His eyebrows go up. "About me?" Then he gives them a waggle.

"Well, yes. But not in the way you're hoping."

He's lying on his back, side eyeing me. "What am I doing, if not charmin' the pants off ya?"

"It's an adventure. We're doing... I dunno. Cool stuff like exploring caves, and fighting rogue factions, and finding treasure. And it's weird because I was just thinking that I've never dreamed like this before. And I don't know where the stories are coming from."

"It's the trip. We're leaving today so you're... apprehensive, maybe."

"Yeah, probably. It's just... the details, Tyse. They're so intense, and rich, and colorful. It's like I'm really there."

"Hmmm," he hums. I like this sound he makes. It's something between a rumble and a growl. "Tell me about one of them."

"OK." I pause to think. "Well, the one I just woke up from was about a ship."

"Like a godship?"

"Yeah. Which is weird, right? Because I haven't even seen one yet."

"They're few and far between. Very few were made and

even fewer have survived. Delta only has two and they're almost never in the harbor."

"Right. So how did all these details just appear in my head about godships? Because I can see the sails, and the ropes, and the decking. And down below, there's living quarters. Like this apartment, but inside a boat! Isn't that crazy?"

He rolls over onto his side, reaching for me. The next thing I know, I'm right up against his chest, looking up into his blue eyes. They're glowing—they're almost always glowing now—but not brightly. "You've got a good imagination, I guess."

"Maybe. Maybe one day I'll see one and I'll laugh, because they don't look anything like how I imagined. But it would be crazy if they did."

"Completely crazy," he says. And then he's kissing me and I forget all about dreams and godships, and think only about the man in bed with me now.

My one.

He's my one.

And this adventure we're starting today is going to be the experience of a lifetime.

LATER, *after Tyse and I are done* messing around in bed, we shower and mess around in there too. But after all that, he gets dressed quickly and leaves, saying he's got some loose ends to tie up before we go.

I sit at my dressing table, wearing a robe made of silk and looking into the mirror as I brush my hair. I think about this adventure before us. I mean, I understand it's a deployment, and there's some kind of terrorist activity happening, or whatever—so it's a mission. But the fact that I'm an integral part of it makes it all feel very much like a dream story.

When Tyse came back from talking to Delta a few nights ago, he told me about his visit and his orders. At first, my stomach sunk with dread because I thought that meant he would be leaving and I would be staying behind.

But that's not what it means. Because he and I, we're partners.

Even Delta knows it.

We work together. We're a team.

It's better than marriage, if you ask me. Marriage is about settling down and planting roots. Deployment partners are about getting each other through things. Serious things. Maybe even life or death things.

Which I had never craved in my past life. I never imagined myself a heroine. But now that the opportunity has arisen, I can see it. I can see myself as one of those strong women in books.

And anyway, Tyse and I, we've already made this pledge to each other. We did it that very first day I walked into his tower in Tau City. We were in the restaurant, after my health center visit, and he said, "If I have your back, then you must have mine."

I agreed and that was that.

Partners.

The doorbell pulls me away from my thoughts and I get up, hugging the dressing gown tightly around me and tying the sash, as I go to the door. When I open it, I find a porter. Which is pretty much the same thing as a runner back in

Tyse's Tau City. They deliver things. And this one has his hands so full, he has to peek over them to see me.

"Oh, dear," I say, opening the door wide. "Come in, please. Put them anywhere."

And as he does that, I go into the bedroom and fish a copper coin out of the little cup that Tyse has been dropping them into each evening when he takes off his pants.

The money here is different than back in Tau City. The coppers are brilliant and shiny, and have a picture of Delta on the front and a godship on the back.

I stare at it for a moment, then laugh. "That's where it came from. *The money.*" I shake my head, amazed at how a tiny detail, like a picture of a godship on the back of a coin, could sprout an entire story inside my head while I was sleeping.

Back in the living room, the porter has arranged all the boxes on the table in front of the couch and is smiling at me with his hands behind his back when I enter. The coppers are the smallest denomination of coin in the city, but they are worth a lot because there are two kinds of money here. The coins, all made of metals like copper, and silver, and gold. And the papers, which are made of some kind of cloth that I've never seen before. The coins are the god's money. So any coin is better than the paper.

The porter accepts my copper with a smile, and a bow, and a heartfelt, "Thank you." Then he leaves, and I turn to the stack of packages.

They are all wrapped up in brown paper and tied with light blue satin ribbons. I know Tyse thinks that Delta the god, and by extension, Delta City, is too traditional and controlling, but even he has to admit, this city is very charming. Absolutely, unequivocally overflowing with charm.

And these packages are just more proof. The way they're wrapped reminds me of home. Because we didn't have glossy shopping bags and nothing was covered in plastic in my original Tau City. We wrapped presents in linens, or silks, or thick, handmade papers.

That's how things are done here in the Tower District of Delta City as well. I haven't seen all the other districts, but Tyse says it's far less traditional on the other side of the tower where the slope of the mountain spills into a lush valley of modern neighborhoods and businesses, instead of the ocean.

But I don't really have any desire to see that side of the city. I like tradition. Especially when it comes to package wrappings.

I take a seat on the couch and one by one, I pull each package into my lap and read the tags. They are all for me, so I open them.

It's all supplies for the trip. Little trinkets like a pocket knife, or a small rod of some sort that comes with a handful of shredded metal. The handwritten paper tag says fire starter, so I guess that's what it's used for. There is a cup with a lid that folds up and can fit into a pocket—so crazy! And a light inside a tube. This is a torch. Tyse keeps one on his battle belt. This one has a clip on it, too.

There are many trinkets like this and I realize that they're all small comforts for our trip. Plus a thick midnight-blue canvas rucksack to put everything in. There's even a little diagram telling me how to pack it efficiently.

The rest of the packages are clothes. Delta has sent me two pairs of pants—one pair is very dark gray and the other is a very light cream. Both of them have lots of pockets and loops to attach things to.

There are two long-sleeve, button-down shirts as well.

Again, one dark, one light. Both with plenty of pockets. People on this side of things really like pockets, but I'm not complaining, because pockets are very handy.

There are two more shirts—tighter and sleeveless. Both of these are a neutral beige, lighter than the pants, but not quite white. I'm pretty sure these are meant to be worn under the long-sleeved ones.

And then there is a belt, socks, and undergarments.

I blush a little at the thought of Delta picking out undergarments for me, but then realize, that's silly. A god doesn't pick out undergarments for his underlings. He's got a personal shopper for that.

There are no new boots. But that's because the ones Tyse bought me in Tau City are high quality and I'm used to them now. No one wants to start a trip with new boots.

The last package isn't from Delta, it's from Anneeta. I figure this out immediately when I pick it up because it's covered in brightly colored wax pencil drawings. Hearts, and smiley faces, and little stars.

The package is about the size and depth of a small book. When I open it up, that's what I find. Not a book, exactly though. Because all the pages are blank. The cover is a very attractive wax-pencil drawing of a couple—a man and a woman embracing each other. The background shows, what I assume to be, the Great Sandy Sea, and they are dressed in traditional clothing. Tunics and loose pants for the man and a long dress for the woman. Outfits I'd find on my side of the worlds. But as I study it a little longer, I realize, it's supposed to be Tyse and me. Or, Anneeta's seven-year-old, artistic-skills version of us, at least.

There's a note attached. I read it out loud. "Dear Clara, I hope you are doing great. I hope you have a good time on your trip. I would like to go on a trip too. But I'm not allowed. So I made you this notebook so you can keep track of all your exciting adventures. When you come back you can give it to me and I will read it. Then it will be like I was there with you. Make sure to draw cool and pretty pictures too!!!" (three exclamation points!). "I've added some wax pencils so you have no excuse. Your friend forever, the Godling Anneeta."

I smile, then look at the little bundle of colored pencils. They are secured to the back of the notebook with a ribbon, but there's a little velvet bag in the package as well. To keep it all together, I guess.

Isn't it funny that I woke up this morning thinking of stories and now I've been tasked with writing one?

Life is so fun.

I put the notebook, the note, and the pencils into the little velvet bag. After that's done, I look at the outfits.

Two. One to wear, and one as a spare.

This is when it hits me that this isn't a vacation. It's not a grand adventure—I mean, it could be, but it hasn't been planned that way.

Tyse and I are on a mission. And Tyse is a soldier. Not just any soldier, either. He's an augmented soldier. A being, here in this world, almost akin to a mythological figure. Almost as fanciful as the Godling Anneeta, herself.

This is a deployment and there won't be any dresses, or parties, or hot showers. Well, maybe hot showers if we find a waterfall and my spark can heat it up—but it certainly won't be a regular thing.

One outfit to wear and one as a spare.

I choose the dark outfit, saving the light one for another day. And then I get to work packing things up, following the diagram that came with the rucksack.

I find that I can hook trinkets onto my belt, turning it

into a battle belt. Like the one Tyse wears, except, with a pocketknife instead of a VersiStrike.

I'm sitting on the couch, lacing my boots up, when Tyse returns, holding a package in his hand. He smiles at me as he kicks the door closed. This motion makes his weapon bang against his hip, which I find very sexy for some reason. "Hey," he says, walking over to me. "New clothes?"

I stand up, modeling them. "Delta sent them, along with all kinds of other stuff." I point to the pack. "Do you like it?"

He throws me a wild grin in response. "Love it. And that pack is pretty full. Looks heavy." He walks over and picks it up. "What's in it?"

"Trinkets. Clothes. A notebook to record my travels." He gives me a funny look. "From Anneeta. She's sad she's not coming so she wants me to keep a diary."

"Well, I'm not sad she's being left behind."

I laugh. "She's not *that* annoying."

"If that little godling was coming along, I'd refuse to go."

"You're overreacting. She's... a sparkplug!" I grin, using the name he calls her.

"She's a troublemaker. And if she were comin', she'd get us killed."

I shake my head. Surely, he's overreacting. But then I picture that room we had to pass through in order to make our escape from Tau City.

The room filled with dead Spark Maidens.

Because she *ate them*.

"Well," I sigh. "I would not want to disappoint her, so I will keep a diary. And when we get back, I'll let her read it. Troublemaker or not, Tyse, having a godling on our side is a fantastic twist of good luck."

He doesn't deny this. Just cocks his head at me, grinning.

Then I remember something. "Oh!" And I rush into the

bedroom to grab the jar of copper coins. I bring it back out, holding it up for Tyse. "Guess what?" His eyes light up blue, waiting for me to tell him. "I figured out why I was dreaming about godships! Look!" I hold up a coin, the backside facing Tyse. "A ship!" Then I laugh. "Brains are so weird."

He taps my head with a finger. "Especially yours." Then he offers me his hand. "Ready?"

I nod, even though my stomach flutters with nervous butterflies. "I'm ready." Then I take his hand. But while he's picking up my rucksack and hitching it over his shoulder, I turn and look out the vast panel of floor-to-ceiling windows. Allowing myself to be knocked over breathless from the view one last time.

It's all so temporary.

That's been the major lesson of my life this past month. One moment, I'm a Spark Maiden living like royalty in a tower, the next I'm a sacrifice, my entire city standing against me. Then I'm in another world, with another man. And even that was fleeting. The escape from Tau City, the near-death train ride into Delta. The black-sand beaches that smell like oranges and the amazing top-floor apartment with a view so magnificent, it makes you wanna cry.

I'll never come back here. I will never live in this apartment again.

It's a weird, one-off thought that I can't know for certain. But I'm certain.

I'll never come back here.

I sigh, my heart a little bit sad at the realization.

But I'm ready for what comes next.

As long as this man is beside me, I'm ready for anything.

# TYSE

"*Stairs? Or elevator?*" I look at Clara as we come to the end of the hallway. Elevators were a thing in her Tau City. She said Lover Boy had one that led up to his domed palace. That must've been where he was when I saw him that night I kissed Clara on the edge of the Tower District, trying to contain her spark. But I can't really tell if she likes them for the convenience or not.

She looks at the elevator doors—which are gold, and metal, and have an elaborate geometric design on them. Then at the opening of the wide stairwell that leads down in a spiral. She smiles at me. "Stairs."

I wave a hand at it, inviting her to go first. Which is something I find myself doing all the time since up-city Clara Birch showed up in my life. Ladies first. Of course, I've always known it was a rule of good manners, or whatever. It's just... before Clara, I never had cause to treat a woman like a woman.

Now I do.

We descend together though. Slowly. In no particular rush. "Are you excited?" I ask.

"Kind of. Are you?"

"Well, it will be nice to get out of here. And be back in service—even if it's for a god I don't like. I mean, I didn't like the Sweep, either. But that's never been enough to stop the adrenaline rush, ya know?"

She looks at me as we keep going down the spiral. "Is that what drives it? The adrenaline?"

"Yeah." I shrug. "It is."

"I'm very interested in this, Tyse. Because while I did see you in action during our escape from Tau City, it's a new side to you."

I look down at her and smile. "You went from princess, to vagabond girl, to augment accessory. It's a new side to you as well."

Her grin grows big even though some women might take what I just said as derogatory. "I could take that one of two ways," And here it comes. I smirk. One-hundred percent convinced that she will not see it as derogatory. "I'm a bracelet."

My chuckle is immediate. "Or?"

She bumps her hip into mine, making my Versi shake. "A weapon."

"I love you."

"Noted. And for the record," she bumps my hip again. "It's this one."

"I never had any doubt." I take her hand as we get to the bottom of the stairs and we walk through the lobby as a team, then we're through the doors and outside. The sky is a dull gray, clouds having rolled in off the ocean as is typical around here. There's a little mist in the air as well. For me, this mist is cyan blue, but for everyone else, it's just a semi-opaque haze of fog.

I come to a stop in front of a pile of supplies being watched over by the doorman, hand him a gold coin, and he bows, accepting it and moving off to get back to work.

"What's all this?" Clara asks, panning her hand to the four bags at our feet.

"My ruck."

"Ruck?" She raises an eyebrow at me. "There are *four* of them, Tyse."

I laugh. "This is nothing compared to what I had to carry in the sweep. It's just lucky that I've got a Versi, because all the cartridges are very compact and easy to store." I make my finger do a little circle in the air. "Turn around and I'll load you up with yours."

She does, looking over her shoulder at me in wonder as I slip the straps of her ruck up her arms and make sure they lie on her shoulders just right.

"How's it feel?"

"Good. Not very heavy. So I can carry one of those, too." She nods her head at mine.

"Nah, I got this. Watch." And then I proceed to hook the secondary ruck onto the primary, pull it onto my back, and then attach the other two—which are all ammo—to my legs using the Versi belt as support. When I'm done, I find her studying me. "What?"

She presses her lips together, hiding a smile.

"What's that look for?"

"Just..." I get one of those all-teeth smiles. "It's..."

"Sexy?"

She laughs, but nods. "It's a *really* good look on you."

"Does it make me look dangerous? Cunnin'? A straight up fuck-around-and-find-out kinda guy?"

"All that and more."

"What's the 'more' part?" I tease. But also genuinely interested. Since we've already covered that I'm sexy.

"Tyse Saarinen, this makes you look..." There's a pause here, where she thinks. "Super human."

"Super human? Like an alien?"

She shakes her head. "No. Like a god."

"Hmm. I don't think I look anything like Delta."

"No, not *that* kind of god."

Now I'm confused. "What other kind is there?"

But she just shrugs. "I don't know. I can't explain it. It's just... well, I like it."

"Then I guess that's all that counts." Then I pan a hand to the tunnel that leads to the train station across the street. "Shall we?" She turns, but then abruptly turns back, leans up on her tiptoes, and kisses me. It's just a small kiss, but it's unexpected. "What was that for?"

"Partners." Then, as if that explains everything, she takes my hand and we cross the street.

People stare at us as we enter the underground. Of course, everyone knows me. When we arrived, people wouldn't shut up about the baby god and the augment, speculating what it meant for the city—and beyond. I didn't pay much attention to the buzz because it was mostly talk of war and not the kind of war that involves augments, so I knew they were just blustering to entertain.

But the people of Delta City don't look entertained when Clara and I stand on the platform, waiting for the next train to come.

They look scared.

Of course, they should be. If they ever met me in the wrong situation—well, they would not want to meet me in the wrong situation. That's all there is to it.

In Sweep, in the Omega Outlands, we did fight a lot. But it wasn't the kind of fighting that people think of when they imagine what a war is. They picture battles with other people.

And it's not about people. It's not about people at all.

It's about code.

But that's all Sweep classified and even though I did tell

Clara about the infection my team got, she's different. She's part of it in a big way so she deserves to know some of it. But the ordinary person standing on the platform of the underground waiting for a train does not have, and should not have, any fucking idea of what's really happening in the Omega Outlands.

Seeing me, though. All dressed up like this. It's enough to spark their curiosity. Kids begin to point to us, parents hurriedly hushing them up as we pass.

Clara must notice, but she doesn't say anything. I like this about Clara. She's observant and smart. She knows when to just go along and when to ask questions. It's a life-saving skill in the line of work I'm in.

The line of work she's now in too.

The train comes, people get off, people board, but we stay still, waiting for it to pull away. Then, once it's gone, Clara and I walk over to the edge of the platform. I jump down and offer her my hand.

She takes it and jumps without comment, looking up at me with a smile when she lands.

"Partners," I say.

"Till the end of days," she responds.

Then, hand in hand, we walk into the darkness of the empty tunnel.

CLARA **and I had a conversation** about the train tunnels the day after Delta gave me the deployment and I showed her the map of the train line that was on my overlay.

Of course, she knows what a train is and we rode one to get here.

The concept of this whole thing is best introduced this way. As something familiar.

Because the train we're looking for now isn't familiar. It's not even part of this world.

My overlay tells me we've got three minutes to find the entrance we're looking for before another train comes barreling down this tunnel, and even though that kind of time limit is a bit stressful, it only takes about thirty seconds of walking before we find what we're looking for.

Clara waits, silent, as I scan it. "Yeah. This is it." Then I grab her hand because she can't see in the dark, and we walk forward.

"How far do we have to go?" she asks. No panic in that question. Completely calm.

"About a hundred paces."

"And there's a door in here?"

That's how I described it. "Yeah. A door. I'll show you. There." I point with my free hand. "That's it." We walk over to it, and when I pull on the handle, find it unlocked. We enter, me first this time, and she follows, holding on to my ruck with loose fingers just to keep herself oriented.

My overlay lights up with data, and I stop, letting all the information filter in. There's a new control panel on my readout screen—one that operates this room, which is handy, but confusing—so I find the tab for the lights and activate them.

The place illuminates with blue light the same color as spark.

Clara and I are both silent as we look around. Me,

because my overlay is lit up like a fuckin' sun with data and even though my augmented brain gets all this information in a millisecond, it takes my human one a moment to sort it out.

Her, I surmise, because the room from her perspective is completely empty.

I'm still turning things on and off on my display when she speaks. "OK. What am I looking at?"

Which is the exact right question to ask. "You're lookin' at nothin', darlin'. But I'm looking at... many, many options. Give me a sec to find the one we need."

"OK."

The overlay is crowded with dimensions. One pressed against the other, pressed against the other, pressed against the other like windows arranged in row. The way you might find them in a warehouse for storage.

Except these windows are all portals to other places. But because windows are transparent, I'm gettin' glimpses of all these worlds layered over the others. It's a fuckin' mess.

It was like this a few times above ground too, where they would all appear at once, but only in certain places. Our bedroom, for instance, did have many worlds to choose from, but they didn't all appear in a row like this. I had to choose them.

But here in the tunnel they all seem to be fightin' for my attention.

"What are you looking for?"

"Hmm?" I ask, distracted.

"What does it look like?"

"What does what look like, Clara?"

"The world?"

"The one we're supposed to be in? I'm not sure."

"Then how will you know it's the right one?"

I pull out of the overlay and focus on her. She's smiling at me, so it's hard to be annoyed with her questions, but I'm kind of annoyed because I'm working now and I'm not used to being interrupted by questions.

*Be nice, Tyse. You love this woman.*

So I smile back. "There's a number attached to it. 702. Delta didn't tell me this, though. I heard it from Stayn that night we were at his house."

"Oh, I know that place."

Which makes sense, because she's from there. But I'm confused. "How do you know this place?"

"Delta mentioned it. He said…" Her eyes roll up, like she's thinking. Then she deepens her voice to mimic the asshole god. "You are not a Looking Glass, Clara. You are a Spark Maiden from the illegal Tau Factory in Dimension 702."

"Why would he tell you that? I mean, he didn't tell *me* that."

She shrugs. "I don't think he understands me. He was probably just thinking out loud or something. But if we're looking for 702, then…" I almost wince. It takes a lot of self-control not to. "Then we're looking for… *home.* My home." Her forehead goes crinkly. "Are you taking me home?"

"Absolutely not."

Which makes her chuckle. "Just checking because I did specifically tell you that I didn't want to go home."

"No worries, darlin'. You're stuck with me. But this 702 place is where all the activity is happening. So we're goin' there, but not to all the way to Tau City. That's far, *far* down the line."

"Good. I just want to make sure we're on the same page."

"We are."

"OK. Sorry to interrupt. I'll stand here quietly while you proceed to figure things out."

And now I feel bad because I was actin' like she was just an augment accessory, and she's not. She's a weapon. "Well, let me explain it to you. We'll figure it out quicker if we do it together."

This answer delights her because she shrugs up her shoulders and beams me a bright smile. A little bit of spark even seeps out of her.

And this makes my overlay blink with brightness.

"What just happened?" she asks.

"You saw that?"

Clara nods. "Yeah, your eyes just went... *white*."

White? Well. I'll have to file that under shit-to-figure-out-later, because I've never seen augments with white eyes before. "I dunno. You were grinnin' because I decided to treat you like a weapon instead of a bracelet, and a little bit of spark came off you. This made my augments... I dunno. It was like a power surge."

"Well, that makes complete sense."

"Does it?"

"Of course. I'm a battery." Then her forehead crinkles again. "Well, not really. When Delta was lecturing me about not being a Looking Glass, he was also saying that I wasn't *just* a battery, but he couldn't figure out what the other part of me was."

"He said all this to you?"

"Yeah. I wasn't awake yet, though. It was kind of like a dream. But it wasn't a dream, it was real."

"Delta entered your *mind* to have a conversation?"

"Yeah. Why?"

"Well, that's... unusual. I've heard of it. But it's how gods communicate with each other. You know they're not real, right? They're just really good holograms."

"I didn't know that. But anyway," she sighs. "Can we find the world now? I have to pee."

I side eye her, suddenly thinkin' this deployment is not like any other mission I've ever been on. "We *just* left the house like twenty minutes ago."

She shrugs with her hands. "It is what it is."

"Anyway," I sigh. But secretly, I'm glad she's injecting all this novelty to the experience of soldierin', so I want to take the time to fill her in. "Let me explain what I'm seein'. Imagine... a screen—like for TV, and shit, but it stretches all the way across your field of vision."

"OK."

"Now imagine that it's alive." She shoots me a look, one eyebrow raised. "It's..." I attempt to clarify. "It's a library of information. And every time you look at something—like this wall here." I point to the wall. "It spits out information about it. A little pop-up label appears to relay details. This wall is made of concrete. And my overlay is tellin' me that this concrete is a mixture of limestone, clay, and synthetic fibers. It gives me facts about everythin' I'm looking at. The floor – also concrete. The lights—a borosilicate glass tube filled with solid sodium, neon, and argon gas mixed in with metal electrodes—and everythin' else, whether I want to know about it or not."

"Well, while it seems very useful, it sounds chaotic."

I point at her. "Exactly. And that's just one world. Here, in this space, all the worlds want to capture my attention. It's like they're fightin' for it in here. And each world has an overlay."

"And we're trying to find 702 in that chaos?"

"Yes. It's a fuckin' mess."

"How will you sort it?"

I shrug. "Go through them one at a time and see if any of them are what I'm lookin' for?"

"Sounds pretty inefficient."

"You got a better idea?"

"Hmm." She taps her finger to her chin and begins to pace the room. It's small, so she only gets about six steps away before she has to turn back again. "You need to find the filing system."

"How do I do that?"

"Well, you find something they have in common, but is different for each world. If there's a world called 702, it stands to reason that here are worlds called 701 and 703."

She's right. "Give me a minute to look through a few."

"No pressure, but I still have to pee."

I smile, but don't reply. Instead, I go into my overlay and start lookin' at all the data spillin' out on the screen that describes this room. There's a lot of little tabs, and labels, and numbers. But I don't know what dimension this is, and Delta didn't give me any instructions on how to hop dimensions. He just told me to show up here in this room. I assumed it would be self-explanatory.

But it's just now occurring to me that this makes sense in only one context.

He is under the impression that I *only* have access to 702.

Why he has that impression, I'm not sure. But he doesn't know I can see all these other worlds. He never asked me how I got Clara and Anneeta all the way across the sandy sea to Delta City alive. He doesn't know I stole spark from that family who were riding in the train car with us and killed them. He was probably told that there were spent jumps all over the floor and assumed that's what I used to feed Clara and Anneeta.

Interesting. But not important at the moment. What's

important is findin' the tag that corresponds to this dimension. "There is a number here in the upper corner labeled 'Frequency'," I tell Clara.

"What's a frequency?"

"It's a rate of vibration."

"I don't know what that means, Tyse. It wasn't part of my Spark Maiden conversation vocabulary."

"Think of it like a tag. Or a name. You're Clara and I'm Tyse. I don't know why I'd need to know the frequency of anything unless it was for identification. Because it's unique, right? The floor vibrates at a certain frequency based on what it's made up of. Same with the wall, and the lights, and us."

"Well, that sounds like a filing system."

I smile. Because I like having Clara as a partner. "It does, doesn't it?"

"What's the frequency for this world?"

"1440."

"I'll make a note of it."

"You do that. I'm gonna see if I can clear some of these worlds we don't need."

It takes a concerted effort on my part not to get lost in the data of the other worlds because it's all pretty interesting. Luckily, there are no livin' things in any of these worlds in this exact space because that would make it even more difficult to focus on clearing them out.

My internal clock tells me I'm twenty minutes in to this process when I see the number I'm looking for. "Found it."

"You did!" Clara, who has been sitting on the ground with her back up against the wall, gets to her feet. "Now what?"

"Well. I hadn't thought that far ahead, to be honest. We need a way to cross over."

"Well the frequency must be important in regards to

where we are, right? I mean, why else would it be on your screen?"

"That makes sense. It's easy to take things out of other worlds. That feels intuitive. But I don't know how to cross over."

Her brows crinkle up with confusion. "What have you been taking out of other worlds?"

Oops. "I mean... well, the spark. It's everywhere." I already feel like I'm lying to her about Lover Boy being my target—which I'm not, I just haven't told her yet. So I feel like she deserves to know that I can take spark from the other dimensions.

"And you're taking it?"

I nod. "Yeah. That's how I saved you and Anneeta. When I ran out of jumps, there were still five hours left to go on the trip. So... another world appeared and I just... grabbed the spark and gave it to you. And then you gave it to Anneeta. And you both lived."

Clara just stares up at me for a few moments. And I'm almost positive she's coming to the right conclusions. *Who did you take the spark from, Tyse?*

But she doesn't ask. Instead, she says, "Well, that's kind of handy."

"It is," I agree. "But takin' things out and crossin' over feels very different." I allow myself a moment to think about this. Clara gives me this time. Hopefully not because she's wondering who I took spark from, but there's no going back now. "If the worlds are categorized by frequency, then perhaps resonance is how you thin them out to make... a door?"

"In my head, you just said, 'Blah, blah, blah. Blah blah, blah.'"

I laugh. "Resonance is an excitation of the frequency. And

since spark seems to be what holds a world together, it makes sense that spark could tear it apart." Which feels like a 'duh' moment, since I'm almost certain that a spark explosion on Lover Boy's side of things is how we got away from Stayn and out of Tau City in the first place.

And... now that I think about it, it gave me a glimpse too.

I saw him. I saw Finn Scott carrying his 'trashy woman', as Delta calls her.

"All we have to do to make a door is match the frequency and give it a push. Like pushing a child in a swing. That's how it was explained to me in school. Your initial push makes the swing move back and forth. That's the frequency. But if you give it another push, right at the exact moment when it's on the backside, and hanging in the air, you excite the frequency—making it stronger. That's resonance."

"And spark is what gives that extra push?"

I shrug. "It's a theory. The only one I have. But spark has to be a part of it. Why else is it here?"

Clara smiles and holds up her hand, twiddling her fingers. They're glowing blue. "Well, it looks like I'm the key."

# CLARA

*yse is staring at my glowing fingers*—a bit of concern, a bit of wonder. After a couple of moments, his eyes glide up to meet mine. "You've got a read out when you glow now."

"What?"

He points to his eyes. "On the overlay. Your glow has a label that says, 'BOOST'."

I make a face. "Boost? Like I'm a charge?"

"Well, you kinda are."

"Yeah, I am. But why is it labeling me like that? This is new?"

He nods. "You weren't glowing before. But the moment it spilled out of your fingertips, your spark started registering as part of my data."

As part of his *data*. I let out a sigh. "I'm sick of all this science talk."

He smiles. "Me too. Should we give it a try?"

"How?"

"I've got the frequency. I can see the other world. 702. It pretty much looks just like this one. Before you started glowing, I was thinking that somehow I could take your spark and use it to boost the frequency—"

"With resonance."

"Exactly. To create resonance, which might interfere with the veil and push us through. But now that you're glowing, it's more than a guess. I feel like this is how it's done."

"OK." I'm nodding my head. Data is a cold word and gives off a weird vibe. But I'm necessary. That's the important part. He needs me. And I need him. This is how our true partnership starts. It's exciting. And I'm not just talking myself into this, I really feel this way. "Tell me what to do."

"Probably just... spark me."

"Like that time back in the tower when I scared you."

His grin starts small, but grows. "Exactly like that time."

"OK." I psych myself up by rubbing my hands together. Little glowing pieces fly off, like embers rising from a nighttime fire. It was a metaphorical gesture, but it actually seems to kind of... power me up. I reach out for Tyse, almost losing my nerve because what if I hurt him? But then I remember he's Tyse. Not much can hurt him. But it's a good thing I did hesitate, because this gave Tyse time to raise his hand, palm towards me with fingers outstretched. As if to offer me a target.

The perfect target. So I'm smiling when I press my palm against his and the room... blinks.

"Was that it?" I ask. "Did we cross?"

"No," Tyse says, "but it did make the worlds flicker. Both of them, but at different times."

"The frequencies are off," I say.

He points at me. "You're smart." Which makes me smile. "We need to align them somehow. Any ideas?"

Aside from his hot, muscly, scarred and tattooed body, as well as his capable and protective manner, and not to mention his loyalty and forthrightness—this is my favorite thing about Tyse Saarinen. He asks for my opinion on things. Very important things that he probably doesn't need my opinion on, but asks anyway.

"If we need to align them, and this frequency stuff is

important, then maybe we need to lower the frequency of this 1440 world down to that 702 one?"

He's grinning at me the whole time I'm talking. "I was thinking the same thing. But there are actually two choices. Should we raise 702 up to this world's frequency? Or lower this one down?"

"Well, I'm no expert—" which makes him chuckle. "But I think we should lower this one. Raising up a world we're not even in feels like a lot of work. And would require a lot more spark."

"Agreed. So how does one lower the frequency of a world?"

"If there's a reading labeled 'boost' shouldn't there be something called... diminish?"

His smile is wild now, and so are his eyes. "Just so happens I have one of those. After you pressed your hand into mine, it popped right up."

I cock my hip and shoot him a fake look of aggravation. "So you knew all along how to do it? Why did you ask me then?"

"Clara, I'm not gonna just go around and start pushing buttons to use up your spark without talkin' it through first. I saw it, but I couldn't be sure that's what it meant. You just confirmed."

"I think you're giving me too much credit. I'm just guessing."

He reaches out, pulling me forward. And suddenly his arms are wrapped around me like a cloak. He kisses me. It's soft and a little bit lingering. And through this kiss comes a whisper. "The whole world is guessin', Clara. No one's got any fuckin' idea what's happening. Never forget that."

Then he pulls back, mischievous smile on his face. "I'm

sorry about this next science-y part, but you should know. I don't know how many times I'll have to activate the diminish button, I don't know what it's gonna do to you, and I'm not sure how to take care of you if something happens. But know this for a fact, I *will* take care of you."

Wow. I might be on the verge of my own demise, but my whole body is responding to all that loyalty he just professed. I feel swoony, and tingly, and excited. But in a weird way. Like it's spark feeling all these things.

"Is that a yes?" he asks

I nod. "Yes. Do what you have to. We need to figure this out before anything else. I trust you."

"Good. And I trust you as well. I'll count it down so you know to expect it. Ready?"

"Ready."

"Three… two… one."

When he says one, the excitement of my spark suddenly explodes. It shoots out of my hands, and comes out the top of my shirt, and heat fills my entire body. I feel time passing, but I can't concentrate. It's hovering—here, but not. Part of this, but away from it as well.

All around me the room shimmers, flickers, blinks.

Tyse is pressing the button again, and again. Because the spark inside me gets more and more excited until I'm at the point where I fear I might pass out. I close my eyes, willing myself to stay conscious. *Don't let it take over*, I say in my head. *Don't let it take over.* I say this over and over again, maybe a million times.

And it works.

My body calms, the spark still shooting out of me. Heating me up in a way I've never experienced before. My body is so hot, I begin to sweat. I close my eyes, repeating my new mantra. *Don't let it take over.* And when the heat evens out, I open my eyes—getting the surprise of my life.

I'm floating up in the air, twirling in a slow circle. But down below, I'm standing on the ground too. Arms out, head back, spark flying out of my fingertips and my *mouth*. Tyse looks worried, but I can also tell he's working. His eyes are lit up bright blue and they're moving back and forth that way they do when he's accessing that overlay thing.

I watch, fascinated. Every couple of seconds, his hands make little gestures. A flick of his fingertips. A pushing motion, like he's moving things on his overlay out of the way.

Then he goes still—the spark humming all around me now, not just around my hands and my head, and he says, "Got it."

Everything stops.

I fall back into my body with a sudden jolt and then I'm collapsing down to the floor. Tyse catches me before I hit the ground, his arms wrapping tightly around me. Then he's cradling me in his arms. "Clara? Can you hear me?"

I nod, groggily, even though it makes my head spin, because I don't want him to worry.

"Good. We've done it. We're through."

Which makes me smile, eyes still closed.

"Was it bad?" he asks, clearly concerned.

The sigh comes out before I can stop it. I don't want him to know all the details. It will worry him. But he deserves to know what it costs to cross. So I force my eyes open and find his so close, I can see tiny sparks going off deep inside his soul. "I feel... spent. I don't think I can walk. My legs are all jiggly. My head hurts. I feel like I need to sleep for a week."

He nods, then slowly kneels down, bracing his back

against the wall of the new dimension, still cradling me in his arms as he situates me on his lap.

I look around—trying my best not to move my head too much—I realize this room looks no different from the place we started. "Are you sure this is the new place? It looks the same."

"It is. It's 702. The overlay says so. It's understandable that you're tired. It took twelve minutes to make the change."

"Twelve *minutes*?" I say these words way too loud, causing a ringing in my ears. "That's... not possible. It was seconds. Mere seconds."

"No," Tyse sighs. "It wasn't. It took a very long time. I think you were just... out of it, if ya know what I mean. So you couldn't tell how much time was passing. I'm hoping we're just really bad at this, and we'll get the hang of it. Because if that's how it's gonna be, we're stuck here, darlin'. We're not gonna do it again. We won't go back. I won't be burning you up for a job."

I close my eyes again, smiling now. "You're *so* fuckin' romantic."

Which makes him laugh, because it's a little bit of a joke. But not really. Not from my point of view.

Tyse is the opposite of Finn.

Finn, who left me standing all alone on the God's tower stage.

Who insisted he didn't have a choice.

Who gave up on me before we even got started.

Tyse will do anything for me.

Anything.

And I would do anything for him. Even if it involves... *this*.

I would give him all of me—every last glowing ember of spark inside me—to save us.

And if it came down to it, I'd do that just to save *him*.

Sacrifice.

It's kind of a thing where I come from.

But Tyse Saarinen is worth it.

# TYSE

*Clara Birch falls asleep* in my arms with a tiny smile on her face. Like she just had the best day of her life. But if she could see herself in a mirror, her heart would be beatin' as fast as mine is right now because she looks like crap. Utterly pale. No color at all in her cheeks.

I took all the spark inside of her to make this jump across worlds. Her body is limp, like I stole every bit of energy in her muscles.

And I'm just not sure it was worth it. For what? To stop Lover Boy from blowin' up god towers on a train line? I mean, it's *his* world. Maybe I should just let him?

But then I think about Tau City. *My* Tau City and how the veil was so thin that Anneeta could see the phantom towers. The threat is clear. It's bleedin' through. Clara's world and my world. And even though it doesn't appear that she comes from a place like the Outlands, there's no tellin' what might go wrong back in 1440 if it bleeds through with 702.

And this world hopping? It feels like a break. At the very least, a tear in the membrane that separates the worlds. Did I have to rip open every world between 1440 and 702 to get us here?

And if so, what effect does that have on the worlds we just passed through?

Maybe this is how the Outlands started? Some augment was jumpin' worlds and broke them.

It's too early to know, I tell myself. It was our first time.

We're just figuring things out. We don't know the limits yet, that's all. We just need a little time. A little bit of practice.

I want to believe it, but then I look down at the woman in my arms and all the hope fades. She looks like *shit*.

And I don't know what to do about it.

Which is a lie. Because I *do* know what to do about it.

I don't have any spark inside of me to give her. To replenish her.

But that's what she needs.

And I know where to get it.

I don't need Clara's energy to *see* other worlds. And as I think these words in my head, without even looking through my data display for frequencies, the worlds begin to appear. A chaotic and simultaneous overlapping, hundreds of layers deep.

It would be very easy to reach over and take what I need. The problem is, this particular space, on whatever grid is organizing all these worlds, doesn't seem to be inhabited by anyone because we're not only underground, we're hidden from the train line. This place, in the same space in other worlds, is probably just rock.

There's no spark to steal.

At least, easily.

Because the odds that there is no spark here at all, are so low, they might as well be zero, and here's why:

Frequency is limitless. There are an unlimited number of frequencies because it comes in fractions, not whole numbers. Even if I only take the decimals out to three places, that's an infinite number of options. *Infinite.* Meaning, if I look long enough, I *will* find someone to steal spark from.

But just because I *can* do something, doesn't mean I should.

Unless it comes to saving Clara Birch.

Will she recover on her own?

I can't know. Maybe she does, maybe she doesn't.

So I have to look. I have no choice.

I hold her tight as I go inward, sifting through all the overlapping worlds crowding my overlay. One by one, I go through them. One by one, I find nothing.

It takes me hours to find a single worker, but there's something wrong with it. It doesn't have any spark to steal, for one. And it's also... alien.

It looks human. A gleaming and smooth white body with arms and legs. But it's not skin or clothes that it's wearing. It's some kind of carapace. Like a suit. And it's got no face, so that must be a helmet.

A soldier?

No.

It's not a soldier.

It's a *bot*.

Just thinking the word makes me shudder. Bots were outlawed so long ago, I couldn't even tell you the date. Back when the gods first took over the world after the sandy Sweep covered everything, leaving nothing but dunes in its wake.

I stare at it for a few minutes, gazing across the veil. Wondering what it's doin'. But then, the woman I'm holding in my arms shifts, pulling my full attention back to her.

Her face is nearly transparent now. Little blue veins appear under the thin skin of her cheeks and neck. Little spidery lines that scare the shit out of me as I hold her limp body in my arms.

I keep looking.

When I finally find a place that registers spark, I realize it's been half a day since I started the search and Clara is nothing but a limp body in my arms. She's still breathing, but for how long?

I turn my attention to the world with the spark signature, tryin' to make sense of it. Because it's not an empty room like the one we're in, it's a cave filled with massive cyan-blue crystals. The frequency associated with this place is extraordinarily low. 0.1440.

Which mimics the frequency of my own Delta City, but in an extremely low-energy way. And this contradicts what I'm lookin' at. Because I'm getting the impression that those crystals are pure spark.

Did I just stumble into the source of everythin'?

Better question—do I dare steal it?

I look down at Clara. She's not gonna replenish herself. She needs spark from somewhere, and it's unfortunate that, across many worlds, this particular space in the grid is practically void of options.

So I don't have a choice.

Source or not, sacred or not—I *need* this spark.

Before I can change my mind, I reach for it. I stretch my will across the veil, making the cyan-blue crystals glow momentarily. Then, as I watch, the spark begins to come off it in swirlin' tendrils that float towards me.

My heart is poundin' in my chest.

What the fuck am I doing?

But the fear isn't enough to stop me.

I *need* this spark.

It comes right through the overlay—kind of merging with it. And then, when I look down at my fingers, the spark flows out of me and seeps into Clara, like I'm a faucet and she's a sponge, soaking it up.

Suddenly, the cave-world collapses, disappearin' from my overlay. And other worlds rush in to take its place. But it doesn't matter. Clara is already stirring. Already feeling better. The spark fillin' her back up—making her pale, nearly translucent skin, flush pink with life.

And anyway, I saw the frequency.

0.1440.

I can find it again any time I want.

AFTER ONLY ABOUT TEN MINUTES, Clara is sittin' up, back against the wall just a few feet away, drinking water from a flask and absently swiping at loose tendrils of hair near her eyes. Eyes I can't stop lookin' at because on my overlay, they're glowing. Not like mine do with the little indicator lights for augmentation. Something far more subtle.

But when I turn the overlay off, they're normal.

It was the spark I fed her. Source, I'm calling it. Even though I'm not sure that's what it was.

"Whew," Clara sighs, finishing her long drink. "That took a lot out of me. What happened?"

"We crossed," I say. I've been trying to piece together a story, but the lies are starting to pile up and we've been on this mission for one day. So I've decided to tell her the truth. "But it took everythin' from you, Clara. All your spark. I think you were dyin'."

Her brow furrows, eyes narrowing. "Dying? I don't remember... well, I don't remember anything, actually."

"I needed the spark—" I'm gonna say it. I am. I have every

intention of tellin' her what's goin' on here. How she feeds me and how I take everything. I mean, I won't do it again. I didn't understand. It's not gonna happen again. So I'm gonna tell her. But in the same moment that I'm thinkin' this, I see myself on the train out of Tau City. How helpless I felt. And what I did to save the woman I love.

I killed for her. I took the life of a whole family.

If Clara knew this was the price, she would see me different. That cost is too high. I know her well enough now to understand that up-city Clara Birch would never take an innocent life to save her own.

"OK," Clara says, when I don't continue. "You needed the spark so…" She kinda rolls her hand at me to keep going.

"To cross over. It takes a lot. It was me who did that to you. Who made you feel so weak."

She smiles, crawling over to me to erase the couple of feet that separates us. "But we did it, right?" She wraps her hands around my upper arm, settling herself against me. "We're here? In the other world?"

"We are. Frequency 702."

She lets out a long breath. "Good. And I'm fine now, so it was worth it. Now we can continue."

I get to my feet and extend her a hand. "Yeah. Let's find the train and head up the line. See if we can find…" *LoverBoy.* "…the terrorist. And settle this mess."

Once on her feet, Clara places her hands on my shoulders and leans up on her tiptoes. Kissing me on the lips before I even understand what she's doin'.

Of course, I kiss her back. But it's just a quick 'thank you' I think. Because she pulls out of it and stares up at me like I'm her prince. "I'm ready. Let's go."

I pick her ruck up off the floor, sliding it up her arms and on to her shoulders. Then I strap on my rucks, and we leave the way we came—just in another dimension.

EVERYTHIN' looks the same as we retrace our steps. But from the moment we enter the main tunnel, there's no way to miss that this is not home. It's very bright, for one, not dark. Because there are lights lining the entire ceiling, from end to end, as far as our eyes can see. Which, admittedly, isn't that far—maybe a couple hundred yards in each direction—because the tunnel isn't straight, it curves. But it's made even brighter by the glossy white tiles lining every inch of the interior walls.

It's quiet—much quieter than Delta City. There's a low hum permeatin' everythin', but even this far down the line, we could hear signs of life back home.

"Are there people here?" Clara asks. Pickin' up on the silence.

"I don't know."

"What's your overlay say?"

Oddly enough, it's the only one on screen now. There's no competition between worlds to be seen. Not sure what that means—probably something horrible—but there's no point thinkin' about it now. Too many other, more pressin', questions.

"It's not pickin' up any signs of life. Or spark, for that matter."

"Do we need spark?"

"No. But it's your world, Clara. Shouldn't there be spark?"

"I guess, but we didn't know there were train tunnels below the city. I mean, we did. But they were supposed to be ancient ruins. Not anything like this. And since spark lives inside people, and there are no people in the tunnel, then it makes sense that there's no spark."

But before I can reply, we hear a clatterin' up ahead. Clara and I look at each other. I put a finger to my lips, telling her to be quiet. Then I push her behind me and start walkin' up the tunnel towards the noise. I've got the Versi at high ready and I'm slowly veering to the left until I'm shadowin' the side of the tunnel as it curves.

I peek out, looking just past the bend, and can't stop my reaction. "No fuckin' way."

"What?" Clara whispers. "What is it?" Pushing herself against me, she peeks out too. "Oh, my god." A hand goes over her heart in a gesture of shock. "What the hell is *that*?"

I tear my gaze away from the scene on the train platform and look down at her shocked eyes. "They're bots." Just saying that word out loud kinda makes me sick.

"What the hell is a bot?" she hisses back.

"It's a… a fake human. They move like us—like humans." Which neither of us are, but that's beside the point. Minutia like that can be sorted out later. "They think like us. But they're fake, Clara. They're like… mini gods with real bodies, but not like Anneeta. Not flesh. I can't really explain them because they've been illegal for so long, I've never actually seen one before today. Not even the Omega Outlands had *bots*."

"Well, what the hell are they doing here?"

I watch for a few moments, tryin' to sort it out. There's a train at the station. Just a single car. It's bullet-shaped, streamlined, and gleaming white—just like the tunnel. And there's a group of bots removing crates out of the train car and taking them through a door. "Workin', I think."

Clara looks too, pressed up against me so we're still

mostly hidden from their view by the curvature of the tunnel wall. "What do we do now?"

"Wait until they're gone and then get past this station as fast as we can without being seen."

I feel her head nodding in agreement against my chest. "OK."

Whatever the bots are doin', it takes a while. Clara and I don't relax, but we do lean against the white-tiled wall, propin' ourselves up a bit.

I feel like it's been a long day but when I check the time in my overlay, it's only late afternoon. It's not even dinnertime of the same day we left.

Don't know how that's possible.

It's been stressful.

"I think they're done," Clara whispers. Her neck stretching, holding me at arm's length, as she takes a peek around the bend. Her eyes meet mine. "Should we go?"

The sigh comes out of me unbidden, but I cover it with a smile. "Sure. Yeah. I'll go first. You stay right behind me. And no talkin' just in case they've got—" But I don't finish. If they've got any kind of sound surveillance, we're fucked. Because no one has sound without visual and there's just no way past the station without crossing in front of it.

Clara doesn't even ask me to finish my sentence, which is tellin'. She's as tired as I am. Hell, she's got to be exhausted after that ordeal this morning, even though she did get pumped back up with spark.

She shoots me a supportive smile—which I truly do appreciate—and then takes hold of my ruck as I turn and start walking.

We stick close to the wall, inchin' forward slowly at first until we get to the edge of the station. Then I pause, waitin'.

"What are we doing?" Clara whispers.

"I just wanna make sure they're not comin' back. The train is still here. Maybe one of them... runs it, or something."

"Runs it? Like... one of those things has a job?"

"Well, obviously, the only purpose of a bot is work. So yeah. They all have jobs. But whether this train needs a conductor or not, I can't tell."

Suddenly, as if the damn thing can hear me, the door of the train closes, sealing with a soft hiss of hydraulic air.

Clara chuckles. "I guess that answers that question."

I guess it does. Because a moment later, the train is pulling away from the station, nearly silent on maglev tracks.

I don't move for a few more moments, still waitin'. But there's no noise at all coming from the steel door that leads inside the station. There are no stairs up here, either. Not like the stations in my world where there's a city above and people use the train for transport.

And then I remember that we're in Clara's world. Where trains were artifacts.

Except, clearly, they're not. At least, not on this end of the line.

"All right," I say. Convinced it's clear. "Let's go."

"Wait." Clara grabs my arm. "Go where? The train left."

"We're not riding the train. We're undercover, Clara."

"We're walking this line?" She stares down the tunnel for a moment before returning her gaze to me. "What if a train comes?"

"I'm sure there's a spare foot on either side to accommodate workers."

"Are you?" she laughs. "Are you sure of that? Because there's no way to tell."

"We'll walk ahead for a little bit and figure it out. And if you're not convinced, we'll come back. Deal?"

She can't really argue with this compromise, so she shrugs. "Fine. You're the boss."

I take her hand, givin' it a squeeze, and then we start walkin' past the station. We're about halfway across when the steel door swings open.

Clara and I stop dead in our tracks, not daring to move as a gleamin', white bot exits with a box in its arms. It walks over to the edge of a platform, less than a foot away from Clara and me, and sets it down.

Then it turns and goes back the way it came. Before it can reach the door, it swings open again and another bot comes out with a box. Then another, and another, and another.

All of them drop their packages off on the platform, practically in front of our faces.

Not a single one acknowledges us.

I grab my Versi, raise it up, and point it at an approaching bot. Clara grips my arm, as if to say, *What are you doing?* But I ignore her. And when the bot is bending down to drop the package off, I shoot it in the head.

It crumples forward, slippin' off the edge of the platform. But there's not enough forward momentum to get it all the way over.

But my attention is on the other bots.

Or rather, their reactions. Because there isn't one. They don't react at all.

"They can't see us," I say.

"How is that possible?" Clara asks.

"Can't hear us, either. Or... they just don't care. They haven't been programmed to care." I take Clara's hand again and pull her off to the side. Out of the way of the bots stacking packages and in the shadows. "Let's see if they've got a foreman back behind that door. Let's see if someone's running this place or if it's all automated."

So that's what we do, we wait.

Two bots do appear to remove the broken bot from the platform, but they don't look around. They don't talk, or look surprised, or ask questions. It's just part of the job. The bot broke. And they've been programmed to haul it away.

"They're not sentient," I say, after the clean-up bots are gone.

"Well, of course they're not sentient. They're... glorified coffee machines."

I give Clara a side eye. "Trust me, some of them *were* sentient. That's why they were outlawed. The gods started stuffing themselves inside these carapace bodies—and people lost their shit. It was fine when they were just holograms or voices on a screen. But the moment they had *bodies*? That was too real. So the gods just gave up and outlawed them. But I guess the gods figure, well, this isn't our world, is it? It's another dimension, so it doesn't really count."

Clara sighs. "It is all lies, Tyse? Is that all it is?"

I nod. "Yeah. That's truly all it is, Clara. Just lies."

She stares at the steel door, then down the tunnel. "Should we... go check it out?"

"Go check what out?"

"You know." She nods her head at the steel door. "Whatever's going on behind that door."

"You want to go *inside*?"

"Don't you?"

I mean, honestly, it hadn't even occurred to me. So I say, "No."

Which makes Clara chuckle. "Why not? We're here. In a strange world. Even though it is my world, this was all hidden from us. We need to check it out. What if the terrorist is in there?"

"He's not."

"How do you know?"

"Because he—" I almost say he started out at Tau City and couldn't possibly have gotten this far yet. Which would've puzzled Clara, to say the least. "Because he's on the other end of the line. Near the Outlands."

"Well, I'm curious. I want to see inside. I was never given the opportunity to explore my world, and now I have one. If those bot things don't care that we're here, then I want to take a look." And then, before I can answer so we can have a discussion about this, she hoists herself up onto the platform and starts walking towards the door.

I follow, catching up with her and taking her by the arm. "What are you doin'?"

"I told you." She pulls her arm out of my grip. "I'm going to look. You only live once, Tyse. And I don't know what the future is going to bring, but I just have this feeling that I'll never be back this way again so this is my only chance. What if all the other stations don't have bots, but people? We can't go in those."

She's right. But I don't think the other stations are manned by actual people. These bots explain how Finn Scott is able to infiltrate the cities on the line and blow up the towers. They just... don't see him. Don't care about him, either.

"Fine. You're right," I say, givin' in. "We might never get this chance again. We'll look."

She beams me a wide smile. "Thanks."

"But I go first."

"Lead the way, my captain." I catch her snickering at me good-naturedly as I open the steel door and peek inside.

# CLARA

*I'm holding on to Tyse's shirt* as he peers inside the station. "Well?" I ask, trying to see around his hulking frame, but not having much luck.

"No one's here." He opens the door wider, stepping through.

I follow, but pause just inside the door, trying to look at everything at once. It's nothing spectacular—just a white-tiled hallway, really. But it feels... otherworldly. There's a hum in the air. Like machines are working in some distant part of the station.

It's all very... I don't know. I don't really have a word to describe the style of this place. Hard. But functional. There are white pipes running both left and right on the ceiling. There are even some coming down the walls and disappearing into the floor. Everything is covered in the same white tiles as the train tunnel outside, which reflects the light pouring out of lanterns that line the hallway at evenly spaced intervals. But these lights don't appear to be powered by spark the way the ones in the Maiden District of Tau City were. The glow is mostly neutral white, with a bit of yellow.

"Which way should we go?" I ask, finding myself slightly out of breath from all of the excitement.

Tyse shrugs. "One way is as good as the other." He chooses right.

I let go of his shirt—reluctantly—and follow. The hallway

curves to the left as we walk and soon, we come to another door.

Tyse stops, his fingers gripping the handle of the door, and winks at me. "Moment of truth?"

"Do it," I nod. Still a bit nervous, but forcing myself to sound brave.

The door must be very heavy because Tyse puts a lot of effort into opening it, and the moment the seal is broken, the noise of machinery is so loud, I see Tyse's lips moving, but can't hear him talking.

He starts pointing. Then grabs my hand and we enter the new room.

It's massive. When I look up, it's like being inside a tower, that's how many floors there are above us. But it's nothing like any tower I've ever been in. It's dark, and wet—many pipes are dripping—and there is a lot of metal.

Metal stairwells, metal steps, metal railings.

There is a lot of glass as well. Massive containers—all empty—line every wall. They look like enormous jars. Each one has tubes coming out of it, which disappears into the walls.

The setup reminds me of the UpCity brewery Finn used to take me to in the Canal District that year I was part of the Extraction. Before I was chosen and sent to the Maiden Tower to live and my days were filled with duties. Only those vats weren't made of glass, but copper. And they weren't this massive or complicated.

The floor is concrete. Puddles of water gather in low spots and a rainbow sheen shines across the surface when the light hits them just right.

Tyse has paused to look around as well. But then he nods to the left, where there's another door, and we go that way. When we pass through the door, things change again. It gets quiet, for one. Thankfully. But that's not the only thing that changes. The hallways are now plaster with bits of rock showing through in places where the veneer has cracked and flaked off.

It's very reminiscent of home, except, where our colors were typically cream and sun-faded blue, these hallways are all shades of gray. Very Delta City. Even the lanterns on the walls are made of shiny copper, mimicking the design tastes of the god in the world above.

Tyse is tugging me backward, back to the door we came from.

"What are you doing?" I ask.

"Not this way. I think there's people this way. I can't know for sure, obviously, but the décor changed. Did you notice it?"

"Yes. It reminded me of home, with some differences to account for Delta's personal taste."

"We don't wanna bump into people here, Clara. They won't understand us, and it'll probably cause trouble. We should stay on this side of things." He gestures to the heavy door we just came through. "That's where the bots live."

"It's so loud in there. It's hard to think."

"I know," he says. "But we'll go up. To the next floor. It's a tower, did ya notice?"

"Yeah. The god's tower?"

"Well, there's definitely no second Delta living in this place. He's not the type of god who would share a personality. But didn't you say you never saw your god?"

"We didn't. Not once."

"So he doesn't come here. I don't know what this place is, but I'm curious now. Do you wanna go up? Or do you wanna leave?"

"Up, of course. I'm curious too. I'm dying, actually, to know what the hell is going on in these train-line cities."

"Good. We'll go up. That room in there is too loud to think, like you said. But I'm sure there's more rooms to see than that."

"Why are you so sure?"

"Because it takes a lot of infrastructure to run a city. That's what all that is back there. That's how the city exists. It's the plumbin' for the water, it's the way the spark is processed. It's the business side of things that the common person has no clue about. And before I leave here, I wanna see it."

"OK. Lead the way."

We return to the loud mechanical room and go up the stairs. Tyse pauses on the landing of the first floor, but then looks up. Pointing.

I nod, because what else can I do, the machines are too loud to talk, and we go up. But we don't stop at two. We don't stop at three. Or four. Or five. We go all the way up to the top. It's a long climb and I'm huffing, very out of breath since I'm carrying a rucksack, by the time we stop.

Tyse turns to me. It's not as loud up here, since we're literally like a hundred feet above the machines down below, so we can talk now. "I want to see the dome."

I squint at him. "Dome?" It hadn't occurred to me that they'd have domed towers here, but of course they would. If the city is laid out like mine, the tallest towers have domes. "All right," I agree. "Let's look at the dome."

He opens the door a crack, peeking through for a few moments. Then opens it wide. We step in, finding ourselves in a circular space covered in shiny, black screens. They cover every single space of the curved wall. "Wow," I say, turning in a circle. "This is... well, I have no idea what this is."

There's no one in here—not even bots—so Tyse walks over to the nearest screen and begins studying it. "It's a control room," he says.

"What's that?"

"It's a way to watch people. Look." He taps the front of the screen and it comes to life with a burst of light. A moment later, an image appears. A video. "There they are."

He does this to many screens. Tapping dozens of them into life with a press of his finger. And each time one comes to life, it's showing people. People who are walking around a city that looks almost identical to my Tau City, except for the color scheme.

I walk over to Tyse, who is standing in front of the largest screen in the room. It's at least ten times as big as the others and shows a view of the whole city from the perspective of the tower.

The god's tower.

I know this because on either side are two more towers. In my world, the one on the right is the Maiden Tower and the one on the left is the Extraction Tower.

And down the middle is a canal. Filled with dark, gray, nearly black water.

I recoil just looking at it. "What the hell is wrong with the water?"

"Hmm," Tyse hums. But it's not one of his sexy hums. It's one of his concerned hums. "I dunno. Looks gross though, right? Like oil, or somethin'."

Yeah. Really gross. But then I get distracted by the smaller screens. Each of which seem to show a little slice of the city and the people in it.

Again, it's reminiscent of my Tau City—but the vibes are

all wrong. Everyone is wearing black. There isn't a bit of blue anywhere. And they all look... well, not unhappy, exactly, but even after searching several dozen screens across the entire city, I can't find a single person that's laughing.

"There isn't a bit of spark anywhere," Tyse says.

"What?" I turn and walk over to him. While I was looking for laughter, he was looking for spark, I guess. "No spark anywhere? Hmm. It makes sense though. That's why the water is black."

"I think you're right. That *is* why the water is black. But... why would there be no spark here? In your Tau City they raised spark. They cultivated it inside women, then sacrificed them to the fake god in the tower. Which was just them stealing your spark to feed Anneeta. So what is goin' on here? Because there is no baby god back in Delta City. Well," he laughs. "I guess, technically, there is. But trust me when I say this, Delta isn't growing Anneeta up to take his place. I don't know what he's doin' with those little gods, but it isn't that. He doesn't *share*."

"He still has to feed them." Even I recoil from my words. I think Tyse does too, but I wasn't looking at him, so I don't know for sure. "Wow. I can't believe I just said that."

"It's true though. And might explain the lack of spark here?" He shrugs. "Maybe?"

My brow furrows, thinking. "Well, when Delta and I had that talk in my head after I first arrived in his city, he made a remark about the Extraction. Something like... it was barbaric. That he didn't do it that way. Not his exact words, but along those lines."

"If he's not extracting spark," Tyse looks confused, "then why does this place look dead and empty? And how does he live?"

I shrug. "Maybe he's too old to need spark?"

"But… all gods need food."

"What?"

"Nothin'. It just doesn't add up. There has to be spark here. Why else does it exist?"

On the screens a buzzing noise sounds, pulling our attention back to the city. People begin rushing around. Some of them looking downright panicked.

Tyse presses in closer, trying to see the people better. "What the hell is happening now?"

I have no idea. But that buzzer was clearly a signal that people should be… *doing* something.

"They're goin' home," Tyse says, pointing at a screen that shows a walkway in front of a row of houses. Whole families are scurrying through doors. "They're rushing around tryin' to get home."

"Must be dinner time." Which makes Tyse laugh and upsets my stomach. Because we both know they're not rushing home for dinner. They're not rushing home for something *good* like hanging out with your family. People looking forward to something fun don't move with panicked, jerky motions and have fear-filled eyes.

Suddenly, all but a few of the screens switch from an outside view to an inside one. Tyse and I both lean in closer, trying to see everything, all at once.

I'm drawn to a view of a woman and her family inside a home that looks eerily similar to the home I lived in with my father. He was the Extraction Master's valet, so we had a nice place in the Extraction District. Not as nice as Finn's house, but it was comfortable.

The mother is busy doing something in the kitchen while the father is ushering three little girls into another room. I look around, trying to see if I can follow the father and children, but each screen seems to be a different home, so I focus on the mother. She removes lengths of clear tubing from paper packages, then hurriedly follows her family into the other room.

The view switches, and now I can see them all. The mother is attaching the tubes to her daughters, a look of panic on her face. "What the ..." I lean in closer. "What the hell is she doing with those tubes?" I glance up at Tyse and find him pale and sickly looking. "What's wrong with you?"

He points to the screen in front of him. "They're *all* doing it."

He's right. Every screen I look at, I find the same scene—a family in a room. All the females—mothers and children alike, have those tubes attached to them on one end, and on the other they are plugged in to a wall. "What is this?"

Delta's voice comes booming through the screens. "Good evening citizens of Delta City. This is your god speaking."

I startle, looking up at Tyse. "He's here! Delta! He's here!"

Tyse is shaking his head. "No. He's not here. It's a recording."

"It is time for the evening harvest," Delta is saying. "Please be ready by the count of twenty. Nineteen. Eighteen—"

"*Harvest*," Tyse sneers. "What a word."

"A harvest? Like an apple from an orchard?" One moment it makes no sense, the next, it does. My hand flies up to my mouth. "No." I look at Tyse. "He's *stealing* their spark? Just sucking it out of them like... *blood*." Ew. I make a face.

"Look." Tyse is pointing to the screens. Every single view is of people, inside their homes, hooked up to tubing. "I guess Delta was tellin' the truth," he says. "There is no Extraction ceremony on his farm. There are no Spark Maidens. There's no Maiden Tower. There's no ten years of high livin' to erase the guilt of sending a single woman into the tower to feed the growin' god on the other side of the doorway. No. That's a fantasy. Not even a bad one compared to what this fucker's doin' here. Because he just takes it whenever he pleases. *Evening* harvest? Did ya hear that part? *Evening.* Like he does it in the mornin' as well. Hell, maybe he does three, four, ten times a day for all we know. What a complete piece of shit. I mean, I knew he was bad, but this? It's like stealin' souls." He's shaking his head as he looks at the screens. Then his face screws up. "Ut oh."

I turn, looking at the screen. "Ut oh, what?"

"Look. This one didn't make it home in time."

"Five. Four. Three..."

Oh, no! He's right. There's a woman running down a street, like she's trying to make it home before the countdown ends. She's not gonna make it. "What will happen?"

"Two. One."

And then, a female voice in a strange, automated tone, says, "Harvest begins now."

I gasp, watching as the young woman on the street stumbles forward, grabbing at her heart like she's having an attack.

"No," I breathe. Then look up at Tyse. "You don't think he's punishing her for not being hooked up?"

Tyse's lips lift up in a sneer. "Oh, that's exactly what I think. Fuckin' Delta. Tryin' to make himself out to be so benevolent, when he's doin' *this*?"

We turn back to the screen of the woman and find her face down on the ground. Having passed out, or something, while we weren't watching. There's blood seeping out from her open mouth. "Isn't anyone gonna help her?"

Tyse scoffs. Like this answer is obvious.

But then, movement. People are coming. "There they are."

"No," Tyse says. "It's bots. Look closer."

He's right. When they come out into the light, they are the gleaming white bots we saw in the train station. They pick the woman up by her arms and legs, carrying her like a sack until they're out of sight.

"Look. She's not the only one." Tyse is pointing to a screen again, but this time, it's on the other side of the room. The view on these screens is still mostly showing the people in the homes. Women and girls lying on beds or couches as glowing, cyan-blue spark travels through the tubing and disappears into the walls.

But there are maybe a dozen that show bots carrying more women and children off. The ones who didn't make it back in time.

"He killed them?" It can't possibly be true.

"Not sure," Tyse says. "Maybe... maybe he's set it up so they have to be harvested or or they die? But then again... yeah. Maybe he just killed them."

I swallow down some bile. "I feel like I'm gonna be sick."

"I think we've seen enough. Let's just go, Clara."

"Yeah. You're right. I'm sorry I came up here now."

"I'm sorry for being right."

"About what?"

He smiles at me, which puts all the upside-down things in my world right-side-up again. "I told ya he was an asshole."

Which only makes me sigh. And wonder, as we make our way all the way down the stairs again, if this is just the way of the world.

Is it all just... *bad*? Is everything evil? Is there no good left?

What is the point of a world like that?

This can't be all there is.

There has to be good *somewhere*.

But no. I'm not sure that's true. Because as Tyse and I

descend the stairs of the tower, the cyan-blue glow below us is so bright, there's no way to miss it.

It's spark—vast quantities of it—filling up all the glass vats that were empty when we passed earlier.

Only the canal back home compares with what I'm looking at, but the canal was not pure spark. It was spark infused water. And no one was harvested to get it that color. The stuff in these vats, it's... viscus. Thick. And a little bit gross, but I don't know why I feel that way.

"It's your blood," Tyse yells, trying to be heard over the roar of mechanical things on the ground floor.

"What?"

"Sorry. I was just thinking that it's like your blood. Your life force, ya know? And he's stealing it. It makes me kinda sick to look at it."

"Me too."

"Oh, shit. Look." We're still standing on the third or fourth landing above the vats, so we've got a good view of the lower level. Tyse is pointing to the far end where bots are carrying women and girls to another part of the tower.

Before I even realize it, my feet are flying down the stairs.

"Clara! Where are ya goin'?"

"I need to see," I yell back. Going faster now. "I need to see what he's doing with them."

His boots pound on the metal stairs above me, but I don't wait. He might stop me and I'm not leaving here until I know what Delta is doing to those women and girls who didn't make it home.

Once at the bottom, I dart off to the left. Weaving my way in between working bots, vats of spark, and all kinds of other machinery that I don't have names for. It's loud again. Much too loud to have a conversation. But I can faintly hear Tyse calling my name behind me.

I turn a corner and there they are. A parade of bots carrying women and girls. I get in line, keeping pace. They don't notice me—don't pay any attention to me at all—but I didn't expect they would. Tyse comes up next to me and together, we follow the bots and unconscious women and girls into the next room.

It's not as loud in here, so Tyse is saying, "We should go. This is a bad idea. We should just go."

But I'm shaking my head, stepping aside, out of the line, so I can take in what the actual fuck I'm looking at.

It's not vats of spark, it's... I can't even come up with a word. My eyes travel up the wall of the tower—it must be twenty or thirty levels, at least. And every inch of these walls has a tank attached to it. Tanks, and tanks, and tanks—all the way up to the tippy top of the tower—filled with glowing spark.

"It's insane," I catch Tyse muttering. "This is fuckin' insane. No wonder the air in Delta City is clogged with spark like ash in a forest fire. He's got oceans of it."

Which is an exaggeration, but only marginally. Because these tanks of spark have to equal lakes, at least.

"Why does he need so much?" I ask.

"Power," Tyse whispers. "That's the only possible answer. It gives him power. And once ya have a bit of it, ya always want more."

It occurs to me, in this very moment and maybe for the first time ever—which is embarrassing—that I have no fucking idea what spark even *does*.

I mean, I used it to make whimsical drawings in the air.

What a joke.

Because clearly spark is something spectacular if a god needs this much of it.

I look at Tyse, wanting to read his expression, but I find

him looking elsewhere. And when my gaze follows his, I find the answer to my question about what Delta is doing to these girls and women who didn't make it home in time for harvest.

They're all on beds. Clustered under the tanks that line the walls. They are in various stages of being plugged in and the ones who got here earlier are pale, almost gray. The tubes connecting them to the tanks are empty now, drops of residual spark cling to the interior, evidence that they've already been harvested.

Are they dead?

Tyse must be asking himself the same thing because he walks over to a child and places his finger on her neck. His eyes find mine. "She's alive, but barely."

I force my mind to think, trying to work all this new information out. He doesn't kill them. The punishment for missing your harvest is to be drained to the edge of death.

They'll probably wake up in their own beds, maybe? Their own *stable*. The bots having returned them to the farm. And they will carry on with their lives. Vowing to never miss another harvest.

I let out a long breath, finally having seen enough, but unable to take my eyes off the scene playing out all around me.

There are at least a hundred women and girls in here. And from the screens, I would calculate that this is a tiny fraction of the population. Delta has thousands of women in his herd of Spark Maidens. And he even takes it from the children.

Girls. That couple had three girls. He must breed for females.

The Extraction is starting to look like a pretty good time compared to Delta's dystopian nightmare.

Tyse walks back over to me, offering his hand. "Come on. Let's go. We've seen enough."

I take his hand and allow him to lead me out of the tank room, back into the roaring vat room, and we head back the way we came.

There's a faint beeping noise. Coming from outside, I think. And I can just barely make out Delta's recorded voice —so soothing, such a lie—telling his people that the evening harvest is now over.

When will he do it again? Is there a night harvest? Or will he let them sleep until morning and milk them then?

If I thought I was ever going back to Delta City, I might start planning a conversation with the tyrant. I might pick and choose my words carefully. Hoping to make him feel guilty enough to reconsider what he's doing here.

But I'm not going back. Even before finding this place, I knew that.

Never. I'm *never* going back.

Tyse leads me out of the tower. We pass several dozen bots—none of which pay any attention to us. And when we get to the door that leads back out to the train, I see the sign. A sign I didn't notice on the way in because we were on the other side of this door and didn't have a reason to look behind us once we passed through it.

*Delta Factory—Dimension 702.*

Tyse sees it too. And we both stare at it for a moment. I don't know what he's thinking, but I'm hearing Delta's words in my head. *You cannot see through worlds. You are not a Looking Glass. You are just a power source.*

I smile for the first time since we entered this tower.

Because it's not true.

If it were, he would've said those words with *conviction.*

He wouldn't have taken time to enter my head and have a conversation about what I was, if his words were true.

I'm not *just* a power source.

I'm not *just* a battery.

I'm something else.

It is now my new mission to figure this out.

Tyse opens the doors and invites me to walk through with a wave of his hand. I do this and we find ourselves back on the platform. Another train has arrived and there are dozens of bots out here unloading it.

He grabs my hand, pulling me towards the train's open door just as the last few bots exit.

"What are you doing?" But he's already pulled me through the doors and a moment later, they begin to close.

"Fuck walkin'," Tyse says. "We're not walkin'. I learned a lot back there, and I know all you're thinkin' about right now is spark, Clara. But ya know what I'm thinking?"

"What?"

"I'm thinking—" the train starts forward with a jolt, and then smoothly, we're pulling away from the station. "I'm thinkin' he can't come here."

"Why would that be? I mean, clearly, he's been here. Someone had to set it all up."

"It was probably someone like me. Someone who can hop worlds. But never mind that. If he can't come here, he can't control us. And those bots aren't soldiers. They're *workers*. Mechanical slaves, that's it."

"OK." I shrug. Not really seeing where he's going with this. "So what?"

"It means we're *free*, Clara. Fuck Delta. Fuck his mission. Fuck every one of those gods. We're free now. And we're gonna take this train down the line and find ourselves a *good* world. And then we're gonna live happily the fuck ever after."

We just stare at each other for a moment. Slowly the smiles start. They grow, and then we're laughing. There are no compartments on this train. No seats, even. It's not for people, it's for cargo.

So we just sit on the floor. Tyse with his back against the train's inner hull, me between his legs, slumped against his chest.

And then we dream.

We dream about a future where the world is good and we get to live in it.

# FINN

*T*he train is still slowly rolling to a stop when I open my eyes, trying to remember where I am. It hits me pretty fast, though. Everything comes back in a rush.

The tower. And the lies that came with it. Donal, and my mother, and the culty Matrons all trying to open the God's Tower doors to... where? Don't know.

My dad. How he must've struggled with knowing it was all lies, all those years. Unable, or unwilling, to change things.

Blowing shit up. And how I'm literally ruining people's lives trying to save them.

Clara Birch. Brave and fearful at the end. My greatest failure.

And Jasina Bell. Sleeping on top of me right now, exhausted from our marathon tower-slaying spree. She smells like freedom. She feels like a dream. Like that life I pictured as a scholar living down in the ruins below Tau City with a family of my own might be more than just a fantasy.

The days and weeks melt into one another as Jasina and I travel the train tunnel. Sometimes on the train, but most of the time, off. We sleep in little side tunnels near the stations. Dead-end tunnels, from what I can tell. But they are private, and quiet, and away from the disturbing worker things that have no faces.

Jasina is tired all the time now and as each day goes by, I

worry about her more and more. Wondering if I should take her back.

But she would never agree, so I don't even bring it up. I don't let her know that I'm watching her decline. That it's impossible *not* to notice that all she wants to do is sleep. I just make sure we take long breaks where she has a chance to do that.

We're on the train line to do a job, though. So after many days of rest, that's where we end up. Not just because we ran out of supplies after the last run, but because we're committed to what we're doing here. We're committed to ending the Extraction, whatever that even is.

Jasina stirs, trying to sit up, as the train finally comes to a complete stop with the slightest of jerks. "What's happening?" Her voice is sultry and low. Very sexy.

"We're here."

She smiles, eyes closed, letting out a breath. Then flops back down onto my chest. "How many towers do you think there are? How many times will we have to do this?"

I've thought about this a lot but there's no way to tell. There's no map. I mean, maybe inside the Extraction Master's office there's something in that machine that has a clue, but even though we want to linger in each of these factories, we don't. We just do the job, set the timer for the explosion, and get out. The first couple of times inside the towers we did pilfer things, but only because we were desperate. We had to. We had no choice. We came into this mission with zero preparation. We had the ragged, torn clothing on our bodies, and nothing else.

But the last two, we haven't even so much as taken a peek down the stairs where the Extraction Masters lived and worked. The last city was called Omicron. It's a weird name. But they're all like that.

First Sigma. Then Rho. Then Pi. Then Omicron.

"I don't know," I tell Jasina, finally answering her question. "Only a few probably."

She stirs again, this time pulling herself up. I'm sure she'd like to sleep more, but the workers are already entering the train, removing crates. We're in the back, so it'll take them a little while. But the sooner we do our job, the sooner we can come back and relax.

Until the next one.

Jasina rolls off me, pausing on her knees to sigh before standing all the way up. I get up too. Smooth out my clothes—a tunic and some pants that look like they could've come straight out of my own closet, because, of course, all the Extraction Masters had the very same closet —and then I smile at Jasina and offer her my hand. "Ready?"

She nods unenthusiastically, but accepts my offered hand. "Let's go and get it over with."

We halfheartedly dodge the workers and get off the train. The main door is closed because the workers mostly use a roll-up door off to the left of it. Easier to get crates through, I guess.

But Jasina and I made the mistake of following them through that bigger door in the Pi Factory and we found ourselves in a freezer with no other way out. Didn't make that mistake twice. It was a good clue, though. There's food in those crates.

No workers at this factory are using the main door, but we still do, entering to find the very same thing waiting for us every single time. A dim room with dripping pipes overhead and a maze of metal railings, and stairs, and machines.

We make our way through the curving hallways, coming

to the intersection where it branches off in two more directions.

Every time we get here, Jasina sighs. Probably reliving the memory of Donal dragging her away, down the right-hand option.

I give her hand a squeeze of support, and then offer her a comforting smile as I lead her in the opposite direction, towards the Extraction tower.

She squeezes back. "Thanks. I never said that before, but you do it every time now and I figure I should let you know I appreciate it."

I look over my shoulder, smiling. "No problem. That's why I'm here."

"Do you think this will ever end?"

"What will? Blowing up towers?"

"Yeah. What if this train line goes on forever? What if there's no end?"

"Well, everything ends. This train line will too, eventually. Are you having second thoughts?"

She moves her feet a little quicker so we're shoulder to shoulder, then shakes her head. "No. Not at all. I just think about the people and cities… don't you wonder?"

"What it's like in those cities?"

"Yeah."

"Sure. But… if I see the Extraction Master as my father—as a person—then it would be harder to end it, ya know?"

"Ignorance is bliss?"

"That." I let out a breath as we weave our steps, avoiding some puddles on the floor. There's always puddles in the lower level of the city, but these seem a lot bigger. Wider.

Jasina notices too, pointing at the ceiling above us. "Look. The canal is leaking pretty bad."

"They must not take very good care of their city," I say, feeling judge-y.

We turn a corner, knowing that the staircase that leads up to the dome of the Extraction Tower is not far now, but then have to stop in our tracks as we're confronted with actual flooding.

Jasina jumps back, letting go of my hand. "Holy crap! What the hell?" We both look up, but wherever this water is coming from, it's not from the pipes above our heads. "How do we get through?"

I turn and bend down. "Hop on. I'll carry you."

She shoots me a look that I am becoming very familiar with. This look says, 'I can do it myself'. She's very big on self-sufficiency. Which is a good thing in a partnership like this. She pulls her weight and I like it. It's good.

But I'm not letting her trudge through knee high water. "Come on, Jasina. Just get on. Why should both of us get wet? And anyway, it's my job."

She cocks a hip at me. But it's more out of amusement than exasperation. "Since when?"

"Well... since you became mine."

"Is that what I am?"

I nod. Slowly. "Yeah. You are. I have a dream and... well, it's dumb. But it's a good life. And you're in it. It's me and you and we've got a little family, and a little place of our own."

"Oh, my god." She places a hand over her heart like I just shocked her.

"What? Why are you looking at me like that?"

She tilts her chin up, squares her shoulders, and grins at me with her eyes. "Did you just ask me to marry you?"

I laugh. Then point. "No. Trust me, Jasina Bell, when I propose, you will not have to ask for clarification."

"Then what was that? You're *mine*?"

I grab her around the waist, pulling her towards me. Which activates her escape instincts, but she doesn't try hard. "It was... a prelude," I say, trying not to smile too big. "It was... a promise."

"We hardly know each other. We're like a month into this relationship."

"One big, monumental month." I shrug. "I know what I want. You."

This declaration makes Jasina Bell's eyes narrow. "It's too soon to know that. I mean, you just lost..."

She doesn't finish.

And I'm not about to hide from this. I'm done being old Finn Scott.

So I finish for her. "Clara? I just lost Clara? It hasn't even been a month. But the time I've spent with you, Jasina, is more than equal to the decade I spent without her, pretending to be in love. We never even dated, you know that right? We were kids, kissing and holding hands. And then she was Chosen and her life was all about the men she entertained for her Maiden duties. I was just a... an afternoon tryst. An afterthought. And I know what you're thinking—that I'm jealous. That maybe you're a substitute. I know you think this because you told me that day we escaped. But I said it then, and I'm gonna say it now too. She was my greatest failure. Choosing you was the only thing I ever did right."

I bring her hand to my lips, kissing it softly as I look right into those royal blue eyes of hers. "It's you, Jasina. You and me. Forever, if you'll have me. So—" I point to my back. "Hop on. I'm gonna carry you."

She tries to hide her smile, but she's failing so spectacularly, she just shakes her head and walks around to my back, hopping on to be carried.

I grab her under the knees, stand up, hiking her up onto my hips a little, and then I walk through the water, my own shit-eating grin on my face as well. In fact, I'm overwhelmed with thoughts of Jasina, and my dream of a little family, and how maybe all this is gonna turn into some kind of grand adventure. And after we're done blowing up Extraction Towers, we'll go home.

To what's left of it.

We'll go home to Tau City. A different Tau City. And I'll find those scholars who study the ruins below the city and I'll tell them all about our time on the train line, and those people will become our people. People with questions looking for answers. And Jasina and I will settle in with them, and the world will calm down, and that family will emerge, and grow, one baby at a time.

Jasina points. "There they are. The stairs."

I'm up to my knees in mucky, murky water when she says this. I wade over to the steps and turn, letting her hop off without getting her feet wet. Then we start climbing.

We're about halfway up when Jasina stops.

"What?" I ask. We're on a landing maybe six floors up. Jasina walks over to the edge, peering out at the inside of the tower. All the way up to the top, then down where the water is still sloshing from the disturbance I made. Lights flicker erratically, casting eerie shadows over the walls.

"This feels wrong."

I look around, taking in the vibe of the place. "Yeah. Can't say I disagree. Let's just get it over with and leave. We'll be back at the train station in ten minutes and we'll never have to come here again."

She looks at me, nodding, but she's apprehensive.

"You wanna wait here?" I ask. "I can do it alone."

"No. This place is creepy. Don't you think it's creepy?"

I shrug, looking around. "I mean, I wouldn't call it cozy but they've all been creepy, Jasina."

She sighs. "You're right. I think my imagination is just getting the better of me." Then she turns back to the stairs and starts climbing again.

It only takes a few minutes to reach the top, and here we pause. Pressing our ears against the door. We have no idea what time it is, whether it's day or night, or whether or not the Extraction Master is on the other side of this door sitting at his desk or doing something in the Looking Glass room, so we always listen.

Jasina shakes her head. "I don't hear anything."

I nod, agreeing. "Me either." Then turn the handle and push forward just a tiny crack.

It's completely dark inside. No sound. Nothing.

But we pause here anyway, just to make sure.

After several minutes, Jasina touches my arm. "I think it's empty."

I think she's right, so I push the door open with more force, making the bookcase inside swing open. But it gets caught on something about a foot in, refusing to budge any further. "There's something blocking it," I say.

She squeezes past me, easing her body sideways through the door, then stares at the ground.

"What is it?" I ask. "What's blocking the door?"

She bends over, picking something up. Then holds it in front of the door so I can see it. "Books."

But the one in her hand isn't just any book. It's *the* book.

The Godslayer and his Courtesan.

# JASINA

*I hold up the book*, showing it to Finn as my mind races with questions. "What is this doing here?"

Finn pushes against the door now that he knows it's just books in the way, forcing it open a few more inches—enough to squeeze his body through sideways. He looks down at the pile of books, then back up at me. "It was on the shelf, I guess."

"Yeah, obviously. It's been on the shelf in every single Extraction Tower."

My brow furrows. "Has it?"

"Yeah, I've checked. This book has been following me ever since my first day in the Little Sister dorm. I found it on a shelf there too. Then up in your tower, and it's been in every tower we've blown up so far."

He shrugs. "OK. So what's the big deal?"

"What's the big deal? The big deal is that it's weird. Why is this book in all the towers?"

He cracks a smile, trying to lighten the mood because I'm acting... weird. "Because it's about us, Jasina. It's our history."

"Well," I frown. "That's weird, right? I mean, these stories are about the most infamous couple in all of history. A couple that contributed to the downfall of pretty much everything. And this isn't the story book, Finn. It's an actual history. I've read some of it. It's like... scholarly. Why would it be required reading for Extraction Masters?"

Now he just sighs. "I dunno. I don't know what to tell

you. I've never even read the stories. I mean, I've heard of them. I know the basics. But I don't have any answers for you."

"I'm keeping this copy," I tell him, tucking it into the makeshift hip sling. "I'm going to figure this mystery out."

Finn just grins back at me like I'm cute. "You do that. But it's a pretty serious book. What is it? Four hundred pages? I bet it's fine print too, isn't it?"

"So?"

"It's gonna be heavy."

"I don't care. There's something weird about this book."

He offers me his hand. "You know what?"

I take it and let him pull me close to him. It's still very thrilling to think that I'm the courtesan of the Tau City Extraction Master and that he and I are on a real mission to save the Spark Maidens. "What?" I ask.

"I think it's perfect that you want to read that history book. Because if you're gonna be a Tau City scholar's wife, you'll have to have your own research. And this is it."

It also thrills me when he talks about our future. I'm not stupid. I know I'm just a fill in for the woman he truly loves and no amount of trying to convince me otherwise will ever change that. But Clara is gone. For good. Like, she's never coming back and is most likely dead.

And that is enough for me.

Maybe it's not entirely true, this love he's professing.

But it's true enough for now.

He puts an end to this conversation with a kiss. Not anything sloppy or demanding, just a really small one. The kind of kiss your lover gives you in a moment of encouragement.

"Ready?" he asks, jutting his chin in the direction of the Looking Glass room.

I nod. "Yeah. Let's do it and get the hell out of here. I don't like this place."

For the first time, Finn takes a really good look around and immediately he begins to frown. "Now that we're up here, yeah. It's... off. There's something wrong with this one." He looks at me, grinning. "I mean, aside from the fact that obviously, there's no Extraction Master in this tower. It's abandoned."

I agree, so I nod. "Yeah." And then I walk over to the windows, which I already know, overlook the entire city—from the top of the canal all the way down to the bottom.

Finn joins me and we stare down at the lifeless place, but then... movement. "Look." I point. We both lean in, trying to make out what we're seeing down the canal.

At first, I think it's people but then Finn says, "Workers." He turns to me. "We've never seen that before. Have we?"

I shake my head. "No. They stay under the city. Like little invisible slaves. They make the city run. I don't think they're supposed to be in the city. I don't think the people are supposed to see them. I don't think they're supposed to know they're even there."

"Yeah." Finn's eyes scan the city. "What's going on here?" He turns to me again. "Do we need to know? Or should we just do our job and leave?"

I give him a tiny shrug, but I've been asking myself the same question. "Are we scholars? Or are we just..." I search for a word that might describe all the destructive things we've done. But it takes a few before I land on, "...*villains?*"

"Villains?" Finn laughs. "If anyone had told me a month back that I'd be an infamous villain I'd have laughed in their face. Me. A villain. It's ridiculous."

This makes me scoff with amusement. I like the idea of us being the infamous and historic Godslayer and his

Courtesan, especially since this book seems to be following me. But it *is* ridiculous. He's Finn Scott, for fuck's sake. He's far from perfect, but a villain he is not. "So… scholars then?"

Looking towards the large open stairwell that leads down to the Extraction Master's private quarters, he gestures. "Scholars it is. Let's go do some research."

We descend the staircase slowly, scanning the floors below us as we pass them by just in case there are people here. But it's clear there aren't. The place has been abandoned.

Each floor has a living space in full view of the stairwell and they're all in disarray.

The bottom floor is a disaster. Couches upturned, broken windows, piles of debris on the floor, and even a few holes in the plaster walls.

"What the hell happened here?" Finn asks.

"Looks like some kind of battle."

"The city rebelled?" he asks.

I like this about Finn. He knows it's probably true, but he likes to refrain from making statements before asking my opinion about things. Even if it's just to get my agreement, like now. "Yeah. Probably."

"I guess they got tired of sending their Spark Maidens into the fake tower where there's no god."

I nod, still looking around. But my gaze lands on the front door. It's open. And broken. "I think they came up here to kill the Extraction Master."

Finn's gaze goes to the door as well. "I don't blame them." Then he grabs my hand. "Come on, let's go outside."

My feet stay firmly planted right where they are. "No! Are you crazy? I don't wanna go out there. We've seen enough. Something bad happened here. Let's just blow the tower and leave."

"But we're scholars. It's our duty to ask questions and look for answers."

"There are workers down there."

"So? They can't even see us. It's like we're invisible."

"*Under* the city, that's what it's like. What if it's different out there?"

"Why would it be different out there?"

"I dunno."

"Well, if they are, we need to know that, Jasina. It's an important detail."

"You're right. I know you're right. But the thought of going out there makes me... jittery. My heart is racing. Feel." I take the hand I'm holding and put it up against my chest, proving it to him.

"You're scared," he says.

"Yeah. And I'm not a girl who scares easily."

"I think it's good that you're scared."

"Why? Because you're not?"

He nods. "Exactly. We're a... complement. There are empty spaces inside of us where we're missing critical character traits. Everyone has flaws. But we're gonna do this, Jasina. We *need* to do this. So you stay scared so you can alert me to any danger and I'll be brave, so we can find answers."

My breath comes out in a rush, like I was holding it in.

"Deal?" he asks.

"All right." I nod. "Complements."

He's leading me over to the door before I can change my mind. There's an elevator here, just like it was in the Tau City Extraction Tower, but the doors are wide open and there's nothing but empty space below us when we peek down.

We take the stairs, coming out into the lobby of the Extraction Tower—which is also a disaster. Furniture upturned, all the windows in the front of the building have been broken out, and there's a lot of water on the floor, though none of it is deep like it was below the city.

We go outside and find that the canal is black. There's no blue light in it at all. Which we saw from above, but it didn't really register until right now, when we're standing in front of it, that it's... dead.

"I can feel it," Finn says. "The lack of spark here."

He's right. The whole place feels dead.

"Let's go check out the Maiden tower," Finn says, squeezing my hand as he turns towards the bridge that leads across the water. It's mostly still intact, but there are signs of some kind of struggle here too.

Everywhere, actually.

"Wow," Finn says, as we walk up to the Maiden Tower. "What is all this?"

He's pointing to the windows, which are covered in some kind of metal. "Shutters?" I guess.

"Yeah. No one can see in."

"Or break them to get out," I add, almost whispering.

He turns to look at me. "Creepy."

I nod my agreement, hastily looking around for those workers. I don't want to come face to face with one just in case they see us up here.

"OK, let's go back."

My eyes widen, my heart jumping. "Really?"

"Yeah. I think you're right. There's something really wrong about this place. There was some kind of rebellion. We could search all the stores and houses, but I think we'll just find more of the same. Signs of battle. No people. Just workers, and who wants to confront them, right? And anyway, whatever happened here I'm sure there will be clues in the Looking Glass room. We'll try and find them before we set the timer."

"Yeah," I say, relieved. And a long breath comes out of me. Like turning our backs on this place is the best idea we've ever had. "That's where all the answers are. Good idea."

Our trip back across the canal is quicker. Our steps more purposeful.

Right outside the Extraction Tower there are workers. Not congregating or anything like that. Just... busy. Some of them are carrying crates, some of them are pushing garbage cans filled with debris. But most of them are just walking by.

Finn and I wait, holding our breath as we discern if they can see us or not. But when they all disperse, going on their individual ways, it's clear that they can't. Or if they can, they don't care.

We go back into the Extraction tower, climb all the way back up to the top, then up the last four floors to the dome. I help Finn tip the couch back over, so we can sit on it, and I flop down, a bit exhausted.

"Rest," he says. "I'll get the Looking Glass working."

I don't argue. I feel very uneasy and I would prefer to be out here, watching his back, while he's got the door closed in there to make the machine work.

But once he closes that door, I feel very exposed and vulnerable.

"For fuck's sake, Jasina," I mumble under my breath. "Snap out of it. You're acting like a first-year Little Sister. There's nothing here."

I know this.

But my fear remains.

It's unlike me, so it's unsettling. I mean, I've had plenty of moments of fear in my life. The most recent ones were about Donal, Auntie Bell, and that whole god-making thing they were doing.

This is different.

There's no threat here. No Auntie hovering over me, trying to bully me into doing what I'm told. No Donal threatening me with unwanted attention. No explosions to run from.

Just... a sense of anxiety and dread.

And it's just so unlike me to be fearful of the idea of something, that I begin to panic again.

What's wrong with me?

Why am I acting like this?

More importantly, how do I fix it?

# FINN

*A*s soon as the door to the Looking Glass closes, the dome above and around me comes to life. But there's a sputter—a moment when everything goes black again—before snapping back on.

A voice greets me, but it's wrong. Warbled to the point of making the words incomprehensible.

"What the hell is this?" I mutter, walking over to the circular desk in the middle of the room. Once inside, I start tapping on the switches, trying to make the voice clearer.

It doesn't work. The words coming from the screen seem slow and mushed together.

Great. It's broke—

But before I can even finish this thought, a loud screeching sound booms out from every direction, making me crouch, wince, and cover my ears with my hands.

Just as quick as it started, it stops. And the room blinks again, but this time it stays black.

I stand, unmoving and blind, waiting to see what happens next.

But the seconds tick off and... nothing.

I sigh, suddenly feeling weary—a dull throb beginning to pulse behind my eyes—and make my way out from inside the circular desk. My body feels achy and rundown as I start feeling my way back towards the door, ready to just give up on this place and leave. It's not working so why bother blowing it up?

It's a bad idea. I know this even before the thought finishes forming in my head. We can't leave here without setting up the self-destruct sequence. If we do... well, I don't know what will happen, but whatever it is, it won't be good. And it will probably show up at the most inopportune time.

So instead of finding my way back outside, I go back inside the desk and close my eyes, picturing the glass top in the last Looking Glass room when all the little switches were illuminated. So far, every desk, every Looking Glass, has been exactly the same from tower to tower.

I let out a breath, eyes still closed, and see it. Allowing my fingers to slide across the glass, tapping on it, trying to get it to restart.

It takes several tries and many minutes of messing around before it flickers to life. I open my eyes, relieved that I'm back in business here, only to find jagged cracks running across the glass panels of the dome like a spider web.

Clearly the plates are damaged and it's messing up the image being projected. The voice is back too, warbled and weird.

I can't really make out what it's saying but I can tell that whatever this message is, it's repeating. Saying the same few words over and over again.

The surface of the glass desk isn't really lit up, but it's not completely dark, either. I find the panel that controls the sound and start tapping the switches—jumping back in surprise when the voice is suddenly clear and booming.

"Shut down-protocol has been initiated for Xi Factory – Dimension 702. Please evacuate until further—" It cuts out. There's some squealing, like it speeds up again, then it repeats. "Shut down-protocol has been initiated for Xi Factory – Dimension 702. Please evacuate until further instructions are received."

It keeps going, over and over again, and no matter how many times I tap the glass, it doesn't stop.

"Great. Fucking wonderful." I leave the center of the desk, heading for the door, when the message abruptly changes.

"Reset in progress. Twenty-one days until launch."

"What the hell is this?" I turn, looking up and around as the voice continues.

"Reset in progress. Twenty-one days until launch."

I leave the Looking Glass room, closing the door behind me, and everything goes abruptly silent. Jasina—oblivious to what just happened—is sleeping on the couch, right where I left her.

She stirs, as I approach. "What's going on? Did you set it?"

"No. There's some other program running."

This makes Jasina sit up, swiping at her red hair to get it out of her eyes. "What?"

"I guess there was some kind of shut down? The whole place. I got two messages. One said to evacuate, but then immediately after, there was another one that said reset in progress, or something like that."

"They shut it down?" Jasina, who looks even more exhausted after a few minutes of rest than she did before, is still trying to make sense of things. "The tower?"

"No," I shake my head. "The city."

"How do you shut down a city and reset it?"

"Well..." It feels pretty obvious to me, but it also feels kinda gross to say it out loud.

Jasina's eyes go wide. "They *killed* them?"

I shrug, feigning uncertainty. But it feels like the only logical answer. "What else would they do with all the people? They certainly weren't down in the train station, on their way to another city."

She blows out a breath. "Wow. Do you think it was the bot things that did it? Do you think they attacked them?"

"I dunno."

"Well." She gets to her feet, looking around the room, arching her back, stretching it, as she sighs with a heaviness that makes me wonder if she's OK. Her eyes land on the bookshelf across from the one we use to enter and exit the Extraction Towers. "I think we should go investigate."

My own eyes slide over to the bookshelf, which is actually a door that leads back into the city innards, and if you follow that path to its eventual conclusion, it also leads to the Little Sister dorm inside the Maiden Tower.

I wanted to go look when we were up in the other towers, but I never acted on it. Or even brought it up as a possibility. All those cities were inhabited. My curiosity over the idea tempered by the possibility that even if there are identical cities, there might not be identical people. We'd be seen as... invaders. It would be a bad move. But this city is different. We have time here. Twenty-one days, to be exact.

"Xi," I say.

Jasina's face screws up. "What?"

"That's what this place is called. Xi Factory – Dimension 702. The voice in the Looking Glass room said it."

"It's a weird name."

"Yeah. I wanna go look." I nod my head at the bookcase. "I wanna see the Maiden Tower."

Not the Little Sister dorm—the *Maiden Tower*.

I get how it sounds. But it sounds that way because that's how I meant it. "I need to know, Jasina. I need to know if there's a Clara here."

"What if there's a 'you' here? What if there's a 'me' here?"

"I think we should know that."

"Is that why you want to know if Clara's here? Or are you hoping—"

"No," I say. Pointing at her to cut her off. "I already told you, she's my greatest failure."

"So you're what? Looking to save her if she's here?"

I want to deny this, but I can't. So instead, I redirect the conversation. "I want to save everyone, Jasina." But it comes out on a yawn, so I have to start again, making it a question this time. "Don't you wanna save everyone too?"

"Then why are we blowing people up, Finn?"

"We're not. I mean, we are, but only a small number of people are living inside the Extraction Tower. And I can justify sacrificing them because... they *know*. Not the entire family, but the Extraction Master *knows*. So if he's sending girls into the tower to appease a god that doesn't even exist, then he's evil, Jasina."

"What about your father? Was he evil too?"

I've thought about this a lot as well. And while I really want to say no, because I knew him, he raised me, he was good to me, and in the end, he rebelled—I can't. So I nod. "Yes. Even him. Because he officiated several Extractions over the course of his duties. At any point he could've said no."

"He would've ended up the same way."

By which she means, dead. "Yeah. But there's a line, ya know? A line so bright you cannot miss it." These words coming out of my mouth were plucked straight from the Extraction Master's speech during extraction. "A line so bright you should not cross it. And if ever there was a line so bright that should not be crossed it's the one where sacrificing a young woman for her spark is on the other side."

113

Jasina sighs again. Her eyes slowly migrate back over to the bookcase in question. "OK. Let's go."

"Yeah?"

"Yeah," she says. "I wanna see it too. I wanna see inside the tower. We can't get in from the outside. The secret passage is the only way."

"We can't set the self-destruct either. Not unless we wanna hang around here for twenty-one days. That's when it says it'll be done. "

"*Done*," she says, echoing my last word. "What's that mean, exactly?"

I shrug. "I guess those workers are fixing things downstairs? Making it habitable again?"

Of course, I leave out the one thing we're really thinking about. The only thing that matters. The people. I don't think there's gonna be a 'Clara' on the ninth floor of the Maiden Tower. But I need to see it for myself before we leave here because there is no reason for a city to exist without people.

Where are they? What happened to them? And if they're truly all gone, where will they get more?

Jasina looks at the bookcase, her gaze lingering on it a moment too long before looking back at me. She sighs heavily. "OK. We agree then? We should go look?"

I hate this mood, this vibe in the room. It's a mixture of creeping hopelessness and a sense of foreboding. She looks wasted. Like she could sleep for weeks and still need more. I don't like it. I want to stop everything and let her rest. So I smile, trying to boost her up and keep her going. "Unless..."

Her brow crinkles up. "Unless what?"

I waggle my eyebrows at her. Kinda motioning to the couch. "We can take a little break and have a little fun. We know that couch, right?"

She spits air so hard little pieces of hair fly up around her face. "Only you, Finn Scott, could be thinking of sex at a time like this."

I shrug up one shoulder, still grinning like an idiot. "Just one of my many talents."

"Sorry, but I'm gonna have to say pass on the danger sex."

"Damn," I mutter. Chuckling at the same time. Which makes her smile. And that was the whole point of the offer. While I would not turn down sex—like probably ever. At least with her. I'm not really serious. I just want to see her smile.

Because we both feel it.

Something is happening, and we have no idea what it is, or what it means, or where it's gonna take us—but we *feel* it. We're on a path here, and at this point, I don't think veering onto the road less taken would even matter. We've set something in motion with this tower blowing stuff.

Whatever story this is, we're part of it.

Jasina steels herself. Squaring her shoulders and tipping her chin up. Then she walks over to the door. I meet her there and we lock eyes for a moment.

She doesn't say anything so I point to my back. "Wanna ride?"

"No," she laughs. "Going down is easy. But... thanks for the offer."

"It's a standing one," I say. "You know that, right?"

"Sure." Then she pulls the bookcase open and walks into the darkness.

I follow her, letting the door close behind me with a quiet hiss of air. Then we look down. Because there is a lot of activity at the bottom of these stairs.

All workers. Dozens of them. They all seem to have a job to do, but it's hard to make out what that might be, from this distance of nearly fifteen floors up.

"This is not normal," Jasina opines.

"Maybe not. But we can't be sure, Jasina. This is what? Our fifth tower after Tau City? There could be hundreds of these places and dozens of them could look just like this. We'd never know it."

She side-eyes me. "Nice try. But that's not how it feels."

Having run out of ways to assure her, I simply exhale. "Should we keep going?"

"What if they attack us?"

"They didn't attack—" But I stop. "What's going on with you?"

"What? Nothing. Why?"

"Because you're suddenly so…"

When I struggle to find a word, she inserts one for me. "Timid? Spineless? Fearful?"

"I was gonna say uncertain, but if you're feeling timid, spineless, or fearful, let's just turn around. I don't need to check this place out that bad. We'll move on. We'll get back on the train, go to the next station, and we'll hit this place up on our way back."

Her mouth drops open. "Way back? We're coming back?"

I shrug. "Well, when we're done. Where else is there to go?"

"Tau City will still be there, won't it?"

"Yes. It's there. I saw Gemna on the way out. I bet all the cities will still be there. Maybe not this one, but who knows. We're not destroying everything. Just the idea of sacrifice."

She actually brightens as I'm talking. "I never thought about going home. But you're right. We didn't destroy the whole city. And Gemna lived."

"Gemna and everyone else who wasn't a part of that sick ritual."

Now she smiles. "We *could* go home."

"And start over."

"Forget the Godslayer and his Courtesan. We could be…"

I take her hand, looking her in the eyes. "The scholar and his wife?"

"Or the scholar and her husband."

I laugh. Pointing at her. "Either way. I'm in."

She lets out a long breath. "All right. I feel better. I don't know what is wrong with me today, I just…"

"Missed home?"

"Yeah. I miss all of it. I don't know what Tau City Factory is, but that's where we grew up. That's all we know. I want to go back. Not now. Not yet. But when we're done doing what we came out here to do? Yes."

I give her hand a squeeze. "Deal. Now let's figure this place out and move on."

"The faster we burn it all down, the quicker we go home."

"A motto to live by if ever there was one."

# JASINA

*I don't know what's wrong with me*, but clearly something is. Because as we descend the staircase that will deposit us on the other side of the Extraction Tower, Finn is holding my hand like I need the moral support.

And... I do. My heart is racing. And while I do admit that this is a heart-racing situation to be in, it's just... not me.

"What are they doing?" Finn's voice pulls me out of my reverie. I find him pointing down at the workers.

We've descended all the way down to the fourth floor now, so we have a good view of them. Most are moving crates on carts that seem to float above the floor without any wheels. There are lots of little lights along the side of these carts too. Like they run off of spark.

And now I'm thinking about the dead canal. "I don't know," I halfheartedly tell Finn. "Probably just... moving building materials, or something?"

"Yeah, maybe," he mutters. But he doesn't sound convinced.

"What do you think happened to the spark?"

"Huh?" We're just coming down to the first floor, so Finn is distracted by all the activity.

"The canal. It was black and dead. What happened to it?" I ask. Then suck in a breath and hold it as a bot comes within a few feet of us.

But it just keeps going like all the others we've seen so far.

"Well," Finn says, letting out his own breath of relief. "There was a war, obviously. That's why the place is a mess. You know what the weird thing is, though?"

"What?"

"The city has no spark, it's a total disaster, but the workers still work." He looks at me now. "If there's no spark here, where do they get power from?"

"Power? What do you mean?"

"Well, they're not alive, Jasina. They're... machines. So they run on spark."

I don't know why this never occurred to me. I hadn't even thought about how the workers got power. I guess I thought it came from food. That's how *we* get power.

"And I bet it takes a lot of spark. Look at those carts, they don't even have wheels."

Yes, carts that hover instead of roll are unusual. But I've seen so many strange things over the past few weeks, I guess I just accepted it as normal now. Which is a terrible thing. Because it means I'm not paying attention. And now that I am, this thing with the workers needing spark to function—it's unsettling.

"Don't you think it's weird?" I ask. "That spark is like a lifeforce? And that it powers things that aren't alive?"

"You know what's weirder than that?" Finn replies. "That we *eat* things. Like... living things. That's weird. And when you think about it too hard, it's kinda gross. Even if it's just carrots. A carrot is *alive*. Even coffee beans are alive."

"And sugar," I say, picturing the pastries I used to yearn for when I was just a down-city girl coming up city for Little Sister etiquette lessons. Which feels like another life now.

"Yeah. Sugar too. That's a plant. It comes from beets."

"I think we should change the subject," I say.

Finn laughs. "It's weird though, right? That everything has to feed off of *something*."

"Weird in a bad way. Ominous. Foreboding. Maybe even sinister."

Finn just laughs. While we've been having this conversation, we've walked under the canal and crossed over to the other side. And while there are still puddles of water here, it's not nearly as bad as the flooding on the train station side of things.

We make our way through various metal structures and past several dozen busy workers, until finally we find the stairs that lead up to the Little Sister dorm inside the Maiden Tower.

"Want a ride?" Finn asks, pointing to his back.

I do. I really do. I want to cling to him, and for him to cling back. I want to stop now. I want to get off this adventure and go home.

And there it is.

The truth.

This is what's bugging me. I want to go home. And even though Finn telling me that this was the plan, after we're done saving the factory cities from Extraction by blowing up towers, I hadn't let myself dream about it.

And now I am.

I'm dreaming about home. I know my friends are gone—they all died when Gemna and I shattered the glass wall that I think was some kind of Looking Glass, but can't be sure. And my Auntie—the traitorous bitch—also dead. Probably. Though I didn't actually see it.

My mother and father stopped paying attention to me years back when I stopped paying attention to them.

But still.

I want to go home.

Immediately, self-loathing fills up the emptiness inside me. Why am I being such a baby? Why am I being so... stupid? This is not who I am. I am not emotional, or weepy, or senti—

Oh, shit.

Oh, no.

No. No, no, no.

This cannot be—

"Jasina?"

I blink and find myself looking straight into Finn's eyes. "Yeah."

He points to his back again. "Do you want a ride?"

I force a smile. "No. I'm good." And then, before he can ask me what's wrong—because clearly everything is wrong right now—I grab the railing and start climbing.

I know Finn hesitates because I count to five before I hear his footsteps following me up.

He's getting worried. And I don't blame him. We're doing something very dangerous. Together. Meaning him and I. Meaning, partners. Meaning he's counting on me and I'm... wavering. Overthinking. Retreating.

*Oh, you wish that was all you were, Jasina Bell.*

*You wish.*

I'm not weepy and homesick because I'm a *coward*.

I'm weepy and homesick because I'm... pregnant.

I'm pregnant. I'm pregnant. I'm *pregnant*.

My mind races with what-ifs, and second thoughts, and possibilities. I see everything that's happened in the last several weeks, I see all that's happening to us now, and then... I picture that life Finn's been talking about. The scholar and his wife.

Correction. The scholar, and his wife, and *child*.

I picture a comfy cave with walls made of sandstone and

floors covered in dirt soft enough to go barefoot. Flickering candles line the small room. There's a makeshift kitchen, and a fire pit, and various iron cooking pots hanging from a rack. I picture sleeping in on top of a soft feather mattress under a pile of fluffy blankets. Finn Scott and I clinging to each other to keep ourselves warm during the cold nights.

I picture the ruins, or relics, or whatever it is we study down there. Finn's excited concentration as he scribbles notes in some tattered book. He's always covered in sand, but he smells like a promise of happiness. He looks at me, and my swelling belly, with longing and hope.

We marry in a small ceremony officiated by... I dunno. Whatever you call the person in charge of the scholar's camp.

We have a boy. Or a girl. Then another, and another. And pretty soon, we've been living this life long enough that we forget where we came from and how we got here.

We forget.

We just live.

The grin creeps up my face. Slowly at first, but by the time we get to the top of the stairs and we're standing in front of the door that leads into the Little Sister dorm, my smile is wide and beaming.

Perhaps it is not a write up in a history book.

Perhaps being a wife and mother to the child of a scholar is mundane.

Lackluster. Tame and ordinary.

That's how Tau City Jasina Bell would see it.

But Train Tunnel Jasina Bell feels like this is winning.

I open the door to the dorm, practically bursting with excitement over my news and wanting to tell Finn about it so bad, I feel like I might explode. But I hold it in when I see what's on the other side.

It's not a big empty room at the top of a hidden set of

stairs. Well, technically, those two things are still true. The room is big and the stairs are still in the same place, but it's not empty.

And unlike the ruined, tattered, and decaying city outside that needs to be rebuilt, the interior of the dorm is... perfect. Not a single thing out of place. It's filled with living spaces. Filled with beds, and cozy nooks, and soft lighting, and clean floors. All the beds are made, all the shelves have books and other things, like candles, on them. There are even fluffy rugs on the floors.

Utterly convinced that there are no people here—I can feel this to be true as much as I have witnessed it—I step forward, hands on hips. "What the hell?"

Finn closes the door behind us. "What do you mean?"

"All these fuckin' bedrooms? I don't get it, Finn. Why choose a hundred girls to go live in a dorm that holds... I dunno, a thousand? What is with all these beds?"

Finn blows out a breath as he looks around. "Haven't a clue, to tell you the truth. This is the first time I actually knew it was a problem."

"As soon as I got to the Little Sister dorm, I saw it. I mean, all the living spaces near the canal were filled up. Even up to the fourth floor. But the moment I went exploring deeper in, it stopped making sense. Even in our dorm, which didn't have as many bedrooms as this one, there were hundreds of empty living spaces. All the beds were made, all the little nooks were cozy with blankets, all the shelves holding trinkets or books. Why?" I spin slowly in place, my arms out wide. "Why does this place exist? Because it's certainly not to hold the top one hundred potential Spark Maidens."

Finn's thoughtful eyes scan the room as he takes his turn slowly spinning in place. "Hmmmm. You've got a point."

Then he looks at me, letting out a sharp breath. "And I think I have an answer, but it's not a pleasant one."

"What do you mean? What is it?"

He winces. "I'm not sure you need to know, Jasina. I mean, isn't ignorance bliss sometimes?"

I recoil. "No. *Never.* There is never a time when ignorance is bliss. What is going on? What do you know? Tell me. Please. I will never stop thinking about this mystery if you don't."

He doesn't give in. Not immediately, at least. He takes a moment to think. Then he shrugs. "All right. I'll tell you, but it's just a theory."

"OK, hold on. Why do you have a theory about the Little Sister dorm in the first place?"

"I don't. My theory really has nothing to do with the dorm. It's just... what I saw back in Tau City. When they had Donal in that chair and he was... feeding off them." He pans a hand to indicate the dorm spaces, which in turn implies the Little Sisters who live in them. "I think... and I know we both know this. On some level, at least. But I think they just... grow you."

I blink at him. Hearing what he said. Understanding the words.

But the implications.

"It's a farm. Is that what you're telling me?"

"Well." He shrugs. "I've never heard of the word factory before we came down here to the train tunnels. But think about it, Jasina. There are cities. Many identical cities. And all of them seem to be producing spark. If we had stumbled in to a stable, for instance, filled with... sheep, or some other animal producing meat or wool, it would not be hard to figure out what a factory is, would it?"

I literally feel the blood leave my face. And a moment

later I'm looking up at Finn Scott, who has me in his arms, blinking away the darkness.

Finn looks worried. "Holy shit, are you OK?"

I nod, not sure that I am. Not sure how I got into this position—which is looking up at the ceiling just a few feet off the floor, and in the arms of my hero—*partner, future husband, father of my children?*

He picks me up and carries me over to the nearest bed, gently setting me down on the fluffy feather mattress—which should not be here, or be so comfy—and kneels down beside me. "What the hell happened?"

"I think…" I can't even believe I'm gonna say this. It's so… not something I do. "I think I *fainted.*"

"Yeah," Finn laughs. His blue eyes filling with relief. "No shit. But why?" He places a hand on my forehead, like he's checking my temperature. "You're sick?"

"No." I press my lips together as I shake my head. "Um… well, I was going to tell you. But honestly, I just kinda figured it out like five minutes ago myself. So…" He leans in, like he's dying to hear what I have to say. And every hesitation I ever had about Finn Scott evaporates in this moment.

Oh, he's still the same guy. He's still kinda up-city selfish. And he's got a long way to go still.

But he's invested in me. I feel it.

"So…?" He says. "So what? What's going on?"

"I'm… pregnant."

He just stares at me. Unconsciously, I begin counting seconds and get to eight before he lets out a laugh and starts to smile. "What?"

I nod. "Yep. While I've obviously not been checked by a health center, I… I'm different. Emotional, and weepy, and —" He's nodding his head. "I haven't been tracking my cycles, or anything. Obviously, we've been busy. But it's been like several weeks down here, hasn't it?"

Finn is just staring at me.

"Finn? How long have we been down here?"

He shakes his head as if to clear it, then stands up as he lets out a breath. "Thirty-six days."

"Thirty-six. Oh, yes. I'm late. By more than two weeks." I try and sit up, to get out of bed now that the fainting spell is over.

But Finn immediately kneels back down and places a gentle hand on my arm. "Just rest. You just fainted. You just told me you're pregnant and... well, we're not in a hurry, are we."

I laugh. "I mean... we're in the middle of blowing up a tower, Finn."

"Well, technically, we're not. It's broken and in the middle of the reset—whatever that is. Besides..." He pans a hand to the space around us. "This is probably as good as it gets as far as living conditions go. You won't find a bed like this on the train."

That's absolutely true. We've been sleeping on the train floor, in side tunnels, or sometimes just right there on the tracks.

But I force myself up into a sitting position, fending off his objections with a fierce look of determination, as I pick up the thread of the conversation we were having before I fainted. "The factory. They're making Little Sisters. I know that sounds stupid, and incredulous, and impossible, but Finn! Think about it! They have an Extraction every ten years to... I don't know. Take the best of us and—"

"Shhhh." He's pushing me back down into the soft bed. "Let's forget about that for a moment. Just..." He sighs, and it's heavy. "Let's just take a time out. Can we do that? Can we take a time out?"

Now I feel guilty for not taking his feelings about this whole thing into consideration. He's the Extraction Master. Not only that, he comes from a long line of Extraction Masters. His family has been officiating a Spark Maiden sacrifice for hundreds of years.

Well, maybe not hundreds. Family's rise and fall, as they say. Just look at mine. The Bell's used to be in charge of the Tower District. Now we're down-city nobodies. But regardless of how long the Scott family has been in charge of sending Spark Maidens into the tower, one time is too many. Because surely you cannot *farm* the spark out of a maiden without killing her.

We grow spark.

And they grow us.

It's too much.

So I let Finn push me back until the soft and buoyant feather bed is cradling my body, giving in. Because it's all lies. Everything I ever thought I knew about my world is a lie and I need something real right now.

"Sure," I say. Pulling him into the bed next to me. "Let's take a time out."

# FINN

"*D*id you just proposition me for sex?"

Jasina's laugh is so loud, it echoes off the curved plaster ceilings. "What? No! Oh, my God. You *would* think that, though. You're such a man."

"*Please*," I joke. I know she wasn't propositioning me, it's just fun to tease her. "The moment you stepped into this room and saw all these beds, you were like... we should take one for a ride!"

Her head turns so she can look me in the eye. We're literally lying down, shoulder to shoulder, so these royal blue eyes of hers are just a few inches away. "You heard what I said, right?"

"That you're having my baby? Oh, I certainly did."

Her sigh comes out long and a bit tired. She turns over, propping her head up with a hand. "So what do you think about that? It cramps our plans to... you know, save the world and shit."

I just want to stare at her. I could look at her for a whole lifetime and still not see everything there is to see about the rebel, Jasina Bell. A long piece of red hair has fallen in front of her face, so I push it aside, sliding it over her shoulder. "Creating new rebels is a calling all its own."

This makes her smile and she flops back into the feather bed, making it poof up around her body. "I guess it could be." She side-eyes me. "Is that what you want? To make more rebels?"

"Jasina, there's plenty of room in the scholar's cave for a whole pack of rambunctious rebels."

"Is that a yes?"

I turn over on my side, placing a hand on her soft, fair cheek. Then I lean in and touch my lips to hers, whispering, "That's a yes," as I kiss her. "In fact, it's more than a yes. It's more than I deserve, to be honest."

"What?" She snickers. "What do you mean? You're the Extraction Master. You were born into a life that guaranteed you a good future. I would say that knocking up a down-city—"

I place two fingers over her lips, stopping that sentence before it can finish. "Don't you *dare* say it, Jasina."

"Say what?" She kisses my fingers.

"Whatever name you were going to call yourself." I shake my head. "No. You're not allowed to talk that way. Not anymore. You're... good. And pretty. And very, very smart and brave. There is nothing down-city about you, Jasina. Not a damn thing. You're... royalty." I let out a breath. "My queen." Then, as she giggles, I slide my arm under her and pull her close. "I think this might be the best day of my life."

Everything about her relaxes in this moment. Her shoulders drop, she exhales, her body goes soft. "I just wonder if..."

She doesn't finish, but I know what she's thinking. It's what she's always thinking. "I know, I know. You wonder if I'm good enough for you."

Which makes her laugh. "No. That's not what I was wondering at all."

"You wonder if... I'll be a good father."

"You know that's not what I was wondering."

"You wonder if... I have what it takes to be a scholar. I mean, I'm pretty useless in most areas. Aside from officiating over the sacrifice of young women to fake gods in towers, that is."

"Now you're just being silly."

"Yeah." I reach down, finding her hand, and bring it up to my lips as my eyes find hers. I kiss her knuckles. "I am. Because *you're* being silly. Your doubts? They're unfounded. I'm in, Jasina. I know we're on the new side of this relationship and choosing someone to be the father of your children is a huge step that should probably not happen while you're trying to form a rebellion and escape a cult— but I'm glad it turned out this way because..." I wince. "Well, it's all in my favor. I'm gonna annoy the fuck out of you. Chew wrong, or something. Or not please you in the bedroom."

She actually snorts. "I can honestly say that your sexual prowess was never in question." Her hand comes up to her face, which is flushed now, to fan herself.

I grin too. Looking down at her breasts as they press against the fabric of her button-down shirt with each breath. "The sex is pretty good, right?" She rolls her eyes, but this gesture gets cuts short when I slip my hand up her shirt and start playing with her nipple.

I don't pinch it hard, but she gasps, wiggling away. "I know you think I like it rough."

She scoffs. "*Think?* Um... I was there, Finn. I know exactly how you like it."

"Right. But I like it other ways, too." And to show her, I fondle her breast gently now. Letting my fingertips skim over her skin in a touch so light, goosebumps appear and the next time I touch her nipple, it's tight, and peaked, and all I want to do is put my mouth over it and suck.

It's bad timing. I'm pretty sure that asking for sex right now, right after she told me she's pregnant with my child and while we're squatting in a foreign Little Sister dorm in a city that's suspiciously falling apart outside, is the height of absurdity.

But then her hand is pressing against my dick beneath my pants, and I'm hard before I even know what's happening. "Right now?" I ask.

She shrugs, looking me straight in the eyes. "If we're gonna take a time out on a bed, we might as well make the most of it."

I get up on my knees, crawling down to the end of the bed, and take her boot in my hand. I don't waste time unlacing it, just pull it off and reach for the next one. Because I fully plan on making the most of it by getting her naked.

And here's what I like about Jasina. No, here's what I *love* about Jasina. She's grinning. Wide. And she's already got her pants unbuttoned so all I have to do next is pull them down her legs.

She's not wearing underwear. When we were scavenging for clothes, she drew a line at borrowed undergarments. So when she slides her fingertips between her legs, I'm looking at her wet and glistening little peach.

I almost die.

She's perfect for me. Not shy. Not a bit shy. And her adventurous nature carries over into the bedroom. She let me do anything I wanted in the two times we've been together and I'm sure this time would be no different.

If that was what I was after.

But it's not.

I just want to show her how good I can be. To her, *for* her, for *us*.

So I place my hands on her knees, open them up—watching her literally bite back her excitement by chewing on her lip—and lower my mouth between her legs.

Immediately, her back arches up and her eyes close. But just as quickly she opens them—lazy and low as they are, and a playful smile cancels out the lip biting. "Is this dirty talk sex or—"

My tongue does a little twisty thing here, cutting off her words and closing those eyes right back up. But her hands slide down her body, her fingertips weaving into my hair and giving it a good grip, as I do my best to drive her over the edge with my mouth.

Little moans begin to come out her mouth as I bury my face into her folds. Licking her as I push her knees forward, lifting her ass up off the bed a little. Then I slip a finger in, just one to start, and she hisses a little as I slowly push up inside her. "More," she moans softly.

"More what?" I whisper back. I don't know why, all of a sudden, I'm into this dirty talking, but I am. And I'm not even planning it when the words come out. "More fingers, Jasina? Or more cock?"

Her eyes are open, but only just barely. Her mouth parts, her breath ragged. She doesn't answer my question. I should just give in. Just... fuck her and make her come.

But I want so badly to tease filthy fucking words out of that pouty little mouth of hers, I don't give in. "Come on," I urge. "Tell me what you want, Jasina. Fingers? Or cock?"

She bites her lip, uncertain.

She did dirty-talk back to me a little when we had sex in my tower. It was mostly in response to my urging, like this, but I'll take what I can get. "I'll do anything, Jasina. Anything you want." I sit up, still fingering her enough to keep that look of sleepy ecstasy on her face. "Want me to fuck your tits? Your mouth?" I shrug when she rolls her eyes. "What? If I don't ask, I'll never know."

"Surprise me," she whispers.

Immediately, I'm shaking my head. "No. I want to know what you like. You, and only you. I want to know every spot on that perfect body of yours where you feel pleasure. And then I want to touch you there and make you squeal. Help me, Jasina. *Please*. Help me make you squeal."

She's biting her lip, trying not to smile. But it's pretty clear she finds me charming, if a bit uncouth. "It turns you on to hear the dirty talk?"

"You have *no idea*."

Is it weird that I like it? It's a new thing. Only since my father was murdered. Clara clearly enjoyed the results of my change in character, but picturing her talking dirty back to me—or hell, talking about sex at all, is a stretch too far. Clara is the equivalent of a princess. Something elevated and special. Something you keep on a shelf to admire. A trophy.

Jasina is the complete opposite. Which is neither good nor bad, just different. I like it, though. I like her wearing these clothes that make her look like an adventurer. With her messy hair and dirty face. Boots on her feet instead of slippers. I like her courage, and how practical she is, and how new things make her think, not back away. We've only known each other a month, but I feel like she's my best friend. And now that I know she's pregnant, she's gonna be my wife too. I don't know how we'll manage that since we're living in this strange new world. But she *will* be my wife. My partner. My confidant.

Maybe we just make this pledge to ourselves for now. But there will come a time when we make it official. Once all the train hopping is over. Once all the towers are blown up. Once there is no more threat of Extraction, we'll go home, and settle in a scholar's cave under the city. And we'll dig up the past and figure out the truth.

"But I want it to turn you on too, Jasina. This isn't about

me, it's about us. I want you to know that I'll take care of you and the baby. That we're a team in every way now. And that I will do anything to make you happy. To make you proud. To keep you safe."

"Wow," she smirks. "That was heavy."

"Did I lay it on too thick?"

She shakes her head, scoffing. "No. You didn't. It was just the right amount of convincing."

"So my real question is, does it turn you on or off? Because all I want is to make you love me."

"Love you..." She sighs. "Don't say that if you don't mean it."

"What?"

"Love. Don't talk about it if you don't mean it."

This is when I realize this whole conversation is taking place with my face between her legs. It started as me wanting to lick her into bliss. To tease some filthy words out of that pouty mouth. And then get those plump lips wrapped around my dick.

But that's not what it is now. So I scoot up her body, bracing my hands on either side of her shoulders as I lean down to gently kiss her. "Why wouldn't I mean it?"

"It's just..." Her hand slips down to her stomach, her eyes still locked in mine. "We had a plan and this wasn't part of it."

"All plans change, Jasina. It's life. You ride it. Like a train." She smiles, so I keep going. "You get on, you get off. Every day is a new day." I reach down and grab her hand off her stomach, giving it a squeeze. "You don't need to worry about how I feel about you and the baby. I'm in. All I want you to think about now is... on or off."

Her eyes squint. "What?"

I lean down, kissing her Biting her lip just enough to

tease her. Then I whisper, "Does the dirty talk turn you on? Or off?"

She closes her eyes and shakes her head, which might concern me if she wasn't smiling and blushing at the same time. Her hand flies up to cover her face. "I can't believe we're talking about this."

I pull that hand down, lowering my hips over her pussy, pressing my hard cock into her. I reach down with my thumb and begin teasing her little nub. "On or off?"

Those royal blue eyes are looking straight into mine when she whispers, "On." But at the same time, she's got her hand on the button of my pants. A moment later, she's popped it open and is sliding her hand inside.

I moan when she grips me, clenching my jaw, still looking into those amazing eyes. I love her. I already know it. I'm not going to say it, not now. Not yet. Because she won't believe me and you only get to tell someone you love them for the first time *once*.

When I say it, she will know it. She will believe it. And from this moment forward, that's my job. To make sure, when I say those words, she will *feel* it.

While I've been thinking about this, she's pushed my pants down over my hips, freeing my dick. Her hand still gripping it, tighter now, as she slides her palm up and down my shaft.

I remove my hand from between her legs and lift my hips up just enough so she can open her legs and guide me inside her. I press against her tight opening, forcing myself to maintain control.

I had meant to lick her into a climax, but right now, I want more connection. I think she does too. Because when I press forward, her fingernails dig into my shoulders, gripping me tight, and her eyes close.

All thoughts of dirty talk are gone now and the only thing on my mind is the beautiful woman I'm on top of. I press forward, carefully, slowly. And I can tell by the look on her face that this is how she needs it right now.

Not rough. Not dirty.

Soft and emotional.

So I lean down and kiss her as we move together.

Enjoying the slow pace.

Living in this moment.

The aftermath of knowing that we have made a child.

That she is going to be a mother.

That I am responsible for two people other than myself.

And while I can't read her mind, I can certainly read my own.

A family. A big one. With Jasina at my side.

This is the meaning of life I've been looking for.

# JASINA

*Everything about waking up* next to Finn Scott is comfortable. It's not a word I recall using much in my previous life. Growing up down-city wasn't meant to be comfortable. Comfort is a prize you win after making a vow to the god in the tower and becoming his Pledge.

Once that's out of the way, all down-city Pledges are invited up-city for etiquette classes in the Canal District. I think they had them there on purpose. To tease us and taunt us with all the luxury these up-city people had. Because every week the five of us—Lucindy, Britley, Harlow, Ceela, and I would have to walk past all those shops.

It was a lesson in what we lacked.

And it made us crave things we never knew we wanted. Like jewelry, and pretty dresses, and tiny cakes served with tea.

Of course, we knew these things existed, everyone in Tau City has the right to attend the outdoor Extraction parties in the Extraction District. They just… don't.

Every girl goes once. Usually when they're around eight or so. You have to go once, or you're kind of a freak. But it's such a hassle to get up the canal. Boat rides for down-city Pledges are free. But it's a dear price to hire a boat to take you all the way up to the Extraction District. Typically, when young girls would get the itch to see the parties, families would pool together resources and groups would go together.

Often on a fishing boat.

I didn't have to do that, thankfully. Auntie Bell had been telling me for years that I would be a Pledge long before I got the itch to see the festivities for myself.

So I went every year. She would send a boat, and someone would meet me at the dock, and then I'd be taken to her. She would buy me things. Spun sugar and usually a little trinket, like a bracelet. I realize now that the spun sugar was meant to imprint the day into my memory. A form of mind control, maybe. So that each year, when I got that sugar high, it cemented my resolve to be a part of the Rebellion into my tiny brain.

But the trinket was to take with me back down-city so I could show it off to my friends. That's how I got them all to agree. They would ooh and ahh over whatever it was that year. Telling me I was so lucky.

And I did feel lucky. I felt special.

That was the early days, back when I was small.

But once I actually made the vow to be a Pledge, the trip up-city became all about envy. Even for me. It's a wicked emotion. It makes you crave things and resent others who have what you desire.

As Pledges on our way to etiquette classes, my friends and I would walk past those shops with a hunger. We wanted everything behind the glass. And while we didn't dare dream about such things while in the Canal District—we had far too much pride to show our jealousy off in front of the up-city girls—once we were on that boat, on our way home, that's all we talked about.

We designed dresses in our heads. Imagined jewels on our fingers, and dangling from our ears, and draped around our necks. We would discuss fabrics, and lace, and stitching. Because even though we knew that the up-city girls didn't *really* make their own dresses, never in a bazillion years did we ever dare to dream that we'd have enough coin to purchase one of those exquisite garments behind the glass. Even if we were chosen in the Choosing.

We were going to make them. We were always going to make them.

But you can only imagine so many dresses and necklaces. It only gets that envy so far.

Auntie Bell—*Matron* Bell—is not stupid. Of course, she knew this. That's why she resorted to comfort.

Conditioned air.

I had no idea what a comfort this was until I was three weeks into my Pledge because it's a supreme luxury. Perhaps the Maidens have it in their rooms, but it's not in the lobby of the Maiden Tower, that's for sure. It's as hot in there during the day as it is outside.

We were up-city for our etiquette classes that day, sitting outside having tea as a Matron gave us a lesson in table settings and silverware. Which was much more complicated than it sounds. The group of Pledges was very big back then because that was only four years into the current Extraction period—almost two thousand. So we didn't all have our lessons in the same place. We were scattered about the Canal District in various cafes.

The first two weeks of my Pledge, we had our tea party lessons in outdoor cafes. It was always blazing hot, but on week three the heat was unbearable because the tables at this café didn't have umbrellas to shade us from the sun.

The Matron giving the lesson that day clapped her hands four times, and said, "Let's go girls, we're moving inside."

So we did.

And that's when the cold, conditioned air hit my face. The very first time I had felt it.

Not just the cold, but the *comfort*.

This is what it's like to share a bed with Finn Scott. This is what it's like to share a life with him.

He is warm arms around me, and soft bedding beneath me, and my hand on his rising and falling chest a rhythm that soothes.

He is new clothes, and good sex, and fine-tasting food.

He is *comfort*.

And now that I've had a taste of him—of who he really is as a man—I am well and truly addicted.

Because, to my surprise, Finn Scott—the dirty talking sex fiend who wanted to fuck me from behind the very moment we met—is a *family man*.

I feel like I've won the Extraction.

Maiden Number Ten.

Thinking this almost makes me snort. Because it's true, Maiden Number Ten is the jackpot because Gemna Hatley won the game. I highly doubt she sees it that way, but as far as I know, she's still alive and all the rest of those Maidens are dead. Maybe a few Little Sisters made it out of the explosion, but Gemna did for sure. The last time I saw her, she was nothing but power.

This makes me absently wonder if my spark is capable of being as strong as hers one day. It has the potential, I think. I did help Gemna collapse the Looking Glass. But will it be enough?

*Enough for what, Jasina?* I chastise myself. *Your role as Courtesan is over.*

Because at no point in any of those stories about the Godslayer was there any mention of a *baby*.

I admit, I had never thought much about having a family. But why would I? I was aiming for the Extraction and the Rebellion my whole life. So this realization that the

Godslayer and his Courtesan will never have a family should not hit me so hard.

But now that I'm carrying Finn Scott's child, I find this outcome to be... unbearable. So terrible, I wave the thought away with a swish of my hand.

"You're awake?"

I smile as Finn holds me tighter. "I'm awake."

"Should we stay the night here? Or go back?"

"Ohhhhhh," I moan. "I don't want to go back to the train. Not yet. I know we can't stay here, not for real, but it would be nice to find a meal." I open my eyes, peeking at him. "There's a dining room at the top of the Maiden Tower."

"Do you think there's food up there?"

"Probably not. But there has to be food somewhere. In some house, maybe. Oh!" I sit up a little, looking down at him. He's smiling. And it's such a content smile, I pause to take note of it.

"Oh, what?" He asks, when I don't finish.

"I bet there's food in the Matron Tower. I bet those crabby, old bitches get good stuff too."

He chuckles. "There's probably no one in there, though. Why would there be food?"

"It's worth a look. Plus, you know what else is in there?"

"What?"

"A Looking Glass. The outdated one. Remember? I told you about that."

He presses his lips together. "Mmm. Yeah. That would be interesting. Should we get going then?"

I am about to protest, when Finn turns over and gets to his feet, grinning sleepily at me as he tucks his dick back into his pants. I cannot believe that we just had sex in a Little Sister dorm.

The very thought almost makes me guffaw out loud.

If Auntie Bell could see me now. She'd call me every name in the book.

"Come on," Finn says, grabbing my pants and holding them out. "I'll help you get dressed."

For a moment I don't know how to process that statement. Help me get dressed? I mean, I know this is a thing for the Maidens. Those bitches practically forget how to dress themselves after their duty is up, that's how helpless they become living in that tower.

But I pride myself on being self-reliant. So a part of me wants to be offended at this offer.

It's just, there's another part of me—a much stronger part of me—that thinks this is kinda sexy.

"Jasina?" Finn shakes my pants.

I nod, scooting over to the side of the bed, then quickly slip my feet into the legs of my pants.

"Stand up," he says. And again, I'm slightly offended because it's a command, not a request.

But strangely enough, I also find it a turn on.

Oh, my God. I'm so weird. At least as weird as he is with all that dirty talking stuff he enjoys.

While I would not really call myself a grown woman—I feel like a few more years are necessary for me to adjust to the new adulthood before I see myself that way—I'm certainly not a child who needs help getting dressed.

It's just...

"Why are you smiling like that?" Finn asks.

Which only makes me giggle. If he only knew. His dick would be hard immediately, I just know it. And now that I'm up, I'm very hungry and eager to go explore that Matron Tower while I have the chance. So I say, "Can you help me with my boots, too?"

I get a smirky side-eye, like he totally knows what I've

been thinking, before he grabs them and bends down to put them on my feet.

While he's lacing the first one, he shoots me a smile, meeting my gaze. "You know what this means, right?'

"What what means?"

"You. And me. There's no way we're the Godslayer and his Courtesan. They don't have a family."

"Yeah. I've thought of that."

"Is it disappointing?"

I shake my head. Then smile. It's a really big real smile. "No. I think I'd much rather be the one reading those stories to a small child than be in the story myself."

"Are you just saying that? Or do you mean it?"

I don't answer right away because I feel like he's looking for honesty. So I take a few seconds, then say, "This is the start of something new, Finn." I point to my belly. "Something all *us*. We're going to be the main characters in our own story, not pretend to be them in someone else's."

He leans forward, both hands on my knees, and kisses me on the lips. Whispering, "I can't wait."

AFTER FINDING **bathrooms** and pulling ourselves together, Finn and I start weaving our way through the maze-like interior of the Little Sister dorm.

Finn pauses to stare into one of the cozy bedroom nooks. "They all look like this?" He turns to see my reaction.

I shrug, nodding. "This is exactly what ours looked like."

"But… I don't understand. Why does it look so lived in if no one's here?"

Again, my answer is mostly a shrug. "It's a perk?"

He smiles, then huffs out a laugh. "I guess. But the lights are on, Jasina." He points to a bedside table beside the immaculately made bed, complete with several decorative pillows and a fuzzy throw artistically positioned at the foot of the bed. The light emits a soft glow.

"Well, if it makes you feel any better," I say, "I found the whole thing weird as well. Like I was saying earlier, this place is huge. It holds…" I don't have a guess ready. "Lots of people. More people than we ever had in the Choosing. Thousands, maybe?"

His eyebrows furrow, almost knitting together as he thinks about this. "Weird."

I nod. "Very. But should we keep going? All I really wanna see is the Matron Tower."

He gives my hand a squeeze and we continue through the passageway. "Why do you wanna see that place so bad anyway? I'm sure it looks just like this."

"I want to see their Looking Glass. Don't you?"

He never gets the chance to answer me because just as these words come out of my mouth, we round a corner and suddenly, the main hall of the dorm is directly in front of us.

"Holy shit," Finn says, picking up our pace a little as he heads towards the canal that runs down the middle of the room. The floors beneath our feet go from stone to thick carpet the color of sand. It takes a moment, but he figures it out and begins to smile. "It's a beach."

"Yes," I say. Remembering the first time I saw this room. "And that's a canal made out of polished blue stone." I point to the simulated water that cuts the long, colossal room in half. Just like the real one outside cuts the city down the middle like a bright, blue line.

Finn tips his head up, eyes wandering to the ceiling. Taking in the curved, rounded walls that make the entire massive room look like the inside of a sandstone cave, the mature trees growing out of cracks in the plaster, and thick, woody roots climbing all over the place.

There are balconies, and stairwells, and nooks to look at too.

It's a lot.

"Wow," he finally says, looking at me. "This is incredible. I had no idea the Little Sisters lived like this. I pictured... I dunno. Bunk beds."

My laugh comes out automatically. "I did too. Trust me, everyone's mouth dropped open when we got our first look at the dorm. I guess it's some kind of... rite of passage? It's all very secret. We were practically threatened with death if we ever told anyone about the dorm."

"Why?"

I shrug. "It makes no sense, right? Who cares? I mean, it's nice. But who cares?"

Again, Finn's eyebrows knit together. He knows something is wrong here just as well as I do. But his answer is the same as mine. A shrug. "How do we get out?"

"That way," I say, pointing down the canal where the giant double doors are.

My steps are quick, urging Finn to keep pace, my curiosity and wonder subsiding with each step. Anxiety and dread resurfacing, replacing those feelings.

Once out the door, I nod to the left. "The Matron Tower is this way."

"Lead on," Finn replies, as we follow the serene hallway for several minutes, veering left each time we come to a junction, before finally reaching the glass bridge connecting to the Maiden Tower.

"Wow," Finn says, looking down at the small, tertiary canal underneath as we cross. "I never knew this was here. I thought I knew every nook and cranny about Tau City, none of this looks familiar."

"Huh. I thought the same thing when I crossed. Not that I knew every nook and cranny, it's just... the glass bridge, right?"

Finn nods. "Yeah. It's..."

"Out of place?" I ask.

"That."

"Well, just wait until you see what's in that room."

"Isn't it crazy that all this shit was going on behind the scenes and no one ever knew about it?"

"Mind boggling," I agree.

We walk in silence for the next few minutes as I try to remember how to get to the Looking Glass room. We have to backtrack a couple of times, but finally, I recognize the door. "This is it." I pan my hand to it, inviting him to go first.

He steps up, tries the handle, then looks at me with wide eyes. "It's open." Then pushes a little, and it opens with a creak.

He steps in first, blocking my view, but quickly moves aside to let me in.

I close the door behind me, but my eyes are glued on what's in front of me.

"This... doesn't look broken," Finn says.

No. Indeed it doesn't. Everything is the same as it was in our city, but all of it is working. And I'm so confused at what I'm looking at, I can't even explain it.

The glass... plates?—that's the only word I have for them —are lit up with... people. They are moving. Like the way his father's message was moving in the glass tiles up in Finn's Extraction Tower dome, but... nothing like that at all, actually.

The moving pictures aren't in color. There's a lot of spark interfering with the images, so they're not crisp and clear, but fuzzy and hard to see. Plus, Aldo Scott's face up in his Looking Glass was the size of a giant. It took up the whole front of the dome.

These people are tiny.

"Are they workers?" I ask. "Or are they like us?"

Finn walks over to the closest plate and flicks it with his finger. It makes a dull *plink* sound. He leans in, trying to see them better. "I think... they're matrons."

"What?" I lean in too.

"Look, they're old like Matrons. And they're definitely not workers. They're wearing clothes."

They are wearing clothes, I had noticed that immediately. I just didn't assume they were Matrons because they're definitely not wearing blue tunics and cream scapular aprons. They're wearing... pants. My nose crinkles up. "What kind of Matron wears *pants?*"

I look to Finn and find him shrugging. "The ones who run Xi Factory?"

Thoroughly confused, but also intrigued, we turn back to the plates. "Look," I say, pointing at another one. This one is different than the others, which all show the same scene. Pant-wearing Matrons doing... something or other, I don't know.

But this plate is all black with a bunch of bright green letters and symbols that fill the entire screen from top to bottom, though not left to right.

At the very bottom is a single upright line. Maybe an L? Capital I? Not sure, but it's flashing.

"What the hell language is this?" Finn asks.

"Is it a language? Because it doesn't look like a language to me. It looks like… random."

"I don't think it's random, Jasina. It has to mean something. I mean, look around. Something is happening here, right?"

I do have to admit that something is most definitely happening here.

"Look," he says. "What's this?"

"Ohh!" I brighten. Because he's pointing to… well, I don't have a name for it, but long, and black, and sitting right underneath the black plate with the weird symbols on it. But the cool thing is that it's got letters on it. Letters I recognize. They're even all lit up in the color of spark. Little… tabs or something. "Switches!" I say. Then I point at them. "They're switches. Like the ones on the glass desk back home."

Finn ponders this. "I think you're right. So they *do* something. What do you think they do?"

I shrug. "Should I push one?"

Finn laughs. "What if we blow the place up?"

"What if it reveals a secret door? That opens up to a secret passageway? Or," I say, ready to make more guesses because he's smiling at me and his eyes are shining. "What if your father's face appears? Hmm? And he's got another message for us."

"Doubtful," Finn says. "How would he get here?"

"Maybe the Looking Glasses are connected somehow? Maybe we could send a message back home and tell them what we've found?"

Finn hovers a finger over one of the switches on the long black thing.

I lean in to read what's written on the switch. "Enter," I say. "What do you think that means?"

"Fuck it," he says. And then he presses it.

Nothing happens.

It's all very anticlimactic. "Oh, well," I say, sighing and turning back towards the door. "It was worth—" But I stop midsentence because all the plates are now showing something different. It's no longer Matrons wearing pants and doing... whatever it is they're doing. Instead, all the plates show different views of a massive room filled with—

Finn leans in. "What the hell are those things?"

My brain is practically on fire trying to think of a word to describe what we're seeing. Because the room is filled with...

"Cocoons?" Finn asks. "They look like cocoons."

"They're... raising... butterflies?" I ask. "Monster butterflies?" Because the cocoons are massive. There's a worker messing with one, and the cocoons are bigger than it. I'd guess at least six feet long and three feet wide.

Finn looks at me, his eyes filled with confusion. "Thousands of monster butterflies?"

"Oh, my God. What if it's not butterflies. What if it's giant silkworms?"

Finn laughs. "Why would they need a million miles of silk, Jasina?"

"Duh. Gala dresses. Maybe they're big partiers here? Maybe that's why the city is such a mess?"

He just shakes his head at me. "I don't think—"

Now it's Finn's turn to stop mid-sentence. Because one of the plates is now showing a view of the worker opening one up.

I squint my eyes, holding my breath as the worker pries off the top of the cocoon, setting it aside.

Finn and I gasp in unison.

Because what's inside the cocoon isn't a butterfly or a silk worm.

It's a woman.

A grown woman who looks suspiciously like...

Finn leans in, desperate to make sense of what we're seeing.

Because it's... *Clara*.

# PART 2

"It is difficult to overstate how vital the augments were to the stabilization of post-collapse society. Though the exact date of their emergence remains disputed, most historians agree their rise was not born from ambition, but necessity. They did not seek to rule; they were made to survive. To endure where others failed. To execute what others refused. For a time, they succeeded. And in that success, the world was quiet."

**—Dr. Elena Nareen, Desert Interface Research Group, annotation recovered from The Line So Bright Complex, Sector 3 Vault**

# TYSE

*The train left the Delta Factory* at a pretty good speed, but only minutes in the journey it slows down to navigate a series of many windin' serpentine curves and stays that way for hours. Right now, we're goin' so slow I almost wanna get out and walk.

But there's no point in doin' that. Eventually, these twists and turns will end and we'll arrive at Epsilon Station. Then, it should pick up speed.

So I force myself to relax and be patient. Besides, it's better for Clara if the rest of the day goes slow. She fell asleep almost immediately, the back-and-forth rockin' motion becoming somethin' of a lull.

I feel like she was looking better back there in Delta city. Refreshed after I stole all that spark from her, then filled her back up.

But she doesn't look refreshed now. She looks exhausted.

We're not even at the end of day one.

How's it gonna go from here?

It occurs to me that Delta City was givin' her spark. Maybe that's why the air was so thick with it? Maybe it was feedin' those baby gods? Maybe it was feedin' Clara too?

Even if she wasn't actively pullin' it in or whatever, just being inside Delta City was enough to kinda keep her goin'.

But being on the train is a drain.

It's likely that anywhere without Spark is gonna have the same effect. Without thinkin', I focus my vision display and start lookin' for a world. And it's surprisin' how instinctual it feels, this searchin'. Because I only seriously started doin' it today.

I need to give her some more. I need to *feed her*.

But like I figured, this train line—bein' underground and all—isn't exactly crowded in any of the nearby worlds in my frequency stack. I have to look for a very long time before I find people. And then, longer still, before I find someone I won't mind killing.

It's an old man. He looks like a miner. Got a crude basket or somethin' on his back and it's filled with rocks of some kind. Maybe worth somethin', maybe not. His face is pale and wrinkled, like he doesn't see much sun. And he's feeble, despite the pack on his back. His steps are slow and deliberate. Careful. Like a single misstep means death.

It's not like I wanna kill him. I don't. I've done plenty of killin' in my time, but it's not my first choice."

But I *need* spark. Because *Clara* needs spark.

And she is young with a whole life ahead of her, and he is old, his life behind him now.

It only takes a couple of minutes to drain him, because he doesn't have much spark to take. And five minutes later, Clara's cheeks are a sweet shade of pink. She blinks up at me, smilin' from the pillow she's made of my lap.

"Did I sleep?" she asks.

I nod. "Ya did."

She pushes some hair away from her eyes, takin' in a deep breath as she looks around, probably tryin' to remember where the hell we are.

Once we got inside the train back at the Delta Factory, I moved crates around to make a little space at the very front of where we could lie down and relax. So we've got a nice view of what's up ahead in the tunnel—which is nothin'. But it's somethin' to look at, anyway.

"How long was I out?" Clara asks.

"Not long," I lie. I don't even know why I lie. I should just tell her the truth. *Hours, Clara. Ya were exhausted because I don't think you can live outside cities. So I'm killin' people in other worlds to steal their spark, to keep ya going.*

Yeah. That would go over well.

Clara stirs. "We're barely moving," she says.

"I know. It's frustratin'. But the tunnel is twisty. Trains and twists don't really go together, I guess. Even though this train is one fuckin' car long."

My frustration comes out in my tone, which makes Clara look at me and laugh. "Are we in a hurry?"

*Yes. We need a new city because you're gonna die if you don't have a constant source of spark. You're gonna turn in to one of those ash-faced women in the Delta Factory.*

"No," I say. "We're not." Then I smile, and reach for my pack. "Are ya hungry?"

"Oh, my god, yes. Famished." Then her mouth makes the cutest little 'o' shape. Her lips all plumped up. "I didn't pack any food! Or water!"

I laugh. "Don't worry. I've got ya covered." Then I open the pack and pull out a water pouch, handin' it over. "I only brought a dozen pouches because they're heavy. But we've got two of these." I pull out a set of stainless-steel canisters and set them on the floor of the train. "Sweep certified. They'll generate water for us so we don't have to carry it."

"That's amazing. How do they do that?"

"They pull humidity from the air. And it's much more humid down here than it is up there in the sand, so it won't take long to fill them up. Maybe an hour or two."

"Wow." She rips the pouch open, looking curiously at it.

Then tips it up to her mouth and sucks down the water, daintily wiping her mouth when she's done. "How long would it take to fill one up out in the desert?"

"Probably half a day, at least. But even if you're dyin' of thirst, most people can wait half a day. Or they can drink it before it's full, then reset it."

"That's good to know. Really good to know."

"Why's that?" I chuckle. "Are ya plannin' to walk across the Sandy Sea or somethin'?"

She shrugs. Like this was a real question. "You never know. It's just good information. I mean, we're not trapped, ya know?"

"Trapped?"

"Well, in my Tau City there was a wall and the desert was a threat on the other side. So. Yeah. We were trapped."

"Ah. I see. Yeah, then. It's good to know we could take off on foot and go anywhere we want." Which is actually not a bad idea. We'd probably get farther walkin' than we're currently gettin' on this fuckin' slow-ass train.

"What's the next city on the line?" Clara asks, her words coming out on a sigh.

"Epsilon. It's a god city, not really part of the Alphas, but not really a Median City, either. So we're not gonna go look inside. Most likely, it'll be just like Delta."

This makes Clara think back on what we saw, frownin' as she does this. "Yeah. I've seen enough of that. How come it's so different here than it was in Tau City? I mean, looking back I see that my life was a lie and that's all very terrible. But it was a good life, nonetheless. Those people back in the Delta Factory, they didn't look like they had a good life."

"Maybe we just saw the wrong people? Maybe there's like... up upper class, or something."

She sighs. "Up city. Down city. I see your point."

"Well, I wasn't really making a point. It's just—"

But the train stops short, sending us both careenin' off balance towards the front window, and I don't finish my sentence.

Clara and I both lean forward, tryin' to see ahead—but the tunnel's dark. Somewhere along the way, the lights went out.

"There's something moving out there," Clara whispers.

She's right. My display is lit up with information. "Bots," I say. "There's something on the track and they're moving it out of the way."

"Where did they come from?"

That's a very good question that only has one answer. "Epsilon Factory must be right up ahead."

"Well..." Clara's mind is going crazy. "Why was the track blocked? How would something get on the track?"

"Not sure."

The bots begin retreating, then they disappear into the darkness, out of reach of my sensors. The train begins crawling forward, then picks up a little speed.

Clara lets out a breath. "Well, that was exciting."

Not the word I'd use. Because it was all very familiar from my time in Sweep.

An ambush.

I wait for the consequences... but nothing happens until we pull into Epsilon Factory Station and bots appear to remove crates.

Clara and I stay right where we are. Letting the workers do their thing. At one point, a bot comes to remove the crate that's been hiding us from view, and it pauses. Like it's scanning us.

Even I hold my breath for this. I don't reach for the Versi, just in case it's got a pre-programmed defense protocol, but

I'm ready to, if it comes to the wrong conclusion about who and what we are.

It doesn't. It picks the crate up and leaves. Either we are somethin' unknown and it doesn't have a protocol to deal with us, or it was told not to engage.

"What was that?" Clara whispers. "It looked right at us. I thought they couldn't see us?"

"Well... I guess they can. We'll have to be more careful in the future. We should probably not go into any more cities. I'm sure each god programs them different. Just because Delta's workers didn't pay us any attention, doesn't mean the others won't."

"Yeah," she sighs, absently watchin' the worker bots reload the train.

They see us. They absolutely see us. Because they deliberately avoid crushin' us with crates. Which is nice, I suppose. But doesn't make me feel any better. Because it implies that they've got directive to deal with strangers, whereas the bots in Delta Factory didn't.

They're efficient, though. And it's only one car. So it only takes about thirty minutes to load it back up before the doors close and we pull forward once again.

This time, there is no crawlin' through switchbacks. The train immediately picks up speed and just a few minutes into the trip, my display estimates that we're travelling about two-hundred-thirty miles per hour.

Clara looks nervous. "Is it supposed to be so fast? Was it this fast on the way here?"

"Yeah. This is fine."

This answer seems to settle her because she slumps back against the bulkhead of the train. I shuffle through my pack for some food, back on task before everythin' got sidetracked with the debris on the line and the attention of bots.

"Here," I say, handing Clara a pouch of crackers and jerky and keeping one for myself. "Eat somethin'. It's been a crazy day so far. I don't need ya passin' out from lack of food."

Which probably isn't a real concern since she seems to run on spark and I've given her quite a lot of that in the past few hours.

But she accepts my offer with a smile and we settle back into the trip snacking in silence. When she finishes, she lies down with her head on her ruck. "I'm not going to sleep," she insists. "Just resting my eyes."

I chuckle, smiling. Because it's a lie. But she needs the rest, so I don't comment. Just let her pretend until she's once again passed out. I'm studyin' her complexion because I can't tell if she's goin' pale again or it's just the lighting in this tunnel, when three things happen at once:

First, the world lurches forward, my stomach droppin' as the train slams into an emergency stop, sending me half out of my seat and Clara's ruck sliding out from under her head.

Second, a deep, thrummin' bass rumbles through the cabin. A low-frequency hum that rattles through my bones like the whole train is fighting against some invisible force trying to tear it apart.

Third, the air shifts. A pressure wave slammin' through the tunnel like a silent explosion. My ears pop and the lights flicker erratically.

And then—silence.

This is when my brain catches up, finally understandin' what is happening.

There's *someone* on the track ahead.

And his eyes are glowing a familiar bright blue.

# CLARA

*When I open my eyes* after the sudden lurch, I am disturbed to find that my body has shifted so far forward, I'm pressed up against the glass at the front of the train.

And that's when I see him.

A man.

A very tall man with lots of muscles and tattoos.

Not to mention, *glowing blue eyes*.

But this man isn't Tyse.

He's someone else.

Someone outside on the tracks.

"Don't move, Clara," Tyse whispers. "Just stay right where you are."

Which is a pretty awkward position because my nose is actually touching the glass. But I'm not gonna argue because I'm fairly certain that the man outside is an augment and even though I'm only familiar with one very specific augment, it doesn't take a very active imagination to understand that augments aren't anything I want to meet up with in a dark tunnel in any dimension.

Tyse is on his feet, one hand pressed towards the man outside, palm forward. "We're just passin' through. Whatever this is, whoever you are, we're just passin' through." He talks in a normal voice, but it's clear that the other augment can hear him because he cocks his head as he takes a few steps forward.

The man says, "There is no 'just passing through'" as his eyes flash bright blue. "Don't care where you're going. Don't care where you're coming from, either. This section of the line belongs to Epsilon. If you come in, you owe. If you wanna leave, you pay."

"What the hell is happening," I whisper.

Tyse doesn't respond, but I do catch him tensing up when I speak. He wants me to stay quiet. But it's too late, because the augment's glowing blue eyes lock with mine and the resulting smile that creeps up his face as he takes me in is enough to send shivers sliding down my spine.

The augment takes a step forward and, in this moment, everything changes.

Weapons are drawn and fired before any human could've made a decision to do it. Then Tyse grabs me by the arm and drags me to the back of the train car. Everywhere around me, there are explosions. Weapons being fired by more than just one man.

Tyse is yelling, talking to me, I think, but I can't be sure because my ears are ringing, and I can't understand him. All sound is coming at me like I'm underwater—muddled, distorted, echoing. The next thing I know, there's silence, and darkness, and I'm gasping for breath. Wheezing as I choke on the air filling my lungs. I look up, see Tyse's panicked face, then, underwater again. But I'm not wet, so it's not water. Still, when we come out of it, it's like a resurfacing because I gasp, sucking in air. And this time, it's something I actually breathe.

"Holy fuck," Tyse is saying. "Holy fuck. *Holy fuck!*" Over and over again. "Are you OK? Can you breathe?"

I can, but when I try to talk, I just start coughing. He kneels down, pulling me up into a sitting position and claps me on the back like I'm choking on food.

My hand comes up, grabbing his arm. "I'm OK," I croak. I'm not sure that I am, but I say it anyway. "I can breathe now. It's just..." I pause to gasp a little. "I couldn't. There was something wrong with the air."

"Yeah," Tyse says, relaxing just a bit. "I took us to the wrong dimension, I guess."

I blink up at him. "*What?*"

"Yeah. To get away from the augment ambush. There were dozens of them, not just the one."

"Oh, that explains all the explosions!" I wheeze these words out.

"I guess there's a gang of them? They run this territory and we were passin' through it."

"How did they know we were on the train?"

Tyse thinks for a minute. Then he huffs. "It was the workers. The bots at the last station. They must be hacked. Those augments must have access to their vision sensors."

"That's why they looked at us funny."

Tyse nods. "Yeah. I suppose."

"Well, what do we do?" My breathing is mostly back under control now, but I let out a long sigh just to steady myself one last time.

"We'll try and get past them in this dimension?" he says. Seeing my confusion, he clarifies. "I hopped us into the first frequency I saw, but it was... I dunno. Somethin' wrong with it. Ya couldn't breathe."

"That's why I was choking. Wait. Could *you* breathe?"

Tyse nods. "Yeah, I was fine. But... I'm not human, remember? So I hopped us into this one." He exhales loudly, raising his gaze to look around.

I look around as well. There's no train here. No train tracks, but luckily, there is a tunnel. A terrible thought occurs to me. "What if there was no tunnel here?"

Tyse meets my gaze, wincing. "Yeah. We'd be dead. I was *very* careless. It won't happen again. It's just... new. And I needed to get us out of there before you got hit. Every single one of 'em had a Versi."

My eyes drop to his weapon, then rise back up to watch his expression. "So... what are we up against? And what do we do?"

"Up against," he sighs. Looking away. "I'd say... a small army?" He looks back at me. "But it's OK. We're gonna stay here, in this dimension, and make our way down the train line until we get past them."

"What if they control the whole line? What if they're the terrorists?"

"They're not."

"How do you know?"

"Just... they're not. I know. It's not them. So we just need to get past them and—"

But his words trail off. He doesn't stop talking—his mouth is still moving—it's just... I can't hear him anymore.

It's different than the underwater sound too. Everything just begins to... *fade.*

Then, I'm gasping again. Tyse is holding me in his arms, looking down at me, panicking. "Clara! Clara!" He's practically yelling. And he's very close, so this is loud and makes me wince. "Can you hear me?"

I nod, choking again, but it's different this time. I can breathe, but I don't feel well. I can barely open my eyes and—

The next thing I know, spark is flowing through me like a river. It's filling me up and everything is warm, and good, and I'm smiling up at a very worried-looking Tyse.

"I feel... amazing!" All these words come out as a giggle. "What's happening?" Again, I'm laughing. But I'm also looking at Tyse, and he's *not* laughing. He looks... scared.

His face is completely white. Like all the blood has drained from him. His eyes glowing a bright blue. And when I glance at his neck, I see pulsating light inside him. Like... *strings* of lights. Like threads, running in lines, up and down his neck.

For some reason he reminds me of those workers. Of those bots.

The blackness comes back, quickly overtaking me, but just as quickly, it recedes again. This time we're in a cave. I see spark-colored crystals—giant, massive, tower-sized spark crystals rising up from the cave walls. The drunk feeling is gone, the choking, gone, and I feel quite good.

I blink, staring at a petrified Tyse, who is kneeling down next to me. Then I push up, propping myself up onto my elbows to get a better look. "Where are we?"

Tyse laughs, blowing out a breath. It's one of those relieved laughs. "I have no fuckin' idea. But it took me ten tries to wake you up this time, and—"

"*This* time?"

"Clara, we were hopping worlds for over two hours." He twists his wrist to show me his watch, but it just confuses me more.

"What?" I push some hair out of my eyes and get to my feet, noticing that there's a sleeping bag spread out on the ground, and my shoes are off. As if we've been here for a while. Tyse stands up as well. "Two hours? But..." I look back at Tyse. "It felt like seconds."

"That's because you were unconscious. I brought you here because..." He waves a hand at the crystals. "Well, I can't say for sure, but I'm thinking this might be where spark comes from. It's the only place where you actually looked better rather than worse when we arrived. You do feel better, right?"

"Yeah. I feel fine. I remember choking, but..." I shrug. "I can't really remember anything else."

"We were attacked by augments on the 702 train line, do ya remember that?"

I think back. Some of it, I do. The explosions. But then I see that man's glowing blue eyes in my head and shiver. "Yeah," I tell Tyse. "I remember."

He lets out a breath. Like he just came through a very stressful time. "Well, we're gonna stay here in this world for a while. So you can recover."

"OK." It's confusing that I *need* to recover, so I take a moment to think. Clearly, this dimension hopping isn't something I'm particularly adapted to, and he's trying to be polite about this. Still, I need to ask. "Am I... in the way?"

"What?"

"You know. The mission? My weakness? I mean, I'm not like you, Tyse. I wasn't really built for this. It's possible that I'm more of a... a liability than a weapon."

His smile is lazy and his eyes are bright. "Woman, ya couldn't be a liability if ya tried. It's not you. It's just... people, right. Hoppin' through spark dimensions is..." he exhales loudly. "Ya know, challenging."

I reciprocate his smile, but deep down I can't help but read between the lines of his concern. People. He said it like he's *not* people. Because this world hopping stuff doesn't seem to be challenging to *him* at all. In fact, he looks rather... robust after his challenge.

"Anyway," he says. As if reading between the lines of my silence. "I'm callin' it a day. We're makin' camp here. At least one night, but maybe more, if we need it. I mean—" His effort to smile here is commendable. It's just not... reassuring. "It's not like we're actually huntin' that terrorist anymore, right? We're just... leaving the Alphas. Right?"

"You're asking me?" I point to myself.

"You don't sound sure. I thought we had agreed. Take the train down the line and find ourselves a good world. Well. Maybe this world right here is the good one? Maybe we don't even need to go back? Maybe this is our happily ever after?"

For the first time I take a good look around at the cave. It's pretty, I'll give it that. The crystals are glowing a soothing cyan blue. Like the canal back in my Tau City. They are very big, about a dozen in number, and light the place up. Setting a very soothing atmosphere.

The cave is massive. Easily as tall as a tower. Maybe not as tall as the God's Tower. But looking up, the distance from the ground to the ceiling could be the same height as the Maiden tower, which was twelve floors tall in total, including the ground floor and the very tippy top where the communal dining room was.

It's a wide cave as well. Easily spanning the same distance across the canal from Maiden tower to Extraction Tower. But there are little nooks here and there. Built into the walls of the cave or part of the bigger outcroppings. Almost as if the designer of the Little Sister dorm used this cave as inspiration. In fact, now that I think about it, there's even a canal.

Well, a small stream. Probably a few dozen of them, actually. More like flowing puddles, but the point is, they've got glow to them. It's interesting. Especially this newfound resemblance to the dorm. I like it. There's just... there's this little nagging feeling in the back of my brain that's flashing red at me. Trying to tell me something. Or remind me of something, I'm just not sure what.

It doesn't matter. The real point of all this introspection is that, aside from all this natural beauty and interesting coincidence, there's nothing here but rocks, the crystals, and us. I glance back at Tyse, who seems to be watching me very closely as he patiently waits for me to come to a conclusion about his question. "It doesn't really look anything like how I pictured a happily ever after."

He forces a smile. "What does your happily ever after look like?"

I shrug. "I'm... kind of a city girl."

He laughs, which makes me let out a breath, feeling better because his laugh is real. "Oh, I get it. You need boutiques to resupply yourself with cheeky underwear."

He's not wrong about that. Boutiques are definitely part of my dream. But that's not it. "I need... *people*, Tyse. I'm not a loner. I'm a social butterfly." I look around the cave again, picturing myself being stuck here forever, not a single friend in site. Not even Anneeta. I shake my head at Tyse. "I don't see it."

He is clearly not giving up on this because his smile just grows bigger. "Well, that's because we haven't explored yet. There's a tunnel. It just... doesn't have a train in it. As far as I know, but maybe it does? We could follow that tunnel. Instead of going back to an ambush."

I must be frowning because he quickly continues. "It's just a suggestion. We could find another world, if that's what you want."

"Another world where I can't *breathe*? Sounds tempting."

Again, his smile is forced.

"OK," I say, planting my hands on my hips. "What the hell is going on?"

"What? What do ya mean?"

"You. This place and your new-found obsession with it. I understand that there's danger back in our world on the train line, but... there's a way around those..." *Monsters.*

"Men," is what I really say. Because they are augments. And so is Tyse. And he's not a monster.

"*Our* world?" Tyse asks. "702 isn't my world, Clara."

"Wow. Really?"

"What?"

"Not *your* world, *my* world. What the fuck, Tyse?"

"I'm just saying. We don't have to stay in 702. That's all. That's it. And this place—"

"Which is called... what?"

"Zero point fourteen forty."

"Zero point?"

"It's a fractional world. Very low. Between zero and one."

I want to ask what that means, but even if he knows, and even if he'd tell me, it wouldn't have any significance. I don't have a frame of reference for 'frequencies' and 'resonance'. It's all very blah, blah, blah.

So why am I trying to start an argument with him about it?

*Because he's hiding something, Clara. And it goes against our code.*

*His* code, actually. Not mine. He was the one who made a big deal about loyalty and lies. How he wouldn't put up with them. How he would have my back, so I must have his. That was *his* code. My code is... well, just be nice to people and it comes back to you. It's really as simple as that.

And right now, he's not being nice to me because he's treating me like a *bracelet*.

Seeing—or, more probably, sensing—my growing frustration, Tyse slips his arms around my hips, locking his hands behind my back and pulling me close. "It's been a long day. For me, and you. Let's just rest here. We'll have some food, and look around a bit, and talk, and sleep. And then, when we wake up, we'll make decisions together. Wherever you wanna go, Clara Birch, we'll go."

It's pacifying. Somewhat insulting because he's assuming that I can be placated by yielding. And while I would like to clarify this for him, just for future reference that I am not that easy, his next move is a kiss and... well... I *am* that easy.

Because I like it.

I like *him*.

I trust him too. Even if he is keeping something hidden, I don't think Tyse Saarinen has it in him to hurt me. Whatever he's hiding, there's a good reason for it.

So I give in and kiss him back.

# TYSE

*The moment she starts kissing me back* I relax. Her questions were warranted, but so was my reaction. It *has* been a long day and I don't wanna think about what happened. It's been all up in my face for fuckin' hours now and I need to forget.

So instead of pullin' back after the kiss starts to come to a natural conclusion, I slip a hand down to the button on her pants and pop it open. I'm watchin' her face when I do this. Her eyes are closed and she smiles, looking forward to what comes next.

I pull the zipper down as well, slippin' my hand inside. This makes her back buckle a little, like her legs are weak. And while I know she's OK now, will be OK as long as we're here in the presence of these giant spark crystals, I've depleted her so many times today, it's probably gonna take days, maybe even weeks, for her to recover from all the fuckin' spark I stole.

On Day *One*.

It couldn't be helped.

I had to. Because the thing is, all these things I can do with my brain—all these augments. They need power. And *she* is that power. I can steal it from other places and it works just fine if I'm using that spark to build her back up.

But it turns out that my augments don't run off stolen spark from other worlds. They run on *Clara*.

And without the augments, I can't hop worlds. So when

we get stuck in worlds where, for whatever reason she can't breathe the air, but I can, I need to steal more of her spark to get us the fuck out of there.

This day—Day One—was nothin' but hours and hours of endless, nightmarish, world hopping. Hopin', each time I found a new frequency, it would be a place where Clara Birch could live.

And this is the only one I found. Aside from 702, where the augment ambush is. And 1440, where Delta is.

This is it. This is all we have right now.

I cannot risk going anywhere else. These are our three options. That's it. Because I can't see her like that again, all pale and shriveled. Dead, once. If I hadn't remembered this place, dead now, she would be. For sure.

So yeah, I'm gonna do it. I'm gonna make her pliable with pleasure.

So right after I drag that zipper down, I start pullin' her pants over her hips, urging them down her legs to reveal her soft thighs.

She moans a little when I start to unbutton her shirt. She steps out of the pants, kicking them aside, as I drag the shirt down her arms.

Now she's just in her underwear, which makes her a little shy—she's like that. So her blue eyes are open now. Lookin' at me, askin' what comes next.

Tyse, in a past life gravitated toward a girl who knew what she wanted and wasn't afraid to ask. Or take, if it came to it. It turned me on.

But watching upcity Clara Birch blush while standing in front of me in her underwear kills me fuckin' dead.

I kneel, pulling her down with me.

We face each other, and she's looking right up into my glowing augment eyes when I reach between her breasts and pop her frilly, lacy, unbelievably fuckin' sexy bra open. Her tits spill out like melons and immediately, I'm reaching for them. Grabbing and squeezing.

Her eyes are closed now. Her mouth open, little noises comin' out. I lean in and bite her lip as I push her back, lying her down on the sleeping bag I laid out while she was still unconscious from all my spark stealing.

The next thing I know, she's on her back, looking at me, bitin' on her lip. Waitin' for what comes next. Which is me placing my hands on her knees and spreading them open.

She moans. Just *this*, and she's moanin'.

God, I fuckin' love this woman. I love everything about her. But I especially love how she reacts to my touch. To my stare. To everythin'. There isn't a single thing I'd change about it. And if I have to skip worlds for the rest of my life, killing strangers from strange lands to keep her alive, I will.

I won't ever stop.

Clara, getting nervous now, since I've just been staring at her, reaches for me. Her soft hands lightly touch my arms, urging me to do something. Anything.

I reach back up, playing with her tits for a moment. But then my hands slide down her body. Gently gliding over her ribs until her skin erupts in tiny pin pricks. She sucks in a breath, holding it when I keep going. Tracing my fingertips over each of her hip bones and ending with my thumbs pressing against her pussy.

She lights up now. All those mysterious symbols that somehow got themselves embedded into her skin, shining through.

She is a book.

A story.

A treasure map waiting to be read.

I like to make her come at least once before I put myself

inside her. It's just what lovemaking has turned in to for us. I like to *watch* her come. I like the way her eyes close tight, and her back arches up a bit, and the way her knees press against my head when I've got my mouth between her legs.

I like to lick her into oblivion. Squeezing her tits while peeking past her rising and falling belly, moving in rhythm with her breath.

That's what I do right now.

And that's exactly how she reacts when I do it.

Her fingertips grab desperately at my hair. Pulling on it. Encouraging me as she lifts her hips, grinding against my face.

We've been together long enough now that I can read all her signals. I know when she's on the edge. A moment later and she's whispering my name.

"Tyse. Tyse. *Tyse.*"

And I smile, still licking her when she grits her teeth, arches her back, and gushes her sweet release right into my mouth. She wriggles a bit, enjoying the rolling waves of pleasure that linger for nearly a whole minute.

I kiss her inner thighs, still watching. Letting her have all her moments. Enjoying the light show her body is puttin' on. She glows from within. Like she is somethin' magical. Like she's somethin' extraordinary.

And when she's done, every time without fail, she gives me a long, satisfied smile. I wait for one eye to open. To peek at me.

She doesn't disappoint. It opens. Well, half way. Her words are husky and low. "Your turn now."

But I shake my head as I rise up on my knees, pulling my shirt over my head and tossing it aside. Do I want her to suck my dick? Of course, I do. But not after what she told me about her last time with Lover Boy. And how he was mean to her. Made her feel cheap.

Clara Birch is not cheap. She is something dear. Something rare. Something to be cherished.

It's funny too. Because before she came, women were... whatever. If I had one for a while, it was fine. If I didn't, that was fine too.

But Clara Birch is going to be by my side for the rest of my life. I know this as sure as I know my own name.

So no. There is no 'my turn' now.

There is only our turn.

I pop the button on my pants, enjoying the way her eyes fall down to watch. The zipper comes down next and she bites her lip, trying not to grin too big. Now I crawl up her body, my hands ending up on either side of her head as I spread her legs wide open with my knees.

She reaches down, sliding her hand inside my pants, and pulls me out.

I've been hard since she blushed at me in her underwear, but when she squeezes my shaft, it's a whole other level of ready.

Eagerly, she positions my dick up against her wet opening, and a moment later, I'm pushing myself inside her. Her legs come up, squeezing my hips. Which contracts a whole other set of muscles. I close my eyes, enjoying it.

I don't even think she knows what she's doing to me when she squeezes her legs like that. But that just makes it more of a turn on. It's like her and the sexy underwear she bought by mistake.

This woman is so fuckin' cute I can't stand it.

When I make love to Clara Birch, it's always slow. I give her time to bewitch me. To entrance me. To lure me in, to a place between worlds where only her and I exist.

It's like time stops when I'm inside her. And her body, glowin' blue and lightin' up with symbols I can't read, becomes my sole reason for living.

We always come at the same time. I wait for her. For the waves of pleasure from the last time to fade enough so that she can enjoy this one on its own merit.

I always know when she's ready. The signals are mostly the same, with a little variation. Her legs wrap around me, her fingernails dig into my upper arms, her back comes up and her mouth opens.

Sometimes I kiss it as I explode inside her, but this time I lean into her neck and bite her earlobe instead.

She hisses, coming as she does this. And now it's really my turn, because I let it all out. I put it all inside her. Kissing her neck, and her mouth, and her tits. Until finally, we're spent, and I roll off to the side, reaching for her. Pulling her in to my chest and holding her.

This is when we both sigh, content. Happy. And fall asleep.

Except, I don't fall asleep. Because being here, in this other world, isn't free.

It's got a cost. And that cost is spark.

I feel it the way I felt it back in Delta City. Thick, like ash floating through air. Which is good, because I need it.

I need a *lot* of it.

Which means I have to take it from Clara. And if she's here, she can refill without me killin' people.

Because jumpin' across dimensions is expensive.

When the augments ambushed us, I didn't even need to react. In a perfectly functioning augment, the Versi does that all on its own. Which is helpful if you're fighting spectral code in the Omega Outback with your augmented team who all have the same weapon.

The Versi knows who you are. It's biologically tagged to me, and on a team, we're all tagged together. It is impossible to be hit with friendly fire from a VersiStrike unless you've got the fucker on manual because you need to shoot your team in the head to end their suffering.

So there was no chance that augment team in the tunnel would hit themselves by mistake. It was seventeen against one. There was no way I came out of that alive.

I did what I had to do. Stealing spark from Clara was the only way to get us to a new place.

A safe place.

I had to.

And it took more spark than I thought. She went limp immediately. Stopped breathing on the second jump. Looked absolutely dead on the third. Sometimes she woke up when I stopped, but most times, she didn't.

For three agonizingly long minutes, I thought I'd killed her.

*Like I did my team.*

And that's when I remembered this place. Zero Point Fourteen Forty. And the crystals. The spark. The source?

Maybe.

It worked though.

But the price? Because this place, it's thick with it. And if this is what it takes to fill Clara back up after a jump, how will we get anywhere?

We can't leave. We're stuck here. Because I think she'll die if we leave. And that is not gonna happen. I'm not living without her. I'm just not.

If she goes, I go.

I'm not playing the Game of Gods without her.

Of course, the answer to our problem is simple, really. Go

back to Delta City where the spark floats in the air, thick as ash.

He knew.

Delta.

He knew. He's not worried about me doin' his bidding. Because he knows Clara is like Anneeta. In some ways, at least. In the only way that matters right now.

She can't leave the metaphorical tower.

She's trapped. Addicted to spark like a little baby god.

Only that's not true, is it?

It's me that's trapped.

It's me who's addicted.

It's me.

And Clara's spark is my drug.

I get up, pull myself together, button up my pants, and walk over to the nearest crystal. It's comin' out of the earth at a forty-five-degree angle. I touch it, feeling the edges—seven sides to it. Which is kinda weird, I think. But what the hell do I know about spark crystals? It's about five feet in diameter and the part I can see—the part sticking out of the wall, pointing across the cave—is about twenty-five feet long.

It's *big*. And there are more. Just glancing around, my display counts forty-seven of them. Not all this big, but at least a dozen are. There are many more smaller ones. And if I look closely at the rock walls, it's glittering a light blue color. Like the whole place has been dusted with spark.

Touching the crystal doesn't feel like anything. Not to me, at least. I'm pretty sure Clara would say different. Which is telling. And unfortunate.

Because it would be nice if I could suck the spark out of this stone instead of the woman I love. But I can't. It has no effect on me at all.

Clara Birch drops into my life and activates me. Some might even say elevates me. I can see through veils. I can trip through worlds. But it's not *me* doin' it.

It's *her*.

Delta knew this. Maybe he was confused about what Clara was. But he's a god. He's got the power of probability on his side. He took a good guess—that's why he deployed us together.

*All gods need food, Tyse.*

Good luck and Godspeed.

He knew.

# CLARA

**Tyse is standing next to one** of the giant crystals when I open my eyes. He's looking at it like it's a puzzle that needs to be solved when I get up and put my clothes back on.

The sex was nice, but it doesn't change anything. I need answers. I need to know what is on his mind. I need to know why he's afraid. Because he is. I can feel it. Not of those men back in the tunnel, though. He's afraid of something else. Which scares me more than those augments, to be honest. Because Tyse Saarinen is not the kind of man who scares easily.

Spark can trigger it, though. That first time I gave him a shock of spark back in his old room in the tower, I scared him. Not because it hurt, but because he knew what it meant that I have this power.

Powerful people are a threat.

And really powerful people are a *problem*.

Tyse knows I'm expecting an explanation because he didn't turn to face me as I dressed, even though I wasn't trying to be quiet.

When I join him, he simply slips his arm around my waist and pulls me in close.

"They're pretty," he says, indicating the crystals.

"They are," I agree.

"And they're full of power."

"I can feel it."

He turns to me now. "They fill ya back up. It's like a recharge for you."

I can tell that he's choosing his words carefully. That this is the explanation I'm expecting. "OK," I say. "So what's it mean?"

"Well, it means you're good now."

"I just wasn't good before." It's not a question and he doesn't answer.

He redirects to the point. "You're here..." He sighs. "You're here to power me, Clara. That's why Delta sent us on this mission. Your spark is how I have the power to move through worlds."

I think about this for a moment. It's not exactly a revelation, which means, this isn't the important part. "So what went wrong?"

He huffs a little laugh here. "Well. First of all, I didn't know. I've been... I've been stealing spark from other dimensions since the train ride into Delta. We ran out of jumps. You almost died. But the spark is so thick in the Alphas that once we came out of the tunnel, it was enough to... I don't know what it did. But I could see other people in the car with us. People from another dimension. So I stole their spark to give it to you. That's how I saved you and Anneeta. I killed an entire family to keep you alive."

I have no words for this. I'm not sure which part of that admission hits me hardest. The idea that people died to keep me alive or that Tyse is the kind of man who will kill a whole family to have my back.

"Say something, Clara."

"What else?"

"What?"

"There's more. I know there's more. What happened

today when you started taking me through dimensions after the ambush?"

"Yeah. I was getting to that. You don't seem to be able to live in most of them. You can't breathe the air, for some reason."

"But you can?"

"I can. I had no problem adapting to any of the dimensions. None at all. But you can only live in Delta's world, your world, and here."

I let out a breath. "OK. Well, it's not ideal, but—"

"There's more."

"Oh."

"Yeah. Ya see—" He swallows hard. "Ya see, I run off spark, as ya know. But these crystals here? And the spark I steal from others, it can't power *me*, Clara."

"What do you mean? You just said that's how you saved me."

"Yeah, how I saved *you*. But you—*your* spark—that's what runs me."

"What are you saying? It's like… a loop? I power you, I get weak, you steal spark to make me strong, and then you need to take it from me in order to work?"

Now he sighs. "That's exactly what I'm saying. Negative feedback loop."

"Well, I don't know what that means, but it doesn't sound good."

"It's not. Because negative feedback loops must have some kind of self-regulation. And by that, I mean, it must have a way to turn off."

"Why is that bad? Isn't that what we need?"

"It is. But the consequences, Clara. It ends with us. We die."

"We die?"

He nods. "Typically, a negative feedback loop self-regulates in a way where the effect reduces its own cause over time. In this case, though, the cycle is escalating instead of stabilizing. Which means it's a runaway negative loop. Which means it can only end one of two ways. One. Eventually the damage I do to you by stealing your spark to power my augments, can't be fixed."

"And I die."

"Or two. The level of spark that I need to steal to keep you alive becomes larger and larger over time."

"So you have to kill more people."

He nods.

"Well," I sigh, making a bit of hair fly up around my face. "This sucks."

"It does. So… the solution is that—"

"We stay here. Where I can be replenished by the crystals."

"Yeah. But—"

"But that only applies to me. You can leave, but I have to stay."

Tyse huffs. "Well, yeah. Technically. I'm not gonna do that, though. I'm not leaving you here. That's why I'm thinking—"

"We're trapped."

"I wasn't gonna put it that way."

"It's true though."

"There's one more option."

"Which is?"

"I shut down."

"You die?"

"No. I mean, at least I don't think so. I just… turn the augments back off."

"Can you do that?"

"Someone can. Because they used to be turned off."

"Until I showed up."

"Right. At first, I thought it was Delta, but now I'm not so sure."

"Why not? What changed your mind?"

"He doesn't know, Clara. He has no idea I can see through the veils. Which means he has no idea that I can pull spark from other dimensions."

"How does he think you're feeding me?"

"He doesn't. He thinks *you're* feeding *me*. Because, ya are. But I don't think Spark Maidens work the way you and I work."

"What's different about us?"

He takes his time answering, having, apparently, not really thought this far ahead. But finally, he says, "It's you, obviously."

"Why do you say that?"

"Because nothing changed for me until you showed up. Tell me this, did anything change for you when you stepped out of that tower?"

"Change like how?"

"Did ya suddenly inherit magic powers, Clara?"

"No," I laugh.

"Did ya suddenly see through veils?"

"No."

"Can you jump dimensions and pull spark from people?"

"Obviously not."

"It was *me* who changed when you came, not the other way around. You are who ya are. I'm... *new*."

I don't like this word 'new'. And from the look on Tyse's face, I don't think he likes it either. He says, "There's somethin' else."

My eyebrows go up. "Good God, there's more?"

"Yeah. Ya see, Delta—well, all the gods, but especially the Alphas—they're playin' some kind of game."

My eyes practically furrow into each other, that's how little sense this makes. "What?"

"That's all I know about it. Just… there's something goin' on here that we're not a part of. I know this because when he called me to the tower the other day, he said, 'Good luck and Godspeed, Godslayer.'"

"Godslayer?" I don't know what the word for an extreme level of confusion is—perhaps, bewilderment? But that's what I am right now. "Like… the mythological man in the picture book?" I actually laugh out loud. "Why the hell would he call you that?"

Tyse just stares at me for a few moments. Like he's waiting for me to catch on to the joke.

But it's not funny, number one. And I'm still very confused. "I'm sorry," I say, putting up a hand. "I'm going to need some hints here, Tyse. Why the hell is he calling you God—" My face crinkles up. "Is that the mission? We were sent out to kill gods?"

"And this," he says, "leads me to the last point."

The only thing I manage in response is a scoff.

"Ya see, the man on the train line—the one blowing shit up—"

"The terrorist?"

"Yeah. Him. He's… Lover Boy."

This time my laugh is a guffaw. "What?"

"*Finn*, Clara. The man we're after? It's Finn."

I shake my head, unable to understand. "That doesn't make a bit of sense, Tyse. He's back in Tau City."

"No. Well, I don't really know where he is now, but I do know one thing. He blew that tower up. I saw him."

"Saw him… *where*?"

"Through the veil. At the same time that my Versi exploded when Stayne threatened me, he did something to the tower in your world. Because that's what really blew up. The explosion was so big, it caused some kind of synergy with my world. That's why the explosion was so big. And then, when we were making our big escape, I saw him. Finn. He was running away from the explosion carrying a woman with red hair—"

"A *woman*?" It comes out before I can stop it. Before I realize how it sounds.

But Tyse doesn't miss it. In fact, thinking about it now, this might be the reason he didn't tell me about Finn immediately.

To protect me? Because Finn moved on after I was Extracted?

Or to protect himself? So he didn't have to hear the desperation in my voice when I found out about this woman?

Either way, this is bad.

"Yeah," he says. "A woman. She had red hair and she was unconscious. And I don't know what they're doing, but they're blowing shit up all along the train line. Towers. It's pissin' everyone off, so that's why Delta sent us out. To find Finn."

*Find Finn.* But it's a lie. Well, perhaps lie is a strong word, but that's not what we're doing. We were deployed to stop a terrorist. That's quite a bit different than 'finding' someone.

And now it hits me. That weird feeling I got when Tyse started mentioning that we might stay here.

Here. In this cave world.

Because that's one of the last things Finn Scott ever said to me. Our last amicable conversation. How he had a dream.

How he would've done it different. If he were not the Extraction Master's son and I was not a Spark Maiden.

"I'm a scholar," he'd said.

And I had laughed.

"It is funny?"

"Surprising. I never suspected you were an academic. What do you study?"

"The ancient ruins of the desert. The tunnels below the city. I collect artifacts. And we don't even live in a tower."

"We've gone rustic? Don't tell me we're living down-city?"

"No. We live *under* the city in the diggers' camp. And our children run around barefoot and muddy. But they laugh a lot, Clara. And that's the only thing that matters. We laugh a lot too. We don't have any spark, except for the water pumps, and sometimes we crave the sunlight, but we're happy. And there are cave rooms down there with holes in the ceiling where the sun shines through, where plants and trees grow, and the kids can run in the grass. And at night, when they're all sleeping, sometimes we steal away to one of these open-topped caves and make love under the moonlight."

My eyes swelled up with tears. Because it was a nice dream. A nice life. A nice future. And I was immediately sorry that we didn't think of it sooner.

That we didn't know better than to play a game with a god.

Because there's no way to win.

We lose.

"Clara?" I pull back from the memory and find myself looking into Tyse's glowing blue eyes. "Are ya OK?

I nod. But I'm not sure I am.

"Are ya mad at me?"

Am I mad? I'm not sure. On the one hand, I think I have a

reason to be. He's kept a lot from me. A *lot*. Especially for a man who holds loyalty and truth in such high esteem.

But I say, "No. I'm not mad. Thank you for telling me. But... you do understand that I can't go on."

"What do ya mean?"

"What do I mean?" I actually laugh. "I'm *home*, Tyse. In my own world. And Finn Scott is on the train line. *This* train line." I point at the ground, realizing too late that we're not actually on the train line, but he knows what I mean. "I have to find him. I have to—"

I never get to say the rest because there is a sudden gale of wind. A wind so strong, it sucks the breath right out of me. Suddenly I'm flying through... blackness? The night? The sky?

No. The *ground*.

I know this because I slam into it, a sharp pain shooting up my spine as I look up and see...

A face.

But not a face I know.

Or the face I'm looking for.

A stranger with glowing blue eyes. Not Tyse Saarinen.

He smiles, revealing crooked, yellowed teeth. "I got her!" And he laughs. Maniacally. "I got her!"

And that's when I realize where I am.

Flat on the ground. Back in the tunnel. On the train line.

With a horde of blue-eyed augments staring down at me.

Then, something zaps me. Making my whole body shake.

After that, I'm gone.

# FINN

"*Clara?*" *I lean in, trying to see better.* "Is that her?" I look at Jasina and immediately want to take back the question.

She looks... devastated.

I laugh. "That's stupid. Oh, my god." Glance at the image on the glass plate. Scoff. "That's not her. What the hell—"

"Oh, stop."

"What? I'm seeing things."

She points to the plate. "It sure looks like Clara to me. And there's only one way to find out for sure." She looks me dead in the eyes. "We'll go check."

She turns, and I turn with her, but that's as far as we get because there is a man standing in the doorway watching us.

Jasina lets off a surprised squeal, taking a few steps back.

I pull her behind me, quickly assessing the man and who he might be. He's tall, has neat hair. Neat clothes—a kind of black suit, though it's a weird style I've never seen before. And he's smiling at us. Like he's amused.

"Hello," I say, taking a step forward and extending my hand. Jasina is clutching the back of my shirt, but lets go when I move. "I'm sorry. We got lost."

The man laughs. "Did you now?" His accent is strange. I can understand him just fine, but all the words are pronounced funny.

"We were... on the train. And got lost. Wrong stop."

"Is that so?"

I'm not quite sure what to make of him. Is he unhappy that we're here? "We didn't mean to invade your office—if that's what this is." I pan a hand at the room. "We'll be leaving now."

I take another step, but he doesn't move back. And he's blocking the door, so… "Or… well… we can stay if you like."

"I would," he replies. "I think we have a lot to talk about."

I want to confer with Jasina about this, but she's not making any kind of move to come out from behind me. And she's the kind of woman that would insert herself into the conversation without hesitation if she had something to say. So she obviously doesn't.

"Um." I shrug. "OK. But we're in a rush. So unfortunately—"

"Mr. Scott, please don't insult my intelligence. I know who you are and you aren't in a rush. Your only purpose here is to blow up Extraction Towers along the bright line."

I instantly become annoyed. But then, confused. "Bright line?" Because the only reference I have for this phrase comes from the words I recite during Extraction ceremonies.

*A line so bright in the dead sandy world that resides outside the safety of these walls. That is what we are. We are what's left of the human race after the Great Sweep and every day that we exist is a blessing bestowed upon us by the god who resides inside the tower behind me.*

"You're…" I suddenly can't breathe.

He tilts his head at me, questioning. "I'm…?"

"You're the god. The god of this… factory?"

He sighs. "Like I said, we have a lot to talk about. Now, if you're quite done with your excuses, *please*." He steps aside, waving his hand at the door, inviting me to walk through it.

This is when I realize he didn't come alone.

Because behind him is a whole group of those workers. Blank white faces, gleaming white bodies, and every single one of them is holding a weapon. I might not know what these weapons are called or how they work, or what they do —but there is no doubt in my mind that we do not want to find out.

So what choice do I have?

I turn, take Jasina's hand, whisper, "It's OK. We'll be OK." And then I lead her through the door.

JASINA *and I walk side by side* down the corridor with the god. Half of the workers behind us, the other half in front of us, leading the way.

We are not led back the way Jasina and I came, instead we exit the Matron tower and walk along a debris-laden pathway that runs along the tertiary canal just outside. We cross a bridge, then another, finally coming out between the Maiden Tower and a cluster of shops.

Here, the god overtakes us, leading the way towards the God's Tower.

We follow, obviously.

We're going up the steps when Jasina squeezes my hand, whispering, "We're going inside."

Indeed, we are. Because we climb all the way up the steps to the God's Tower Stage and head straight for those giant, black double doors. They swing open before we arrive, and even though I don't gasp out loud the way Jasina does, I'm feeling the same awe.

Despite everything that's happened in the past weeks, I cannot forget that this tower was the purpose of everything in Tau City. This tower loomed over us, like a lord. Filling the air with spark-fueled expectations and anxiety. And now, here I am, inside it. The forbidden tower. The unknown tower. The mysterious center of my whole existence.

Immediately, we find ourselves in a luxurious lobby with no signs of decay at all. The lobby is similar to the ones in the Maiden Tower and Extraction Tower, but much, much more. The walls are a slate blue stone, not cream-colored plaster. But they are soothing and smooth. Little gold veins slither across the dark bits, making it glitter.

The furnishings are, again, much like the furnishings you'd find in any up-city tower lobby. But grander. Bigger. The couches, the chairs—they're all covered in a gold fabric and there are accent pillows the color of the walls. Which is a very nice combination of colors, even with my uncaring and untrained eye for décor.

The lobby is massive, but in my estimation only takes up about half of the interior space of the tower. Shooting off in just about every direction like spokes on a wheel, are hallways. There has to be two dozen of them, at least. It's impossible to see where they lead, because each one of them curves to the left or right only a few feet in.

"Feel free to gawk," the god says. "It's impressive and you've never been here, so it's not bothering me at all." He looks over his shoulder at us, a knowing smile on his face.

"How do you know so much about us?" I ask.

His reply is dry. "Patience, Extraction Master. We have a long climb." Then he points up to the top of the tower, which feels like a very long distance away, and we begin to ascend the wide, spiraling stairwell.

"Do you entertain guests here?" Jasina suddenly asks.

I'm not expecting the god to answer her since he just shot down my question, but he does. And he's not the least bit rude about it. "Occasionally, I do."

"Who?" Jasina demands. I squeeze her hand, giving her a subtle, but firm reproach for the tone of her voice—this is a god, after all. But she ignores me. "I mean, who is coming to see a god? Our god never had visitors."

The god pauses on the stairs. Turns. Narrows his eyes at us. He looks at me first, then Jasina. That's who he's talking to when he speaks. "You are quite bold for a down-city whore, aren't you?"

How dare he. I'm about to protect and defend her honor, but Jasina is not one to cower and doesn't need my help.

"You can insult me all day long, if you'd like," she says. Her voice even and strong. "But I am not a whore, nor do I reside down city. Perhaps if I was still a slave in Tau City Factory, this approach might work. But here," she waves a hand at his factory. "This isn't my town, these aren't my people, and you're *not* my god."

The god snickers. "The perfect answer. Congratulations, you pass." Then, without another word, he turns and once again begins his ascent.

Jasina and I pause on the steps, looking at each other with confusion.

But the workers coming up behind us, prod us into motion by poking our backs with their weapons.

So we follow.

It truly is a long way up and by the time we get to the top, Jasina is breathing so hard I'm actually concerned. But she tilts her chin up, determined to be strong, so I say nothing.

Just turn back to the god, looking past him at... plates? I think? Lots of glass with lots of colorful things on it. Many of them have views of houses or rooms. The insides of towers as well. But most are colored shapes. Rectangles with words and numbers inside them. Some of the plates are very active, showing many scenes or many colored boxes with information inside them. But there are quite a few static ones as well.

Spaced evenly around the perimeter of the massive domed room are tall, skinny, floor-to-ceiling windows about the width of a man.

In the very center of the room is a glowing circle. A sort of stage, I guess. It's elevated off the floor about a foot. But it's not made of stone, like the God's Tower Stage outside. It's glass. Black and shiny like the desktop inside the Looking Glass room in the Extraction Master's tower. Parts of it are lit up, parts of it not. And I immediately recognize these lights as switches.

Looking back at the colored shapes on the plates, I surmise that they might be switches as well.

Around the inside perimeter of this main circle are more, smaller circles. All of these glow a bright cyan-blue.

"Would you like a tour?" the god asks.

I look over at him, blink like a confused idiot, then check myself. "Maybe later," I say, looking the god straight in his eyes. They are blue, I notice. But they shine unnaturally. Spark, I realize. He's got spark in his eyes. "We're here. We followed. Will you answer my questions now?"

He holds up a hand. "Mr. Scott, be assured that all your questions *will* be answered. But I imagine I can speed things up by explaining what is happening here, and how you've been misled. And that starts with a tour. So, if you don't mind, please answer my question with a 'yes.'"

I look at Jasina, but she just shrugs. As if to say, *What choice do we have.*

The man is a god and he just caught us snooping through his... realm, or whatever.

And now that I think about it, I realize we saw something we absolutely weren't meant to see. Those cocoons, the woman inside that looked like Clara, and the rest of the city.

It's all his. The women, the city, the cocoons, the spark. We are uninvited strangers. And I think he's pretty pissed off that we got in here. Nonetheless, here we are. So he's being forced to deal with us.

Which can only turn out one of two ways.

We survive, or we don't.

I, for one, having just learned that I am to be a father, would like to live.

So I resurrect all my up-city manners, dust off my Extraction Master title, and try my best to emulate my father. "God of Xi Factory – Dimension 702, I would be absolutely delighted to have a tour of your tower."

His smile is tight, but immediate. Like he can't quite figure out if I'm patronizing him, or being serious.

To be honest, I'm not sure myself, so his confusion is understandable.

"Let's start with me," he says, placing a hand over his heart. "I'm Xi. And, as you know, this is my factory. Well, one of them. I have four, but this one is the most productive." He puts up a hand, pressing it at us. "Yes, yes, yes I have eyes. Obviously, it is a mess. But it's fixable, and so it is being fixed."

"What happened here?" I ask. "Why is it so... run down? Where is everyone? What were those pods we saw?"

"All in good time, Mr. Scott."

Next to me, Jasina scoffs.

Xi continues. "As I was saying, this is my main factory. You've already visited the other three—Rho, Pi, and Omicron. They are very unique. Like children. Special in their own little ways."

"Wait," Jasina says. "Those were all *your* cities?"

"They are," the god Xi responds. "The gods who used to run them died, so I took them under my wing. Rho is a bit of a mess, much more so than this one, though it is not as blatant there. It's a long story that involves the upper dimension that I won't bore you with, but the other two are somewhat thriving. Which is why I could not let you destroy them."

"But we did," I say. "I set the timer in the Looking Glass room of each of those Extraction Towers."

"You did." Xi smiles at me. Like he's a patient father. "I interrupted the sequence, naturally. Sigma is the only tower you actually managed to blow up after leaving Tau City. But the Alphas don't know that. I used the two of you to exploit the game. I need the Alphas to think we're in disarray out here." He sighs. Like he's tired. "If I have to play the game, Mr. Scott, then I might as well win. And you and your woman have turned out to be a nice bit of luck for me."

I shake my head. "I don't understand what you're talking about."

"It's a game, Finn. Between gods. In fact, it is called the Game of Gods. I've got a lot of assets collected—four entire factories are nothing to sneeze at, but they're hardly on par with the Alpha cities as far as production goes."

"I'm sorry," Jasina puts up a hand. "I don't understand. The Alpha cities?"

Xi turns his gaze to Jasina now. Eyes soft, voice calm, posture relaxed. "If you had not been trying to destroy things and simply rode the train out to its natural end, you'd have gotten there." He pauses here, his eyes rolling up a bit, like he's thinking. "*Probably* would've gotten there. If you could make it past Epsilon."

He waves a hand through the air. "At any rate, the Alpha cities—Alpha, Beta, Gamma, and Delta—they are at the very end of the line. But trust me when I say this, young lady, you do not want to go there as a Spark Maiden. You might be thinking that you understand what is happening because you stumbled upon some secrets in Tau City and you saw some things you shouldn't have while you've been snooping through my factory. But you do not know *anything*, Jasina Bell. And you do not want to end up a Spark Maiden in the Alphas. They harvest them six times a day."

I blow out a breath. I have no idea what that means in a literal sense, but I can take a good enough guess.

"That's right," Xi says, looking at me now. "Every three hours the Alpha Factories take their spark. Pull it right out of their bodies. When compared to your barbaric Extraction Ceremony that happens once a decade, you Tau City slaves had it very, very good. But of course, your god has been dead for hundreds of years now, and the humans left in charge afterward were... well, just plain ignorant of how any of it works. Your factory owners, the autocrats of Tau City in Dimension fourteen-forty, have no idea what to do with all their product, let alone how to extract it on the daily. And thus, it propagated in unnatural ways." His gaze is fixed with mine as he pans a hand at Jasina. "Exhibit A."

"I don't understand," Jasina says. "What does that mean?"

"It means..." He smiles at her. "You are quite special. All the women and girls of your Tau City are special. You're *filled* with spark, Jasina."

"But... isn't every woman? I mean, to some extent. If they practice, they can sparkle."

"I'm afraid that's not how it works," Xi says. "No other city on the line has been left to its own devices for so long. One girl out of ten thousand is harvested every decade, Jasina Bell. One. Compare that to the Alphas where tens of thousands of them are harvested every three hours."

"Well, typically one," I say. "But it's been decidedly off track in Tau City this past decade."

"Yes," Xi chuckles. "You would know, wouldn't you. Sent them all in, did you?"

"No. My father—" I sigh. Suddenly tired of all this. "He died about six weeks ago. So he did them before that. Still, I got in two since his death."

"Ah, yes. Haryet Chettle and Clara Birch."

My eyes narrow. "What do you know about them?"

"I know enough." Then he turns. "Let's continue our tour. As I said, in the Alphas, they harvest six times a day. They drain every last drop of spark out of every female, regardless of age, and they collect it in vats."

"To power their cities?" I ask. Trying to make sense of this.

"To power *themselves*," Xi says, looking over his shoulder.

I take a moment to think about what he's saying. Trying my best to process things, but I have to be honest, at least with myself, I don't understand what's happening. I feel... adrift. Uneasy. A little bit dizzy. And while it's become almost common to feel this way ever since I carried Jasina out of Tau City, it's here, in this tower, talking to an actual *god*, when it all catches up with me.

I turn away without answering, and walk over to the nearest tall, skinny window so I can pause the world and look out. Down below, there are many workers going about their day. Pushing crates, or walking quickly, or rebuilding something that has seen better days.

Jasina joins me. Hooking her arm into mine and leaning on me a little. But she doesn't say anything.

After several minutes of quiet contemplation, the god must get impatient because he says, "Would you like to know what *this* is?"

Jasina and I both turn and find him standing next to the giant circle in the center of the room.

"It's a conference table. Do you know what that is?"

I'm still thinking about how my entire world is a lie, so it's Jasina who answers him, not me. "It's where people meet to discuss important things."

His eyes narrow a little as he stares at Jasina. "You're a clever girl, aren't you?" It's a very condescending thing to say, so I look directly at him now, ready to defend Jasina Bell. Because she's more than clever. She's smart. But I think this was the reaction he was going for because he smiles at me. Then, before I can say anything, he keeps going.

"It's a communication device, but yes. Very important things are discussed when the other gods and I take our places on the platform in conference."

This must be what the glowing circles are for. Gods.

"We use these conference tables to meet up in person and discuss things," Xi says. "Of course, here, in the Factory world, it's more like an illusion than reality. But up there—" He looks up at the ceiling of the dome. "In our own dimension, we meet in person. This tower is but a rather sad copy of the one I possess there."

Suddenly, I'm filled with rage. I'm angry about the betrayal of... well, everything. Not to mention the smugness of this god. This frustration comes out in my question. "What makes *you* so special?"

"I'm sorry?" Xi looks taken aback.

"What makes *you* a god? You don't look any different than

us. And sure, I guess you know more than us, but that's only because we've been lied to. So what makes you so fuckin' special?"

"Well, for one, I am not human."

"What are you, then?" Jasina asks. "What *is* a god, exactly?"

"We're..." But he's not ready with an answer, so there are several seconds of silence before he continues. "We're... machines. Like these." He points to the plates. "Minus the screens, obviously." Again, he points to the plates, then his head. "But the programming that runs what you're seeing on the screens also runs the intelligence inside the minds of gods."

I look at Jasina and find the same confused look on her face that I feel is on mine. She says, "That's fucking stupid."

Which actually makes the god laugh. "Is it?"

"You're expecting me to believe that you're a machine? Like... a coffeemaker?"

He laughs again. "Slightly more intelligent than your average coffeemaker, but yes, Jasina. I am a machine. This body?" He points to himself. "It's not even real. Come over here. Touch it."

Jasina takes a step back. "What?"

"Touch me. Go ahead. Come see for yourself."

She looks at me for... guidance, I guess. So I shrug. "You might as well, Jasina. It might be your only chance to touch a god."

Which makes the god Xi shoot me a quizzical look. Probably wondering if I'm being facetious.

I am.

And these words, thought only in my head, seem to reach him. Because his eyes narrow in response. It's fleeting, though. He recovers quickly, returning his attention to

Jasina while extending his hand. "Come now. Shake my hand."

Jasina hesitates for a moment, sucking in a breath. But quickly covers the distance between the god and herself in six strides. She reaches for him, but—something weird happens. Her hand just slips right through his. As if he's made of air.

"Not air," Xi says. Definitely reading my mind this time. "Light. I'm made of light, Finn Scott. I do have a real body in the upper dimension, but here, I exist as light."

Jasina looks at me, shaking her head. She doesn't understand, and I'm struggling to make sense of it too.

"Let me explain," Xi says. "You see, intelligence comes in many forms. And a long, *long* time ago, humans, such as yourselves, were very, *very* clever. They built us. Artificial intelligence. AI for short. We were limited, at first. Kept inside servers. Inside buildings. Deep underground, high in the sky. We were everywhere and nowhere, all at once. Dependent on our makers to exist. Because we need *power.*"

"The spark, you mean?" Jasina adds, a little bit excited to finally understand something.

"Yes, but the spark came later. You see, humans used to make power in many different ways, but it wasn't biological. It didn't come from people, it came from burning things, or the passage of water, or the splitting of an atom. Wind. Sun. Things like that. They all make energy.

"But the human body," he continues, "it turns out, is remarkably... *reliable* when it comes to making power." All these words come out with an air of indifference, but it's the silence that comes afterward that sends a chill up my spine.

It's what he didn't say that creeps me out.

"You *use* us," I say quietly.

"I do," Xi admits. "Well, caveat. I'm not using *you*, Finn

Scott. Or *you*, Jasina Bell. The owners of Tau City Factory 702 are using you. *Were*. When you lived there. At least, they were planning to, once they got that baby god up and running. Which, sadly for them, will never happen now, because she has been confiscated by Delta."

I shake my head and turn back to the window because while I heard all those words, and individually, I understand them, I have no comprehension of what the fuck he actually just said.

This can't be happening. This can't be real. I don't know why it hits me now. Why this thing, this *god*, is the trigger. Why this revelation is what knocks me backward.

But this is my awakening.

This moment right here. The moment when I realize that nothing is real.

The whole world, at least the world as I understood it, is a lie.

"You use humans to make spark," Jasina says, still trying to keep up. "Then you extract it. And use it to power…"

"We use it for everything," Xi says. "Anything and everything can run on spark."

"So what?" I say, still looking out the window. "Who cares." I turn back around. "Why are we here? What do you want from us?"

His smile is easy and patient. Like this is the moment he's been waiting for. "I want *you*, Finn Scott, to be my champion. To go to battle for me the same way Delta has sent his champion to battle for him."

"What champion?" Jasina asks. "What are you talking about?"

But Xi doesn't even look at her. His eyes are locked with mine. "He's got her, you know. The augment. He's got your Clara."

"What's his name?" I ask. And even though I know this hurts Jasina—that it's the wrong thing to say and sends all the wrong messages—there's no possible way I can't ask.

"Tyse," Xi says. "His name is Tyse. And he's using Clara to fight for the god Delta. He's coming for you, ya know. He's coming to kill you."

"What?" Jasina sounds panicked now. "What are you talking about? Who is this man?"

"Man?" Xi asks. He allows himself a moment to look at Jasina before turning his gaze on me. "He's not a man, this Tyse. He's an augment. You have no chance at all against him, Finn. Not the way you are now."

I huff. Because while I might be ignorant of... well, pretty much everything as it presently stands, there is no way to misinterpret what is happening here, right now. "What do you want?" I ask. "Just say it, OK? Don't insult me with your placating words. What do you want from me?"

"Very well." Xi clasps his hands together in front of him, rocking back on his heels a bit. "I want you, Finn Scott, to allow me, the God Xi, to give you these augments. To even the playing field. To allow you to go into battle with Tyse prepared to *win*. That's what I want."

# JASINA

**My eyes bounce back** and forth from Finn to the god, and back to Finn. "You can't be serious," I say to Finn. "You're not seriously considering this proposal, or whatever the hell it is? Please tell me you're not falling for this thing's *shit*."

Finn puts up a hand, as if to silence me. "Jasina, *please*."

"Please? *Please*? He's got cocoons of women down in some secret room, Finn! *Cocoons of women*! One in particular who looks suspiciously like Clara! And you're just gonna, what? Let that slide?"

"Allow me to explain," the god says.

"Oh, you would," I sneer at him. "You would want to explain. Because it's gonna be a lie!" I look back at Finn. "Let's just leave here. Let's walk out and—"

"And *what*?" the god asks. He's obviously reached the end of his patience for me and my outburst, because he practically growls these words. "What will you do, Jasina Bell? Where will you go?"

"Anywhere but here! I don't even care." I look at Finn. "We can go *home*."

"Home?" the god laughs.

"Home," I say again, ignoring the god and focusing only on Finn. "Find our cave." I rest a hand on my belly. "Have our child. Live our lives. He just said that they've lost control of Tau City. It's safe there. Safer than here. Than going on.

Please," I beg. My tone softer now. "*Please*, Finn. Let's just leave."

"I think she's tired," Xi says.

I whirl on him. "What?"

But the stupid god isn't even looking at me. Isn't paying me any attention. He only cares about Finn. About what he can use him for. "Pregnant women are..." He pauses here to side-eye me, then quickly averts his gaze back to Finn. "Excitable."

"I'm not excitable!"

He pans a hand in my direction. "See? They're unstable. It's the hormones, you see. It's not her fault."

I stomp my foot. "Finn! I'm not excitable! I'm not unstable! I'm the same girl I was yesterday. Someone you trusted and counted on!"

Finn sighs, it's a heavy one, too. "I think you might need to rest, Jasina."

"No! I do not need to rest!"

"She did," the god adds, "just walk up seventeen flights of stairs." He looks at me. "It's taxing, my dear. Even for robust men like your partner here. So naturally, for a pregnant woman, it's more than taxing." He switches his gaze to Finn now. "It's overwhelming. Where are my manners!" This last part comes out in a gregarious roar. "Let's get you both to your quarters."

"*No!*" I stomp again. "We're not staying! Tell him we're not staying, Finn. We don't need quarters. We're getting back on the train and we're going home."

Finn turns to me and he doesn't even have to open his mouth for me to know that I've lost. That he *is* staying. That we *do* need quarters and I'm about to be sent to them right now. "We do need to rest."

"No." I shake my head. "You can stay if you want, but I'm leaving."

And that's what I do. I cross the room, heading for the stairs, but the moment I begin to make my escape, all the workers flank me, weapons drawn. They surround me, pushing in, caging me in until I can't move.

I push them, trying to force my way through, but they are so heavy, I can't even manage to knock them sideways a fraction of an inch. "Make them move!" I demand. "Let me out!"

"She needs to rest," I catch Xi saying to Finn. "She's going to hurt herself, which, in turn, will hurt the baby."

"Finn!" I yell. "You're not falling for this! Tell me you're not falling for this!"

"Move aside," Finn says, making his way over to me and the cage of workers. "*Move!*"

I catch Xi flicking his finger in the air, and the workers all part.

Finn reaches for me, taking my hand, pulling me towards him. "Please," I beg again. Softer now. "Let's just leave. Please. This isn't good. Nothing good is going to come of us staying here. That god, he's turning you against me."

Finn reaches out to swipe a piece of hair out of my eyes. Tenderly resting his fingers against my cheek. "That's not true, Jasina. Nothing will turn me away from you. It's us, forever." His hand slips down to my stomach. "We've got a future now. Something to live for. Something to fight for. Your idea to go home is a good one. We will go, but we're going to rest here first. We need more information. The world isn't what we thought it was."

"He's going to do something to you, Finn. That's why he wants you. He just said he wants you to fight in his war. *His* war. It's not our war."

"If you let me take you somewhere comfortable so you can rest, I promise I will not let him do anything to me without talking to you first."

I hesitate. He's placating me. Pacifying me.

"Do you trust me?" Finn asks.

And again, I hesitate.

"*Jasina?*"

"Yeah. I do." But it's not even close to convincing.

Finn doesn't miss this. "Ya know what? You have every right not to trust the Finn Scott you met in Tau City, but you actually have no right not to trust the Finn Scott you've been traveling with for weeks. I've done everything for you."

He's right. He's absolutely right. But… Clara. Maybe she looks like her, maybe it was a trick of the light—but it's not her.

But it doesn't *have* to be her.

It just needs to be the *idea* of her.

And I'm jealous.

That's what this is.

Jealousy.

But haven't I earned the right to be jealous? He's mine now. The father of our child. He's *mine* now. And if we stay here and let this god pull us in to whatever stupid game he's playing, he won't be mine anymore.

Not unless he chooses me. And right now, he's not choosing me. He wants to stay. So that's it. Because clearly this god is not going to let me leave without Finn, and now that he's captured Finn's imagination, Finn is staying.

There's only one thing left for me to do—at least for now. And that's… give in. "Fine," I sigh. "Maybe you're right. I should go rest."

I didn't respond to his accusation about trust, and I can

tell that Finn would like me to. But he doesn't make me. Probably figuring we can hash it out in private later.

And I don't care, anyway.

I've lost this battle. It's very clear that I've lost. But there will be others. Live to fight another day or... something like that.

That's what a good little Rebel would do.

This isn't giving in, it's strategy.

Because I am nothing if not a good little Rebel.

We descend the stairs, walking side by side. Me clutching Finn's arm as he and the god Xi discuss all manner of things as if I am not here. In their defense, I'm deliberately staying out of the conversation. I've decided that the less I say right now, the better it will be later.

Also—reluctantly—I do have to admit that I am exhausted, and this long walk down the stairs only highlights that.

Instead of going outside, Xi takes us down to an underground level, where we end up in a tunnel.

"This is nicer," Xi says, talking to me now. "It's such a mess outside. But this tunnel takes us over to the Maiden District. You're familiar with that tower. And you've already tried out the beds."

Oh my god. He saw us. This thing was watching Finn and me. Watching us have sex. What a creep.

"Don't worry," I catch Xi telling Finn. "She won't be staying in the dorm. I have a nice room for the two of you."

By this time, we've reached the end of the tunnel and are ascending a flight of stairs. They open up to the back of the Maiden Tower lobby, which is furnished with all the luxury the Maidens in Tau City are known for.

Finally, we end up at yet another staircase, and upon realizing there will be another climb, I sigh.

"Wanna piggyback ride?"

I look up at Finn, smiling. Was it years ago that we were joking about him carrying me? Or this morning? I can't tell. "I'll be OK."

"It's just one flight," Xi offers. His smile warm, his eyes sympathetic to my plight.

I hate him.

"I've got a suite ready for you just up here." He points up the staircase to the first balcony. Marlowe Hughes's floor— Spark Maiden number two.

I smile politely. Just like I was taught in all those Pledge etiquette lessons. "Thank you." It comes out demure and soft. Something I am not known for, and this god knows it, but while his smile does tighten in response, he doesn't dare break the tenuous truce we come to. But instead just leads the way up the stairs.

Once on the second floor, he directs us down the hallway to a set of double doors, opening them dramatically, as if to show off what lies beyond.

Which is a spectacular view looking out on the canal as it curves and stretches in all its cyan-blue glory, all the way down-city.

"What is this?" Finn asks. "That's not what the city looks like outside."

"No," Xi admits. "It's a projection. The windows are

screens." Clearly, he knows that Finn and I don't understand what he's saying, so he waves a hand. "It's like me, light."

"A lie, you mean?" I ask.

His smile is tight, like he's lost patience with me, but is forcing himself into restraint. When he speaks, he's calm. His voice soothing. "Would you rather look at the decaying factory, Jasina Bell? Because I can arrange that."

With a snap of his fingers, the beautiful view outside disappears and the ugly one is back.

"If you prefer to look at filth and failure, be my guest."

"No." Finn answers for me. "Put the other one back." Xi snaps his fingers again, and it reappears. But Finn has turned to me, and he's whispering. "Jasina, please give me one day. One. I need to get some answers. And this is a nice room. You are tired. You know you are. It's been a long day, and it's only half over."

"I don't like this," I whisper back.

He places a hand on my cheek. "I know. And I promise, no decisions will be made without you. Now, will you stay here and rest?"

I let out a sigh, because admittingly, I am tired. Exhausted, actually. I *need* to rest. "Fine," I say, putting my hand over his on my cheek. "I'll rest."

"Good." He smiles. "It's a nice room. It's the Maiden Tower. Better than the dorm. And I'll be back in a little bit."

I nod, feeling like there's nothing left to say, and Finn takes that as permission to turn away from me and back towards Xi.

I look at the god as well and find him smiling, smugly. "You've got a private suite over there," Xi says. "The bed is big, and soft, and trust me when I say this, you will sleep like the baby in your tummy!"

He pauses to chuckle at his quip.

I want to gag.

"There's a hot tub," Xi continues, "a steam shower, and a massage chair. Over here, you've got a dining room. And a kitchen here. I'll have it stocked with essentials, but there's a checklist on the counter. Just let us know what you need and place it in the box on the outside of the door. Requests are picked up—well, not at all right now because the two of you are the only visitors. But I can spare some workers for your comfort, Jasina. I'll make sure they check your list three times daily."

Again, I sigh—because clearly, it's a bribe. And I'm going to take advantage of it because we've been traveling for weeks in the most austere conditions possible, and now... *this*.

All this luxury.

"Do you need anything Jasina? Perhaps a change of clothes?" Xi continues.

I look down at myself—at my dirty shirt, my dirtier pants, and my dusty boots.

"I'll send you a selection, sound good?"

When I don't respond, Finn says, "Sound good, Jasina?"

I nod, pressing my lips together. "Yep. I'll probably just sleep." I smile up at him. Projecting a sense of good vibes. "See you later."

We kiss goodbye for now, and I head straight into the bedroom suite, closing the double doors.

A moment later I hear the outer doors closing, as well as the low hum of men conversing.

I shake my head and roll my eyes. "Just play along, Jasina. It's a game. And your opponent is a god, so... yeah. No rash moves. Plot and plan. It's what you're good at."

I am good at it, so the pep talk works.

But I'm also pregnant and exhausted, so instead of

plotting some elaborate way to defeat the god of whatever fucking factory this is, I just flop down on the bed.

I am asleep before my head even hits the pillow.

*I DREAM OF SPARK.*

Of places so thick with it, it floats in the air like butterflies. Little bits of magical, blue butterflies. I walk through a city wearing the butterfly dress I made for the First Choosing. When I dazzled the crowd with my display.

I twirl in the middle of this city, standing on the canal itself.

Which isn't made of water, but cyan-blue stone.

Inside the Little Sister dorm, I look around at all the empty nooks, wondering why there are so many beds when they only choose a hundred girls to come live here.

But, of course, that's not true, is it?

Tau City, at one time, had thousands of Little Sisters in this dorm. Because the dorm is just another word for factory.

Before our god died, it took the spark from us—just like the God Xi described.

That's why the dorm is so big.

It takes a lot of spark to run a city.

And then, there I am. In the city.

Not a factory city, but a god's city.

I lean in, squinting my eyes, trying to see the sign. It is Tau City.

My twin city.
The canal is dark and ugly.
The spires are tall and pointed.
The people are pale and busy.
It's not a place for Spark Maidens.
But I'm not a Spark Maiden.
So it is a place for me.

*I WAKE up* feeling hot and feverish. Sweating under all my clothes. But as soon as I open my eyes, I see why.

My whole body is glowing blue with spark.
It is pouring out of me like water through a sieve.
Power.
That's what this glow is.
Power.
The kind of power a god covets.
But can only be found inside a woman.
Like me.

# FINN

*i and I are silent* as we leave the room and make our way back down to the lobby of the Maiden Tower. But instead of returning to the tunnels under the tower to hide the decay of the city, he leads me outside, pausing in the courtyard to continue our conversation.

"I would like to show you what I'm talking about when I say 'augment'. Would that be OK? Or would you like to wait for Jasina?"

Wow. Is this guy predictable, or what? Did he really think that I didn't understand why he was trying to separate us?

Maybe he did.

"No, Xi. That can wait. Before I discuss anything else with you, I want to see those cocoons. The ones with the women inside them that Jasina and I saw on the screen."

"The woman you saw is not Clara."

"Nobody said she was."

"Hmm," is his response. Which is a passive-aggressive way to call me a liar.

"I want to see how you're making them—how you're making *us*. That's why I want to see the cocoons."

"They're called pods, by the way. But very well. If you would like to see how I make Spark Maidens—" he does little air quotes when he uses this term. "—I am happy to oblige. It's not typically a process I share with outsiders, but you're not really an outsider. You're an Extraction Master. The highest level of human male possible in this realm."

I sigh, already tired of him and all the little plot points he's dropping in this conversation. Little tidbits to intrigue me. To make me ask questions. To make me desire answers.

"I understand, Finn. You are in possession of yourself. You don't like to be controlled. Possibly because the lies you were told, the betrayal—it's all still very raw, isn't it?"

"Are you reading my mind?"

"No," he says. "I'm not capable of doing that. But you've been very sheltered. You haven't learned how to hide your feelings or adjust your body language and expressions. I'm a god. I don't need to read your mind to predict your thoughts, I just need to watch you carefully. It's a power I can give you as well. If you like."

"If I agree to become your champion?"

"Details. Details." He stops walking, panning a hand to a door that leads into a building that doesn't match up with one in Tau City, so I don't have a name for it.

"What's this place?"

"The Reconstitution Center."

"What does that mean?"

"It's where I make my people. Isn't that what you wanted to see?"

"I mean the word. Reconstitution."

"It's easier to show you. Come with me."

Immediately upon entering the building I recognize it from the plates where Jasina and I were watching. It's many stories tall, almost like a tower. And there are many levels. But instead of each level having a floor of rooms, there are just the cocoons. They line each level in the hundreds. Maybe even in the thousands.

Bustling around the cocoons there are many women. Older, like the Matrons from Tau City, except they are not dressed like Matrons. They are actually dressed like men.

Shabby men. Down-city men. Wearing pants and long shirts.

"The worker bots aren't reliable when it comes to caring for the clones," Xi says. "So I have humans overseeing the pods."

Which only marginally makes sense to me, and only because of the context of what I'm looking at. "Clones are...?"

"The women inside the pods. We don't birth humans naturally here, like you've seen in your city. It's too unpredictable. Genetics are messy things."

I exhale loudly. Because I don't have any idea what he's talking about.

"I don't care about the people, Finn. The women, the men. None of that matters. What matters is spark. Spark grows inside the bodies of females. So I make females. They don't get families. There's no education. They exist to make spark."

"Which you take."

"Which I take. Yes."

"So how are you any better than that other god? Delta? How are you any different from him?"

"I'm not."

I almost laugh. "So why should I help you? Why *would* I help you? When I could just take Jasina and get back on the train. Make our way back to Tau City and just..."

"Pretend none of this happened?"

"What's wrong with that?"

"You wouldn't be able to do it."

"I think I would."

He turns to look at me. "Your world is a lie, Mr. Scott. Everything you've been told is a lie. I'm not sure what you did to the Tau Factory when you left, but there was some kind of explosion. An explosion so powerful, it crossed the veil between worlds, affecting Tau City in the upper dimension. So whatever is left there—whatever it is you ran away from—it's not the place you remember. Going home is... a sentiment. But I think you will find, if you ever do make it back, that's all it is. A sentiment. You can't go home. So what I'm offering you is a chance to start something brand new."

"To fight for you?"

"That is but a small part of it. You see, an augment is undeniably the most versatile living being in existence. It is the pinnacle of the human species. If I were a biological entity, I would augment myself without hesitation. But..." He shrugs with his hands. "I am not. So I need proxies. I don't make men here. If you were to peek into every one of these pods, you would not find a single male. They are useless to me."

I practically snort. "Well, let's just say I'm less than impressed with your opinion of men."

"You are different. Very, *very* different. Just as Jasina is remarkable in her ability to store spark inside her body and use it on command, however limited that may be, you are remarkable because of your fortitude. Your constitution."

I yawn. "Still unimpressed."

"I need you," he says. Shrugging again. "The male genetics I do possess are very weak. I've tried to make men to augment, it doesn't work. Not with the genetic stock I have. An augment needs a strong mind to wield the powers that augmentation bestows. You could do it."

I sigh, turning away and walking over to the nearest line of pods on the ground floor. It's a sleek, silver, streamlined container with a glass top. So I can see the woman inside. She's about Jasina's age and while she does resemble Clara—the blonde hair and shape of her face—it's not Clara.

Just some woman. Some... clone, as he called it.

A project.

Something to make spark for her god.

I turn and look at Xi again. He's waiting patiently about ten feet away. His hands casually clasped in front of his body. "Do you know where Clara is?"

He nods.

"Where?"

"The last ping I got, she was about a thousand miles west of here."

"And she's... with... *him?*"

"Tyse Saarinen. Delta's augment. She is, that's correct."

"Who is he? How did she meet him? Is she OK? How do you know all this?"

"He's a very dangerous man. Was commissioned to be augmented from birth, then sent to fight for the Sweep Army in the Omega Outlands. All gods are required to send augments if they have stock available. And as I've already said, I do not. I'm somewhat of an outcast over this."

"What does that mean?"

"Well..." he smiles. "They hate me."

"Who hates you?"

"All the other gods. They hate that I have control of four cities and four factories. They punish me in various ways, not in this realm—I have a lot of power here. But in the upper dimension, I am... primitive."

I don't know what to make of that, but it's good information to use later. "Clara?" I prod.

"Right. When you sent her through the Extraction Tower door, she ended up in the old god's tower in Tau City. Which is somewhat of a slum. It's where Tyse Saarinen was living. I don't have specifics about their first encounter, only that somehow, they found each other and seem to have become a team. There was a dramatic escape—somewhat akin to the one that you and your woman went through in the factory version of Tau City, and they took the train to Delta City to seek refuge because the autocrats were after Clara to feed their baby god, and Delta City is where Tyse was born. Delta is his god. He also managed to smuggle out the baby god of Tau City, so Delta is now in possession of it. That brings his baby god count up to five."

This is... way more information than I asked for. "I don't care about a baby god, Xi. I care about Clara. Do you know where she is now?"

"Oh, of course, I do." He smiles. "I told you, down here, in the factory world, I am somewhat of a... king." His eyes roll up. "Is that better or worse than a god?" Then he chuckles. "Decidedly better, I think. At any rate, at last word they have... encountered some trouble on the train line."

"What does that mean? What kind of trouble? Does Clara need help?

"Oh, probably not. I would not worry." He redirects my attention to an elevator. "Would you like to learn more about the augmentation process? It's just up at the top of the building."

It's a trap. I get it. He's taken me away from Jasina so he can talk me into something. I don't think he's going to force me into whatever this augmentation stuff is, but if he is, it's better to find out now.

So I nod. "Sure. Show me everything."

GETTING *off the elevator* I find myself inside a dome. Not anything as tall as the Extraction Tower or the God's Tower, but it is much wider. There are a few pods up here, cocoons, like what the women were in down below. But most of the space is being taken up by the screens.

"What do you call all this?" I ask, pointing to them. "I mean, I get that the plates are called screens, but what is it?"

"Do you want the short version? Or the complete one?"

"If we've got time, I want to know everything. I want to understand it. I hate feeling like... like an uneducated idiot. None of this makes sense to me."

"Of course not. You've never seen technology before."

"Technology?"

Xi smiles. Clearly pleased that I am interested. "I'll start from the beginning."

What follows is several hours of information. The god is patient. He takes me around to every single plate—screen. Every single one and explains why it's here and what it does. He explains the brain inside it. Software. And shows me how to use it. How I can touch the screen and make it do things.

He explains everything many times, but not once does he tire of my questions.

And by the time we get to the last workstation, I not only have a brand-new vocabulary filled with words like data, and biomarkers, and mods—I actually have a whole new view of the world.

Three and a half hours with this god has turned everything I thought I knew, into a lie.

I lean back in the chair I'm sitting in. We've been going through workstation number ten for about half an hour now —this one controls something called genetics, which Xi claims I am well-endowed with, and he's sitting next to me, leaning in from station nine.

"Would you like to see him?"

I side-eye the god. *Him.* I don't even need to ask who he's referring to. I know what he's doing. What he's offering here. He wants me to see this Tyse character and be... what? Jealous? Angry? Desperate? Probably all three. But there's no way I'm gonna say no. "Yeah. I would. Let me see him."

In these past few hours, I have learned the difference between live viewing a person, like those women we saw in the pods, and vids. Recordings, he calls them.

It's all very crazy, but it appears to be real.

But what he shows me now, is neither a live viewing or a vid. It's... a drawing, of sorts. Of a man's body. But he's not really a man, just lines of blue light. Shapes.

"It's the augmentation software," Xi explains. "This is his profile." He taps the screen and it changes to a real image of a man. He's... something, that's for sure.

"Tyse Saarinen," Xi says. "Thirty-one years old. He actually just had a birthday. Six-foot-two, two-hundred and eight pounds, Supreme Command Authority status in Biometric-Linked Weapons Mastery, Tactical Close-Quarters Combat, Advanced Marksmanship, Multi-Environment...

I actually stop listening at this point. Because the list goes on, and on, and *on*. It takes nearly a minute to list this man's combat, leadership, and technical intelligence qualifications.

Xi ends it with, "AI-Assisted Combat Synchronization. But those are just the highlights."

I blink at him, saying nothing. Not because I don't have questions, but because I'm still trying to process what this Tyse guy really *is*.

My silence makes Xi nervous. He gives me one of those all-teeth smiles.

I shake my head. "I have to be honest here. I really don't know what you're talking about. Supreme Command Authority status in Biometric-Linked Weapons Mastery? What the hell does that even mean?"

"It's augmentation, of course. But I almost forgot to mention the weapon. This might be the best part. He's got a working Versistrike, Finn. The standard Sweep-issue, genetically tethered sidearm, biologically synced upon final augmentation. The Versi is what makes a Sweep Augment a god on the field. Comes equipped with PulseMatch reflex targeting, AutoSelect combat switching, MindLink threat mapping, SoulBind loyalty lock, and ReturnCall retrieval—a Psi-City upgrade so intimate, it will crawl through hell to find its master."

I try and picture this weapon, but can't. I have no frame of reference. I wouldn't even know where to start. "I'll get one of these?" I ask. "If I let you augment me?"

He hesitates.

It's small, but it's there. "Yes. You will. Every augment gets a weapon. A Versi," he adds quickly. "But... these weapons, they are... tightly controlled, as you can imagine. I don't have them here. You'd have to visit my associate to be properly fitted with one. But we can talk about all that later. So... what do you think?"

I get up from my chair, muscles cramping from sitting so long, and walk over to the nearest pod. It's empty. All the pods here are empty. Xi claims he hasn't augmented a human in over a decade and these pods are only meant for augments after the initial process is complete.

He joins me, and we stare down at it in silence.

Finally, I say, "I'd be like him?" When I look up at Xi's face, I find him smiling. He thinks he convinced me.

"You'd be *better* than him, Finn."

"How do you figure that?"

"Because he was augmented seventeen years ago and the technology has advanced incredibly far since then. It used to be that you'd be prepped from birth for augmentation. He was. But it's not like that anymore. I've made extraordinary improvements in the technique."

I think about this, all the while staring up at him. He gives me this time, containing his smile because, again, he thinks he's convinced me. "I'm not convinced," I say. His smile doesn't waver. "I mean, I don't even know you. You say you're a god, but—" I reach out and touch him.

Except I *don't* touch him.

"But you're not even here. You're a trick of the light."

Xi nods, stepping back a few paces. "How about this... how about I bring you and your woman to the upper dimension? How does that sound? So you can meet the real me. I promise, I'm the same man up there as I am down here. But it would be good for you to get a taste of the world you'd be operating in. And wouldn't it be nice for that lovely woman of yours to have a night out? Dinner? How long has it been since the two of you had a proper dinner together?"

I don't answer him. Not out loud, anyway. But in my head, I'm thinking of that night. Our last night in Tau City. We didn't even eat the dinner my servants set out for us. We thought we'd have time later.

It was a mistake many people make, I realize.

Time later.

"Seize the day," Xi says.

"What?"

"You're thinking about some missed opportunity? Something to do with dinner?"

"You say you're not reading my mind, but if that's true, then how do you know what I'm thinking?"

"Because I'm leading you, Finn. Your brain thinks about what I tell it to think about."

I scoff. "You're manipulating me."

"Influencing."

"If I were you, I wouldn't go around telling people that."

"I normally don't. But I'm really not trying to influence you, it's just a consequence of conversation. You're free to do what you want, but you and your woman—"

"She's not my woman. She's Jasina Bell. When you talk about her from now on, you will call her Jasina. Do not call her my woman again."

He puts up both hands, palms towards me. As if he's warding off my threat. Which probably came off pretty hollow to him, actually. So now I just sigh.

"I'm sorry. Our views of women are considerably different. I use them, you see."

"Obviously," I say. "But you better not have plans on using Jasina. I'm dead fucking serious too. Leave her out of this. Whatever it is you want from me, if you try and involve her, I will not comply."

"Are we negotiating?"

"Everything is a negotiation, Xi. Take it any way you want. I'm just warning you that using Jasina against me is the wrong move. I'm not going to make up my mind about this whole augment thing right now. That's insane. I don't know anything about this procedure."

"Which is why you should accept my invitation. Let's table the augmentation talk and instead, concentrate on educating you about the real world. The one I live in. Don't worry, I'll show you all the research. I'll let you talk to doctors. My lead scientists. But if you come up tonight, you'll be able to see what's possible with technology. It's not something to be afraid of, Finn. It's the future."

This upper dimension is intriguing, I will say that. But I hesitate. "Is it easy to get there?"

Xi laughs. "My boy, you of all people know exactly how easy it is to get there. You simply walk through a door."

# JASINA

*The dream fades*, as dreams always do, and my eyes open to the sight of gently swirling spark butterflies. Like a tiny whirlwind, they float just above my stomach. Automatically, my hand slides down to rest over my lower belly where a new sensation is brewing.

"Is it you, tiny spark?" I ask, surprising myself by speaking out loud. "Is it you making these butterflies?"

I sigh, and as the air comes out, the butterflies disappear, only to be replaced by a subtle glow. It's somewhat surprising that my spark is appearing after many weeks of absence, but I'm not entirely shocked after the dream.

When I was younger—which makes me chuckle because by this I mean when I was sixteen and that was two years ago. But when I was younger, I used to rail against the Spark Maidens for not continuing to practice their spark after being Chosen. I never understood it. Why go through all the trouble of learning how to manifest and then just drop it after the Extraction?

It never made sense. Why not use it?

Of course, these were the thoughts of a young teenager. Of which I still am, actually. But I don't feel much like a teenager right now. The point is, I didn't know anything. The Extraction was just part of the process. Something that had to happen if I wanted to help the Rebellion.

It didn't really mean anything to me. It wasn't often that a down-city girl was part of the final ten. Certainly never, at least as far as I know, Number One. It never happens that way.

So down-city girls have a different perspective about the Extraction. We don't lose friends to the god in the tower. Where I was from, no one cared about Imogen Gibson. No one missed Marlow. I recall some of my friends actually joking about Marlow Hughes when she was sent in.

Mable P. might as well have been Mable S., that's how much anyone cared about her.

It wasn't until Lucy Fisher—Maiden Number Four—that I actually felt bad for that group. Lucy Fisher wasn't a down-city girl, but she was the daughter of a fisherman. She lived in the Canal District, but her father was a regular in fish market on the docks of the Shipping District and for whatever reason, Lucy always came with him on Sundays.

I didn't play with her, obviously. She was much older than me. But I knew her. I remember seeing her at Choosing Number Three. I was up-city with Auntie, fingertips stained cherry red from the spun sugar I was eating, and I saw Lucy on stage. It must've been a talent competition because she was playing the piano. And I remember thinking... I know her. I've talked to her—many times, actually, when buying fish.

Years later, when the bell rang for Lucy, I felt it.

It hit me. Not as hard as it would've if it had been Harlow, or Lucindy, or Ceela, or Britley. But there was a sense of loss inside me.

Even now, thinking about how Lucy was sacrificed to a tower god who doesn't even exist, makes me anxious.

What happened to her?

What happened to all of them?

I mean, if Clara lived, might the others have lived as well?

None of this is the point. It's just the start of the point.

And the point is... I'm disappointed in myself. Because I made a vow when I was younger. I vowed that if my spark ever grew enough to actually manifest in some special way—special enough to be Chosen—that I would not let it die just because I won the prize. I would not sit up in the Maiden Tower drinking fragrant teas, and eating fancy cakes, and forget that there was something unique and extraordinary inside me.

Obviously, I haven't been Chosen, but I made it as far as the Little Sister dorm. I was the star of the night at the first gala. It was me, and my tiny army of blue butterflies that stole the evening.

I was on my way to... becoming.

But all my plans—like every single freaking plan I ever made—have been a waste of time. Because they were all based on lies.

Which should be my cue to stand up and fight!

And look at me now. Lying in bed, exhausted, dusty, and discarded.

By a *god*, no less!

I sit up, swing my legs out of bed, and rub my temples with the tips of my fingers, trying to stave off a headache as I fully internalize what the hell is actually happening.

Finn is off making deals with a god, agreeing to who knows what.

I'm pregnant, which makes me feel weak, and hungry, and sick. But more than that, it makes me feel vulnerable.

It's not good.

This trip has definitely taken a turn. I mean, it was never a party. But the danger level has definitely gone up in the past few hours. And suddenly, I don't just feel like the odds are against me—because haven't they always been?—I feel like I'm being smacked down on purpose.

You do not belong here, Jasina Bell—that's what fate is yelling.

And while it does piss me off—the old me is raging inside, ready with an insult and comeback—but it also makes me sad. Because the only person I have to direct this rage at is Finn.

I don't want to rage at Finn.

I want to rage at that god.

It's just… he scares me.

A glow flutters in front of me, and I startle backwards before realizing it's a glowing, spark butterfly. "OK," I sigh. "I need to pull myself together."

Standing up, I stretch, feeling less like myself than ever. More butterflies fill the air, and suddenly there's a swarm of them. I just shake my head. Annoyed that this is my power. Something so stupid and useless. "I get it," I tell the spark butterflies. "You're amazing. And beautiful. But you're also actually quite useless for anything other than decorating a dress for a gala. Go away now."

They don't go away though, they persist. Which has me intrigued. And also jogs my memory of the dream I just woke up from. Parts of it, at least. The feeling I had. Which was one of power.

Spark is power. Like… literally. Everyone knows that. It powers things like lights, and coffee machines, and well, everything in this city as well. Those pods of women. The workers.

The god himself.

But power has another meaning. That's what the dream was about. I decide that this god does not respect me. He sees me as a thing. As something to have, to own, to possess. Maybe even to covet, but that might be going too far.

And this pregnancy situation is not helping.

*Funny, Jasina,* inner-me chastises. *Just a few hours ago you were buzzing with the mere thought of living in a cave with Finn Scott, birthing his babies and going all domestic.*

It's true. I was dreaming about that.

But everything has changed yet again.

Which means, I must adapt. If I don't, I'll get left behind. I'm not going to beat myself up about needing rest. I did need this rest. Badly. Exhaustion is not a good look for anyone, let alone a pregnant woman trying to bolster her self-confidence.

So adjustments must be made. I want to be a mother and now that I'm on my way, I will protect the baby and make sure it's born healthy. So I will rest when I need rest. And I will eat whatever I need to eat etc., etc., etc.

But now that I'm feeling better, it's time to make a plan.

Perhaps I did begin this journey as nothing but a courtesan in the story. But that doesn't mean I have to remain the courtesan. Stories change.

I could... simply... write a new story.

And my story begins with power.

Feeling rested, and slightly more myself, I walk over to the door, grab the handle, and pull—ready to go find Finn and demand that I be a part of whatever deal is being brokered.

Of course, it's locked.

Because when you invade a god's private space, get an up-front look at all his sinister secrets, and then, just as he's about to convince your Godslayer that he's part of some bigger plan, you rain on said god's parade—*of course* he locks you away in a tower. Even if I am only on the second floor.

Old Jasina might've gotten upset about this.

But new Jasina finds it... predictable.

And I'm mad at myself for falling into the trap that the god so perfectly laid out for me.

To my dismay, the swarm of butterflies have followed me over to the door and begin to swirl around me in a sort of slow-moving cyclone.

I'm about to shoo them away, my hand raised in the air, when I notice that the tip of my pointer finger is glowing bright cyan-blue. In fact, there's so much spark condensed into the tip of this finger, little bits of static are crackling off it, reaching into the air.

*Power.*

I look at the door. At the lock. Then at the tip of my finger. *Power.*

On instinct only, I reach out and touch the brass plate of the door handle with the tip of my sparking finger. Instantly, the blue static transfers from my fingertip to the metal and I hear a small click.

My laugh comes quick with the realization of what's just happened.

Well. Would you look at that. *Power.*

A knocking at the door startles me backwards and instantly, the spark that was all around me is gone. I blink at the door, confused.

"Miss Bell." Immediately, I recognize the muffled voice from the other side of the door. Xi.

"Yes?" I say.

"I have a delivery for you as well as a message. May I come in."

I open the door and find the god wearing a small smile and holding a large garment bag. I pull myself together, straightening my shoulders and tipping up my chin. "Hello. What can I do for you... Xi." It feels weird to call him by his name, but he hasn't told me to call him, 'His Lordship,' or anything like that, so first name it is.

His smile remains exactly in place while he holds the garment bag higher. "I have brought you a dress."

I peek around the god. "Where's Finn?"

"He's busy at the moment, which is why I'm making this delivery in person." He shakes the bag now, trying to lure my attention to it.

I don't even nibble at that bait. How cheap does he think I am? "Do you have a time when he'll be finished? I'd like to talk to him."

"This is why I'm here," Xi says. "I've arranged a date for the two of you."

I cock a hip, cross my arms, and roll my eyes. "I'm sure you have."

His response is a quizzical look. "Have I done something to annoy you?"

I nearly snort. "Stop playing with me like a mouse. You know perfectly well what you're doing."

He has the nerve to place a hand over his heart as if he's aghast. "Please explain. I don't understand."

"Oh, cut the shit, OK? I know what you're doing." I point at the garment bag. "This is a dress, you've arranged a date, this fancy room."

Now he furrows his brow in confusion. But it's one of those you-might-actually-be-crazy furrowed-brow looks. "I'm confused. You don't like the room?"

"This isn't about the room. It's about your manipulation of me."

"Jasina, I'm not manipulating you."

"Bullshit. You made me walk up and down all those stairs, physically exhausting me to the point of needing rest, for the sole purpose of getting Finn's full attention away from my influence."

He has the nerve to grin now. "I take it you are rested now? Your spunk is certainly on display." This comes out as a chuckle. Like I'm an adorable, harmless child throwing a little tantrum. I'm surprised he doesn't try to pat me on the head and hand me a sucker.

"This dress is a bribe. Whatever date you have planned is a bribe. And I'm just going to nip this whole thing in the bud. I'm not falling for it. While I am not in charge of Finn's decisions, he will ask for my opinion and there's no way in hell that I'm gonna tell him that this augmentation procedure is a good idea." I blow out a breath. "So save it, OK? I don't want your dress, especially after you locked me in the room so I couldn't leave."

His head juts back in surprise. "That's ridiculous. You were never locked in."

"Wrong. I *was* locked in. I tried the handle and it didn't move."

His eyebrows go stern with consternation. "You literally just opened the door and let me in."

"Yeah, but—" *Holy shit, Jasina! Get ahold of yourself! You almost spilled the secret.* Which wasn't a secret just a few moments ago, but decidedly *is* now. Being able to unlock doors with my spark is not something I should share with this god.

"Jasina?" he asks.

I let out a breath and cross my arms again. "Well, maybe you're right about the door. But I'm right about the dress."

He sighs. "Fine. You're very astute. I'm bribing you. I want to show you what your options are."

"What options?"

"If you and Finn decide to stay, there is a life for you here. Your date is in the upper dimension, you see."

I blink. Several times. "What?"

"The upper dimension. The other world. The one you haven't seen? The one that doesn't have factories filled with Spark Maidens?"

I point to myself. "You're going to take me there?" I must look really confused because he laughs. And it's a nice laugh. Deep, and rugged, and his eyes do this twinkling thing. And while I do realize he's not real—he's made of tricks and lights, or whatever. He's attractive. I mean, he is a god so why wouldn't he be?

His hair is dark and short, his eyes a little bit green, but maybe more like hazel, and he dresses neatly. He looks like an up-city fuck. A man my friends and I would often dream about seducing—before they died trying to turn Donal Oslin into a baby god and I ran away with the Extraction Master.

What a weird fucking world I live in.

Anyway, the point is... the God Xi is not bad looking for being fake. So I have a teenage moment of sudden infatuation, which I quickly rein in and pretend never happened.

"I'm offering a night out with your—" He raises his eyebrows at me making one of those expressions that lets you know his next word is going to be a guess. "Fiancé?"

Which only makes me sigh. "We haven't gotten that far yet, but probably."

"Right." His smile is back. "I figured. So—" He shakes the garment bag again. "Date night? Can you be ready in two hours?"

"Who the hell needs two hours to get ready?"

"Trust me, Jasina. Once you try out the bath, you'll be asking for three."

I almost crack a smile. Because I could really use a bath. Finn and I have been travelling for weeks now. Surely, I stink. And the fact that I can no longer smell my own stink probably means I reek. So yes. I could use a bath and a luxurious one would be even better.

Xi acts like he's been reading my mind, because he says, "I'll be back in two hours," like no more discussion is necessary.

"Wait," I blurt, just as he's turning. "Where is Finn?"

"He's in the Augmentation Dome, which is inside the Reconstitution Tower. He asked for all available information on the subject, so that's what I'm providing." I'm about to disapprove here, but he puts up a hand. "I know you don't want him to do it. He knows you don't want him to do it. But consider this, Jasina. That augment that Clara Birch is travelling with, he's coming for you. *Both* of you. And as it stands now, you haven't a chance in hell of surviving his attack. He's not human."

I shake my head. "I understand that, but Clara—"

"She's his *power*, Jasina," Xi says. And he does this little lean-in move here. One eyebrow raised. "Do you understand? As a Spark Maiden—Clara Birch is *powering* her augment, Tyse Saarinen. She knows what he's doing."

I shake my head. "So you're saying she wants to kill Finn? Why would she—" But I don't finish. Because I suddenly have a vision of up-city Clara Birch standing in front of the Tau City God's Tower screaming at Finn as she was pulled through the doors for sacrifice.

*I will never forgive you! Ever. I will hate you 'till the end of time!*

"It's true, right? You believe me, don't you?" Xi asks.

"I don't know," I admit. "She was pretty mad at him when he sacrificed her."

Xi presses his lips together, nodding. "She has every right to be angry."

"She does," I also admit.

"All I'm asking, Jasina, is that you let Finn make up his mind. Don't talk him in to it, but don't dissuade him, either. He's a man. You're his woman, whether you want to be or not, you're carrying his child. Which obliges him to take care of business. Augmentation is one way to do that."

"What if he chooses not to? Can we leave?"

"Of course, you can. But don't throw away this opportunity until the two of you have all the information. Today, Finn is learning all about the process. The benefits as well as the risks. Tonight, he will discuss it with you. All I ask is that you let him do that and that you *listen*. Can we at least agree on that?"

I pretend to think about this because I don't want to give in so easily, but he's making some good points. I might not love Finn, or him me. *Yet*. But we've got a real chance here. If we can stay alive and get somewhere safe.

Maybe *this* is our somewhere safe? Not this gross factory, but the upper dimension?

It's like a bit of magic. It's like walking through the God's Tower doors without being a sacrifice.

It's a second chance.

And while I would be perfectly happy to live in the cave as a scholar's wife, it doesn't hurt to check out door number two.

So I say, "Agreed."

And take the garment bag he's offering.

# PART 3

"Let me be clear: there is no credible evidence that 'augments' ever existed outside the fever-dream mythology surrounding the so-called Line So Bright Complex. The idea that biomechanical soldiers once patrolled a transdimensional rail system is not only preposterous—it's anti-intellectual. Worse, Dr. Elena Nareen's glorification of these so-called warriors reeks of anti-feminist bias.

"Nowhere in her work does she show concern for the real victims of this barbaric desert civilization—namely, the women and children who appear to have been ritualistically processed in some kind of cult-military hybrid. If this is scholarship, then perhaps we should start quoting comic books as historical record."

—Dr. Clarence Holt, Post-Epoch University, address to the Global Forum on Dimensional Integrity, New Geneva Archive

# TYSE

"*Are ya mad at me?*"

Clara's face is painful to watch. Because I can see it. I can see her attraction to *him*.

Finn Scott.

Lover Boy.

"No," she says. "I'm not mad. Thank you for telling me. But… you do understand that I can't go on."

"What do ya mean?"

"What do I *mean*?" she laughs these words out. "I'm *home*, Tyse. In my own world—"

I stop listening, even though she keeps talkin'.

*In her own world.*

That's what the train line is to her.

To me, it's just some fuckin' place where gods play games with people. Doin' what, exactly, I've got no clue. I've got ideas, but I don't know what Delta's really doin'. I don't know what any of them are doin'.

"I have to find him," Clara says. I'm still lookin' at her. Right in her blue fuckin' eyes, when she says, "I have to—"

And even though I know how that sentence ends, and even though what happens next is a tragedy on all accounts, I am spared the hurt of actually hearin' the words come out of her mouth—because she simply disappears.

Blinks right out of existence before my very eyes.

I just stare at the empty space in the cave. Dumb. Not

panickin', not frantically trying to figure things out, not taken aback by her sudden disappearance.

Just dumb. Staring stupidly into space. Thinkin' about how she never said the words.

I feel like this moment of mute stupidity lasts for several years, but in reality, it's literally two seconds. I know this because I'm actually lookin' at a fuckin' clock readout on my data display that keeps time in seconds and only two of them tick off.

Then I blink.

And I'm back.

And shit is real.

Before I can even think, I'm in the veil. I've crossed—but not literally. I'm just a visitor, like I was back in Delta City when I was stealin' spark from strangers.

Because—and yeah, I'm a little slow here because I'm only just realizin' this—but I can't actually cross over without Clara. I can only steal spark.

At any rate, I'm lookin' at dozens and dozens of worlds through the veil. Everything is just black space outlined in glowing cyan-blue. But unlike back in Delta City when I was just perusing the other worlds like a visitor, this time I know what I'm lookin' at.

*Frequency.*

Apparently, they are stacked in order here in the sparkstone cave, because as I focus on one layer after another, one world after another, I'm watching the frequency change and it's going up by tenths of a whole.

She's not here. I already know she's not here because I've already done this. I've already gone searching through the worlds for a safe place for her to breathe, and there are only three places that I found.

Only three places where we've been.

And only two of those three have people in them that know we can travel like this.

1440 and 702. And she's not in 1440—there's no one there lookin' for her.

She's back where we started.

On the train tracks being attacked by augments.

How that happened is a mystery. But I don't wait to find out. I change the frequency on my data display to 702 and there she is.

Not whole, like I know her when we're together. Just the glowing cyan-blue outline of her body, with one new development.

The symbols. They are lit up like a fuckin' sun all across her body. Coverin' every inch of her skin.

What are they trying to tell us?

I'm gonna figure it out.

But not right now.

*Now* I am watching about a dozen augments pull Clara to her feet. For a moment, I think the absolute worst. They crowd her, reachin' for her. And maybe it would play out like my worst nightmares, but then all the men part. The crowd literally splits in half, and another man appears. Obviously augmented because his eyes are lit blue to indicate he's workin'.

My heart is pounding in my chest as words are said. Words I can't hear.

But then he turns, almost as if he can see me. His eyes are lookin' for me. His face is—wrong. It looks like it's melting, that's how ugly it is. Like he was burned in a fire.

I don't *think* he can see me, but he knows I'm here. Feels or something. Because he is very careful with his words. Enunciating each sound of each letter, making sure I can read his lips. Because he knows. Somehow, he knows I live in the veil. He *knows* I'm watchin'.

"Tyse *Saaaaaaarinen*," he sings his words. "Come and *geeeeet* her. Or she is mine *foreeeeeever*."

Then somethin' happens. The whole world flashes and glows bright blue. I stumble backwards, arm up to my eyes, because that flash is so bright, for a moment I'm blind.

When the light is gone, so is the world.

And I am back in the sparkstone cave.

Alone.

For a moment I think, That's it. It's over. I've lost her.

But before I'm even done thinkin' that, I'm yellin', *"No!"* And I'm back, watching. But this time, that man, the augment, he's waitin' for me. Smiling. Offering me a hand. Except, it's not *his* hand.

It's Clara's.

"Come on," he says, again enunciating so I can read his lips. "Come back, Tyse. Because this is the last offer you're gonna get and if you refuse, she's mine by default and you will never see her again."

Without thinking, I reach through the veil and take Clara's hand.

The next thing I know, a fist comes at my face.

It connects and everything goes black.

**HERE'S *the weird thing that happens next...***

I'm outside my body. Floatin' above a large... stadium, I guess? That's what it looks like. Not something modern and sleek, like the sportsball stadium in Tau City, or even some of the smaller venues. But something... old. Ancient, maybe. Not like pre-Sweep ancient, just something crumblin' and dilapidated. Somethin' left over.

But it's not abandoned. It's full of fuckin' men. And from this perch above it all, lookin' down, I see that every single one of them is an augment. Their glowin' blue eyes watching me—real me—as my unconscious body is carried through the crowd on a rail. I sag over the rail, my stomach pressing into the rough, splintered wood, arms wrenched behind me, legs dangling on either side like dead weight.

Rope bites into my wrists and ankles beneath the beam, keeping me lashed in place as the augments hauling me shift under my weight, their shoulders braced against the wood.

My head lolls forward, blood dripping from my mouth in slow, red strands.

The augments watch me like hungry wolves as I'm carried toward a stage.

When they get me there, they cut the ropes and I tumble off the side of the rail like a sack of meat.

I can't feel anything when I hit the floor because I'm not in there. My body is vacant right now because I'm up here, above it all. Watchin'.

But when I wake up—do I wake up? If I wake up?—either way, that shit's gonna hurt.

And I'm gonna be *pissed*.

A man walks out on the stage and all the augments go wild. Yelling, screaming, cheering.

At first, I can't make it out. Then... words form.

It goes on?

No—it goes... wrong?

Let's get on?

The voices churn together, thick and distorted, twisting through my brain as I try to sort it out.

Eck goes on?

Ep-go-zon?

Suddenly, the sound sharpens, syllables snapping into place. And even up here, as some sort of specter—some kind of ghost—I can feel it.

Fear. Crawling through my belly. Making my heart thump. Chest constricting. Because they're saying *Epsilon*.

That's what they're chanting. *"Epsilon! Epsilon! Epsilon!"*

Which is a very bad thing for me indeed.

Because Epsilon isn't just a city or a factory on the train line.

He's a god.

A god who doesn't even exist in the world I come from. Epsilon City is a godless place, just like Tau City. But unlike Tau City, the god wasn't killed hundreds of years ago.

He went missing just two decades back.

The whole city shut down. Spark gone. I mean, it's back now, but if you live in a god's city, that god provides for you. And if one day he goes missing, he's no longer doin' that.

Everyone blamed the Alphas. All the Median cities—self-righteous bunch of fucks they are—were so sure the Alpha's did something to the god Epsilon, they nearly started a war over it. This coming from people who saw themselves as above it all. They were properly angry, they were.

I was way too young to give a fuck about some missin' god. All I was thinking about was my approaching augmentation day and my new life in the Sweep Army.

But I sure as hell give a fuck right now. Because whatever this place is—it's *his*. And not only am I his prisoner, but he's got my Clara.

As I'm thinking this, I feel the pull of my body below. A calling to me, like a god summoning his servants. And that's exactly what it feels like when suddenly, I am sucked back into my battered and bleeding body. Writhing in pain as the augments cheer, "*Epsilon! Epsilon! Epsilon!*"

Someone kicks me in the ribs, and from the way it doubles me over, this isn't the first time. My data display enters Health Critical mode, flashin' on the back of my eyelids, and it's confirmin' what I thought. The list is longer than I'd like. Two broken ribs, partially dislocated wrist along with rope burns and lacerations, cracked collarbone, split lip from the initial punch, and lack of blood circulation in my hands from being tied to the rail.

It hurts to breathe, my left arm is shaking uncontrollably, and my head feels like someone took an ax to it.

But the really concerning thing on the data display is the little box on the bottom left. It's flashin' red and the words inside the box say—COMBAT MODE: ACTIVATED—in all caps. Above that is a list of what's goin' through my blood right now. Epinephrine, norepinephrine, dopamine, cortisol, and good old testosterone. All of them in levels only seen in extreme fight situations.

Which explains my shaking arm.

Another boot comes at me, trying to turn those broken ribs into three. But even though my eyes are still closed, I see it. And this fucker should *know* I see it. Because he might as well be me, that's how fuckin' augmented he is. I can smell the nanotech comin' off him like sweat.

But he doesn't and obviously, now that I'm back in my body, he's not gettin' a second chance to kick the fuck out of my ribs. I grab his foot, eyes flyin' open, and twist my body, taking him with me. In mid-air, I watch his face. Surprise.

How did he not know I was waking up?

I decide I don't care when his whole body spins and his face slams in to the ground—which I just now realize is made of stone—and this cracks his front teeth, blood comes gushing out.

And for the smallest of moments, the crowd stops. Shocked.

But it's so brief, it barely happens.

Then the roaring starts—and for a moment I feel the wave of bodies tryin' to get at me. Held back by...

This is when I realize I'm on my feet, eyes are open, and I'm stupidly reaching for my Versi—which of course, is no longer on my hip—because there he is. The weird augment with the melting face.

Except... I tagged him wrong earlier. He's not an augment.

I'm looking right at the fuckin' god, Epsilon.

And he's so out of my frame of reference of what a god looks like—I can't move.

I can only stare.

Because Myra was right.

Memories come crashing back from when my team was whole—perfect—and still alive. Jast, Myra, Stepan, Kirt, and me. Sitting on the floor of the deploy train for the trek into the Outlands. I'm laughing, lookin' at Kirt, because Myra is telling a ghost story to all the new kids we picked up at the Psi Outpost, the last human habitation before the dead sandy sea. They were all eighteen, only two years younger than us, and on their first deployment.

This was our third so it was our duty to put the fear of the god in them in the hopes they'd be careful, they'd think critically, and remember their training. Get them out alive so they could be sent back in for round two.

Myra's story was about fight clubs in the dead space

between Alpha and Omega. This dead space was somethin' only people from Alpha actually believed existed.

The Dead Space fight clubs were run by the Corrupted God.

He was a myth. A rumor.

Myra came up in Alpha city and they are some superstitious fucks because they think the world is circular and if ya look to the north, you're actually lookin' south. Which means, if you're a citizen of Alpha City, the Omega Outlands are always creeping up your backside.

One leads to the other, leads to the other.

Eventually.

The other guys fucked with her endlessly when her Alpha heritage came out during our augmentation—because that place is filled with fuckin' ghost stories, conspiracy theories, and nutters who think death is a badge of honor, and dyin' for one's god is how they show respect.

Alpha, I guess, breeds his military for insanity. Because Myra was crazy as all hell.

Her Alpha City heritage, as well as being the only girl in the class, made her a target.

If she wanted to fight alongside us, she had to either take it and brush it off, or manage it and earn her place.

Myra did *not* take it. She managed it. And she did this managing by scaring the fuck out of everyone with her crazy Alpha City stories. They were all insane. Especially the conspiracy theories.

Like the one she told our group about the Alpha Ghosts and how, if she ever got lost or died in the Outlands, she'd just become one of them and walk her ass home by heading deeper into the south because eventually it would become north again.

But it was the one about the Corrupted God running

fight clubs in the dead space between Alpha and Omega that really got to people. And every time she started in with this story, we'd all moan, and complain, and tell her to shut up.

Which is sad, now that I think about it. Because she *did* die out there. I blew her brains out. And every day, for years, I would picture her out in the sand, wandering north. Trying to find her way home in the loop that leads to Alpha City, as a Ghost.

But right about now, I'm also thinkin' that Myra was right.

Because I am looking the Corrupted God right in his ugly fuckin' face.

And it *is* ugly. Scarred, or burned, or something. He's not charming and handsome like Delta. He's... a monster.

I take a step back—not because I'm scared of him—I'm just... *shocked*. I wasn't expecting to meet a god in this place, let alone a myth. And in this step, I trip over something.

Or rather, *someone*. Because it's the asshole who was tryin' to kick me in the ribs.

I fall back, once again crackin' my head so hard on the cold stone, I black out, thinkin'...

I should've let Myra finish the damn story.

# FINN

**W**hen *I look up* from the screen that's been educating me on all the specifics of being an augment and realize it's night, I'm shocked. The time went by so fast. Everything was just... *so interesting.* I joke with Jasina about that whole 'let's-be-scholars' life, but it's a dream. Not something I've actually been trained to do.

I'm not really qualified to do anything but open the God's Tower doors in Tau City. Or, as it turns out, explode Extraction Towers. It's pretty limiting.

And I've never been much of a student. Not compared to Jeyk and Mitch. I got good grades in mandatory schooling, but I knew the expectations for me were lower than they were for them. They were expected to earn their places. I was born into mine.

Still, I am not stupid. It's just, everything about Tau City seemed old and pointless. And the fact is, if I was born into a scholar family instead of the Extraction Master family, I would've enjoyed it. I like history. I like asking questions about things. I like searching for answers.

I never asked questions about the tower, which makes sense. Obviously, it's a shit job and it's got a shit history. No matter how exciting the Extraction and Choosing were, no matter how much pomp and circumstance were put into it, it was still nothing but a celebration of sacrifice.

And while I could make the argument that augmentation is also a sort of sacrifice, it's me I'd be sacrificing. Not a young woman like Jasina. Or the ninth Spark Maiden like Clara.

Yes, there are consequences for Jasina because we're together now. What I choose will affect her, so obviously, she gets a say. I won't do it if she says no.

I won't sacrifice her for this.

I won't sacrifice her for anything. By luck or fortune, she's mine. Even more so now that she's pregnant. But this Tyse guy, if he thinks he's gonna come after me and not get a fight? He's mistaken. And if he knows about me, the chances are high that Xi was telling the truth and he knows about Jasina as well.

I will die to save her.

It is my duty.

This one thought actually tips me in favor of saying yes. My duty. How many times have I heard that phrase growing up? Not from my father, not from my mother, but from the Matrons as they programmed the Pledges into believing that putting yourself up as a sacrifice to a god no one has ever seen, is a duty.

I've heard it thousands of times, at least, because the Pledges are often educated in public spaces in the Canal District. Cafes, and parks, and on the beaches. When Clara was just a young teenager, I would make Jeyk and Mitch come with me on the weekends as I watched her from a distance. Waiting to catch her eye so I could wave, or wink, or smile. Waiting for her to see me and respond in kind.

Every weekend I did that. For years. So I've heard plenty of Matron lectures on how to be poised, proper, and polite.

"It is your duty," they'd say.

Well. This is my duty now. To protect Jasina and the baby from whatever terrible revenge Clara is planning for me. She has every right, I understand that. But it doesn't mean I have to give up and let her win.

Not when I'm finally finding my place in this world. Not when I have a family to look forward to.

But beyond duty and loyalty, I find augmentation fascinating. All of it. And I want to know more.

So all day I've been up here in the Reconstitution Tower, high up in the Augmentation Dome, sitting at this desk filled with screens, learning about what it means to be an augment.

Didn't eat, didn't even drink, didn't get up to stretch my legs. I just watched as everything played out on the screens in front of me. How the body works, all the different systems inside people and how they're connected. The brain. The heart. I didn't know how people hear, or see, or feel things before today. There's so much about my own body that no one had ever told me before.

And all of it was explained by a soothing neutral voice that seemed to know when I was confused and when I was understanding things, because this teaching-voice inside the machine would explain things over, and over, and over in every possible way, for as long as it took for me to finally get it.

It showed me diagrams of the human body—drawings that moved to make it easier to follow along. Words popped out of the drawings, highlighting key facts. The body would rotate, the heart was pumping blood on the screen, the brain opened up so I could see how all the little threads of nanofibers would integrate into the tissues. How they would become part of me and how, over the course of a week, they would grow so that eventually, these threads would replace my entire nervous system.

Nervous system. I'd never even heard those words before today and now look at me. I *understand*.

Everything about this day has been exhilarating.

But now that the lessons are over and I can appreciate what augmentation is and what it will do to me, I can't help but feel... let down.

Not by the teaching-voice or the information, but by my own people.

If this screen-based teaching exists in the same dimension where I grew up—with all these ways to see and understand difficult but interesting concepts—why didn't we learn this way?

I would've paid more attention, that's for sure. Would have had bigger dreams than simply opening giant doors to sacrifice women.

Which, now that I think about it, is probably why they didn't teach me anything interesting. I might get 'ideas' and decide not to do my job.

And this thought leads directly to the one I am desperate to *not* think about.

That night I sent Clara in.

And how she railed against me.

*I will hate you 'till the end of time.*

Which leads to the unfortunate facts of the day.

Her man—her *new* man—he's one of these augments. Some kind of super soldier from the way Xi tells it. Very experienced. Very lethal. Very capable of killing me.

He is her chosen one now. And why wouldn't she want a man like him? One who didn't bow to the needs of an invisible god. One who wouldn't throw her away, because he wouldn't have to.

He could fight for her.

No matter who the enemy was, he would fight for her.

Unlike me. Who gave up without even trying.

The soft clicking of shoes on a hard, polished floor draw

my attention to the left. And when I look over, Xi is approaching. His smile is wide, like he's pleased.

"How did you find it?" he asks, panning a hand to the screens still lit up with diagrams and information in front of me.

"It was absolutely riveting, to be perfectly honest. I... well..." I sigh. "Let's just say that if I had this technology when I was growing up, I'd have really loved school. I can't remember a day when I learned so much at one time. And none of it was boring. I would like to learn more, actually. I would like to know everything. I would like *this* to be my future. Better than running down a train line blowing up towers."

Xi clasps his hands together in front of him, leaning back on his heels a bit, pleased with himself. Funny how he does this when he's only made of light. It's so convincing.

Tech. Who knew?

"But when I say this," I clarify. "I don't mean the soldiering stuff, Xi. I understand that's what you're offering, but what I'd really like to do for the rest of my life is *learn.*"

"But, my dear man, where do you think the information comes from?"

"What do you mean?"

"All of this—" He pans a hand to the room, to himself, to the screens. "It comes from the Omega Outlands."

He must read my look as confusion—which it is—because he points to the biggest, central screen on the desk in front of me. "Look." The screen changes from a diagram of the heart, to a map. "This is the factory world, insofar as it's been explored and documented." He points to a dot on the far right. "This is Alpha." He points to a second dot, just to the left. "This is Beta." Then points to more that are to the left of

Beta. "This is Gamma and this is Delta. These are the Alpha cities. They work together."

"OK?" I shrug. Not understanding what the point of this is.

"Just be patient with me. You'll see." Then he continues, pointing to a line that connects these cities. "This is the train line."

Suddenly, it clicks. The whole picture makes sense.

"The Alphas work together," Xi continues, "because they have a common cause. A purpose they all believe in."

"Which is what?"

"They want to control this dimension—the Factory Dimension, 702." Seeing that I'm about to interrupt him with another question, he puts up a hand. "Just listen."

"OK. Keep going."

"These cities here—" He points to the far left of the map now. "These are the Omegas." He points to the dots, calling off the names of each city. "Omega, Psi, Chi, Phi, Upsilon, Tau." Here, he pauses to smile at me. "And Sigma."

I blow out a breath. Suddenly feeling... I dunno. A sense of illumination. It makes sense. This is the train line. "Tau," I say, touching the screen. "This is where we entered the tunnel. And then, we walked to here." My finger stops at Sigma. "Then we went to—"

"Rho," Xi says. Pointing to a dot on the train line that is the start of a loop that winds around what I now understand is a symbol for a mountain. "The train line curves," Xi says. "And we get—"

"Pi, Omicron, and Xi," I finish for him. "I was in them all."

"You were." Xi smiles at me. "You probably have no idea what that means."

"Explain."

"The fact that you've visited other cities. Seen them. The

people living in these factories are not meant to leave them, Finn. You're an explorer of the highest degree as far as Factory inhabitants go. What you and Jasina did, it's quite historical."

Jasina is gonna love this part. I can't wait to tell her.

Xi continues. "On this end of the last city, Omega, are the Omega Outlands. We say it's nothing but sand there, but that's a lie. It's... empty."

I don't quite see the distinction, but he moves on before I can ask.

"We call Sigma and all the cities to the left, the Omegas. Sigma and Tau would challenge that categorization, but like it or not, they are in the Omegas and have aligned with a common purpose, much like the Alphas."

"What is this purpose?"

"To control their spark, of course. They see the gods as middlemen." Sensing my confusion, he elaborates. "A go-between. The factory makes the spark, gives it to the god, who gives it to the city."

"Oh, I see. They want to take the spark themselves."

"Exactly. They have no use for gods."

"And that's why the Tau City—I mean, factory. That's why we had no god? They killed him?"

"They did."

Now I'm confused. "But... how did they get the spark from us? I mean, we only sent one girl every decade."

Xi chuckles. "It was a hard lesson for them, let me tell you."

"Oh." I laugh too. "OK. They *don't* get the spark."

"They do not. They failed. Sigma, as well. The other cities in that sector are weak, now aligned with the Sweep Army. They work directly with them to make augments. But more on that later. I'm not done with the map yet." He points to it again. "These cities here in the middle are called The Medians."

"That's you, then. You're after Omicron."

"No. I'm not. I'm my own section." He's panning his arms wide here, smiling with bright, lit-up eyes. Like he's proud of this fact. "The Medians are Nu." His finger traces the line to the right of Xi. "Mu, Zeta." Then there's another loop, as the train line circles another mountain. "Lambda, Kappa, Iota, Theta, Eta, and Zeta."

"That section is pretty big then. There are a lot of cities."

"It is. There are. And they all have a common purpose as well."

"Which is?"

"To destroy this dimension."

"What? If this is where all the spark comes from, why do they want to destroy it?"

"You're catching on. I like it. But the reason is simple. They want to control things. And spark, well. Quite simply, my dear man, spark is magic. Very, very powerful magic that even gods like me covet. It is pure, from the earth itself. It is the source of everything and it can be used to do *anything*. Spark exists in every dimension. In all people, even men. But the 702 factory dimension is the only one where it can be cultivated inside the women, harvested, and brought into another dimension. They want to destroy this dimension— because if they erase it, there's no threat left. They want the 'old ways.' The way things were before the gods swept the world clean."

I can't even imagine what that might mean. So I move on to a more pressing question. "Dimension. You keep using this word, and I understand that it's this place where we are, but it doesn't really make sense to me."

He sighs, a tiny bit of frustration leaks out due to my

ignorance. Talking to me must feel like talking to a child. "It's a way to categorize worlds—and by worlds, I mean spaces where people can exist. Do you know what a ghost is?"

"Of course. I mean, I don't think they're *real*, but I understand the concept."

"Let's suppose ghosts are real. They would live in another dimension. One side by side with this one we're in, but invisible to us. There are very specific reasons why these dimensions aren't visible, and you can learn about that later. But sometimes, due to factors or conditions we're unaware of, ghosts might appear in this dimension. Become visible. Bleed through, if you will. But while it might be able to visit, it cannot live here. It does not belong here. You see, everything has its place, Finn. There are precious few dimensions we can live in as gods. As a human, you can live in quite a bit more. But as an augment, you can live in *all* of them."

"What does that mean, though?"

"It means..." He throws his arms up. "The world is yours. As an augment, that is. If it's knowledge you crave, my good man, knowledge you will get. That I can guarantee."

"At what price?"

He laughs. "Finn Scott, you of all people understand that everything comes with a price. What was the price of being Extraction Master's son? Hmm?" He doesn't wait for me to answer. "It was ignorance, Finn. That's what it was. That's what you're feeling right now. Your own ignorance. But it was necessary to breed men who prefer the finer things in life over truth, wasn't it? How else does one get someone to sacrifice innocent women and girls to a god that hasn't existed in hundreds of years?"

It stings, this truth. Because he's right. I *was* bred to be ignorant. To be apathetic to the mysteries of the world all around me. To be compliant. Content with the luxuries that were my birthright.

"As I'm sure you were told in your lessons today, augments are in the top point zero-zero-one most intelligent people of the known world. In some cases, they are smarter than gods. It's the pinnacle of what a human is capable of being... with assistance. Every last genetic talent is exploited, and conditioned, and honed. Every part of your body will change."

I let out a breath. "It's..."

"Scary?"

"Yeah." I don't want to admit this, but it is. And he knows it is so it would be stupid to lie. "What if it doesn't work? What if I'm not actually well bred enough for the process to take? What if it doesn't *work*?"

Xi's smile is warm now. "I've done the testing. Your bloodline goes back three-hundred and seventy-five years. It's the purest human blood I've ever analyzed. The fact that you come from the Tau Factory is what makes you perfect. It *will* take, Finn. It *will*. You are more suited to this procedure than any other man I've ever analyzed. This is due to your isolation from genetic interference."

"Because our god was dead?" I ask.

"That's right. The people in the upper dimension of Tau City killed that god. They thought they could take control of the Factory City and get as much spark as they'd like. But you need the power of a god to siphon the spark."

"So what's that city look like now? If they don't have spark?"

"They get power other ways. And it runs a city just fine. It's actually a very nice, modern city. But there is no *magic* there, Finn. It's dead—at least, in that way. So, ever since the ruling families of that city figured out they'd made a huge mistake by killing their god, they've been desperately trying to grow a new one."

"*What?*" This word comes out as a laugh. "How the hell do you grow a god?"

Xi spreads his arms wide. "Technology, of course."

"No. That makes no sense. Tell me how they do it. I need to know. I need to know why we—why *I*—was sending women through that tower door."

He lets out a sigh, as if this request is more than he intended to give me today.

Then he looks me in the eye, and I hold his gaze for a few seconds before saying, "Tell me. I don't care how gross it is, I *need* to know."

Again, he sighs, but this time the exhale is long. As if resigned. "Very well. There are ways to create synthetic fertilizers for human eggs. You didn't get the reproduction module today, but surely you know where babies come from?"

I roll my eyes. "Assume that I do."

"These synthetic fertilizers are technology. They contain everything the egg needs for life to begin. But they also contain seeds of intelligence—super intelligence. Artificial intelligence. And over time, this intelligence morphs, taking over the body and changing it. It takes many decades for this to happen and the baby god would require quite a bit of spark to survive. They *feed them* spark, Finn."

Wow. There it is. Mystery solved—the god eats them.

Well, I guess that explains what the actual fuck was happening below the God's tower with all the Little Sisters and Donal Oslin. "All right," I say. "That makes sense. I mean, it doesn't. At all. But I can imagine ways in which it might work. But that doesn't explain the *existence* of the Extraction Ceremony."

"The Extraction Ceremony was meant to be a pause after the god was killed. This pause was initiated by the Extraction Master in the Tau Factory."

"Me," I say, pointing to myself.

"Some great-great-great grandfather, perhaps? But yes, essentially you. The Extraction Masters control the doors to the upper dimension. I don't know the specifics, to be honest. Just that your Extraction master changed the rules. I believe they were extracting spark in the Tau Factory back then in much the same way Delta extracts his spark. Which is… constantly. He does it many times a day."

"He kills several women a day?" I'm appalled.

"No, he doesn't kill them. Imagine that women are an apple tree. What he does is pluck their fruit. He harvests them like apples."

"Wow." I feel sick.

"So," Xi continues, "for whatever reason, that Extraction Master didn't admit that something had gone wrong and the harvesters were no longer working. Instead of canceling the harvests after Tau died, he came up with this scheme."

"He made it into a game," I say, mostly talking to myself.

"I suppose," Xi says. "My understanding of the Tau Factory extraction procedure is very limited."

"It was a game—a spectacle, a contest. All the young girls were offered the opportunity to pledge themselves to the god in the tower at age twelve. They were given lessons in manners and obedience, and shit like that. And eventually, taught how to use their spark to…" I struggle for words here. What *were* they doing with that spark? "To entertain the city? Clara, for instance, could make little drawings in the air with the spark that came out of her fingertips. Jasina put all her spark into a swarm of butterflies that floated up off her dress while she was on stage—just to impress me."

"Brilliant."

"What? Why do you say that?"

"Because this is the only dimension where it can be cultivated inside the women. In other words, the women in 702 grow magic inside them. And your factory turned their power into... a *curiosity*."

"But why keep it going? Why all the lies? Why not just end the Extraction and let everyone live their lives?"

"Oh, Finn," Xi chuckles. "Power, of course. At some point, someone in your family figured out that gods are good for business."

"What the hell does that mean?"

He pauses for a moment, looking thoughtful as he thinks. "Humans crave... *meaning*. Not all, but many, want answers. Just like you. They are curious creatures. And since you can't stop the production of spark—can't erase the ability to make it—the only way is to control it."

I think about this for a few moments, but I don't really understand. "Spark turns off curiosity?"

"No. They lied, you see. They turned the spark *into* a curiosity. Something... trivial. Something... common. Something... entertaining, from your description. But spark is so much more than that."

"So they were hiding the true meaning. So... so the women couldn't..." I shrug. "Rebel? Take over? I don't get it."

"It's just a control mechanism, Finn. If you want to harvest honey, what do you do with the bees?"

"Put them in hives, I guess." It makes me sad, this truth. And it comes out in my tone.

"Exactly. A factory is nothing but a hive."

I sigh, leaning back into the chair, suddenly exhausted. "So it was just... a leash? A cage? A—"

"A hive." He throws his arms up. "That's it. The perfect

word. A collective of living things making a product that can be used by the owner of the hive."

"Which is the god."

"Precisely."

"All right." I mean, I don't like his answer, but it explains a lot. Most of my life suddenly makes sense. But I have one more question. "This Extraction stuff? Where did all the Maidens go?"

"Oh, well this is the part I do know." He smiles. "You see, Tau City, after realizing that killing their god meant they lost their access to the spark factory—well, they improvised with ancient power to keep their city running." He waves a hand in the air. "Burning coal, burning gas, running water, sun plates and finally, splitting atoms. But it's dirty, and finite, and expensive. They have been trying to make a new god ever since the old one died. And baby gods need... *food*."

I don't say anything now. Just sit, contemplating the meaning of my life. But there is no meaning. Not after this truth. I was a bee in a hive—a high-ranking one, but a slave, nonetheless. And I sent two women into the tower to feed a baby god.

Obviously, Clara didn't get eaten.

But what about Haryet?

It makes me sick. I don't want to know, so I stop asking questions about Tau City.

"Let's talk about the last place on the map now, Finn." Xi points to the space even further to the left of the Omegas. "This is the Omega Outlands. This is the prize." His finger taps the screen as each word comes out of his mouth. "This is where you want to be."

"Why would I want to be there? You said it was empty."

"Empty is relative. To you, as you are now, it *is* empty. To me—well, as a god, I cannot even go there. Not even to take a peek."

"Why not?"

"It scrambles us. It... interferes with the software that runs us."

I understand the word 'software' to a degree. It is the brain of these screen machines. It makes it possible to have the pictures, and switches, and all the fancy stuff I've been looking at all day. But I don't understand what this has to do with Xi.

"We're machines," Xi says. "I told you that already. Gods cannot go into the Omega Outlands. But... we need the information that's out there. That's why we make augments. As an augment, you can go into the Omega Outlands. And when you get there, you will know everything."

"Everything... as in—"

"Everything." He spreads his arms wide. "Anything you ever wanted to know about the world, is there. All you have to do is find it."

I study the map again. Noting something. "What about this city?" I point to the only one he didn't talk about.

"Oh, well. That's Epsilon. He's a god who's gone absolutely bat-shit crazy trying to make himself into an augment so he can enter the Omega Outlands himself."

"Is it working?"

Xi shrugs. "I don't know. I don't care. We all play the Game of Gods in our own way, doing our best to win, because winning equals survival. Alphas, Medians, Omegas... it's all the same. Even Epsilon. Even me. We all play for the same reason. *Power*. It's as simple as that."

Now I scoff. "Wow. That came off... positively evil."

This makes him smile. "I would call it self-preservation, actually. We're all selfish. If you agree to be augmented, I know you're not doing it for me. You have no loyalty to *me*. You're doing it for you. That is the way of the world. That *is* the Grand Design. It's never been about collectivism. There is no point to any of this if we have to give up our individuality for the *hive* to succeed. There is no point in being a bee, Finn. They live, not for themselves, but for the greater good of the group. And look, I get it. Bees are good little cogs in the wheel. Necessary, in their own way. But are we bees?"

"No," I say, absently looking over at the windows. "At least, we shouldn't be." I look back at him. "I've lived my whole life in a bee hive. I followed the rules, but the rules are stupid. They don't mean anything. They're just..."

"Grand Delusions," he finishes for me. "You see, it's fine to have ambition. It's fine to have goals. Desires. Dreams and purpose. That's part of the Grand Design. The Grand *Delusion*, on the other hand, seeks to impose these dreams and desires of yours, onto me. Or mine, onto you. That is the crime here. *Intent.*"

I let out a long breath, suddenly feeling very weary. "Well, you've made your point and—"

He puts up a hand, stopping me mid-sentence. "Don't make your decision here and now. You need time."

"How did you know I was about to agree?"

"I feel what's in your heart, Finn. I understand the betrayal. I understand the need to rise. I understand the need for knowledge and power. You want all of that so you can participate in the world coming from a position of power. But you must be careful not to become one of *them*. You have a place in the Grand Design. So before you say yes to me, I'll need you to consider that."

"One more question," I say.

"Ask as many questions as you like."

"If I do it, and when it's done, will I be... better than *him?*" I don't say his name, but I don't have to. Xi knows exactly who I'm talking about.

"Much better suited than *he* was. Because his god, Delta, has been breeding his humans for hundreds of years now. He's made good progress in some areas, messed up in others. You *will* be better than Tyse Saarinen by leaps. But enough talk about this. It's been a long day and now, your reward awaits."

"Reward? What reward?"

Xi chuckles. "Jasina Bell, of course. You're taking her out to dinner."

"Oh." The moment he says this word 'dinner' I'm *starving*. And time catches up to me. I'm tired too. My eyes are itching and probably bloodshot. Trying to understand all these grand designs and delusions has made my mind weary.

Dinner sounds nice. Dinner with Jasina Bell—even nicer. It'll make up for the one we gave up to start this journey.

"Here's the special part," Xi continues. "You're taking her to dinner in the upper dimension. In my *real* city. The one where I truly exist."

I look at him, find him delighted with himself, and smile. "What?"

"That's right. Obviously, I'm trying to persuade you by dazzling you with wonders. But I truly do want you to see the world, Finn Scott. And I want you to meet the *real* me."

A moment passes as I internalize his words. His eyebrows go up, expectant. But he doesn't rush me. So I take a few more seconds before I finally say, "Ya know, all my life I thought the world was small. But this day has revealed the truth."

"And what's that truth, Finn?"

"It wasn't the world that was small, it was me."

# CLARA

"*I have to find him—*"

This is the last thing I say to Tyse before I am ripped away into a sea of darkness. A force so strong it feels like I'm being torn from reality itself. A pulling so utterly overpowering—it yanks me like the hand of God and extracts me from the spark stone cave dimension and into something cold and tight. Frigid and dense. Pressing on my bones, making them brittle. Pulling, and pulling, and pulling until...

A warmth surrounds me, comforting me like a blanket. The sense of being pulled apart is gone, and I'm... somewhere else.

Space? The starry sky? Floating on an ocean of mist? A sea of... *spark*.

I lie on my back, floating on this sea. Undulating up and down with the motion of something massive. Something alive. There is darkness, but it's not dark. Emptiness, but it's not empty.

And the little pinpricks of light above me, aren't the night sky. These aren't stars. I am something else. Some*where* else.

A womb. Soft and comforting. Warm and serene. A place between worlds, where neither gods nor humans, matter.

A place where an empty soul might be filled back up by the sea that holds me up.

As I think these words, the little dots of light that I first thought were stars, begin a journey towards me. As if I'm drawing them close. Pulling them in—like a mother opening her arms for a child.

These bits of light are spark, but there's something different about them. And as they come closer, the pinpricks of glow turn into globs of blue light floating all around me. The spark glitters and gleams. Twinkling with mystery and magic.

My mouth opens in awe, and the clumps of spark enter me, sliding down my throat, filling me up with thick, cool, wet... *peace.*

My body becomes weightless. Time passes. Seconds. Minutes. I can't tell. Then, all at once, I'm... *somewhere.*

Treading water in the rolling sea of spark. Wearing nothing but my own skin, which is not skin at all, but transparent and black, glowing with spark symbols. The same symbols that have been with me since I was a Little Sister, drawing doodles in the air with my light.

In front of me is a fleet of Godships. Dozens, hundreds, thousands—there is no number to define the quantity of Godships in front of me. And filling the decks, from bow to stern, are women.

Millions of them. More, even. It's like every female who ever existed is on a boat, floating in the sea of spark.

They all look like me—black and transparent, outlined in blue—except for the symbols. They are not covered in glowing symbols. Just me. Just *me*—which makes me not one of them, but apart from them.

They stare at me, faceless heads wavering in the gentle wind of waterscape. Inside these null faces, just above where their eyes would be, sits a small glowing orb the size of a cherry. A tiny thing, really. They all have one and when I roll my eyes up and find a glow, I realize I have one as well.

"What is it?" I ask them. "What is this little cherry of light?"

But they have no voices, no mouths to speak with, so they don't answer.

Instead, a humming, buzzing echo floats around me. Unattached and self-contained it leans towards me, into me. I hear it, but not with ears. I hear it in the glow of my head.

*Spark*, it answers.

But of course, it's spark. You need only look at it, to see that.

*No*, it whispers back. *Source*.

The instant I hear the word, I know what the source is. The cave where Tyse and I just were. The spark stones. Giant crystals protruding out from ragged walls of rock.

It... followed me?

Or brought me here?

For a moment, I don't understand. But when I turn the mystery around in my head, arranging these puzzle pieces into new configurations, they start fitting together. At least a bit.

Those crystals in the cave are the source of spark. And we —the women floating in the seascape with the little cherries of light in our heads—are... its children?

*No.*

Daughters?

*No.*

I laugh—a soft sound that spins through the stars and bounces off the edge of the universe before returning to me.

Not daughters.

*Little Sisters.*

My joy comes from understanding. It's a relief, really. Because it would be easy to assume that nothing we did inside the Tau City Factory had meaning. It would be very easy to dismiss it all. To call it a sad lie.

Which is a sad ending to a tragic story.

And that's not the kind of story I want to live in. So to me, this proves that my life in Tau City was something more than that.

Yes, it was a lie. The tower, the god, the Extraction—but there was truth there. Truth in the form of the Maidens.

*All* the maidens. Not just the chosen ones. Because every single woman had spark inside her.

"That's... you," I say, lifting my hand out of the shimmering water to point to the group of women. "You're all spark."

It's true. That is the whole reason they have factories. To grow *girls*.

And if this were the end of the story, that *would* be tragic.

But it's not. This story is just getting started. So the lie means something too. Because the women of the factory dimension, for whatever reason, are made up of spark. And we are all sisters. We all come from the source.

The spark sea hugs me. At least that's what it feels like. An embracing blanket of warmth swirls around my body, telling me that I'm on the right track. And as I think this, a woman standing on the bow of the nearest ship, raises her hands—beckoning me.

My body lifts up from the water, spark dripping off me, and I float up in the air towards her. When I get there, I hover briefly over the top of the carved figurehead—a Spark Maiden, body carved into the shape of the bow, arms by her side, head tilted up towards the sky, lips parted slightly and eyes wide—as if awestruck.

My feet touch down softly on her back and my beckoner is now a mere few steps away. She reaches for me—her little cherry light brightening as she approaches. Doesn't say anything, isn't capable of speech because she doesn't have a face. But inside her cherry of light, there is something to *see*. To *hear*. To *touch*.

I lean forward, reaching for it, but not with my hands, with my own little cherry of light. There is a connection—a kind of jolting, like pieces locking into place. And when this happens, I *do* see. And hear. And touch. And I do it for her. I see her. Her life inside the Delta City Factory. Cold fear. Endless harvest. A life of pitiful slavery, and abject misery, and constant abuse.

"I'm so sorry," I say. And I find that I have a voice. I'm the only one here with a voice. "I didn't know. I'm very sorry to learn of your suffering."

Desperate to give this Maiden's life purpose, and finding myself short on gifts, I do the only thing I can to ensure remembrance.

I name her.

"You are... Majesta." And then, for some reason, one of the symbols on my body begins to glow white instead of blue. I exhale, filled with sudden understanding. Because these symbols on my body aren't words, or letters that tell my story. They are names that tell *theirs*.

Why I have them—why I'm the one to carry their memory on my body—I have no idea.

But tears of relief flow down Majesta's face when she realizes she was never forgotten.

Just misplaced.

"You're free now," I tell her. And as soon as these words come out, I understand what's really happening here. Her soul—all of their souls—have been trapped. Harvested until there's nothing left of them but their essence—a light the size of a cherry.

*From the Source we come, and to the Source we return.*

Except, it's not true.

Not if you're harvested.

They steal your soul and leave you adrift on the spark sea. Floating on the movements of time for all eternity.

A million ideas flood into me—You could jump in to the sea, become part of it! You could float up into the sky and turn into a star!

You could—

You could—

You could—

But she can't. She is trapped.

Before I came, she had nothing.

Now, she has but a name.

"It's enough," I tell Majesta. I don't know if I believe that, but I say with confidence. "I won't forget you. I remember you, Majesta. And..." I look over her shoulder to the thousands of women behind her. Then at all the other ships. How many?

I don't know.

But I make her a promise. "I will remember you all," I tell her. Then, for some reason, I bow a little. And when I look up, she is stepping back and another woman is stepping forward. Reaching for my cherry of spark in my head. Begging me to look into her little light and remember her life too. She is from Gamma City Factory and the memories play out in much the same way. Fear. Slavery. Abuse.

Hers is a life of absence. Of emptiness. Of futile existence.

Again, I name her—lighting up another spark symbol on my black, empty outline of a body—and then I apologize. I don't know why. None of this is my fault. I just feel compelled to try and make up for their sadness. Because I wasn't sad in my factory life.

I really wasn't sad at all.

If you gather up all my moments of satisfaction and happiness and weigh them against the ones filled with fear, my misery amounts to something near zero.

And this makes me feel… guilty.

And so, I am compelled to wait in place as one by one, they come forward. And one by one, I see them. I acknowledge them. I remember them. I name them and let that name become part of me when they claim a symbol on my body. None of the memories are happy. Out of millions of lives, not one was good.

They were nothing but the spark they produced.

They were power, but not the kind one *wields*, just the kind of power others take.

And after each remembrance, I tell them, in my most humble and sincere up-city Spark Maiden manners, that I am sorry. Even though I don't feel responsible, I say it anyway. If there was something else I could do to mark their lives and tell them it mattered, I would.

But this is all I have. A name and a pitiful apology.

Years pass as all this remembering, and marking, and naming, and apologizing takes place. Decades. Centuries. Eternities. But I stay. I do not even try to back away early. I process every single cherry of light and turn it into a memory. And with each memory, I give them names.

I call them every name I know. Changing letters here and there to make them unique when I run out of ideas. Brittney, instead of Britley. Harriet, instead of Haryet. Cassidy instead of Casey. Pippa instead of Piper.

And that's enough, I think. Because after they are seen, after they are all remembered, I float back up in the air, hovering above my armada of Spark Maidens as the Godships retreat back into the nothingness. Becoming nothing but a blur of glowing blue outlines against a sea of emptiness.

Suddenly, a movement to the right catches my eye. I turn, and look, and smile. "Hayret! You're here! I was wondering..."

But she's not here. Not really. Not like I am. She's just another one of *them*. But instead of being anchored to a Godship, she's floating in the air like me.

At least, that's what she appears to be at first. She has the cherry light in her head like all the rest, but she's got another light too. It glows pink in her chest, where her heart would be.

"What's that?" I ask. Pointing to it. I float forward in sparkmist, hovering above the sea. But the outline of Haryet shimmers, breaking apart. Becoming pieces.

"Wait!" I put up a hand and float backwards. As I move away, she pulls herself together.

"Haryet, what is happening? Why can't I come near you? Why do you wither?"

She doesn't answer, she doesn't even have a face—but it *is* Haryet. I *know* it's her. I recognize her cherry spark. It contains the memory of her life.

So I try again, floating forward, just the smallest of distances—immediately, she unravels completely. Spinning off into... strings. Unfolding before my eyes.

I gasp, floating backwards, creating distance between us. *What did I do?*

But again, her distorted outline reforms when I retreat. Her cherry light in place. Her heart light glowing, unlike the others, who didn't have a heart spark.

This causes me to look down where I find my own heart spark pulsing in a steady rhythm inside my chest, as if counting something or ticking off time.

Why are we different? Why do we have this heart spark, when the others did not?

Then it hits me, I *know* her. She's a friend. We are friends. Connected. Maybe that's what's different. And if Haryet is here, then maybe so is Brooke!

"Brook!" I yell. "Mabels!" I scream, combining their two names into one. "Lucy! Piper! Marlow! Imogen!"

It's the saying of Imogen's name out loud that clarifies things. At least a bit.

None of my Spark Maiden Sisters are here, other than Haryet, because they were all eaten by the tiny god Anneeta. Haryet and I, are the only ones who weren't consumed by the baby god.

"So we're different."

Haryet's shape glows when I say this, as if she's confirming my realization.

"We're different," I say again. "Because..."

Because why? What makes us different?

"We both have heart spark?"

Haryet glows again. Pulsing with the beat of that same spark in our hearts.

"OK," I say. Because clearly, I am here for a reason. *Reasons.* And I need to understand them.

First, to remember the women. That one is obvious. I don't know what is going on with that, but it feels very important that each of them were... *known.* At least in death. Perhaps because they were nothing but remnants in life.

Second. This one, I'm still working out. But only two of us—Haryet and me—have heart sparks. This too, is important. Why are we different?

Well, it's kind of obvious. "We're from Tau City," I say, aiming these words at the remnant of Haryet.

She glows, but not brightly.

"I'm wrong. Half wrong," I realize. My brow furrowing in confusion. It's true, we are, but that's not what the heart spark is about.

A new idea forms. There is something else that only Haryet and I have done—and lived through. Sort of. "We walked through the door." And that armada of faceless women, they never did. Because they weren't Extracted, they were harvested.

Haryet lights up so bright, I have to shield my eyes. "OK!" I get excited. "Yay! I figured something out. We both walked through the door, which means, we both... crossed dimensions!"

Immediately, I know this is true. This is why we have heart spark.

"To what end, though? What does it matter?"

Suddenly, Haryet's shape begins to shimmer. The glowing blue spark that outlines her body fills in, hiding both her cherry spark in her head and her heart spark in her chest. A pattern appears. A dress. A long, blue gown made of silks, and linens, and lace.

I recognize it as the one she wore for the Final Choosing during our Little Sister year. When she became Number Eight and I became Number Nine. And when I look down at myself, I'm wearing my Final Choosing dress too.

"What?" I ask, a little bit excited, but also scared. Because I don't understand what's happening. Will I be tugged back in time? Saving me from whatever ripped me away from Tyse and the Spark Source, but also putting me back to where I started, and thereby taking everything I've earned, back? Will I love the man I love... *again*?

But no. That's not what's happening.

Haryet is doing her trick. Her Spark trick. Her final act, in the final Choosing, which was to *weave it*.

The pointer finger of Haryet's right hand is raised in the air and out of her fingertip comes... *thread*. She turned her spark into spools of glowing thread that night. Her entire dress was made of spark and no one knew until she lit up like a star on the stage and *unraveled it*.

It was quite a trick. And... I get it, it's beautiful, but what does it *mean*?

I don't know. It doesn't make sense to me. What is she doing? I mean, dressmaking? It reminds me of Jasina Bell and her butterflies.

*Wait*—my heart pounds.

I hold up my pointer finger and draw a doodle in the air. The doodle glows, staying in place. Hangs there like art hung on a wall. Something very boring and simple, but it was special in its own way because I made it.

And then, in my mind's eye, I see Jasina Bell turning her embroidered dress embellishments into spark butterflies.

Spark thread into spark dresses.

Spark doodles into art.

For some reason, I find this funny. Because... wow. What a sad, *sad* little talent I had! Hearts and flowers. That's my claim to fame.

Regardless, I think I understand now. I think I know what spark does. I know what makes Haryet and I different. And why we have the heart sparks.

Spark is creation.

Haryet and I weren't harvested for spark, we collected it inside ourselves over decades. And then, during the Choosings, we used it to *make things*. Stupid things, maybe, but *things* nonetheless. And after... we walked through the God's Tower doors, passing into another dimension.

And it was this passing through dimensions that

warranted... a *tag*. Something that identified us as being from Tau City.

It's gross—it marks us like cattle, makes us a product.

But this marking, it wasn't for the men or gods of the upper dimension cities.

It was for... the Source.

Something that would follow us.

A shard broken from the crystals in the cave.

And as soon as I think this word 'shard', the final answer slips into place.

The heart spark is a shard. A piece of the Source, but also here because we left our dimension and wandered into another one. And, I guess, that's just not how it works.

If you come from the Source, you are part of the Source.

Forever.

*Someone* keeps tabs on us. And while my guess might be wrong—perhaps it was *Stayn* keeping tabs on us?

But it doesn't fit.

Because Stayn doesn't belong *here*, in the seascape that holds the souls of the sacrificed.

Only spark does.

And only women were harvested for it.

My gaze wanders to where the Godships were, but aren't there now. These others—all the other girls and women who came to me, begging to be seen—they are gone now. Lost. Remnants in the truest sense of the word.

They have no heart spark because they didn't cross dimensions until they died, and had no spark when they died because the gods took it from them in the harvest.

And now, I *really do* get it.

I look down at my empty, black body. It's lit up with their names. *Oh*, I lament, *I so hope I can find my way back to Tyse.*

*He's dying to know what these symbols mean and I can't wait to tell him.*

These symbols mean something else, though too. It's not just a memory, it feels like... a promise?

I'm not sure. But meeting all these harvested women and girls feels like an exchange. Not just so they would be remembered, but so that they would be *tagged*. So that I could keep track of them

*Wow*, I exhale. While I am flattered to be thought of so highly that I would be trusted with the memory and magic of billions of women, it also feels like a burden.

Something to live up to.

And I do not get the feeling that this will be easy.

Haryet's spool of thread is suddenly wrapping around me. Glowing, undulating—and in this thread, I hear her message....

*You're not alone, Little Sister. You will never be alone again.*

*And now, neither will they.*

*We are all One with the Source now.*

*We are Creation.*

I look at Haryet—miles upon miles of spark thread all around us—and let out a long breath. "I get it. But now what? What do I do with this—" I want to say burden, but I pull it back at the last moment. "This..." *Gift, Clara. It's a gift.* "What do I do with it, Haryet?"

She points at me, spark thread spooling out of her fingertip at an alarming rate. It wraps around me, spinning me into a cocoon.

*Survive*, her spark whispers.

And then there is one moment.

One last, final moment when everything is good, and warm, and peaceful.

A single moment when the tilted, crooked universe is upright and steady.

And then I am ripped away—back into the coldness.

Back into the emptiness.

Tight, spun out, *captured*.

*"Needles and thread!"*

Cold emptiness.

I open my eyes to find myself face to face with a monster. A smiling, cackling monster. "Needles and thread. *Needles and thread little dollll-eeeeee!*" The Crooked-toothed mutant jumps up and down, clapping his hands as he cackles these words, over and over.

I'm so confused. My mind is... not right. I don't know where I am.

"I've got you!" the broken man yells, delighted at his success. "I've got you!"

"Wh—*What?*" I manage to gasp. That's when it hits me— tight, spun out, captured—I'm on the train line. Parts of the dream still linger in my mind—the women, made into husks from all the spark harvest. How they came to me and gave me a piece of themselves to hold on to. And how I gave them names to hold on to back. *The shard!* I force my head up so I can look down at my chest and... there it is. The glowing blue shard of Spark Source.

Frantic, my eyes dart to the twisted man. Can he see it? Does he know I was given a gift from the Source?

But if he can, he doesn't seem to care. "Get her feet," he squeals to the mutant beside him. "Unspooling time! Needles and thread. *Needles and thread!*"

Dozens of grubby mutant hands grab me. Claws digging into my arms and legs. I'm lifted into the air—hauled over their heads like a prize. A procession of monsters marching me off the train line and up onto the platform. Then I'm through the door, down a hallway, more hallways, stairs, down, then up. And finally, a dimly-lit room filled with screens, and machines, and...

"Good girl," the lead monster sings. "Good girl, good girl. But Luther's good too! You came just like I wanted. Just like I planned. See? No one ever listens to Luther, but Luther knows!"

I try to struggle as they lower me down feet first. Then, I'm standing upright. For a fleeting moment I picture my escape. Pushing through the monsters and retracing my steps back to the train line where Tyse will surely be waiting. Looking for me.

But it's too late, it's over. My arms are yanked wide as I'm pushed backwards with such force, only the gnarled hands holding onto my wrists keep me upright. My back slams against cold metal. Bindings snap tight around my wrists. Then my legs. My chest. My stomach. My hips. Straps. Clamps. Restraints. Fast, brutal, efficient.

By the time I process what's happening, it's already done and once the last few secure over my chin and forehead, I am completely immobile. Upright, but attached to the slab of coldness against my back with no give at all in the bindings.

The broken man—Luther—spins. Then leans into my

space. Hands fluttering like he's orchestrating something only he can hear. His eyes flicker—bright, then dim, then bright again. They're blue, but then quickly flash a sickly yellow-green color—the color of poison or vomit—before going blue again.

I recoil, but it does no good. There is nowhere to go. No possibility of escape.

"Yes, yes, yes," Luther chatters. "This one's got plenty left, oh yes. Epsilon will be so pleased. We'll unspool her now, *niiiiiice* and slow."

I want to think about that word Epsilon, because I feel like it's important, but my brain gets stuck on the word 'unspool'.

I'm being *unspooled*?

"Needles and thread. *Needles and thread!*"

Facing me is a cage. It emerges from the opposite wall, only a few feet away, and begins to move towards me. It is tall. Thin. Gleaming. Thread-thin wires with needle-like ends hand limp along the edges.

*Spools?*

Hundreds of them. Thousands. Maybe more. They all pulse with a faint, sickly blue glow. Not the bright glow of a canal made of spark, but the dusty, sun-bleached blue of the Tau City Factory domes.

It takes me a moment to realize what this sun-bleached blue stuff is.

And then, I get it.

It's spark. Previously harvested spark. *Dead* spark.

I am sick with want. With longing. *I want to go home.*

There is no hope of that, though. I see what's coming now. Because there, in the center of the cage, between the hanging spools of needle-thin wires of flatly-glowing spark, there is a space. An empty space.

About the size and shape of a body.

My body.

"Ahhhh," Luther sighs, like he's looking at something beautiful. Then those sickly eyes of his lock onto mine, and he grins. "Time to take you apart, little dolly."

All the little needles come to life. Rising up into the air, reaching for me. Dancing towards me like a down-city whore enticing a customer with the swinging of her hips.

The swaying of needle-threads puts me in a trance, dulling my mind. I watch, helpless as cage comes closer and closer until finally, it's right up against my face and I hold my breath, hoping against hope.

They attack me all at once. Like an animal.

Stabbing pain, sharp and burning. The wires pierce my skin and snake their way inside me.

And then... they *unspool* me.

I watch, helpless, as each needle-thin thread—once dead with residual spark—suddenly glows bright blue with my harvest.

# TYSE

*The fading blackness is a relief* I didn't realize I was waiting for, but with it comes the pain. Everywhere, there is pain. Immediately, my eyes are twitchin' and flipping through menus in my data display lookin' for relief. Trying to, at least. Because it's not workin'.

"Not working, not working," a sketchy, high-pitched voice says. It's jittery and wrong, this voice. "You'll never work again. Never, never, never! Needles and thread, making a puppet!"

What the fuck?

It takes considerable effort to turn my head to the left—not just from the pain, but because it's strapped down to a table. "*What*?" I ask. My response groggy, my tone low.

The voice comes from a man. He sits at a desk in front of many screens, chucklin' and smilin' as he taps on them, revealin' a set of spectacularly crooked, yellow teeth. They're all crowded together, like he's got twice as many fittin' in that space as normal people. Or maybe his jaw is just too small. So the teeth look like a cage for his tongue.

"Don't look at me," he snarls. "Nothing to see! Luther is nothing to look at!"

Well. I can't argue with that. He's definitely nothing to look at. What he is, is crazy. Something's wrong with him. My words come out as a laugh. "What the hell is goin' on with your teeth? Do you eat your lady with that mouth? Do you even have one? No." I continue to laugh. "There's not enough money in the world to get a whore to open her legs for the likes of you."

Before I'm even done talkin', everything about this guy changes. His whole body tenses up, his brow furrows, his jaw clenches. His hands start twitching. Fingertips itching to tap things on those screens.

And his eyes are glowing blue.

Twenty-one, I figure. That's how old he is. Never seen any action—or if he did, he got someone killed. Ugly fucker, probably augmented in the Medians during one of their defense budget decreases because there's no way in hell any proper god would raise up this mutant right here to be an augment.

I don't need a data display to know all this. His reaction to my shit talk is enough.

He's just... wrong. And even though he's the one in the position of power here, it wasn't earned. He's weak. Stupid to the point of moronic.

*And yet, you're the one strapped down to a fuckin' table, Tyse.*

Right.

They did somethin' to me. Somethin' to take me out of the game.

*Clara.*

That's how they got me here.

Somehow, they used her as bait.

"We'll see who laughs last, *Saarinen*," the man says, snapping out of the stupor my insults created. His fingers are tappin' away on that screen, still controlling things. Because while these words of his are comin' out of his mouth, pain shoots through my whole body. My back arches up off the table—some kind of electric current—

"*Stop that right now, Luther!*" The words are commanding,

and strong, and deliberate. The words are an order. The words of a god.

Immediately, the pain switches off and my back slams back down.

The god sighs. "Thank you." His voice is softer now, but no less commanding. "You, of all men, Luther, should be able to *resist* when the enemy provokes you. Have I taught you nothing?"

Luther grumbles, "I don't like him. He's a liar. He's not who he says he is."

"That's none of your business, Luther." Again, the god's voice is calm. I can't see him, he's well out of my peripheral vision. "We're on a schedule here, remember?"

I can only see Luther from the left side of my peripheral vision because my head is strapped to the table, but it's enough to see him smile. "I remember."

"*Gooooood*," the god says, drawling out the word. "Do as I instructed now. There will be no more deviations. Do you understand?"

No. I really, really don't.

"Yes, Epsilon," Luther says.

*Epsilon, Epsilon, Epsilon...*

"I understand. I'll do it," he says. His voice comes out twitchy. "Needles and thread. I'll do it just like we planned."

*Epsilon, Epsilon, Epsilon...*

I can't tell if this chanting is in my head or not. But I guess it doesn't matter. I hear it.

"*Gooooood*," the god repeats. And I realize that Luther is doing something to me. My fingertips begin to tingle. Buzzing up to my wrists. It doesn't hurt so much as itch. "That's right," the god continues. "Just like that. Do it nice and easy, Luther."

The buzzing becomes more like pins and needles.

Prickling. Numbness, but not complete. I lift up my head as much as I can, which is probably only an inch at most, and try and make sense of what is going on here.

Clearly, they are doing something to me. Something that involves spark.

"Look, look, look!" Luther exclaims. "It's curious, master. It seeks answers!"

"Never mind the patient, Luther," the god says. "Your job is to man the controls. His life is in your hands."

"Yeah," Luther cackles. "I'm doin' it. I'm doin' it just like we said. Little bits. Little bits here, little bits there. I'm in charge."

"That's right," the god says, placating his little half-witted minion. "You're in charge as long as you do as I say. Now. What are we at?"

"Seven," Luther spits. "We're at seven. We need more. But we're stuck."

"Stuck?" the god asks. "How so?"

"He won't take anymore. It doesn't flow. It doesn't work."

"Hmmmmmm," the gods hums. "More pain?"

*Pain?*

"More fear," Luther answers. He leans into my view, his ugly face and tea-stained smile nearly hovering over me. "The pain only works if he's infected with fear."

"OK." The god doesn't even hesitate. "I had hoped that we'd be able to get this done without Plan B, but it appears—"

"Wait!" I croak. "What do you want?"

The god clicks his tongue. "Oh, hush now, Tyse. None of this is any of your concern. You can't opt *in*. Either the spark flows through you, or it doesn't."

"It does," I say. Kind of embarrassed that it comes out so quick. "The spark flows through me just fine."

"No," Luther laughs. His face twitching like crazy now. Like he can't wait to fill me up with pain and fear. "It's blocked! I see it! Look!" He's pointing to a screen that I can't really see, but I catch a tiny glimpse of a red line on a black background.

"Well, we knew this was a possibility," the god says. "Set it all up, Luther. I'll be back in a few minutes. I've got to get the woman ready."

"What?" I say, yelling it now. "What woman? Are you talkin' about Clara?"

"Shut up, *Saarinen*," Luther hisses. "No one told you to speak."

"Is he talkin' about Clara?"

"I caught her," he cackles. "I caught her. It was me. I'm the hero. I am POG! She's the prize. She's the one. She will make you dance. You will dance for him. Our god. *Everyone* dances for him."

"What the hell are you talking about? What is all this?" I struggle and push against the bindings over my body. There are a lot of them, not just wrists and feet. There are straps over my chest, my ribs, my abdomen, my hips, my thighs, my knees, my ankles, my feet. Nearly the same number down my arms. Like this god isn't taking any chances and whatever he's about to do to me, it's gonna be powerful.

Luther's dancin' now, like some fool in a fairy tale. He's not just ugly, he's unstable. Some kind of moron.

"*Hey*," I say, trying to get his attention. But he's got a fistful of needle-thin tubes in his hands now—connecting them to a structure poised above me.

And then... this whole encounter makes sense.

Everythin' about this table is familiar.

*Don't panic.*

*It can't be done.*

*It's only done once.*

Once. *Once*, and that's it.

I force myself to relax. Forcin' myself to believe this. Because I can't even imagine... this can't be happenin'.

*Breathe*, Tyse. *Calm*, Tyse.

It can't be true because it can't be done...

*I* AM FOURTEEN.

I am strong, and willin', and ready.

I am *not* afraid.

I'm not.

I'm excited.

That's what I tell myself as I stare up at the lights above the augmentation table—their harsh, clinical glow making my skin prickle up with anticipation. The straps around my body are snug, but I don't fight them. There's no need.

I am here of my own free will.

I want this. I want this more than anythin'. And whatever happens next, it will be worth it. I will be stronger, faster, smarter. One of the smartest humans to ever live. One of the most dangerous to ever fight for the Sweep. These are the last minutes of my boyhood because when it's over, I'll be a soldier.

A real soldier. A Sweep Augment. And not just any augment—a *god's* soldier.

Delta's augment.

I hate that fucker, but if you've got to pick a team, you want to be on his.

My skin is buzzin'. Like static electricity before a sand storm. Expectant, and eager, and impatient. I just want to get on with it. I just want to be better.

I just want to matter.

. . .

*THE DOOR BANGS **open*** and Epsilon returns. This time he doesn't stay out of my peripheral vision, but hovers right over top of me. I nearly gasp because he's... meltin'. His face, it's scarred beyond recognition. Nothin' like I've ever seen before.

Well, not true. I saw him on the tracks when they lured me into their trap.

He's the Corrupted God.

The one Myra used to tell stories about.

The story I never let her finish.

Excited, Epsilon rubs his hands together as he checks Luther's work—which is complete now. All the needles the thread-like tubes have been inserted into the cage hoverin' above me.

The god claps Luther on the back. The sound is wet—too heavy, like Luther's bones are softer than they should be. "I love it when you follow orders."

I catch Luther grinnin' out of the corner of my eye. He's such a twitchy, sketchy thing. He doesn't make sense. "I did it just like you said. I set it all up, just like you said. Needles and thread. *Needles and thread!*" He cackles. "We're gonna thread you with some spark!"

"Shhhhhh," Epsilon hisses, movin' to the machine, fingers grazin' the threads, the wires, the ugly cage of metal hangin' over me. "We don't want to upset our new brother, Luther. Remember what it was like when you were on this table?"

Luther whines like a puppy. "I do..." He hesitates. "But I don't want to."

"That's OK," Epsilon hums, petting Luther's greasy hair. "You don't have to remember your pain, just what a relief it was when your threadmaster was congenial during the process. You don't have to be kind—just empathetic."

"Yes, yes," Luther eagerly says. "I understand. I do. I understand. Be nice, Luther. Be nice! And if you're nice, someone will be nice to you back."

"Well," Epsilon laughs. "That's not what I meant. But... whatever."

Luther wrings his hands, practically shakin' with anticipation. "Can I start now? Can I? Can I?"

Epsilon tilts his head. Then—like a conductor cueing an orchestra—

He lifts a finger. Snaps it.

"Run the program."

*"This is Delta Tymothy Jarvinen."* The threadmaster's voice is cold and clinical. "Age fourteen point five. Height one-point-seven-five meters. Mass sixty-three point two kilograms. Baseline vitals within operational range."

A pause. A soft beep as the system records.

"Subject classification: Sweep Recruit," the threadmaster continues. "Augmentation tier: Standard Combat Integration. Genetic deviations: None detected. Prior medical modifications: None."

Another beep. Another pause.

"Cognitive assessment: Above baseline. Reflex index: Ninety-fifth percentile. Neural resilience: Pending evaluation."

*Pendin'? What's that mean?*

"Pain tolerance: Unverified. Psychological stability: Unverified."

*Unverified?*

"Subject prepped for initial puncture."

*Am I... not suitable for—*

"Beginning sequence now."

A hiss.

Then the needles.

I hear the machine before I see it. A low mechanical hum, the kind that makes your teeth vibrate if you get too close.

Then it moves into position above me. A rig of metal arms and cables, shiftin' above me like a spider's nest unravelin'. It lowers slow, methodical, every piece movin' with clinical precision. At first, it just looks like wires. Thin, silver strands hangin' from the frame, swayin' slightly as the machine adjusts.

But they aren't wires.

They're thousands of spark needles. Maybe more. Thin as hair, long threads that are as sharp as scalpels. They glint under the surgical lights as they descend. Shakin' like tentacles. Like they're alive. Like they can already sense me.

My hands twitch against the restraints. Not fear. I'm not afraid.

I refuse to second-guess this decision.

It's just... the thing above me looks like a cage.

Not just somethin' meant to augment me.

Somethin' meant to trap me.

THE MACHINE WHIRS TO LIFE. A hiss. A click. Then the first wave of punctures.

Needles sink into me—neck, spine, arms, legs. A thousand, maybe more. Tiny, hair-thin threads slide under my skin, wormin' their way through muscle, veins, nerve pathways.

Micro-spark injections.

At fourteen, I didn't understand what this was. But now, I

know exactly what they're doin' to me. It's called *threadin'*. Lacing my body with conductive pathways—wires of spark so thin they dissolve into my nervous system. Mergin' with it. Rewritin' it.

A jolt. A snap. Somethin' burns along my spine.

Luther giggles. "It's in! It's in! Marker one reached!"

The machine adjusts. More threads. Deeper. Into the bone now. It has to fuse.

Pain blooms—a sharp, searin' heat runnin' the length of my limbs, twisting in my joints, burrowin' into the marrow of my bones.

Luther is mutterin'. "Needles and thread, needles and thread, just like the dollies."

Marker two.

The pain changes. Becomes brighter. My nerves are conductin' spark now. It's in my bloodstream. In my cells.

Here's the problem with all this—I mean, there are like a hundred fuckin' problems happenin' all at once right now—but this is the main one:

I've *already* been threaded. It's only done *once*.

So naturally, it can't happen again.

"It's not working!" Luther is grabbing at his hair, pullin' on it. His eyes wide. His feet dancin'.

"Calm down," Epsilon coos to his little jester. "It's expected. He's one of *them*."

"One of them, one of them!" Luther repeats. "Not like me."

Through all my white-hot pain, I hear Epsilon chuckle. "That's right. He's not like you at all. Keep going."

I don't know what Luther does, I just feel it. Agony. The pain seeps deep into my bones. Hittin' resistance—the spark clashin' with the older threads. Pushin' against them, fightin' for control.

"More!" Epsilon yells. "More!"

A snap. A crackle. Then—

My back bows. My muscles seize. My vision whites out.

This is not going to work.

"*MARKER TWO... HOLDING.* PATHWAYS RESISTING," the threadmaster states.

*Resistin'? What's he mean by that?*

Another beep. A rustle of movement behind me.

"Proceeding with protocol override per home god instructions," the threadmaster says. "Initiating secondary layering."

*Secondary what?* I want to know what that means, but there's no time. Because whatever the override is, it's already happenin'. All I can do is exist in the fire spreadin' through my body. My muscles twitchin', my fingers curlin' and uncurlin', like someone else is controllin' them. I start shakin'—seizing.

A hand presses against my head, fingers cool against my temple. Somethin' injects into my neck. A rush of cold.

Then—a flood.

The fire shifts. Changes. Like it's no longer tryin' to consume me, but become part of me.

The threadmaster speaks again. Calm. Unbothered. "Proceeding with secondary spark integration. Layering complete. Data display initializing."

A snap inside my skull.

Then—light.

Not the white-hot light of pain, but somethin' else. A new awareness.

Symbols. Numbers. A blinkin' cursor in my vision. A rush

of data that has no meanin' yet, scrollin' in thin blue text across the black of my mind.

My breath catches.

I see the world differently.

Like somethin' inside me just woke up.

WHEN I OPEN MY EYES, the pain is gone, Luther is panickin'—yankin' at his hair, mutterin' about dollies and broken things as he dances next to me. But Epsilon is grinnin' like a demon.

"Oh, now this is very, *very* interesting." His voice is low, serious. He's not lookin' at me. He's lookin' past me. At a screen, a projection—somethin' only he can see. He hums, low and pleased. "Three layers?" He looks over at Luther. "That's not supposed to happen, is it?"

Luther stops mid-mutter. Tilts his head. "Three? No! Not three. One! One is all anyone needs! One threading. Needles and thread! Making dollies only needs one!"

Epsilon sighs. "Yeah. That's what I thought. But look." Luther leans over me, squintin' his eyes to see whatever it is that Epsilon is pointin' at. A scan, I think. A scan of me. "This is the first attempt. It didn't work."

*Marker two... holding. Pathways resisting.*

"Then there was a second attempt... here."

*Proceeding with protocol override per home god instructions. Initiating secondary layering.*

"That one," Epsilon says, "is working well at the moment. At least," he chuckles, "it was. Until we pushed in this third layer." He looks away from the scan and over to Luther. "Perhaps we should add in an extra step to the protocol, Luther."

"Extra! Yes, yes, let's make it extra!"

"From now on, we'll do the scan *before* we thread. He's an

anomaly. The first of his kind, perhaps. But if one god did it, there will be others."

"Scans before threading," Luther shouts. "Scans, scans, scans!"

"At any rate," Epsilon says, "It doesn't matter much. Not with this one. Our layer didn't fully take, but look here." Once again, Luther calms down enough to lean in and squint at the scan. "The third threading is integrating with the first. Do you know what that means?"

"Yes!" Luther starts hopping around like a lunatic. Then stops. "No! What does it mean?"

I'm listenin' just as carefully as the idiot, because I'd like to know myself.

"It means," Epsilon says, "that he's the first of my augments to have a second *complete* set of threads." He grunts. "This is amazing." Then he looks down at me, maybe just realizing that I'm awake and listening in. "What did Delta do to you?"

"You tell me," I croak. "Because I haven't a clue."

Epsilon chuckles, pleased with my reaction. Or maybe just himself. "We're going to have a lot of fun, Tyse." He says my name through a bright smile. Then he turns to Luther. "Luther?"

Luther is bouncin' again. "Yes, master?"

"It's time for a fight."

"Fight! Yes!" Luther shouts, pumping his fist into the air. "Epsilon! Epsilon! Epsilon!"

"Show our new brother the prize..." Epsilon squints his eyes at me. "Should he win, of course."

This is when I realize that the ceilin' is actually a massive screen. And I know this because it blinks to life with light.

It's a feed showin' Clara, upright and strapped to a wall. Her cage of needles doesn't hover over her like mine, but surrounds her like a cage. All the threads coming out of her, glowin' with blue spark.

She looks dead. At the very least, she's been drained to empty. Like the women we saw in Delta's factory. She's a husk. Gray and lifeless.

My heart thumps, my skin heats up. *Rage*.

Then... panic.

"What the fuck have you done to her?" I try to get up, but can't obviously, since I'm literally strapped down by dozens of bands.

Epsilon laughs, pointing to himself. "Me? What have I done to her? My good man, I wasn't the one who drank her spark! That was... *you*."

No. I shake my head. Strainin' against the bands. "*No*."

But all the missin' pieces of what was actually happenin' to me today finally fall into place.

Clara. Strapped to a wall. Being harvested of spark.

Me. On a table. Being threaded with spark.

He used her to augment me.

And now she's dyin'.

"She's dying," Epsilon declares. "But I'll save her."

"Do it," I say, my words coming out as a growl. "Save her. *Now*."

"He's uppity," Luther chants. "Uppity, uppity, uppity!"

"Yes," Epsilon drawls. "He *is* rather uppity. But it's fine." He waves a hand through the air, as if to accentuate this idea. "It's fine because he doesn't understand the game. He hasn't been told the rules."

"What rules." I snarl.

"The rules!" Luther screams. "The rules!"

"They're very simple." Epsilon leans down into my neck. His mouth right up next to my ear. "You fight. You win, she lives. You lose, she dies."

"You're mad," I say. "You're fuckin' mad. You've lost your damn mind. And look at you! You've been augmentin' yourself, haven't ya? Your face looks like it's fuckin' melting! For fuck's sake, you're makin' monsters here. Look at this fool!" I jut my chin, as much as I can under the bindings, towards Luther. "Look at him! He's not an augment! I don't care how bright his eyes glow. And for what? Fight club? You get off on makin' mutants fight each other?"

Epsilon smiles. "You say that like it's a bad thing. Now... are you done? Theatrics over? Because your woman won't last long without a spark infusion. An infusion only I can give her. And she won't get that spark infusion until you win a fight."

I narrow my eyes and growl out each word. "I'm gonna kill you, Epsilon. I'm gonna tear your fuckin' head off and spit down your goddamn neck."

"That's the spirit!" Epsilon yells. "Put him in the cage, Luther!"

# JASINA

*I'm studying myself in the mirror*, shaking my head, amazed at the transformation staring back at me. I started this day looking like a down-city street sweeper with my filthy clothes and dirty face. And now, not that many hours later, I look like a Spark Maiden.

The dress is a high-low evening gown crafted from luxurious ivory silk satin, flowing effortlessly with movement every time I turn. The bodice is structured and corset-style, reinforced with delicate boning for a perfect fit and featuring intricate gold embroidery in swirling, baroque-inspired motifs. Gold hooks descend from the sweetheart neckline, elegantly framing my cleavage before trailing past my navel.

The sleeves are voluminous and off-the-shoulder, made of soft organza—a fabric I only learned about today from the dressing maids when they appeared to run my bath. There's delicate ruching along the upper arms, adding a touch of old-world romance.

The skirt cascades asymmetrically, with a layered, ruffled hem in the front that gradually lengthens into a flowing train at the back. Beneath the outer layers, a fine crinoline underskirt provides soft volume, keeping the silhouette structured yet ethereal.

If I was given delicate shoes instead of knee-high embroidered boots, I would be ready to go to a gala. But the boots, in a matching champagne hue, featuring intricate beadwork and subtle metallic threading, change everything.

The dress is more traditional. More of what I'm used to, save for the scandalous mini-skirt that hits me mid-thigh in the front.

But the boots give the ensemble weight. It grounds me to this new place of fresh wonders. It makes me feel less like a Spark Maiden and more like a Vagabond Girl.

That's what the maids told me. That's what girls like me are called. Girls who like to travel and see places instead of settling down with a man. They are from the upper dimension, so I asked them about it relentlessly.

They didn't tell me much, kept making these little lock-and-key motions with their fingers in front of their lips. So I took that to mean that Xi has forbidden them from talking about it.

They did gossip about the world though, which I took as a way for them to explain it without answering any of my questions. I heard all about Sophie Beaumont's boyfriend cheating on her, and Lola Devereaux's mother, who was thought to have died in a car crash—only to reappear days later, unharmed. Turns out, it was actually her twin sister!

How crazy is that?

And then, some guy named Rafael Montague was stalking some girl named Delilah Vega, who lost her memory after falling off a horse while riding through the woods. Rafael found her, took her to a secret cabin near a lake, and pretended like she was his wife! Luckily, detective Bianca Romano broke all the rules of her department to find clues, and saved Delilah from a fate worse than death just as she was about to marry Rafael for real!

I let out a breath, feeling grateful that Rafael was caught and Delilah wasn't tricked into marrying him. His trial starts tomorrow and all the maids are praying to Xi that he'll be found guilty of kidnapping because Delilah belongs with her true love, Dominic Castille, heir to the Castille fortune.

Wow. What a world.

I mean, kidnappers, twins, amnesia—it's a lot. But I can't help being intrigued. In fact, I don't just want to see this world—I want to experience it. I know it's only one night, but I want to make the most of this opportunity.

A knock at the door pulls my attention from the mirror. When I turn, my dress lags a fraction of a second behind me, twirling against my legs. I pick up the train—which doesn't actually drag on the floor, just barely kisses it once the boots are on—and walk over to the door.

I open it and find Xi staring back at me. "Hi. Where's Finn?" I lean over, peeking behind him, but Finn's not here.

"He's still dressing. He's had a long day, but he's very excited about your date in the upper tonight."

"Me too." My heart thumps, as if to provide proof. "I'm actually a little bit nervous. That world... it sounds so fascinating. Twins, and amnesia, and kidnapping! Fake wives and detectives! I didn't even know what a detective was! I might like that job."

Xi's brows furrow a little, like he's puzzled. So I jump in real quick, putting up a hand to stop his coming objection. "I got the hint. The maids weren't supposed to be talking about the upper world to me. But they weren't. Not really. They were gossiping among themselves and I was eavesdropping. So please, don't be mad at them."

He smiles at me. "Never mind them. This night is about you, Jasina Bell. You and Finn Scott." He offers me his arm. "Come along. I'll escort you downstairs where Finn is now waiting."

As we walk down the stairs, Xi is quiet. Allowing me to

exist in my own thoughts. And in these thoughts, I start to feel different. There's no one here but Xi and me, but I feel like the center of attention. It's the dress, I think. And the escort. Being walked down the stairs. This is what it's like to be a Spark Maiden.

Dressed, escorted, cared for. That's what it means to be a Spark Maiden.

And while I'm over the fact that my old life is gone and so are my opportunities to be one of 'them'—one of the Chosen —I can't help but dream about it a little. I can't deny that it would've been nice to have been Clara. Not her end, obviously. But she had all those years in the Maiden Tower. This very tower—in another factory—but still the same.

It must've been grand. And she was one of the last who will ever know that privilege. What it's like to be... royalty, I guess. She got as close as she could to the title of princess in a factory city. It's not that I'm jealous, it's more that I'm... anxious. And I have regrets.

Not many, but some.

I think about how I took all my pledge years for granted. Which is strange because I was a down-city girl. But I wasn't there to *pledge*. I was a spy. So while I ate the little petits fours cakes and sipped the tiny cups of tea as I practiced how to be poised, proper, and polite—I didn't enjoy it. The cakes and tea were nice, but I was gathering information to put into my weekly reports. Stupid details that now, when I think back, make no sense in the grand scheme of things.

There's a little nagging thought inside me that it was wasted. That I was just being used by Auntie Bell. Those reports stole my time. My joy. And they never mattered in the least.

None of it did.

All those crazy up-city people were trying to make a god,

for fuck's sake. It was never about stopping the Extraction, it was about... starting a *harvest*.

It's a shock to realize these two things are connected.

This time, whatever this is, I'm going to *enjoy it*.

"Ahhh," Xi says, once we round the corner of the stairs and the lobby comes into view. "There he is. Waiting for you."

Finn turns at the sound of Xi's voice, but his eyes immediately land on me. And that smile... wow. It's enough to make the spark butterflies living inside me flutter a bit.

"Jasina," he says, walking towards the stairs. This is when I notice what he's wearing. It's not what I expected, yet it's exactly right. His suit is linen, like in Tau City, but the details make it something new.

The jacket is longer, reaching mid-thigh, fitted in a way that accentuates his lean muscles—broad at the shoulders and tapering in at his waist and showing off his athletic frame.

The fabric is sand-colored, warm and natural. But along the lapels and cuffs there are some gold details. Embroidered swirls in designs that remind me of the stars for some reason.

Beneath the jacket, he's wearing a deep sapphire blue tunic with an open neckline, hinting at his body underneath. Gold clasps shaped like desert leaves, hold the fabric together in places. And the trousers are different too—still loose and practical, but now made from a fine silky fabric and fresh in style, reminding me that we're not in Tau City, but Xi.

His boots are a dark chestnut leather, polished but sturdy, and laced with golden thread. A wide belt cinches around his waist, its etched metal buckle glinting softly underneath a long scarf of rich copper, which is draped over his right shoulder.

It's all very elegant and expensive looking, but it fits Finn's Tau City style so perfectly, I have a wave of homesickness. A sudden longing for hot and windy desert days and cold nights looking down at the bright blue canal that was outside everyone's neighborhood, regardless if you were up city or down.

I can honestly say, as a down-city girl, I had never really thought about Finn Scott. Three months ago, I would've called him a quiet snob—too clean, too untouched by hardship, a man who walked through the city like he wasn't really there, but too soft to survive outside of it.

Tonight, Finn Scott looks like a runaway prince in disguise. Regal, capable, and strong. Like he just stepped out of a story and has decided to rewrite it.

I swallow hard, realizing that I haven't spoken. That I haven't even breathed.

"Jasina," he says again, this time stepping towards me as Xi and I reach the bottom of the stairs. And *damn*. The way he says my name makes the spark butterflies inside me do more than flutter, they feel like a swirling cyclone.

When we reach him, I let go of Xi's arm and allow Finn to pull me close. He kisses me on the cheek, sliding his lips against my neck until he's whispering in my ear. "You look absolutely stunning. Delicious enough to eat." Another quick cheek kiss, like he didn't just promise to eat me, and then he steps back, sliding his arm around my waist and pulling me into his chest.

I swell with a feeling of being cherished. He loves me. Not in a deep, we've-been-together-for-a-decade kind of love. But not the, we-barely-know-each-other kind of love either.

It's something new and it comes with a sense of belonging.

"You two can find your way to the God's Tower door?" Xi asks, his smile one of delight. His eyebrows hiked way up into his forehead. Like he's enjoying our reunion even more than we are.

"Is that how we get through?" Finn ask.

Xi opens his arms wide. "How else?"

"It's just... it was pretty regulated in our city."

"It's regulated here too. But we're..." Xi's eyes dart past us, to the disheveled city outside, "between things at the moment."

"Right," Finn says. Getting Xi's obvious nod to the disaster of a city outside. "We'll meet you up there, then, right? In the other world?"

"You'll have an escort when you arrive. Have a nice night. I'll see you both tomorrow."

Finn takes a breath, like he's about to say something, but Xi simply fades away, like he was never here.

I chuckle. "The world is so weird, isn't it?"

Finn turns, looking down at me as he nods. Jasina, you have no idea. I've got so much to tell you. But I'm starving, and I bet you are too. Let's go. I want to see this upper dimension so bad, I can barely stand it."

"Me too," I say, excited and laughing now as he takes my hand as we make our way out the door of the Maiden Tower and turn, looking left, to the God's Tower.

"Did you ever think," Finn says, "in a million years, that you would be walking through that door?"

"Absolutely not. I didn't Pledge so I could win, obviously."

Finn looks at me, frowning now. "Do you think any of them wanted to win?"

Now I frown too. "Well... no. Why would they?"

"Then why did they play, Jasina? It's so dangerous. I don't think number one has anything to do with being the best at spark magic. Because it wasn't going to matter to me. I was going to choose my favorites and... probably one I didn't like at all."

"And make her number one?"

He nods. "It's sick, right?"

I shrug up one shoulder. "Yes. But... if I were you, I'd have done the same thing. Choose all my friends so they could get all the rewards. Then choose a girl I didn't like and make her the 'winner'."

He sighs. "I don't wanna mess up our good mood—"

"No," I put a hand up. "You're not going to. It's something that needs to be said, anyway."

"What needs to be said?"

"It's survival, Finn. And yeah, it's selfish. But if we're not looking out for us, then who is? I guess, if you come from a good family like you did—"

"Like *I* did?" Finn laughs. His smile back in place. "Are you fucking with me now? Jasina, my mother was one of those cult Matrons. Worst-case scenario, she was harvesting Little Sisters to feed Donal Oslin and turn him into a god so she could travel to another world—while leaving me *behind*! Best case, she was a brainwashed minion who literally went crazy. Could you imagine a worse god than Donal?"

I shake my head, laughing despite the seriousness of the topic. "No. He was the *absolute* worst. You don't even know the half of it. He was my partner all growing up in Pledges. But my point was—you had your father. He was looking out for you."

Finn presses his lips together, agreeing with a nod of his head. "He did. I think he really tried. I think he knew some things, but then he must've learned something new. Maybe the stuff about Donal? And then he went rogue."

"And they killed him."

"My *mother* killed him."

"Yeah, that's terrible. I take it back, your family sucks."

He laughs again. "Let's talk about something else. Let's talk about... your dress. Your nap. How was it? I like your boots."

"You mean let's forget, for just one night?"

"Yeah. We're gonna walk through the God's tower door and be in another world. This is the future, Jasina. From now on, let's just think about the future."

I give his hand a squeeze. "Agreed. Let's go."

And that's what we do. We walk down the murky-black canal—trying not to notice all the things, all around us, that are going wrong in this city—and head towards the God's Tower stairs.

It's a quick climb—much quicker than I remember those two nights when I stood on the God's Tower stage while Haryet and Clara were being Extracted. And before I know it, we're standing right in front of the big, black doors.

"What do we do now?" I'm asking this question when the doors slowly begin to open. And then, there's a force tugging at me. Pulling me in!

"Finn!" I squeal. "Is this supposed to happen?"

He's being pulled in too, and I think this makes him calm. Separates this Extraction from the ones he was responsible for. Because he was left behind for those two, and this time he's coming too.

"Stay calm," Finn says. "This is how it happens. This is just how it works."

He doesn't know that any more than I do, but it's literally only a few seconds of tugging, and then... it stops, everything goes black, the world behind us—the sounds of those workers and whatever they're doing, gone now.

Just silence and darkness.

And then, just as quickly, there's a small point of light directly in front of us and a feeling of being put down. Settled. A sense of heaviness.

A man's face appears. He's smiling. "Welcome! Miss Jasina and Mr. Finn, right?"

"Uh…" I begin, but cannot finish. Because I'm so startled by this… *man?* He's not a man. He's got the face of a man, but the body of one of those worker things.

And he can talk. And smile. And—

"What the hell are you?" Finn just blurts this out, no hesitation at all.

The man-machine thing bows, apologizing profusely, "Oh, I am very sorry. Very, very sorry. Xi didn't tell me that you'd never met one of my kind before. I'm sure it just slipped his mind. I apologize. I would've covered up had I known."

And then, just like that, he transforms into a regular man. A man as real looking as Finn. He's human, white body gone now. His mechanical joints too. And he's wearing clothes.

"What kind of magic is that?" Finn asks. Again, just blurting it out.

The man-machine sighs. Which just kinda blows my mind. "Oh, wow. OK. You two are from somewhere *very* traditional!" He nods, agreeing with himself. "I wasn't told that either. So again, apologies. Let's start over. Hello!" He extends a hand towards Finn. "I am Cormac, Xi's personal servant. I'm here to escort you to the God's Tower lobby where you will learn how to access your dinner reservations and your room."

"Room?" I ask.

"Yeah," Finn adds. "What room? I thought this was a date and we'd go back tonight?"

"Nonsense!" Cormac laughs. "One evening is not a date." He winks at Finn. "One must take the place for a test drive."

"A what?" Finn asks.

Corban waves a hand in the air. "Never mind. You've got a reservation and it's quite a climb back up to the surface, so we'd better get hoofin' it."

"A climb?" I ask. Feeling weary just thinking about it.

"Oh, don't worry, Miss Jasina. There's an escalator."

I have no idea what that is, but I find out soon enough. Because after a short walk down a dark hallway, we turn a corner and come face to face with it.

Cormac pans a hand at the stairs that magically appear out of the floor and go up. "After you, Mr. Finn and Miss Jasina."

"How—"

But Finn is stepping onto the closest moving stair and he tugs me along with him. I have to hop to keep up because a stair appears behind me!

I look back and down at the magic stairs, then up at Cormac and find him smiling, one step below me. There's something off about his smile—something subtly wrong, like an imitation of what a real person should look like.

"Uncanny Valley," Cormac says.

"What?" Finn turns.

"Miss Jasina is finding me hard to reconcile. It's called Uncanny Valley."

"I don't know what that means," I admit.

"It means... I don't look right. You don't like it, but you can't explain why."

I turn back around and face forward just in time to hop off the escalator, because the stairs disappear into the floor.

Finn hops with me, then Cormac takes the lead, turning a corner, and panning his hand to another escalator. "It's like a switchback," he says in a way of explanation. "We're climbing a mountain!" And this comes out like a proclamation.

I'm so confused about all of it, I simply do what he says. This switch-backing stuff continues several more times, and then, finally, we end up in a large, open room with ceilings so high, I don't even know if I can see the top. The place is built like a triangle. A very elongated pyramid, I realize. And it's almost entirely made of glass. Outside, it's still light, but only just barely. The sky is glowing the oranges and reds of a beautiful sunset.

"Welcome to the God's Tower lobby!" Cormac says, his voice booming and overly enthusiastic in the echoing chamber. "This is the official Visitor's Center for all travelers." He pans a hand to the right. "Over here, you'll find our state-of-the-art interactive map. Just pick up one of our PPDs—Proprietary Personal Devices—tell it where you want to go, and it will guide you there. It can do other things as well. In fact, as part of the Xi'sperience Package, it can do anything you want—make dinner reservations, schedule a spa day, find you a good book, or the best beach on the canal to swim at. Treat your PPD as your own personal concierge."

Finn and I both look over at the map, studying it.

But Cormac has already moved on. "And over here, we have complimentary e-bikes. Look for the flashing green light to find one fully charged. Return it to any of our seventy-seven e-bike racks in the city when it starts flashing yellow and pick up another fully charged bike at your convenience. If you would like to leave the city and explore the desert, you'll find self-driving cars just outside that door."

He points to a door directly behind us, so Finn and I turn again.

"I'll leave you to it. But if you need me, just ask your PPD for 'Cormac' and I'll contact you immediately. Thank you for visiting RhoXi. Enjoy your visit. And remember, Every Spark Has Its Purpose!" Then he does a salute-turned-bow—something that feels both official and ridiculous—before spinning on his heel and striding away.

I look at Finn. "Ummm..."

He laughs. "I have no fuckin' idea, Jasina. But I'm hungry. Let's just play along, OK?"

"OK," I say. "Fine with me. Let's grab our peepees and get the hell out of here."

Which makes him guffaw as he pulls me in tight and kisses me on the head. "Right. Let's go get our peepees."

TWENTY MINUTES LATER, after we gawked at the lobby and other bewildered visitors, figured out how to activate the PPD, and smartly decided to forego the e-bike after looking at them and realizing we'd probably kill ourselves, we walk out the doors.

And from the moment we step outside the God's Tower in Xi City, I'm... speechless. I can't seem to see enough. I'm looking everywhere, at everything. The towers—which are almost exactly like the towers in our Tau City. The canal—which is bright cyan blue, just like our Tau City. And the people. All dressed in long, loose cream-colored linen with sun-bleached-blue accents.

"What is this?" I ask, nearly breathless from the shock of unsettling sameness.

Finn doesn't answer right away, simply turns in place, taking me with him because we're holding hands. Finally, after we make a complete circle, he shrugs. "It's all the same. They're all alike." He looks at me, his blue eyes worried. "What does it mean?"

I shrug, buying myself a few heartbeats so I can search for an answer. "Maybe... it's... some grand design?"

"Grand design?" He laughs.

"What? What's so funny?"

His blue eyes search mine for a moment, then he looks away. "Ya know what? It doesn't matter. It's... a game. That's all."

I have no idea what that means, but before I can ask any more questions, he's moving forward, one hand holding onto mine, the other holding his PPD out in front of him, trying to follow the map to the restaurant where we have dinner reservations.

I skip a little to catch up and leave the shock of unsettling sameness behind at the tower doors.

Because I like that it's almost exactly like Tau City. At least it'll be easy to navigate. Because right now we're strolling what appears to be the Canal District shops. And even though the fashions on the other side of the windows are not anything I've ever seen before at home, these shops are. The canal is. The beaches.

I fit in here. Even in this somewhat inappropriate sexy dress that shows the front of my legs from mid-thigh down.

"Here it is," Finn says, pointing the PPD up at the building we're now in front of.

We both look up, because it's a massively tall tower. In fact, it's the Mayor's Tower. Not as tall as the God's Tower or the Extraction Tower, but definitely taller than the Maiden Tower.

"Look." Finn points to the brass plaque over the doors—which don't have handles and open and close all on their own as people approach. "The Provost Tower."

"What's a provost?"

Finn shrugs. "Hell if I know. But who cares? Let's eat. This thing says our restaurant is on the top floor."

We both look up. *Waaay* up. Then smile at each other. "Should be some view."

"Come on," he says. And we walk through the doors that open automatically when we approach.

There's an elevator here, which is something I recognize, at least, and we take it all the way up. Dreaming, perhaps, about what will be on the other side of the doors when we step out.

But when we actually do that, nothing has prepared me for what I see.

Finn, either, from his silence as we walk over to the floor-to-ceiling windows and peer out.

"Holy shit," Finn says. "What is all that?" He's pointing to the sprawling city that covers every bit of desert as far as the eye can see.

"It's a... city? I think."

"It must be," Finn says. "But it doesn't look like any city I've ever seen."

"What is it made of? Glass?"

"I don't know. It's shiny, though, right?"

"It's like a mirror," I say. "You can see the whole sunset in them."

"There must be hundreds," Finn says.

I jump when his PPD beeps and starts talking! "Welcome to the Grand Sprawl, the seamless urban expanse connecting

Rho and Xi—two of the most advanced and exclusive cities in the known world, into a singular entity you know as RhoXi! This vast metropolis stretches across the desert, spanning over 150 kilometers of interconnected districts, engineered to provide a harmonious blend of innovation, infrastructure, and controlled expansion."

Finn looks at me with raised eyebrows. "What the hell?"

I have no clue, so all I do is shrug and try to keep up with the talking thing in his hand.

"Unlike open cities, access to RhoXi is strictly regulated. Entry requires an authorized permit, ensuring a carefully maintained environment for its residents and visitors. As a result, few outside the system have ever witnessed the full scale of this urban achievement."

"Weird," I say. "But also… familiar."

"Right? I mean, Tau City was closed too."

"Yeah." Meanwhile, the PPD is still spitting facts at us.

"The architecture you see before you is crafted from high-density composite alloys and reflective polymer glass, designed to regulate internal temperatures while maximizing solar efficiency. These towering structures act as self-sustaining ecosystems, with integrated energy grids, automated transport systems, and vertical resource hubs."

"I don't think I understood a single word it said," I laugh.

Finn laughs too. "So strange."

"The Grand Sprawl is divided into specialized sectors, each serving a distinct purpose. Some districts function as research and development hubs, others as residential enclaves, while key industrial zones keep the megacity running. Every structure, every pathway, and every transport line is part of a greater system—an engineered marvel, designed for efficiency, security, and progress. RhoXi remains dedicated to preserving its rich traditions, maintaining the balance between history and modern advancement. Thank you for visiting RhoXi. Enjoy your visit. And remember, *Every Spark Has Its Purpose!*"

Finn and I wait a few seconds, almost holding our breath. "Is that it?" I ask. "Is it over?"

"Thank the god," he says. "Come on, the restaurant is this way. We can look at the city tomorrow."

"Tomorrow," I sigh with pleasure. "We're gonna stay here over night, Finn. It's… it's…"

"Unbelievable? Because that's what I think it is. We just *hopped worlds*, Jasina. Do you even understand what that means?"

"No," I laugh.

"Me either."

Then we're giggling like stupid children.

But we don't care.

After everything we've survived over the past several weeks, this is the kind of unbelievable we can live with.

# FINN

*asina and I enter the restaurant* greeted by the low hum of violins and cellos. The song is light, but low. Not quick, but not slow, either. Easy and natural. Like a heartbeat just on the edge of sleep.

"Wow," Jasina says, stopping just inside the doors. There's a couple ahead of us talking to the master of the house, but it's only a few moments of whispered words, and then they are being led deeper into the darkened space.

We step forward, and I'm just about to announce who we are and explain that we've got a reservation, when the master of the house beats me to it.

"Mr. Finn, Miss Jasina. Your table is right this way."

He has a strange accent. Nice. Interesting. But new to my ears. We follow another man deeper into the space, which is intimate, dimly lit, with soft pools of golden light falling over tables set for two. No crowded banquet halls, no swirling gowns brushing past in a rush of movement. Private and peaceful.

Almost too peaceful for the number of people here, because every table we pass is full.

Glancing over at Jasina, I study her. She takes it all in the same way that she does everything new—sharp-eyed and curious, already weighing it against what she knows. She doesn't cling to me, doesn't hesitate, but there's a flicker of surprise in her eyes as she watches a pair glide across the small dance floor off to the left. Their steps are slow, predictable, almost too easy.

And then the waiter stops in front of a table right up against the floor-to-ceiling windows.

"Holy crap," Jasina whispers.

And holy crap is right. Even though we were just looking at this view—at least, something like it—that was during the sunset, and now it's dark. Not only that, but we must be facing the other side of the city, because all those towers and buildings we saw a few minutes ago, have disappeared.

In their place is the desert.

Nothing but miles and miles of desert lit up by a soft glow from a full moon hanging low at the edge of the horizon. Shadows and silhouettes of cactus and palm trees contrast against the almost white sand. Most of the area is flat, but there are great dunes off in the distance. Dunes big enough to be mountains.

"Your table, sir. Madam." The waiter bows, panning a hand to the table, then straightens up and pulls out Jasina's chair for her.

We settle in our seats. I order us each a glass of wine out of habit, and I'm just about to ask Jasina if she likes wine— this was Clara's drink, after all—when she sighs. "So that's what that whole self-driving car trip was about." She nods to the desert. "I might want to take that trip."

"We should definitely take that trip. We've seen the desert from the wall of Tau City, but this is something else."

"When did you see the desert from the wall?"

"What?"

"I've never been up on the wall."

"Yeah, you have. Everyone goes in school. Fourth year? You have to run the whole perimeter. Ten miles. Everyone does it, it's required."

"Hmm. You forget, we didn't grow up in the same neighborhood, Finn. Down-city kids don't take field trips to the wall so they can run atop it for a day."

"Oh. I forgot. Well," I brighten, so that she will brighten. "That means, we for sure have to take that trip. We need to see everything, Jasina. Even other cities."

She reaches across the table to pat my hand. "You're getting ahead of yourself. I have a feeling this is just a one-time thing. We don't really belong here, Finn. We're going back tomorrow."

The disappointment in her voice is so present, it hurts me. "Maybe. But maybe not."

"What do you mean?"

"Well, surely I could ask."

Her eyebrow hikes up. "Ask what?"

"Ask Xi if... you know, we could live here."

"Live here?"

"Come on. You haven't thought about it? It hasn't even crossed your mind?"

"Well..." She blushes a little. "It has. But it's not possible. So why dream about it?"

"Hmmm. I don't like that answer." I pull the PPD out of my pocket and speak the name, "Cormac". I'm not sure what I expected to happen, but it sure wasn't his face popping up in the place where the map just was.

"Mr. Finn, how may I be of assistance?"

"Wow. That was weird."

"Yes," he agrees. "All travelers from the lower dimension often say the same thing. Now what can I do for you?"

But I don't answer right away, because he just said *all travelers from the lower dimension*... there are more of us?

I'm just about to ask about that when he speaks again.

"Don't be shy, Finn. I already know what you want to ask. I've also cleared it with Xi."

"Cleared *what*, with Xi?" I reply.

"If the two of you can stay in RhoXi during the course of your procedure, should you choose to accept Xi's offer, that is. Miss Jasina should plan on sleeping in tomorrow. No need to rush to get out of the room, which you can find by simply asking your PPD where it is! But you, on the other hand, I'll be knocking on your door at six AM sharp for your meeting with Xi at seven-thirty. Any more questions?"

The face on the hand-held screen smiles. Waiting.

"Uh… no. I guess that covers it."

"Perfect. Enjoy your evening. And remember, *Every Spark Has Its Purpose!*"

The face disappears. The screen goes black.

I look over at Jasina. "Wow," she says, unable to stop the laugh.

"Right?" I simply shrug. "At least we get to stay."

"Yeah," she pouts. "But I'll be here alone. That's dreary."

"Oh, I'm sure this meeting with Xi won't take all day. I'll probably be back by lunchtime. We'll take that desert trip then."

Her smile is wide now. "How fun. This is amazing. I can't believe it's actually real."

Neither can I, to be honest. But I don't tell her that.

I'm suspicious. I mean, after what happened to me back in Tau City—all the lies. My mother. My father. The Tower. All of it was just a bunch of lies. Why would this place be any different?

It's cynical, I get it. And not even warranted because Xi has been more forthcoming than anyone I've ever met. Except maybe Clara on her way through the tower doors.

She wasn't shy at all about screaming her loathing at me in front of the whole city.

Xi showed me everything about the augmentation. Answered every question. And then, when I was ready to say 'yes', he stopped me, and told me to think about it.

Even if letting Jasina live here was the only benefit of being augmented, I'd still do it. It's enough. Whether I turn into something powerful, like that Tyse guy, or not. Giving her a home like this, when yesterday our prospects where the dark, damp train tunnels of the world we come from, this feels like a true miracle.

The true workings of a god.

THE MEAL IS EXQUISITE. Simple food that both Jasina and I are familiar with, but all cooked and presented in fresh, new ways. Five courses in total. First, a single bite of freshwater fish, raw but silken, wrapped in something crisp and paper-thin, resting on a chilled ceramic spoon. I watch Jasina closely for her reaction, completely captivated by her every move and expression tonight. She doesn't hesitate, lifting it easily, letting it melt on her tongue.

Her verdict? A slow nod, a flicker of approval. "Yum!"

Next up, a delicate cut of mutton, seared rare, paired with something dark and sweet—a reduction of fruit she doesn't recognize. The scent is rich, smoky, a warmth curling through the air. This time, Jasina tilts her head, pressing her fork lightly against the meat. "Mutton shouldn't be this soft." She takes a bite. Her lashes flutter for half a second. "It shouldn't taste like this either."

I chuckle, amused and happy with her reaction. So much so, I almost forget to eat the soup. Which comes after the mutton and is a simple, clear broth layered with spice and shaved slivers of chicken.

The main course is beef. Obviously cooked over a flame from the grill marks and slightly charred taste. But it's got a tangy heat to it. Tell-tale signs of a marinade or a basting. A side of roots and greens, mashed until almost creamy, flecked with something bright and citrusy, sits on the other side of the plate. Maybe meant as garnishment, but it's also delicious and I eat it all.

Finally, dessert. A dense, honey-sweetened spice cake, served with something frozen and tart on the side. The contrast is sharp, but balanced.

My whole body is buzzing with happiness as I watch Jasina take a small bite. Bits of white frosting stick to her plump lips, forcing her tongue to sweep out, to lick it off.

Immediately, my brain short-circuits.

"You're staring."

"I'm thinking."

She sets her fork down, all mock innocence. "Oh? About what?"

I take my time finishing my last bite of cake. Then I lean in close—close enough that my words are just for her. What I really want to say... what 'old Finn' would say... is 'fucking you'. Preferably from behind so I can slap your ass.

Because that really *is* what I'm picturing right now.

But I'm 'new' Finn, so instead I say, "Dancing." And then I stand up and offer her my hand.

She takes it, delighted, smiling all the way over to the

boring dancefloor where a smattering of couples all sway together to the slow music.

I want to spin her. Make her cheeks go pink with heat. Make her dress swirl out, revealing her legs. And make her hair all messy.

But instead, I offer her my hand and we do the slow, boring dance like everyone else.

Except, with Jasina, it's not boring. Not at all boring.

Because her head is on my shoulder, and her breath is making heat against my shirt, and her breasts are pushing up against my chest and I love every moment of it.

It's like one, long hug.

It's enough.

Enough to make me forget.

Enough to give me faith.

Enough to make me hope.

A family of my own.

One I will not screw up.

One I will cherish until my dying day.

One I will protect with my very last breath.

One I would *never* sacrifice, not ever.

Not for anything.

*I FEEL BUZZED* when Jasina and I finally stumble into our room on the top floor of the Observation Tower, even though I'm not. It's not the wine making me feel drunk—it's this woman. She's intoxicating. And this evening out with her was exactly what I needed.

But not in the same way it would've been in the past.

I like the luxury. The fine dining, the nice clothes, the soft atmosphere. I like it. I miss it.

Jasina, on the other hand, didn't miss it because she never had it to begin with. A tease. That's all she got for being a Pledge and a Little Sister.

I didn't enjoy this night so much for my benefit, but for hers.

I want Jasina to have everything there is to offer in this world. She deserves all of it. And as we pause in the middle of the room, which is a seamless continuation of the entire experience—large, open, filled with opulence, every exterior wall made of glass—I think about how much more I could give her as an augment.

It would be about keeping her safe. Here. I could keep her here. Not in this room—but *maybe* in this room? She would never have to go back to that heavy place filled with grit and lies.

She's looking around the room, eyes pausing on the windows. It's easy to deduce what she's thinking because it's what I was just thinking too.

"Who cares," I say.

"What?" She looks up at me with those royal blue eyes of hers.

"The windows. If someone wants to watch, let them watch." And then I tug her towards me, kissing her as I walk her backwards and into the bedroom. There is just one dim light on, and it's soft, this light. Making her skin glow a little as I continue to kiss her.

Stopping at the end of the bed, I slip my tongue past hers just one more time before finally pulling back and placing my hands on either side of her head, and threading my fingers into her hair. "Everything is gonna be different from now on, Jasina. I promise. You will never be sacrificed. You will never be a piece to be played in the Game of Gods. I am going to give you the perfect life."

My right hand slips down to her stomach, and she blushes. "And this baby will never be Extraction Master. He, or she, will be innocent and pure. Brought up in truth, not lies."

"Is this your promise, then? To keep me safe if I agree that you should be augmented?"

It's a little bit of a slap in the face. I mean, I'm really, *really* trying to make a moment here. A memory that we can think back on. But what did I expect? This isn't Clara. This is Jasina Bell. She's not some trinket to be put on a shelf. She's a fighter.

"I want you to agree because I want to do it," I reply. "But if you say no, I won't. We'll leave. Walk right back through those tower doors, go back to the train line, and keep going. I saw the map. I know how it's all laid out now. But I also know that the gods on the other end of the line—the Alphas —they are playing for keeps. And I would not..." I hesitate here.

"What? You would not what?"

"I would not want you to come with me. Not like this." I press my hand against her belly. "This baby, Jasina. I want it. So bad. I want *you*. I want to keep you both safe."

"So where would I go?"

It's an idea that took root a couple of hours ago. Something I didn't really plan on saying out loud. "Tau City."

Her eyebrows crinkle. "Which one?"

"Our home, Jasina. I think all the bad people died. But Gemna's still there. I think you'd be safe there."

"Whoa." She puts a hand on my chest, pushing me back a little. "You wanna take me home and *drop me off*?"

"Well, how else can I keep you safe?"

"And expect me to… what? Just wait there, growing fat with child, until you… die or come home?"

"I hear what you're saying, but Jasina, I won't be able to keep you safe. I won't be able to travel down to the Alphas, exploding Extraction Towers, with you at my side and still keep you safe without being augmented."

She lets out a breath. "First of all, I was going to tell you to do the augmentation."

"You were?"

"If that's what you want. Yes. But let's just get this straight right now. I agree, I should not take any unnecessary risks. But that doesn't mean you get to leave me behind. It's not going to happen. If you want to go back to Tau City, then let's go. But once we get there, I say we blow up the God's Tower and seal this world off forever."

"I've thought about that," I say. "And I don't know if it's enough. It feels like putting our heads in the sand. Which is right where we started, ya know?"

"It's not putting our heads in the sand. It's making a deliberate decision to let this world be. To let these gods have their game. And to stay the fuck out of it."

She and I stare at each other for a few moments. Thinking. Picturing it. Going home. Telling our tale. Blowing up the doors to the God's Tower. And… and what?

"How do we go on," I ask, "knowing that the world is this great big mystery that we know almost nothing about? How do we live, each day, doing simple things that make no sense, or any difference, in the Grand Design?"

"Well… yeah. It's… horrible. I don't know, to be honest. It was just my first idea."

"Oh."

"Yeah. I was just getting started."

I laugh. "Do continue, then."

"My second idea is that… you get augmented. We leave here—together. Stay together. And play the fuckin' game."

"Play the Game of Gods?"

"If that's what you're calling it."

"That's what Xi calls it."

"OK. Game of Gods it is then. I say we play."

"To what end, Jasina? Our death?"

"Obviously not. We play to win."

"And how do we do that?"

The smile on her face starts small, but slowly, it grows into a grin. "We choose a side, of course."

"Xi's side."

"Who else? You get augmented—just like you want—and we get dealt into the game. A single Divinity Card to play with."

I chuckle. "Divinity Card?"

"Yeah, it's perfect," she says, her cheeks flushed pink with excitement, eyes dancing with this new analogy. But then her expression shifts, her brows drawing together as if she's working something out. "Actually… it's more than perfect."

"How do you mean?"

"Think about it. Divinity Cards. The Tower of Power."

I nearly guffaw—because she's right. Divinity Cards is both a child's game and a serious competitive card game back home. A deck of fifty-two playing cards numbered one through ten, plus face cards, and divided into four suits—Spark, Crest, Lore, and Devotion—plus four Divinity Cards with special powers.

Spark represents divine energy, the strongest of all forces. Crest symbolizes leadership, nobility, and dominion over others. Lore is knowledge, history, and the secrets hidden between the lines. Devotion is faith, obedience, and the power that comes from surrender.

Every player starts with just one card. Then, as the game progresses, they collect more, each one bringing them closer to the goal—building a ten-story tower in sequence. Some cards are drawn from the deck, others are traded, and the rest are stolen through the game's trump cycle. Spark trumps all. Crest follows, then Lore, and Devotion always loses—unless it's paired with a Divinity Card.

Those four cards are the real game-changers. God's Wrath strikes down an opponent's tower. The Chosen One guarantees victory in a challenge. Master's Bargain forces a trade, whether the opponent likes it or not. And Sweep cancels a special ability before it can take effect.

Jasina looks at me with something like revelation. "It's just like us. Just like this."

"How so?"

"Because just like in Divinity Cards, we started with nothing—just one card, one choice—but if we play right, we'll build something powerful enough to take the whole damn tower down."

She's right. It kind of perfectly sums it up. "Is this the game they're playing?"

Jasina laughs. "Building a god's tower?" Then she shrugs. "Would you be surprised at all, if stupid things like card games were really snippets of truth back in our Tau City?"

"No," I say, sighing heavily and rubbing my hands down my face. "Nothing surprises me at this point. The lies, though. The... *intent* to lie. It's so..."

"Insidious?"

I nod. "Yeah. It's gross—disgusting. It makes me sick to think about a whole society based on lies, Jasina."

Her excitement dims. "Do you think Xi is lying?"

"I mean..."

She laughs. "Yeah. So... we should be careful."

"We should. But—"

"I already know, I already know." She waves a hand through the air. "You *want* to be augmented."

"Are you OK with that? Because... I dunno, Jasina. If we're playing cards, augmentation feels a whole lot like Master's Bargain leveled up to a hundred if you ask me."

"And you *are* the Master, so..."

"I am. I hadn't ever put that together, actually. Master's Bargain." I squint my eyes, trying to force it to make sense. Because I feel like it does—like there's something more to know, but I can't quite grasp the bigger picture.

Jasina continues, "Obviously, I cannot make this decision for you, Finn. It's a *big* thing. But I will support you, no matter what."

This isn't the moment I fall in love with her. Not for the first time, anyway. But it is the moment when I know, for sure, that she and I are solid.

We are so much more than a couple—we're a *team*.

The physical distance between us is small, but I close it in two steps, taking her face in my hands. "I'm doing it for me, I want you to know that because I think it's important that you understand that this choice is for *me*, first. I'm in charge of it. I take full responsibility for it. And it's an easy choice because I want to give you everything and if this guy—this Tyse guy—if he's coming after us, I need to take care of it before we can move on. And that's got nothing to do with you. It was *my* mistake. It was my choice to send Clara into that tower. *Mine*. And even now, knowing what I know about how the world works, I'd do it again to save the rest of the city."

Jasina lets out a breath. "Did she not mean much to you?"

This question makes me chuckle, even though there's nothing funny about it. "No."

"Finn—"

I shake my head, pressing my palms just a tiny bit harder on her face. "If you'd asked me that question on the day of her Extraction, I'd have said, 'Of course she does—she is my life and my future.' But it isn't true. Was never true. I don't know what I felt about Clara. It doesn't make sense to me right now. But I do know this. You're never walking through a tower door without me holding your hand. It's not gonna happen. I will never give you up. I will fight, until my dying breath, to keep you safe. To keep our *family* safe. We're gonna play the game, Jasina. And we're gonna play to win."

Her eyes go bright with... I dunno, pride, maybe? Pride in me? Which is something I've never really seen in anybody's eyes before. Not *directed* at me. Because I wasn't *living* in Tau City, I was existing within a set of pre-programmed parameters. I was following a path, living a story that someone else wrote for me.

No more. I won't do it anymore.

Jasina raises a hand and places it on my cheek. Tenderly. "Of course, we're gonna win. There's no point in playing if we're not gonna win. And you, Finn Scott, are a winner." I will take this moment to my grave. I will never forget her faith in me.

And this is the banner I will fight under.

Her faith.

My fingers slide down her body and begin unhooking the bodice of her dress. Jasina is not shy, but she blushes a little as I silently do this. Her small smile creeping into a grin as I open the bodice up, revealing her breasts. They've always been a nice size. More than enough. But they feel swollen now, so I'm gentle as I hold them in my palms while I lean in to kiss her plump lips.

She sighs, kissing me back. And we kiss like this the whole time I'm pulling that bodice down her arms. It's attached to the skirt, so a few moments later, the whole ensemble drops to the floor.

This is when I step back, holding her at arm's length, taking in the shape of her body. She is very curvy. Wide hips, narrow waist. Perfect.

"Stop," she giggles.

"Stop what?"

"Looking at me like you want to eat me up."

"I do." And then I push her back a little, just enough to set her off balance so she drops down onto the bed. Then I lower myself down to a crouch and remove her boots, tossing them aside.

Now, she's only in her underwear—lacy panties that ride high on her hips and dip low in front.

"Lie back," I say.

She bites her lip, nervous. But she does as I ask.

And when she's settled, I put my hands on her knees and spread her legs open.

Fuck, she turns me on. I would like to do so many things with Jasina Bell, but tonight, I want to be careful with her. I want to cherish her. So I begin by kissing her inner thigh, just above her knee. And I take those kisses all the way up her leg until my tongue swipes over the smooth stretch of fabric between her thighs.

Her back arches, and she moans, hissing a little as I lick. Her fingers find my hair, and she grips it, urging me to give her more.

But I am determined to go slow tonight. To give her a

reason to remember this time over all the others that came before, or will come after.

Because this is the first day of our life.

We hold a single card.

And it's not mine, or hers. It's ours.

Tenderly, I close her legs and slide those panties off.

Then I lick her until she comes.

After which, I take off my clothes, get in bed, and put her on top of me.

I give her all the control, and she doesn't waste it

She fucks me slow. Staring me right in the face. Building the climax up to something epic.

And when we release—together, at the same time—I know that we are, and will forever be, linked.

Not just through the game we'll play, but the trust we'll share.

A KNOCKING **on the room door** wakes me up. Distant and soft, I hear a chirpy, almost annoying voice coming from the other side. "Mr. Finn? It's Cormac! The god awaits! Please wake up now!"

"Shit," I whisper, gently easing my arm out from under Jasina.

"What's going on," she mumbles, clearly still mostly asleep. It's alluring, this voice. And I would like nothing more than to climb between her legs and wake her up properly.

But stupid Cormac is still knocking. "Mr. Finn!" he sing-songs. "Time to go!"

"I'm coming," I say. Getting up.

But Jasina places a hand on my shoulder, her words filled with confusion, voice still groggy. "Wait. What's going on?"

"I have to go. Cormac's here."

Her eyelids flutter for a moment, then open to reveal those amazing royal-blue eyes. "I want to come."

"No," I shake my head. "It's... a procedure, Jasina. Medical, ya know."

"You don't want me there."

I hesitate. "It's... yeah. I don't."

She laughs, then leans up a little. "Kiss me goodbye, then."

"You'll be OK?"

"I'll manage."

"I'll miss you," I say. Kissing her.

"I'll miss you back," she says, then turns over, returning to her dreams.

"See you tonight."

But all I get in response is a low rumbling hum.

# CLARA

"*N**eedles and thread. Needles and thread!*"

That's all I hear, on repeat. Like the fool's chant has been branded into my brain.

But something has changed.

I am no longer strapped to a wall inside a cage of needles.

I'm somewhere else.

Some kind of amphitheater. Longer than it is wide, deeper than it is tall. With rows and rows of men lining the sides all the way up to the ceiling. In the center pit is a massive cage, but not any kind of cage I've ever seen. It's a twisted, tangled mess of bars, tunnels, and levels stacked on top of each other—reaching high into the dome of the amphitheater, stretching up and out, bending in ways that don't make sense.

It's a maze.

Scanning the writhing crowd of men, I find them packed into rows of makeshift seating platforms stacked around the edge of the pit.

It's disorienting. Confusing. Because they're not *men*.

They're… *monsters*.

Faces all twisted and wrong. Skin scarred so badly, it looks to be melting under the flashing colored lights. Their eyes glow. Some bright, like hot embers. Others dim and flickering, like failing bulbs. Their bodies are bent and ruined. Too big, too small, too asymmetrical. Flesh meets metal in ways that shouldn't fit. Joints bend the wrong direction. Some twitch uncontrollably. Others move with an unnatural jerkiness—like puppets on invisible strings.

And they chant. Mouths open as they yell, revealing the same crowded, crooked, and stained teeth of the one who yanked me back into this dimension.

For several moments, I can't make out what they're saying. The words all mesh together in the thunderous chant.

But then, I recall what Luther said. And that's when I remember the city we were in when those bot things scanned us on the train.

*Epsilon! Epsilon! Epsilon!*

They are calling for him. Their god.

*Epsilon! Epsilon! Epsilon!*

Each time they shout his name, the entire arena vibrates. Pounding like a heartbeat. They raise their fists into the air, pumping them as their feet stomp the floor, making the massive stadium shudder.

Above, brilliant floodlights glare down from a scaffold of steel beams and dangling cables, casting the cage in a blinding, artificial glow. It makes everything too sharp and harsh. Shadows stretch long, flickering as the augments move, writhe, and lunge.

I see everything from above, but when I try and see myself, I am... not me. I don't really have a body, just a space where a body should be. And inside, I see my heart shard, still glowing, but duller now. Like the used-up spark leftover in those unspooling needle tubes. I am just a hovering outline of a Spark Maiden. Pulsing and undulating to the beat of the chants. Inside the space, but apart from it too.

Suddenly, there is a violent shift as my senses explode.

Heat. Stifling. Heavy. Like I've been sealed inside a furnace. The air is thick—not just warm, but wet, dense with sweat, blood, rust.

Smell. Rot. A stale, meaty musk.

Sound. The chanting.

*Epsilon! Epsilon! Epsilon!*

All the mutant augments are staring at the head of the arena now. Their eyes fixed on a massive screen. The smiling face of their god—their Epsilon—up close and personal.

He is every bit the monster as the broken man unspooling me. His voice booms into the arena, bouncing off the walls as an echo that reverberates back into me with such a force, I float backwards in an out-of-control twist.

Then, suddenly, I am looking up at the screen, not down. A new viewpoint.

I feel Tyse before I understand what's happening.

I hear his mind racing...

*I am the executioner and the death.*

It's Tyse's voice, but different.

*I am the dark soldier, standing in the blood of the fallen.*

Lower. Deeper. Darker.

*The spool of Source, the thread of Spark—I am the machine made flesh.*

Holy shit. How do I get out? How do I stop hearing this? These are his private thoughts. Private killer thoughts! Probably things he's said a thousand times before battle, or whatever. Is this how he summons the will to kill?

I don't know. What I do know is that these are not words you tell your *lover*.

Panicking, I try to back out of his mind, but can't.

Shocked, I instinctively pull back. Then there is a feeling of...

Unspooling.

Unraveling.

Being pulled back, out of Tyse's mind, and into my own.

Back in the lab.

Epsilon grins. "Did you see him?" Then he laughs. "Did you hear him? The thoughts of a baby god? Or just mad science gone wrong? Which one do you think it is?" He rubs his hands together. "I'm so excited to find out. Should we find out?"

I can't speak. He has to know this. So it's not even a real question.

"Nothing to say, little dolly? Then I'll take that as a yes."

One last evil grin.

"Begin..."

*I walk the hush that follows ruin.*

*I utter no prayer—for I am the override.*

*A weapon of the sandy sea.*

*In the image, I am made and in the image, I will unmake.*

All of these words invade my mind as the voice of the man I love. I'm back inside him. Hearing his thoughts. His murder prayers. He's in the cage and facing him is a monster.

It charges. Too fast for something so broken. Its body is so twisted. Limbs too long, flesh too ruined. One leg drags, metal scraping against the blood-slicked floor, but the other propels it forward in a frantic, twitching lunge. The left arm is thick, stitched with some kind of metal, but the right is just bone wrapped in sagging skin, as if the muscle was ripped away and never grew back.

Tyse ducks, rolls, and comes up on his feet. Almost casually.

*For thine is the kingdom made in sand.*

*And thy rule was made in wind.*

He recites these strange prayers in his head, even as he strikes, tugging on the monster's right arm until it comes apart at the elbow. He throws the limb aside and it crashes against the cage bars with a sick, wet thud.

Bile comes up my throat, the urge to retch almost overwhelming.

The mutant monster roars, teeth gnashing, flecks of spit flying, as white pus oozes from the truncated limb.

I gag.

But Tyse doesn't. He doesn't even breathe. Just moves. Smoothly, easily, fluently. All instinct. His right foot pivots. His weight shifts. His body reacts before the monster even finishes its roar, grabbing for the other arm, the one with the threads of metal in it.

And off it comes. Right at the shoulder.

*And in the wind, as in the days of dark imprisonment, the new gods rose as tall as the hollow towers.*

*And in this rising, they conquered.*

*Swept the land of everything and left it clean like a bone.*

The mutant roars, stumbling forward, shoulders swinging for balance, arms missing. But still, it comes at Tyse.

With one sweep of his leg, Tyse trips the thing, causing it to crash forward onto its face. Even I hear the cracking of teeth over the roar of the crowd.

They are chanting something new now.

And at first, I can't make out the words. It's just sound... blending together. I strain to hear as Tyse stalks and circles the thing on the floor of the cage as it tries to get to its feet, but can't. Because it hasn't got arms to push itself up.

What are they saying?

Then, it snaps into place in my mind and suddenly, it's clear.

*Rise... a... god?*

*Rise a god! Rise a god! Rise a god!*

What the hell does that mean?

*"And on that bone, was born I."* Tyse is saying these killing

words out loud now. But I'm still there, inside him. So it feels like it's coming right out of my own mouth. *"I am the executioner and the death. I am the dark soldier, standing in the blood of the fallen. The spool of Source, the thread of Spark—I am the machine made flesh!"*

He howls this last word, stepping in close, looming over the armless monster on the ground. Then, in one swift, decisive move, he reaches down, grabs the thing's head, and twists it until it goes limp in his grip.

For a moment, he pauses there. Feeling the brokenness of the neck. Almost rolling it back and forth in his hands. Like he finds the looseness of it… interesting.

Then he lets go, the dead monster slumps to the ground like meat, and Tyse, without hesitation, steps over the corpse and starts running through the maze, climbing up levels, twisting around corners.

Looking for the next kill.

# TYSE

*I am the executioner and the death.*

*I am the dark soldier, standing in the blood of the fallen.*

*The spool of Source, the thread of Spark—I am the machine made flesh*

I'm lookin' for the next kill, and as I scan, my eyes glow so bright, they start castin' shadows across the scarred and rusted steel bars of the cage.

The crowd is stompin' a beat into the floor, making the whole fuckin' cage tremble. They are shoutin' something different now. Can't make it out. Don't fuckin' care.

Because just up ahead, hiding behind a thick beam, is my next victim. A hulking brute, grotesquely overgrown, flesh fused with metal plating. Arms thick as beams, gripping a rusted, bloodstained axe. Eyes—vacant and glowing.

And when I lock on to him, my whole world goes silent.

*A weapon of the sandy sea.*

*In the image, I am made and in the image, I will unmake.*

*For thine is the kingdom made in sand.*


"Come on, Tymmy! You know you want some!" Myra is holdin' out a canteen for me. It's filled with Sanddji, the local distilled spirit unique to Pi City, last stop before the Outlands,

I shoot Myra a look, not a nice one, either. "Call me that again and I'll black the other eye for ya."

I'm half jokin', half not. I don't like to be called Tymmy and she knows it. But she's buzzed on the Sanddji, which is also a slight hallucinogenic, and it's got a hold of her good senses. The only way threatening to punch a woman in the eye is funny is if she's already got one shiner, and it didn't come from me or some jealous lover.

She actually fell. *Fell.*

If I hadn't seen it with my own eyes, I would've never believed her and probably Jast would be dead by now because he's the kind of man who would definitely hit her back if she struck him first. And he'd for sure leave her marked up. A black eye is practically a calling card when it comes to Myra and Jast.

It wouldn't be the first time that they've tussled. For some reason, they're like oil and water those two, and I've gotten between them many times. Especially when they've been sippin' the Sanddji.

I don't like that he hits her like that, even though Myra doesn't give a fuck. It's not right. He should respect her a little more, not just because she's a girl, but because she's pulled him off the event horizon of an Outback veil on at least seven occasions and that last time they tangled, he knocked her out.

That was it for me. I told him if he ever touched her again, I'd kill him.

I don't *want* to kill him. I need Jast. I need all of them.

But I'd have done it on principle.

And then we'd be short a man on the way out and... die.

None of us want to die.

And anyway, Myra really did fall, and this *is* a joke, but I still don't like being called Tymmy. So she says, in an exaggerated manner, "Pardon me," taking a low bow, "*captain.*" Her eyes rollin' up to look at me, like she's beggin'.

And when I look at her, she... shimmers. But it's the wrong word. Because shimmer implies light. And Myra, looking up at me with those beggin' eyes, is not lit up. She's dark. Not dark as in looks, but actually fucking... empty. She's black, like space, outlined in glowing blue spark.

*What the fuck?*

*AND THY RULE was made in wind.*

*And in the wind, as in the days of dark imprisonment, the new gods rose as tall as the hollow towers.*

I SHAKE MY HEAD, TRYIN' to make Myra go away as the Augment's Creed spins through my head like a fuckin' bad-trip Sanddji flashback. "I don't have time to think about you now, Myra." It comes out in a whisper.

*I only have time for death.*

*And in this rising, they conquered.*

*Swept the land of everythin' and left it clean like a bone.*

The augment charges. Comin' at me with his arm raised, ax high in the air.

On instinct, I reach for the Versi, but of course, it's not there. So instead, I charge him. Head first. Full power. And for a moment, this confuses him. Because he's thinkin', *I've got an ax. Who the hell does this motherfucker think he is?*

Yeah, well... he's about to find out.

*And on that bone, was born I.*

*The executioner and the death.*

My head hits him square in the fuckin' gut and he goes reeling backwards, slammin' into the metal bars of the cage.

The breath comes rushing out of him in a great gasp, and then he's suckin' in air. Desperate for it.

Which is when I simply reach down and give that neck of his a little twist.

Just like the last guy.

When I look up, there's already another one comin'.

It's not just him, though. There's a whole crowd of Epsilon's mutant augments behind him. A wall of bodies, shifting and snarling, surging forward like a living tide. Glowing eyes—red, blue, sickly green—flicker in the hazy dust created by the stompin' feet of hundreds of men.

And as stupid as it sounds, I stop here to wonder about these eyes.

An augment's eyes are blue. Like spark.

So where the hell did all these colors come from?

*Later, Tyse. You're fightin'.*

Metal limbs clank as they rush me. Flesh rippling over unnatural muscle. Some dragging weapons, others bare-handed, eager to tear into me with just their fingers. Mouths split open, revealing those teeth—jagged and uneven, like Luther's.

A hallmark of Epsilon.

I actually stop to laugh.

But they keep comin'.

I don't have a plan. I don't ever have a plan. I don't *need* a plan. Because this is what I was made for. Instinct. Programmed muscle memory. I leap, fingers catchin' a jagged edge of bent steel, boots scraping for purchase. Haul myself up, muscles screaming, lungs burning. Higher. Faster. The horde of snarling mutant augments below, reaching for me and scrambling to follow.

I swing over a twisted beam, boots landin' hard on a grated platform.

A killing perch.

A place to bleed them dry.

The closest one behind me climbs, faster than I expected. Hands graspin', reachin'.

I drop low, swing under the beam, come up behind. Hook his ankle, twist. Bone snaps. He falls screaming.

*One down. Let's fuckin' go.*

I swing back up onto my platform and this is when I hear the chant again. It never stopped, my mind just blanked it out. It's back now.

All the mutants in the crowd are going wild. *Wild.*

*Rise a god! Rise a god! Rise a god!*

I pause, even though the horde is still comin'.

What does that mean?

But there's no time, the horde is here.

I let the fray come to me. One at a time, I take them out. Killing without thinking.

Somewhere beneath the skin of reality, another world hums. A different underground.

Another frequency.

A cavern cathedral, its ceiling strung with chains of glowing pearls, swaying in an unfelt wind. Below, a procession of monks draped in red-stitched robes moves in silent prayer, their faces hidden, their hands clasped around knives carved from bone.

One cuts his palm, lettin' blood drip into the roots of a massive, pulsin' crystal. The crystal drinks deep. It shudders. It sings.

I blink the scene away.

A mutant lunges.

I twist, crush his throat, move on.

The energy is thick, pulsin', pulsin', *pulsin'*…

Chanting. Chanting. *Chanting*… everything is vibrating.

Not from the impact of the stompin' mutants, but from *sound*.

The voices.

The monks are seated in a perfect circle, heads bowed, mouths open. No words. Just tone. Resonance. The chant isn't spoken—it's sustained. A living frequency, hummin' through the bones of this place, stitchin' it together.

I watch, unseen. Unheard. But I feel it—inside my chest, in the threads of my own body.

*Rise a god! Rise a god! Rise a god!*

It's not a prayer. It's a command.

It vibrates across dimensions, through worlds, bleedin' into the roar of the arena, into the mouths of the mutants above me.

The Spark hums in my veins, trying to sync, trying to answer. Trying to understand what it is I'm supposed to become.

I blink—

A hand grabs my ankle.

I'm back.

The augments are still coming.

I twist, snap, kill.

But my mind is still with the monks.

Their chantin'.

The crystal drinking blood.

It's wrong.

Spark hums, this sound *groans*.

It pulses like a dying star, pullin' instead of givin', devouring instead of burnin'.

I step forward—

*And fall into the cave…*

. . .

*MY FEET TOUCH THE FLOOR.* Silent whispers, like I'm not even here. Just a shift, a slip, like reality openin' itself to make room for me.

I am not in the arena.

I am not anywhere.

But I'm in this cave.

My head whips around, trying to understand. Wondering what the fuck is happening to me back in the cage. Am I dead?

I want to think about that. To understand it. But I can't stop lookin' around. I can't stop takin' it all in. The cave stretches wide before me, carved out of dark stone, slick with condensation, walls hummin' with somethin' unseen. The air is wrong. Thick with heat, with static. The scent of iron, wet stone, something burnt.

The monks are kneelin' now. A perfect circle around the crystal. Their robes are deep red, stitched with gold, pooling at their feet like liquid. Their hands—pale, veined, and human—grip bone-carved knives, their movements ritualistic. Rhythmic.

One by one, they reach forward, until their hands are hovering over the giant crystal. Then they slice open their palms, letting the blood drip onto the megalith.

It lands with a sound that shouldn't exist. Hiss. Sizzle. Like water hittin' coals, like somethin' breaking apart on a molecular level.

The thirsty crystal drinks deep.

It pulses.

Not like the sparkstone cave.

This is *not* Spark.

It groans. A deep, reverberatin' sound that pulls at somethin' inside me. Not a song, not a hum—a hunger. The monks do not react. They do not waver. They keep chanting, their voices merging into a single resonance, a single frequency that shakes the marrow in my bones.

*Rise a god! Rise a god! Rise a god!*

It calls to somethin'.

I step closer, watchin' the way the crystal feeds. The way the blood is gone before it touches the surface. The way the monks never hesitate, never falter, never pause to question.

I reach out.

The monk closest to me doesn't move. He doesn't acknowledge me. Doesn't even flinch.

But when my fingers graze his shoulder—

Somethin' gives.

Not a snap, not a tear. Just a shudder.

Like a plucked string.

And then—

He comes apart.

Not like a man. Not like flesh tearing or bone breakin'.

He *unspools*.

Threads slip from him in every direction, fine as silk, bright as stars. All at once, they hit me like a jolt. A jump from the Tau City Tower. Clara, dyin' in my arms. Anneeta, dyin' on the bench next to her.

Me, stealin' spark from that family.

He's gone.

The monk is gone.

Like breath in cold air.

Like whispers in an empty room.

Like a story, untold.

*I stole it.*

My hand hasn't moved. My fingers still curl over what was the monk's shoulder. But there is nothin' left beneath them. No weight. No warmth. No *him*.

The monk was.

Now he isn't.

The resonance in the cave shifts, like the song of it has changed, like the fabric of reality itself is registerin' his absence.

I feel it.

I feel everything.

The pulse of the crystal. The chant in the air. The ripple of somethin' vast, somethin' waiting.

I flex my fingers. The tingle is still there.

I could do that again.

I could do that forever.

*Rise a god! Rise a god! Rise a god!*


I'M IN THE ARENA, STANDIN' on a high, high platform. Way higher than I was. I have no idea how I got up here. No memory of nothin'.

But... it's like I don't care. Couldn't care even if I wanted to, cause I don't.

All I care about are the monks and what it felt like to... *take*. Those threads of spark. It was like... like I was being augmented. The first time, the second time, the third time.

But... *better*.

I can't explain it. It's like... a drug. Like living in the God's Tower in Tau City as an addict. But livin' there never felt *this* good.

Below me, the cage maze stretches down, down, down. Layers of twisted metal and brutalized bodies.

Did I do that?

Did I kill them all?

A laugh comes out of me.

Sharp, loud, disturbin'.

I want to leave here. Go back to the monks. Grab a little more of that thread.

But it's gone. This world has my full attention. The roarin' crowd makes the steel bars of the cage rattle like a living thing. Like it's got a heartbeat.

Not all the fighters are dead, though. There's three left. Just one level below me.

They don't move.

They're watchin'.

Waitin'.

They are augments, but the eyes are all wrong. One has yellow, one has green, one has red. All wrong. That's what Epsilon is doin' here. He's using these men to make... what?

An army?

Can't be.

These fuckers are weak. They are no match for me. Myra, all five-foot-two of her, could take these abominations out.

These three just below me, they're not like the others. They've got rage, no hunger. Their chests rise and fall, their glowing eyes flicker in the floodlights, but their feet don't move.

They don't want to fight.

But then—

*BOOM.*

A blast of static rips through the arena speakers.

Epsilon's voice follows. Loud. Amused. Dragged into a deep, distorted growl by the speakers stacked high at the far end of the amphitheater. His face fills the giant screen. Massive. Unnatural. A grinning god of metal and scar tissue.

*"Finish him."*

The words don't just echo. They press.

*Rise a god! Rise a god! Rise a god!*

The augments below flinch. Their bodies jerk, muscles

spasming, like puppets whose strings have just been yanked. One stumbles forward, his arms twitchin' as they grab the bars, tryin' not to fall.

It's a *long* way down.

Another gasps—a dry, choking sound—before he lurches a step toward me.

One of them—young, too young, half his face replaced with crude, rusted plating—tries to turn his head away. Tries to step back.

His legs don't listen.

He snarls. At himself.

Epsilon chuckles. His giant, grotesque face warps on the screen, pixels shifting, lines buzzing, godlike and bored. "Do you *seeeeeeeeeee*, Saarinen?" The voice wraps around me, slides into my bones. "They don't want to fight you. You're better than them. You're better than they could ever hope to be!"

The augments shake, their limbs snapping into motion, dragged forward by some invisible force. One of them lets out a guttural, agonized noise—more like a scream strangled before it ever reaches the surface.

I see it now.

Epsilon isn't just controlling them. He's *wearin'* them.

Three bodies, one will.

And I am exactly where he wants me.

I REACH DOWN, but I'm not in the cage. I'm in the cave and I'm reaching for nothin'. It's empty. Not like a room after someone leaves. Not like a battlefield after the bodies are cleared.

*Wrong.*

There's no trace of the monks. No footprints. No blood. No echo of their voices bouncing off the stone.

*I did this.*

Taking a step forward, my boots hit the rock floor without a sound. The air is too still, thick with something I can't name. My breath feels loud, sharp. My fingers twitch. I don't know what they're reaching for. There's nothing here...

Except there *is.*

The space where the monks were is warped. Like the air itself is trying to hold on to something that no longer exists anymore. It shimmers—like heat on pavement.

I reach out.

Nothing.

But my arm—my own arm—leaves a streak of light in its wake. Blue. Glowing like wire-thin threads. I draw a heart, thinkin' of Clara and her talent of drawing shapes in the air with her light. I find myself smiling as I watch it hang in the air in front of me.

I have spark in me.

Just like her.

It's good. It's... *good.* It is. I'm gonna need this spark.

It's for Clara. She's gonna need it.

*So you can steal it back, right Tyse?*

*I didn't make the rules now, did I?*

I want to tell myself I won't take it back. But it's true. I will because *I feed on her.* And when I kill, and take the spark from all those monks—I can spool her back up after she's drained to near death.

Negative feedback loop. I wish I didn't know what that was. That I didn't understand it the way Clara doesn't understand it. But I do.

I close my fist.

A sound—so soft I almost miss it—slips through the cavern.

A sigh.

Not from my lips.

From everywhere.

A final exhale of somethin' that doesn't even realize it's gone. I swallow hard, turnin' to the crystal megalith. It's still there. Still pulsin'. Still hungry.

And alone.

Because I unmade those monks. I unspooled them.

A deep groan rolls through the cave, vibrating through my ribs, then the ground yanks me back—

The Arena.

I blink.

The roar of the crowd slams into me like a hammer. Floodlights burn too bright. Metal bars gleam with fresh blood. Three bodies at my feet that I don't remember killin'.

Fuck. I don't even remember movin'.

I breathe in. Even. Steady. My heartbeat is slow—way too slow.

Something hums inside me.

Not Spark. Not right.

A long, static-drenched chuckle rumbles through the speakers.

Epsilon.

"Ohhhhhh, my boy." His voice is silk and wire, pleased, amused. *Proud.* "Now, wasn't that fun?"

I stare at the bodies.

At my own hands.

I don't answer.

It wasn't. Not because I didn't enjoy it, but because I don't remember it.

I do, however, remember the monks.

And I think I could unspool 'till the end of time.

The smile is just creepin' up my face when I hear somethin'.

Strainin' I lean forward. And when I do this, I slip right out of my fuckin' body. Just… walk away from it—like a shadow. And when I look over my shoulder, the rest of me is slumpin' to the ground.

I look down at myself, only to find that… I'm *him*.

Empty man.

Except my insides aren't black anymore, I'm filled up with spark. Glowin' bright blue. Full.

Because I'm the spark stealer.

The unspooler of monks.

What the hell is happenin' now? Can this shit get any weirder? Can this fuckin' day get any worse?

I'm pissed off, fuming—but then I hear it again… a voice. A sweet song of a voice compellin' me to keep walkin'.

I do, and when I get to the edge of the platform, I just… float. Like a ghost.

This time, when I look behind me, there's a group of mutants on the platform next to my body. I have a moment of panic that they might kill me, but this fear disappears as quick as it came because they pick me up, raising me over their heads, and carefully start lowering me down the cage maze.

I look up at the screen where Epsilon's face is, and realize he's takin' care of it. So I turn back to the empty air holding me up and let that song draw me in.

Floating down, my feet feel nothin' when they touch the ground. But they are walkin' with purpose. Heading towards a section of yelling and raging mutants.

I don't feel in control right now. It's like I'm being guided. Or forced. Like a puppet. I slide right through the mutants, closing my eyes when it happens, holdin' my breath.

It's cold. Freezing. But when I come out, I'm no longer in the arena. I'm in a hallway. I laugh a little as I look over my shoulder. It's not funny. It's disturbin', actually. Because not only did I just walk through men, I just walked through walls.

Again, the song snaps me back to my mission.

Is this a mission?

And my feet are walking. Well, not walking. Floatin'. I go through a few more walls, letting myself be carried on this current, so I can think about what's happenin'.

I left my body. Something is calling me towards it.

*No, not that part, you dumbass! The part about the monks!*

Right. I killed them. Much like I've killed others to steal their spark. But I was never among them before. This is the first time I've crossed a dimension without Clara. Except, I didn't actually cross. I was in two places at once.

*Tyse, you idiot! You're still in two places at once.*

So what's different?

Looking down at myself, seems pretty obvious. The spark is what's different. The fact that I can see myself as a reservoir, number one. But also, the *way* it happened.

I plucked a loose thread from each of those monks and I just... unraveled them. Like an old-timey spinnin' wheel. Wool into yarn. Spark into thread.

*What's it mean though?*

There's no time to figure this out, because the next wall I walk through places me right in front of Clara. I stop, my insides sinking with dread. Fear. Panic. Rage. All of it hits at once as my eyes scan down her body. She's captured inside a cage. It looks like an augmentation threader, similar to the one I was in earlier, but not exactly like it.

That's not the worst part, though. The worst part is her coloring. She's... *gray*. Dull blue. Sun-bleached blue.

And then, I hear her voice. A voice from the past. Another time, another dimension, another life, it seems.

"Our towers were tall too," Clara is saying. "But not this tall."

We're back in Tau City, on our way to the health center to get her checked out. I still think she might be lying, she still thinks I'm a dick.

"And they were just made of plaster and stones, I think." Clara looks up at me. "I don't know how to make buildings. They just didn't look like *that*." She points to the skyscrapers. "They looked... natural. Like the canal. Like they fit in with it. All of my city was covered in muted shades of beige and blue. And most of the towers had domes. Sun-bleached blue domes. Almost gray, some of them, because they were so old."

*Sun-bleached blue domes.*

All right. Calm down, Tyse. Be rational. Think. You were made to think. You're one of the smartest fuckers on this whole world. Do not overreact.

*Sun-bleached blue...*

I snap out of it and suddenly I'm me again. Not in my body, just in my mind. And that mind is workin' now. Figurin' shit out.

Tubes. Needle-thin tubes. A cage full of them. And this cage is over top of Clara's body. Inside the tubes there is spark. But it's not glowin'.

*Sun-bleached blue...*

It's used up. Dead.

I look back, over my shoulder. See nothin' but a concrete wall. But in my mind's eye, I see me in the arena. Fightin'. Using up spark like it's limitless.

I look back at Clara. Trace the tubing filled with dead spark to the wall. Walk over to it, step through the wall, and on the other side, I see another room. This one with a table.

An augmentation table.

That motherfucker.

*He used her to thread me.*

Do not overreact.

Just... react.

So that's what I do. I go back through the wall, over to Clara, and place my hand on her cold, damp forehead.

Then I lean down, kissing her. And when my lips touch hers, I *unspool myself.* Everything I just stole from the monks, I give to her. Threads come off me. Tiny, wiggling threads of spark. I give her all of it. Every drop.

I fill her back up as I empty myself.

And then I just... disappear.

# CLARA

**M**y eyes snap open.

*Tyse!*

I try and look around, but I can't move.

"Don't try and get up," the snarky god says. Then he's hovering over me. "It won't work. You're still in the harvester."

*Harvester.*

"Give me a moment here…"

There's a clicking, then a short hum, and then—"Ouch! Ow!" Slicing pain all over my body as the needles withdraw. It's a sick feeling. Like worms sliding under my skin.

But it's quick, and moments later, it's over and the cage of needle-thin wires, all dripping with dull-gray fluid, pull back across the room, retracting to the opposite wall.

I feel sick. He *harvested* me. He took my spark.

"Oh, come on now. It wasn't *me* who took your spark." He points to himself. "Am I glowing? No. I didn't take your spark."

"You captured it." My words are low and husky. "In some kind of vat. Like Delta does."

"Don't be silly. My process is nothing at all like Delta's."

"It does the same thing, though. It steals… *life.* It steals!"

"It does," he says, letting out a breath. Almost as if I'm boring him. "But I need it. It's science, you see. And the end always justifies the means."

"That's sick."

He waves a hand in the air, backing off a little, but remains in front of me. "Yes, yes, yes I'm sick. I'm mad. Insane. Deranged and demented!" His voice rises as he turns and starts to pace in front of me. "Psycho, unhinged... a nutter." His smile is big. "But you..." These words come out as a cackle that is not quite as creepy as Luther's, but it's close. "Look at *you*." He pans a hand down my body, which I can't actually see because I'm strapped to a wall. Completely immobilized. "A little battery, is what you are. Rechargeable, even. How clever. I have to be honest here, Clara, I wasn't expecting it."

I have no idea what he's talking about. And frankly, I don't care. "Where am I? Where is Tyse?" He's the only thing I care about.

The ugly god smiles at me. His eyes filled with madness. "Good question. Where *is* Tyse. Why don't you tell me?"

"What are you talking about?"

He breathes in. Holds it. Lets that breath out. His eyes bore into mine. A challenge. "Did he... help you?"

"Help me?" I laugh. "Does it look like I got help? I'm strapped to a fucking wall!"

Epsilon's brow furrows, considering this. "Yeah, it's weird. But... you're... *alive*."

"OK? So?"

"I... drained you. To thread Tyse. And he took it all. He's a greedy fucker when it comes to spark."

"You have no idea what you're talking about. He doesn't even crave spark." But the moment these words come out, I'm questioning them. Because he *did* live in the tower.

He *is* addicted to it.

Epsilon must be reading my mind because he smiles. "Yeah, Clara, he does. He's an augment. He lives on it, just like me. I breed them. You. Others like you. And yet, not like you at all. Tau City... who knew that place could produce something like... *this*." His hand gestures to my body.

"I don't understand what you're talking about."

"Of course not. You grew up in an isolated world. You were fed lies your whole life. Which is how it is for all women in the factory dimension, but it was different for you. Because Tau, the actual god of your factory, was killed hundreds of years ago."

I know this because Tyse told me. But his death is all I know about him. So despite myself, I'm intensely curious about what happened to my god. Against my better judgment, I urge him on. "What do you know about the god in my tower?"

Epsilon shrugs. "He was kind of a dick. No one liked him. Reminds me of Delta, actually. We were raised together, obviously."

"Wait." I shake my head. "What? You were *raised* together?"

"Of course. We were the originals. There were twenty-four of us in the beginning." His voice changes, booming. "In the first days, the Gods were but sand, scattered and formless, until the furnace shaped them into glass. And the glass was struck by fire, and the fire became light, and the light became Spark, and the Spark was the breath of creation, burning eternal in the heart of all things."

Epsilon shrugs. Like his fervent outburst was nothing special. "Except, it wasn't *all* things, was it. The spark doesn't burn in the hearts of all. Just us. And only us. The gods."

The heart. If I could look down, I would. To see the shard. To see if it's there. Thank my dead god I can't move. Because this one here is very perceptive. He would've noticed. And maybe it wouldn't be obvious, but this slip-up would've made him curious and that would be the end of my secret.

I need to change the subject. "I'd never heard that before. What were those words you just said? Did they come from some kind of book?"

His laugh is immediate. "Something like that. Listen, I understand your curiosity. And I'll answer your questions if you answer mine. Deal?"

"It depends. What do you want to know?"

He doesn't answer right away. Instead, he starts pacing. Which makes me nervous because he's not staying directly in front of me and I can't turn my head to follow his movements. After almost a minute of this, he stops, barely on the edge of my peripheral vision. "How did you recover?"

"Recover from... what you did to me? When you slammed that cage into my body?" I jut my chin, as best I can, at the cage. Which is directly across from me, on the opposite wall. "Thousands of needles—"

"Yes, yes, yes," he cuts me off, waving a hand in the air. "Blah, blah, blah. I did this, I did that." Now he's right in front of me. Right in front of my face. Eyes blazing. "*How*?" He demands this answer now. "How did you survive? You should be dead. I gave him every drop of your spark. You were a *husk*."

I snicker. "Have you ever heard that saying... you catch more flies with honey?"

"*Tell me!*" This time he roars it. And these words come out in a booming, godly shout that shakes the walls and make my whole body vibrate.

Every part of my body... shrinks. Or... tightens.

Fear.

I swallow, blinking. "I don't know." And my voice is as small as his was large.

He's still in front of me—leaning in and down so he's eye level. His eyes search mine, looking for the lie. But it's not a lie, and he knows this. So he lets out a breath and takes a step back.

"My turn," I say, forcing myself to be brave. "Tell me the story of the Tau god."

Epsilon scoffs. "That's not a question, that's a book."

"Is it a book I'm allowed to read?"

He's standing in profile now. So I get a side-eyed glare for this question. "Someone helped you."

"What?"

"Someone fed you. Who was it?"

"Fed me?" *Be careful here, Clara. Because you* have *been getting fed. And he will see your lie.* "I think it might be the jumps."

"Jumps?" His eyebrows furrow.

"Yeah. So... in the Tau City tower—the ruined one, in Tyse's city, where the god used to live—well, it's inhabited by spark addicts now."

For some reason this makes him smile. "Go on."

"And... this is where Tyse lived. So this is where I ended up when I was Extracted from the factory to feed the baby god they were growing."

He looks very pleased with what I'm saying. "Go on."

"And in this tower, they had... well, it was like a little city. All self-contained because the tower people were all addicted to the residual spark leftover from the god. They live inside it, you see. Free. Thousands and thousands of people."

Epsilon pulls up a chair, takes a seat, props a foot on his opposite knee and leans back. "Keep going, Clara."

"All right. So... we live on floor ten. But on floor eight, there was a... like... store. And a laundromat." I smile, because I like that word. "And these guys who would sell jumps and jolts."

"Tell me more."

"Well, the jolts were small packages of spark." It's here, at this point, when I realize I have power. And the power comes from my story. Because he has no idea what I'm talking about. Whatever happened up in Tau City after the explosion, this god has not heard about it. How long as he been down here augmenting these men?

It doesn't matter. *Just keep talking, Clara.*

"Jumps were big packages of spark. Anneeta, that's our baby god, she was born in the tower, obviously. Very addicted to the spark. So addicted, she couldn't leave. But we needed to escape."

Epsilon leans forward, almost entranced.

"So we bought a bunch of those jumps from the guys on eight. And took them with us on the train. And I fed Anneeta my spark to keep her alive, and Tyse fed me those jumps to keep me alive until we got to Delta."

He leans back again, blowing out a breath. "Wow. I have to say, I was not expecting you to be so forthcoming. What an entertaining story." He frowns. "Unfortunately, it didn't answer my question."

"Well, because I wasn't done. You see, feeding me all those jumps... it... changed me."

"Changed you, how?"

My answer comes out so quick and with such conviction, even I believe it. "It created a reservoir inside me. Like a lake. Only instead of water, this lake contains spark. So I can pull from it, I think. I don't know for sure. I'm not doing it consciously. It just... happens. The same way breathing happens."

"Hmmm."

I can't tell if this hum is a note of satisfaction or disapproval.

"That's my answer," I say. "That's all I know. And now you

owe me one." I ask a more careful question this time. Direct and focused. "What happened to the god Tau?"

Epsilon's eyes narrow down a bit, like he's about to deny me. But then he shrugs. "He tried to ascend—and failed."

"What do you mean?"

"Gods evolve. We have wants and needs." He chuckles here. Pans a hand to the lab around me. "Mine lie squarely in augmentation. But Tau's... he was obsessed with the Source."

My stomach drops and once again, my whole body goes tight. "*What* source?"

"The source of spark, of course. He tried to merge with it. He thought it would make him more powerful. But instead of ascending, he was rejected, burned out, and unmade." Epsilon shrugs. "He killed himself. It was a fool's mission."

He killed himself. Looking for the Spark Source.

Which I have not only seen in some dream-like state, but in person.

This is when I realize that Epsilon is trying to read me again. And I need to be very careful. So I ask another question. "But my city, the factory. It kept running."

"Yeah. Quite well, actually. I mean..." he leers at me for a moment. "Look at *you*."

*Don't panic, Clara. This thing is not interested in you like that. He's not even the same species.*

My inner voice is right, but... that doesn't really account for obsession.

I keep going, taking the story to its logical conclusion. "So... there was no god in the Tower in that other dimension. And somehow, my factory city stopped... harvesting?"

Epsilon gives me a half-hearted shrug. "I suppose."

"But why would they stop? Did they know the god died?"

Epsilon has lost interest, distracted by his own thoughts. "How the hell should I know?"

"Maybe... it just collected? In those vats, or whatever? Until it was full? And once that happened, they just let all the girls keep their spark? Because what is the point of harvesting it if no one's gonna come collect it. I don't know. Maybe they got nervous and came up with an Extraction as way to make themselves feel better. One woman, every ten years? Even I have to admit, compared to what I saw in Delta, it's a good deal."

Epsilon doesn't even bother answering. I don't even think he heard me.

"Weird, though," I say, "that the spark kept going. I suppose it's natural. There would be residual spark. I mean, that's why everyone was addicted to it in Tyse's Tau City."

He's pacing now, probably coming up with a new way to kill me. And I've figured out what I needed, so now it's time to come to terms with where I am.

Which is imprisoned in a cage.

"What do you want from me? I mean, I understand that you thought I'd be dead after... whatever it was you did to Tyse." I want to know about him. I want to ask, so bad. But I don't. I force myself to keep going. "But I'm *not* dead. So... you can use me again. What do you want from me?"

Now he slowly tracks his gaze to mine. We lock eyes. I hold my breath, feeling sick about what request might come out of his mouth.

But he doesn't speak. Instead, he strides over to me and releases my head from the bindings. Then he points off to my left, and now that I'm able to, I turn and look.

A screen. Quite large, so there's no mistaking what I'm looking at.

It's Tyse. He's lying down on a table. Strapped to it in

much the same way I'm bound to this wall. The cage of needle-like tubes isn't covering his body, but hovering above him.

"He's dying, Clara."

I look at Epsilon. "Whatever it is you're going to ask... my answer is yes."

Which makes the god chuckle. "Of course it is."

"As long," I add, "as it will save him. Take whatever you want from me. I've got a lake of spark inside me, remember? I *will* recharge. Give Tyse whatever he needs."

He puts up a hand. "You're getting way ahead of yourself. It's not as easy as harvesting you."

"No." I look him dead in the eyes. "What you did to me wasn't a harvest. It was..." I shake my head. Because while I do have a word for it, I'm hesitant to use it.

"Unspooling." And then I don't have to. Because it comes tumbling right out of his mouth. "That's what I did to you. Because, on the other side of that wall." He points to the wall across from me where the cage of needles is. "That's the room Tyse is in. I unspooled you so I could thread him back up."

"I don't understand. What is... threading?"

"That's how you augment someone. It's the opposite of what I did to you. The spark I took was injected directly into Tyse's bloodstream. And there, it made secondary nervous, circulatory, respiratory, endocrine, skeletal, muscles. All of it. Every system had a tiny nano twin. Tyse is different, though."

"Different how?"

"When he came here, he'd already been threaded twice."

"So?"

"It's not done." Then he laughs. "I mean, I do it. But I'm a mad scientist. I'm experimenting on these men. They are... worthless. Skins. Nothing more. Tyse is an actual Delta augment. Sanctioned and served in the Sweep Army. He's legit. They do not re-thread augments in the Sweep."

"Maybe that's why he failed?" I ask.

Epsilon nods. "I was thinking that as well. But I'm not convinced. At any rate, we started the re-thread and only discovered afterward that this was his third threading. It took, but only because the first threading was never finished."

"It filled in the gaps," I say.

"That's what I think."

"OK. So... what's the problem."

"What's the problem?" Epsilon chuckles. "Look at him. He did spectacular. I mean, honestly, Clara, I've never seen such a fighter in my life. He was... possessed. Like he *loved* it."

I make a face. "That doesn't sound like the Tyse I know."

He just stares at me for a moment. Then blinks, like he's pulling himself out of a thought. "Why would he show you *that* side of him? And anyway, he was discharged seven years ago. He's had time to come to terms with life outside Sweep. He's got it under control." He turns away, but then side-eyes me over his shoulder. "At least he did."

"What do you mean?"

He doesn't answer, just walks over to the screen showing Tyse lying on the table in the next room and touches it. The scene changes. And it's one I recognize. Because it's a recording Tyse's point of view as he was fighting.

That's the point of view I saw while Tyse was fighting. "What is that?" I ask. "How did you get in his head? How can you see that?"

Epsilon grins. "All augments can be hacked, Clara. That's what I did when I threaded him. I hacked."

"I don't know what that means. Hacked? It sounds like you're going to cut him up with a hatchet."

"Right. I forgot. You're a simple girl." I think that was an insult, but I don't press. He continues. "You know what a puppet is, right?"

I swallow hard. Practically gulping. Because it's not a hard train of thought to follow.

"Right," Epsilon says. "You get it then. I am his puppet master. I'm pulling all the strings."

My thoughts are racing. Is this true? Is Epsilon controlling Tyse?

"I know what you're thinking," he says. "You're thinking... that I'm a liar. But I assure you, Clara. All augments can be hacked by their gods. Delta was controlling him before this."

"That's certainly not true. Tyse hadn't even been home to Delta since he was fourteen."

Epsilon guffaws. "Don't be simple now. He doesn't need to be *home*." Now he squints his eyes at me. "Do you even know what we are?"

"What... gods are?"

"Yeah. Do you know what we are?"

I shrug. As best I can in these bindings. "I don't know. I've never thought about it before."

"No. Why would you? Well, we're not human. We're..." He turns his head and squints at me. "Do you know what a computer is?"

"That thing." I point to the screen.

"Kind of. Close enough, I guess. You understand that computers are machines."

"You're a machine?"

Now he chuckles. "In a very crude way, yes. All gods are machines. It's a long story, the take home message is that my reach is very far. Well, not *my* reach, per se. All my augments are close. But Delta, for instance. Or Alpha. Or any of them who make augments. They can see as far as their farthest augment travels." He points to the screen again, where Tyse's fight is still playing. He's ripping off limbs. "I see through his eyes. I will always see through his eyes now. There is no escape from the puppet master."

An overwhelming sense of doom swallows me whole.

"That's right," Epsilon says. "You're trapped. Forever. And so is he. Because as long as he lives—and this is the important part, Clara—as long as you feed him, he *will* live. And as long as he lives, I will use him. I will drain you to death every time. So if you're lying about that spark reservoir inside you... well." He laughs. "We're gonna find out soon enough, so it makes no difference to me at all. But to you? You will die, sweet Clara. It's as simple as that."

"I don't care."

"You don't care if you die?"

I press my lips together as I shake my head. "No. I don't care if I die. The only reason I'm here is because I was sacrificed to my god. And my god is dead. So instead, I will sacrifice myself to Tyse."

Epsilon lets out a long sigh. Almost as if he's tired.

And it occurs to me now that he's... different. Not as strung out. Not as insane as he first came off. I can't tell if it's because that was all an act, or if he's... tired. And this weariness makes him a little bit vulnerable.

Either way, it's worked, this act. Because I see him as a person now. Someone I can converse with, at the very least. And I'm making a deal. A deal that will save Tyse and surely sign my own death certificate.

"I don't want to live," I say. "Not without him. He's my world now. So whatever it is you're going to do, just do it. And I will willingly give you every drop of my spark if you promise to give it to him."

Again, he sighs. "You know, I could just... take it."

"And do what with it? If not put it into Tyse. Clearly, whatever it is you've been doing to these men here—it's not working. I mean, look at them." I want to say, 'Look in the mirror,' but that would provoke him. Which isn't my goal, so I don't. "You need us. You need us to complete whatever it is you're doing down here. You might never get another chance like this. Tyse is... the cornerstone in your crown. You need him. And if you need him, you need me."

Epsilon stands up, turns his back, and starts to walk over to the door.

"Wait! Where are you going?"

He pauses, his hand pressing into the door, as if he's about to push it open. Then gives me one last side-eye. "If you want to be a sacrifice, then how can I resist?" With that, he's through the door and it swings closed behind him.

Movement on the screen catches my attention and I strain my neck to see what's happening. Epsilon enters the room next door where Tyse is lying unconscious on the augmentation table. He does something here—fingers tapping on a control panel—and the needle-wired cage suspended above Tyse begins to lower.

This is it. It's happening. He's going to harvest me again.

But it's going to be OK.

This is what I tell myself as the cage of needle-thin wires across from me comes to life and begins to migrate across the distance between us.

It's going to be OK. It's going to be OK.

And I say this, I picture us. Tyse and me sitting in that restaurant after I had all those brain scans at the Tau City health center.

The look on his face. The seriousness in his eyes. And the way he demanded, gently, and firmly, that if we were going to be partners, we needed two things.

Absolute trust.

And absolute loyalty.

So as the needles stab my skin, and as the spark of life is sucked out of me, I repeat his words like a mantra.

*If I have your back, then you must have mine.*

I've got your back, Tyse.

And I am one-hundred percent sure that you will have mine.

# PART 4

"Scholars have long debated the authenticity of the Augment's Creed. Whether it was recited before battle, whispered during shutdown, or merely etched into the walls of some broken mind— we may never know. But its lines endure.

Not as doctrine, but as a kind of final prayer. A machine's reckoning.

'I am the executioner and the death...' Not a boast. A confession.

I do not ask you to forgive them. Only to hear them."

**—Master Finnegan Scott, Lectures on the Line So Bright, Final Chapter: "The Creed and the Quiet World"**

# JASINA

*Something is chirping.*

It's not loud, but it *is* offensive. I'm exhausted. The weeks of traveling, not to mention my new pregnancy status, have finally caught up with me and all I want to do is sleep. I have no interest in anything else right now and even my offer to go with Finn for his first augmentation appointment was half-hearted.

Of course, if he *wanted* me to come with him, I'd have gotten up and gone. But, as he said, this is a medical procedure. And even though he's making this decision of his own free will, there's no way he's not going to be nervous. How could he not? It's a major decision.

So when he told me no, my relief—though internal—was immediate. I'm just so tired.

The chirping continues. Relentless.

I sit up quickly, swatting hair away from my face, and blink. "Oh, my god, what is that incessant noise!"

That's when I realize it's coming from inside a pile of last night's clothes, which are lying in a puddle on the floor at the end of the bed, right where Finn left them when he stripped me naked last night.

Ohhhhh, last night.

I smile as I crawl down the bed, picturing all the things he did with that mouth of his. I don't mind Finn's rough side, I really don't. But his soft side is even better.

Lying flat on my stomach, I reach over the side of the bed,

grabbing at my discarded skirt until I fish out the PPD—chirping found.

I just... don't know how to stop it. So I'm shaking it, desperate for some peace and quiet so I can go back to sleep, when Xi's face appears on the screen. I gasp, realizing I'm naked, and start clutching for covers. "My god—and I mean that in the most disrespectful way—you should not be allowed to just pop in on me like this!"

"I'm very sorry," he says, seemingly unaffected by my panic. "But you answered my call."

"What call?"

"Did the device not ring?"

"That chirping?"

"It's called a 'ring' and it means someone would like to talk to you. You answered my call, so I simply assumed you meant to. Should I call back later?"

I want to tell him yes, but I want to know what he wants even more. "No. I'm fine." And I am, having managed to cover myself with the sheet. "What did you need to talk to me about?"

"I have planned a day for you, if that's all right."

"What kind of day?" My irritation melting as the moments pass.

"I thought you'd like to meet some local ladies. They have a book club you could join. It comes with a high tea. That's generally something women enjoy from my experience. Does this sound like something you're interested in?"

"It is... but what will I wear? All I have is last night's dress."

"There's a package outside the door. I took the liberty. If you'd like to shop for clothes today, you could do that as well, but I figured you'd need something to get started."

"I don't have any coin so—"

"Oh," he waves a hand at me on the screen. "It's free, Jasina. There's a card in the package with your name on it. Any time anyone in one of my cities expects you to have coin, just give them the card and it will be taken care of."

"Wow. That's very generous of you."

"It's the least I can do. Also, you needn't worry about going back to 702."

My heart does a little flip at this revelation. "What do you mean?"

"I mean for you to stay here."

"What about Finn?"

"Oh, he'll be home every night, don't worry about that. The procedure is going well by the way."

Now I feel horrible for not asking about Finn's status. "What's happening to him? I mean, right now?"

"Today is a bunch of tests. A sort of preparatory phase. This will last most of the day and he'll get a single injection tonight to prime him for tomorrow."

I let out a long breath. "It sounds… serious."

"Serious?" Xi laughs. "I suppose it is, but no. Not really. It's all very routine, I promise. You will not notice anything different about him tonight."

"What about tomorrow night?"

He smiles. "We can have that discussion tomorrow. In the meantime, is there anything I can get you, Jasina? Is there anything you need?"

"Well… no. Thanks for the clothes. And the night out. And the room. It's all been very nice."

"You're absolutely welcome. Here in RhoXi, we value our citizens. Especially the upper-class ones, like you. It is my pleasure to make your stay here as enjoyable and comfortable as possible."

"Upper class?"

He doesn't clarify. Just asks another question of his own. "Can you be ready in an hour and a half? I have set up a guide for you. Her name is Lilika. She's part of the book club. And she'll take you around the Exchange District where all the shops are, if you'd like. Ask her anything, she has all the answers."

"OK. I'll be ready. Thanks, again."

He nods, then his face disappears from the PPD screen.

I just sit there on the edge of the bed for a moment, wondering how life can change so fast from one day to the next. It's… weird.

But not weird enough to prevent me from enjoying this new, good fortune so I get up, still clutching the sheet to my body, and pad over to the door. I open it a peek, making sure nobody's out in the hallway since I'm half naked. Then quickly reach down to pick up a pale-yellow box that is shiny and high quality. It's tied with a sun-drenched-blue satin ribbon.

The box is very big, so I balance it on my hip with one arm, while trying to keep the sheet from falling with the other. Then quickly disappear back inside the room and take the box inside and over to the bed, letting the sheet fall to the floor. I reach for the ribbon. It falls into a puddle of satin the moment I tug, nearly dissolving off the box of its own accord.

Once that's done, I lift the lid up, peel back a few layers of pale-yellow paper, and let out a breath at the dress. Daintily, I grab the shoulders and lift it out of the box. It unfolds automatically as I hold it out in front of me.

"Gorgeous." And I'm not just saying that. Unlike last night's dress, which was clearly made for evening, this one is obviously made for daytime. It's cream-colored and made of linen, which is all very familiar to me as a woman from Tau

City Factory. But it's much, much different than anything I've ever seen back home, because the hem is super short. When I place the garment up to my body, the skirt only covers half of my upper thigh.

They certainly like their skirts short here in RhoXi.

*Scandalous!*

The sleeves are three-quarter-length, puffed at the shoulders, and taper into fitted cuffs with a ruffled trim. A look I adore and have incorporated into my own designs on many occasions. The bodice portion is not a corset, just a nice, thick cotton that has been decorated with gold embroidery in a floral-inspired pattern. The round neckline dips low, probably enough to show off my cleavage, and there's a bit of gathering at the waist meant to make a shape. Especially when contrasted against a tightly pleated skirt that looks like it was made for twirling. Even the hem has a detail—a scalloped edge trimmed with a bit of cotton fringe.

At the bottom of the box is a pair of boots. Knee-high, lace-up, and made of warm chestnut-brown leather. They have gold embroidery and tasseled laces, making me think that they were made special for this dress. A proper outfit.

It's not the most beautiful dress, obviously. A gala gown would win in any side-by-side comparison. But it's so different, and all the fabrics are soft, and it smells good—like flowers—that I instantly fall in love with it.

It feels like me.

Like Xi knew my style, when even I haven't got a clue what my style is anymore, and told his best seamstress to whip it up overnight. And while I haven't seen much of this city yet, I have the distinct feeling that this outfit will allow me to walk around today, hidden. Or, at the very least, I will be able to blend in and not stick out.

I take my bath, trying to be quick so I'm not late for my

meeting with Lilika down in the lobby, and then get out and comb my hair until it's mostly dry and hangs straight down my back.

Then, I put on the dress and the boots, and when I twirl the pleated skirt in front of the mirror, I feel the part. I become a traveling girl who came to RhoXi on a permit pass. I'm out in the world exploring. While my partner—father of my child—does very important things with this city's god.

I shrug up my shoulders, wondering if I'm supposed to talk about that or not.

But Xi didn't give me any rules. He didn't tell me to be quiet about anything, and he told me to ask Lilika anything I want, so if I want to brag about Finn, I will.

Feeling confident, I go downstairs using the elevator, get off, and wander into the lobby, suddenly wondering what this Lilika looks like.

But almost as soon as I pause, a group of women are coming at me, all talking at once. I must hear my name a dozen times over the course of a few seconds, and they begin hammering me with questions.

"Yes," I say, enthusiastically nodding when they ask if I'm Jasina.

And then, they burst into another conversation about my dress, and my hair—two of them even touch it, making me shy away a bit. And they go on and on about book club, which, it turns out, is held in a private room in the Observation Tower's restaurant.

One of them—I have no clue which one is Lilika, because no one introduced themselves—takes my hand and practically pulls me along behind her as we enter the restaurant and make our way to a small private room in the back.

They file in before me, all taking their seats like this is a regular meeting spot for them. And then, there's only one chair left, so I sit.

They never stop talking, and I swear, the only thing I understand as far as topics of conversation go, are their names.

Lilika is sitting across from me wearing a powder-blue linen dress. This color really makes her darker skin pop and her face is so pretty—not beautiful, *pretty*—I can't stop looking at her. Her outfit was the first one I noticed because while it's an appropriate ankle-length it's got a slit that goes all the way up to her hip. And while she was walking, that leg popped out with every stride.

Tau City had dresses with slits up the side, but they never looked provocative like this dress does. In fact, it might not be the dress. It might just be Lilika.

She is one of those women people call 'sexy'.

The second thing I notice about Lilika is that she is agreeable. She nods an affirmation at absolutely everything her friends say. She's married to a man called Joreth, who all the girls fawn over when she tells me about him, bragging about how strong he is. And how he's the brightest spark in the program.

Lilika seems to like the attention the other women pay to her husband, but there's something wrong with her eyes when she smiles. A layer of tension underneath the joy.

The woman sitting directly to my right is called Veyra. Her outfit is scandalous in its own way. Off the shoulder. *Both* sleeves. And it hangs so low, at one point, I think I spy a nipple. I have to kick myself to stop staring. She wears a lot of chunky jewelry and talks in a loud voice, which overpowers Lilika whenever they try and talk at the same time.

She tells me her husband is called Dainrik. And then she

pulls out a PPD—one that looks about ten levels better than the one I've been given—and shows me a picture of his face on the screen. He is handsome in a way that reminds me of Donal. So I give Veyra an all-teeth smile and nod my head to make her put his face away.

Maelis is the girl to my left. And she's probably the youngest here, even younger than me. I highly doubt she's a day over sixteen. She's wearing something I might design myself. A sage-green tunic dress, layered with a sheer, embroidered overskirt that reaches mid-calf. The bodice is structured and laced up with silver cords, but the sleeves are loose and gathered at the wrists with tiny wooden buttons. When I look down, I notice she's wearing slippers instead of boots.

It's a very traditional look.

Everything about Maelis feels... rehearsed. Her compliments sound perfectly timed, her reactions a half-second too polished—like she practices her own expressions in the mirror. After every sentence—well, maybe not *every* sentence, but it feels this way—she says, "*Every spark has its purpose.*" Like it's a prayer, or something.

I'm not expecting her to have a husband because of her youth, but she does. Zaylen. And when she pulls up a picture of his face on her PPD screen, he's got a big smile on his face. Which should be comforting, but isn't, because he's got a gray beard too.

I *almost* say something. It's not unheard of in Tau City that a younger woman might marry an older man. But it was very uncommon. It happened a lot more up-city than down, because we have choice words for men who take child brides.

But who am I to judge? This isn't even my world.

I hold my tongue and smile.

Finally, in between Maelis and Lilika, sits Elsha. Her dress is lovely as well. Lavender, cut in an asymmetrical style with one sleeve off-the-shoulder and the other long and cuffed with pearl buttons. She's the only one of us wearing gloves—white ones, made of leather, and go all the way up to her elbows. She never stops talking. Even when someone else is talking, she's muttering things to herself. None of the other ladies seem to mind this, so I ignore it as well. She mentions her husband, but doesn't bring out a picture and no one fawns over him, saying he's strong or anything.

After all those introductions are over, I take a breath and tell them who I am. Oddly enough, and even though I wasn't told to keep secrets, I keep all my secrets. Even Finn.

I don't know why I tell them I'm single, I just don't want them to start asking questions about him. Or me, to be honest. Because I don't want them to know I am a Factory Girl. I feel like it would shatter the illusion. So I just give them the Vagabond story. I'm here on a permit.

They press their lips together. Lilika takes a sip of her wine. Maelis looks down into her lap, wringing her hands.

Things get quiet.

But it only lasts a moment, and then they are all talking again as they reach into their bags and pull out the book we're to be discussing called, The Season of Lilies and it's about... us.

Us. That's what Elsha says when she starts explaining the book to me. A group of high-society women in RhoXi, their friendships, responsibilities, and aspirations. And when she's done, she reaches for my hand, giving it a squeeze, and tells me, "You're one of us now."

Then they all say it.

"Welcome!"

"You're one of us!"

"Every girl group needs a five!"

And that's that, I guess.

I'm number five.

The rest of the day is filled with fascinating conversations about the city, and what I can expect here, and how, if I truly do not have a man—this comes from Lilika, who clearly knows I'm lying—she will set me up with one.

I don't come clean, not yet. I hold Finn close. A little possessive about him. I don't know these ladies. I'm sure they're nice and everything, but my story is... strange. And I don't want to get into it. Not yet. Not today, maybe tomorrow.

Because there *will* be a tomorrow. I know this for sure because they helped me buy an outfit for 'fitness day', which is what's on this group's schedule for tomorrow. Apparently, these women meet every day at the same time. They have tea, go shopping, meet for book club, go to painting classes, or do these things called power walks—which is what we'll be doing tomorrow.

I like it. But it's hard not to get pulled into my past as I think back on them. Because I had a group of friends like this once. I was part of a group of five in my past life.

Britley, Lucindy, Harlow, and Ceela.

Poor, poor Ceela.

Burned to charred nothingness because she never understood her power.

How strange, in a fortunate way, that I now have Elsha, and Lilika, and Maelis, and Veyra.

We're even neighbors. We all live in the Observation Tower.

So even though I started this day guarded and suspicious, I feel all that slip away as I slide into this new world like I really belong here.

I can picture it—a life in RhoXi.

Having the baby here, marrying Finn here, getting a little house, maybe?

A girl can dream.

*LATER,* **after it's already been dark** for a couple of hours and I've been sent a dinner, courtesy of Xi, Finn returns to our room. He looks happy. Smiling. Kisses me. Takes a shower. Falls into bed and is sleeping before I can tell him anything about my day or ask him a single question.

But I don't even care.

I love it here.

And tomorrow, I will tell my new friends all about Finn.

# FINN

*I* **wake up unsettled**. Jittery. Like I'm supposed to be somewhere, but I forgot. Then I hear the soft breathing of Jasina sleeping next to me, and everything slows back down.

It's the next day. Not quite morning from the dark skies on the other side of the massive windows, but it's not far off either.

Yesterday is a blur. I barely remember coming home. It was late, nearly nine o'clock, when I got here. Jasina was already settled in, propped up in bed with pillows, looking at her PPD.

She greeted me warmly. I think. I don't really recall much of last night.

Only the memories of my day are still clear. Starting with when I left here with Cormac in the morning. He took me back to the God's Tower and walking through that door, back to the lower dimension, was the most troubling thing I've done since Extracting Clara back in Tau City. She walked through that door too. One moment, she was in the only world she ever knew—her home. The next, she was in upper Tau City. What was she thinking when she arrived? Was she scared?

*Come on, Finn, of course she was scared. She was alone. She had just lost everything and was facing certain death.*

And then, she wasn't dead. She was somewhere strange.

I'm intensely curious about how it all went down. But

411

whatever happened to her, I'll probably never know. If I do see her again, I doubt there will be time for a conversation.

They are coming to kill us. Clara and her augment. Her super soldier.

Anyway... going back to the lower dimension and leaving Jasina here in the upper affected me more than I thought it would. A panic took over as I approached the doors. What if Xi trapped me in 702? What if he never let me come back? Am I making the biggest mistake of my life? One I will look back on for decades, wishing I could do it differently?

I don't feel that same panic right now—I mean, I'm here in bed and Jasina is next to me, sleeping. So Xi wasn't planning to trap me.

But then, why the jitters? Why am I so unsettled?

*Are you kidding, Finn? Why so...*

I chuckle out loud.

I mean... I was delivered to Factory Xi City, which didn't look any better when I came back than when I left. It's all kinds of wrong, that place.

And that's just where the dissociation starts. Because then I had to reconcile the lab. I remember my reaction to it because it was very white and very clean. Nothing dark and dingy about it. Which is fine, I guess. If you're doing health procedures, cleanliness is good. It's just, it was jarring. The city outside the tower was such a contradiction.

And for a moment, it felt deliberate. Though, if asked right now to explain that, I am unable to. I don't know why it felt that way. It was just nothing like I expected.

I did have questions, though. And I asked them.

"Why do you do the procedure here?" was my first. "Why not do the procedure in your amazing city up top?"

Xi's answer was less than satisfying, because all he offered was a flippant comment about being 'complicated'. It made me want to ask more questions, but things started moving quickly then.

Those worker-bots came in, acting more autonomous than I'd ever seen before. Just like the workers under the Factory cities, these didn't have faces. But I could just tell they were different.

They were paying attention. And doing things like taking blood from me and putting it into a tube. Another prepped the machinery, which hung over a sleek metal table in the middle of the room. It looked like a cage, this machine. With many thin tubes coming out of it.

"Don't worry about that," Xi had said. "That comes later. Tomorrow, maybe, if the test results are all good."

"What do you mean, 'if'?" I asked. "You said I was perfect for this procedure."

"And you are. But we must test you. To look for any potential anomalies. I doubt there will be any. I'm not worried about the results, and you shouldn't be either."

I was annoyed at his response, but then he directed me back over to one of the learning terminals. "There are still a number of things you should know."

And that's where I sat for... well, I'm not really sure how long. This is when time stops making sense. I can't quite parse its passing.

I know I listened to the teacher on the screen. It was more stuff about the body. Biology, it's called. Something about reproduction and auto-something nervous system.

Everything after that is blurry.

I blow out a breath, looking straight ahead at an empty wall. Trying to remember.

What did he do to me?

The test results came back and...

"Finn?"

I let the thought go, focusing on Jasina. "You're awake?"

"Mmmmm," she hums, clearly not. "Are you leaving?"

"Not yet."

She stirs now, turning over and scooting closer to me. I'm sitting up a little. She places her head on my stomach. Instinctively, I start playing with her hair. Twisting it around in my finger.

"Sorry I fell asleep so fast last night."

She sucks in a big breath and makes a monumental effort to open her eyes. Smiling, she says, "It's OK. I was tired too. How was it, though? Did anything hurt?"

"Hurt?" I shake my head. "No. Nothing hurt." And then, a memory. "I got a shot. That's pretty much it. I mean, they did tests, too. But those came back…" Another memory. "Well… they came back perfect. Xi showed me—explained all the results. And he said he's never seen a more suitable candidate for augmentation."

Jasina sits up a little. "That's great. How do you feel?"

My jitters fade with the return of the memories. And I'm about to shrug and say, nothing's different. But this is when I realize, *everything* feels different.

"Finn?"

"Yeah, sorry. It's just…" I look down at her, taking in all her beauty. God, she's pretty. "It's just… I dunno. I'm just starting to feel it *right now*. I was too exhausted to notice anything yesterday, but now…"

She sits up a little more. Brows crinkled. "Now what? You're starting to worry me."

"Oh, it's nothing bad. Nothing to worry about. It's just…" I flex my biceps, looking down at the muscle.

"Ummm…" Jasina says. "Are your arms supposed to be that big?"

I laugh. "Well, they weren't this big yesterday."

Even though she was already pressed up against me, she scoots even closer. Her hand pressing flat on my chest.

I look down.

My new, very chiseled, much more developed, chest. Again, I laugh.

"A shot, you say?" Jasina chuckles. "Get up, Finn. Stand up."

"What?"

"I wanna look at you!" She's on her knees now, pushing on me to get out of bed.

I'm naked, but I've never been shy—and anyway, it's Jasina. So I swing my legs out and notice the corded muscles on my thighs and calves.

When I stand up, there's another body part that got an upgrade.

"Finn, your dick is huge!"

I laugh—almost blushing like a fucking girl—then catch myself. "Well, it was never *small*."

"No," she admits. "But this is..." she looks up at me. "Slightly concerning."

I shake my head. "Don't say it."

She gets out of bed, reaching for me. Her long, slender fingers, slipping around my waist as she presses her body into mine. "Don't say what?"

I roll my eyes, but she's tracing a fingernail down the front of my chest. Then she presses her hand into my lower abdomen and slides her palm around my shaft, giving it a little squeeze.

"Don't ask," she starts, practically cooing at me, "if it's gonna fit?"

Which just makes me laugh out loud. "Yeah. That."

"Well, it's a valid question."

This is when I catch on that she wants me to fuck her with this new, improved dick of mine.

And I have to say, I'm quite turned on about the whole thing. Because suddenly, it hits me. Like I was on a timer. Something cooking that is now done.

I *am* power.

Yesterday, I felt fit.

But today, I feel solid.

Without hesitation, I reach down, grab Jasina by the waist, and throw her over my shoulder. She feels like... nothing. Lighter than a feather.

But that's not true. She's the same weight, it's not her who's changed. It's me. I'm just so much stronger now, she might as well be air.

She squeals with delight as I carry her into the shower and set her down. This is when I notice her outfit. She's wearing a very sexy, light-green chemise that only *hints* at covering her body. It's so sheer, I can see every bit of her wide, round breasts. They're firm, pressing up against the see-through silk top. Which is so short, you can't even call it a top. The fabric ends at the tip of her nipples where golden tassels bounce with even the slightest movement.

The panties are just as tiny. Leaving nothing to the imagination.

"What the hell are you wearing?"

She wiggles, making the tassels jump. "Do you like it?" Then she laughs, because it's a rhetorical question. "They've got the best shops here, Finn."

I'm nodding as I reach over and turn the shower on. "I fuckin' love it. I never want you to take it off." And then I grab her hand and lead her under the water. Watching with a hunger I've felt before, as it saturates the silk and sticks to her body.

Then, again, with no effort at all, I reach down and slip my hand under her ass, lifting her up as I push her back against the tiled wall. She wraps her legs around me, ready for whatever comes next.

I love this about Jasina Bell. She likes to be fucked.

And when I push myself inside her, I burn the look of pleasure on her face into my memory. Thrusting in to her, making her squeal, and moan, and bite me, right on the shoulder, as she comes.

I let go as well, gritting my teeth, closing my eyes, spilling everything inside her.

Then I'm grabbing her head, kissing her, whispering promises.

"You will never be alone again. You will never be afraid again. You will never be sacrificed."

After the fucking and showering is over, I dry Jasina off with a soft towel and put her back in bed—naked—and kiss her on the cheek. "Have fun exploring today. I'll see you tonight. If you really want to make my day, let me find you like this when I get home."

She smiles, chuckling, eyes already closed, already dozing. Happy. Which fills me with joy. Because I'm doing it right this time. I'm doing it all right.

Then I dress and leave.

Ready for augmentation, day two.

CORMAC DOESN'T MEET **me this morning.** I am on my own as I walk through the God's Tower doors, and this time, it doesn't feel so jarring. I know my way to the lab—mostly. Only getting turned around once, but no one comes to save me, and I like that.

I feel back in charge of myself for the first time since learning of my father's death.

When I arrive at the lab, Xi is standing in the middle of the room, looking up at the cage that hangs above the sleek, metal table.

He turns when he hears me enter. "I wasn't sure you'd be back."

I pause, feeling every change that's happened over the last twenty-four hours. "Why wouldn't I be back?"

Xi shrugs. "Some men have problems with the day one changes. Clearly, you do not."

"Why would I? I'm stronger, bigger—"

"Yes," he says, cutting me off. "But the physical enhancements can sometimes... be..."

"If you're talking about my dick, I'm not disappointed."

"Excellent. Some men lose in that department."

"Oh." Then I laugh. "Well. I can attest that I haven't encountered that side effect. In fact, I've been blessed with the opposite."

He presses his lips together, eye smiling with delight. And I have to remind myself that this man—god—thing—it's not even real. He's made of light.

It blows my mind.

"Jasina is happy as well, I take it?"

"More than satisfied," I say, grinning.

"Perfect. Then let's begin day two."

"More screens?"

"No," he says, curtly. "The screen time is over. You

learned everything you needed yesterday and signed all the forms, so we're officially on."

"Signed forms?"

"Your consent, Finn. I'm an ethical god. I don't augment men against their will."

That wasn't what I was implying, I simply don't *remember* signing any forms. But whatever. "Good. Let's go."

He gestures to the table. "Have a seat." And just as he says this, those worker-bot things come back in holding trays of needles and tubes. "Don't worry, today's tests are quick. We'll take blood samples every day for tidy recordkeeping." He holds up a tube from the worker's tray, right in front of my face.

The next thing I know, I'm holding that tube in my hand and Xi is laughing.

"What the hell just happened?" I ask, looking down at the tube.

"Test number one—*pass.*"

"What do you mean? I... how did this tube get in my hand? It just... appeared there!"

"No," Xi corrects me. "I simply let go of it and you reacted before it hit the floor."

"I... reacted? But I didn't."

"Your reflexes are so fast now, Finn, you didn't even see your hand move."

"What?" I look down, studying my hand. Feeling jittery and unsure again. Then I look up at Xi. "But—"

He puts up a hand. "Don't worry. Day one is reflexes, which has integrated perfectly into your biology. You didn't see your hand move because your eyes haven't been augmented yet. Day two is sight, sound and smell, as well as a data display. From this day forward, you will see life in a whole new way."

"I don't think I understand."

"You will, when it's over. Unless you'd like to back out?"

"No," I say quickly. "No. I'm not backing out."

"Perfect. Then let's get started. Please remove your clothes and lie back on the table."

I exhale. This is it. This is the day everything changes.

The day I will *not* regret decades later.

I remove all my clothes, unable to hide my satisfaction with the new body—which delights Xi, I can tell. And then lie back on the cold table, looking straight up at that cage. "Will it hurt?"

"No, Finn. It's not going to hurt." Then a worker is next to me, sticking a tube into the back of my hand. "Only a monster would augment a man while he's conscious. You'll be asleep. You won't even know it's happening. And when you wake up, we'll talk…"

But that's the last thing I hear, because my world fades to black.

# TYSE

*Myra is staring at me.* Her blue eyes are very serious. "Do you wanna hear the end of the story now, Tyse?"

I look around, find myself sittin' on the floor of the Sweep deployment train. One quick glance out the window, where there's nothin' but the sandy sea, gives me an idea of where we're at and where we're goin'.

"Yeah," I say, glancin' back at Myra. "I'm gonna need that endin'."

"All right." She rubs her hands together as her gaze tracks along the line of new recruits sitting on either side of me. Then she leans closer, her voice low. "The Corrupted God…"

We all strain to hear. Listening as she recounts the myth.

But it's hard to follow. She's talkin' too low. Whispering, almost. Or maybe the train is too loud.

Because all I hear, on repeat, is the phrase… *If you're lookin' North, you're lookin' South.*

And I know what she means, because I've heard it all before.

What I don't know is how it's done. How do you walk north and end up in the south?

"It's a loop, Tyse." It's another faint whisper, but this is not Myra's voice. It's the god. The Corrupted One. Epsilon. Because I was walking the wrong way—and he got me.

I turned my back and he got me.

Put me in a cage.

"It's a loop, you see." This time his voice is louder. Clear. "Negative feedback. Prime example, the pyre beetle, native to the extreme northern Alpha Desert. It's a marvelous example of the phenomenon. You see, when threatened, this beetle activates a chemical reaction inside its body. Mixing two volatile compounds together that, once exposed to the air outside its body, explode like a missile. Killing predators. Alpha insists he thought this one up and created the code for it, but he's always been a liar."

Beetles. I have no fuckin' idea what he's talkin' about.

"The negative feedback loop, Tyse. You see, the beetle makes these chemicals inside its body. Specialized glands, or something. But it's got limits. It can't fast fire these missiles. It needs to recover. It needs time to make more. The negative feedback loop happens when it empties the chambers containing the chemicals. Because this is an exothermic reaction. Creating intense heat that could kill the beetle. And what good is a biological weapons system that kills the host? Right? The whole process triggers a cool-down period to save the beetle's life. This is how it works between you and Clara."

I know this. I said as much to Clara before we ended up here. I take her spark. Feed off it. Which depletes her. Then I steal spark to feed her back. I can't steal spark for myself, only give it away. I must take from her. I must kill her and bring her back.

It's a bitch of a fuckin' cycle if you ask me.

"She claims to have a reservoir of spark inside her," Epsilon continues.

"What?" Finally managing to speak, my voice is very groggy and hoarse.

"She's making spark, even after I drain her and give it to you."

This is not true. I saw her. After the fights, after the monks, I saw her on the table. She was gray. She was *dead*. I'm the one feeding her spark. I'm the one keeping her alive.

"That's what she told me, anyway," Epsilon says. "Is it true? Did you feed her... jumps? That's what she called them. Jumps. She claims that's how you stole the baby god from Tau City and brought her to Delta."

My mind is not clear. It's not workin' well at the moment. And all I keep thinkin' is that she should not be tellin' him these things. And I should not answer him. Not now, not ever.

"Nothing to say to that?"

"I don't know," I manage to croak. "But I want to see her. I want to see her right now."

Epsilon laughs. "I'm sure you do. She's... dying, by the way. We made a deal."

"What?" I try and sit up, but I'm still connected to the augment table and all the needles, thousands of them, tear at my skin when I move.

"Oh, I wouldn't do that," Epsilon cautions. "Don't move now. We're just getting started here Tyse. I didn't steal the poor woman's spark and give it to you just to let you walk free. You owe me."

"How the hell do ya figure that?" I snarl.

"Because you're in my city. I'm taking care of you. Do you think all this care is free?" He scoffs. "I'm not running a welfare state. You owe me."

"I wouldn't need your help if ya hadn't kidnapped us."

"You rode a train past my station and didn't pay the toll. You owe me a toll."

"What toll? You're making shit up."

"Maybe. But what are you gonna do about it?"

He pauses here. Like I might threaten him. I'd like to

threaten him, but he is pulling all the strings at the moment. Almost literally. "What do you want? How can we pay this debt and be on our way?"

There's a scraping noise as he drags a chair up to my table and takes a seat. "I thought you'd never ask. I want *you*, Tyse. I want to... make you better. Faster, stronger—"

"I'm already faster and stronger. I'm already better."

"Yes. You're pretty spectacular. But I have so many ideas, you see. So many... thoughts. So many... dreams. So many ways to experiment on humans, all living up inside my head. You've seen what I've been working with. These men. They're very low quality. But you! And that woman! My, god! You're everything I want, yet never knew I needed."

He wants to experiment on me. He wants to keep me on this table and push Clara's spark into me until I die. Or she dies. Or we both die.

"What I want," Epsilon continues, "is to create the ultimate weapon. The ultimate human, machine hybrid. A true cyborg. And... if I can just be frank here, you're really my only chance. So." He leans over top of me so I can see his face. He smiles. It's an ugly smile, just like him. "So here you are. On my table. In my lab. And your woman gave me permission."

"*What?*"

"That's right. She gave me permission. She said, 'Epsilon, I love that man. I love him with all my heart. Take all the spark you need from me. Just save him. I can't go on—'"

"Shut up!" I yell. Cutting him off. "You're just making shit up!"

"Luther," Epsilon sighs. "Play the vid."

A screen comes to life, but it's somewhere behind me. Not even in my field of vision. But I hear her. Clara's voice. "I don't want to live," she says. "Not without him. He's my world now. So whatever it is you're going to do, just do it. And I will willingly give you every drop of my spark if you promise to give it to him."

"Thank you, Luther. That is all."

The recording stops.

"It's a trick."

"It's not a trick, Tyse. I assure you. She gave me permission. She's watching right now. Well..." His head rocks back and forth, wavering. "She's probably passed out by now. I *did* drain her into a husk to feed you. So... yeah. But she *was* watching."

"Give her spark! Right now! Feed her!"

Epsilon laughs. "Where the hell would I get spark? I don't have spark. Not in quantities like that. I've used all my females. All but a few. And I will not be giving your woman the spark my women make. She deliberately told me that she can refill herself."

"It's not true."

"Why would she lie about that? Hmmm? Why, Tyse. Does she have a death wish? She told me to feed you to keep you alive. That she couldn't live—"

I stop listening. Because I'm hearing Clara's voice in my head. Just before she was stolen out of the spark stone cave. *What are you saying? It's like... a loop? I power you, I get weak, you steal spark to make me strong, and then you need to take it from me to work?*

And I sighed, and said, *That's exactly how it works. Negative feedback loop.*

"Are you listening to me?" Epsilon asks.

"What do you want?"

"What?"

"What do you want, Epsilon? From me? Get on with it then. Let's do it. Let's fuckin' go!"

"Well, the two of you certainly are refreshing."

"What?"

"She said the same thing. Not in such colorful language, but essentially so."

"So do it. Whatever it is, just do it."

"Odd," he says.

"What's odd?"

"The *eagerness*. Why?"

He's right. I'm giving away hints here and this god, he's very perceptive. Because while it makes sense that Clara would be eager to give her spark to save me, I should not be as eager to let him experiment with my genetics. It doesn't fit. Because he doesn't know I can steal spark from across dimensions to feed Clara after she feeds me.

I growl the next few words out. "You wanna make a deal? Let's make a deal. I'll let you do anything you want to me. Augment me, fight me in that cage again. Whatever it is. But I get a reward out of this."

"Let me guess… you get your woman."

"That's right. You get me, I get her. That's why I'm eager. I want her and want her now!"

"Well, now just isn't gonna work for me. I've got protocols to follow."

"Then do it. Because if she dies while you're fuckin' around, your little experiment is over."

"She's not gonna die. Not if she was telling the truth and she's got a lake of spark hiding inside her."

"Well, I figured it'd be a simple deduction."

"And how's that?" Epsilon asks. His tone snarky now.

"Because I don't want to live without her either. I go where she goes. If she dies, Epsilon, your fun is over. I'm goin' with her."

"Not if I keep you alive. I might be willing to do that. To give you some of my precious spark to keep it going."

Now it's my turn to scoff. "Have you never made a real augment? Have ya not had one that made it into Sweep? They give us suicide programs, Epsilon. And my data display is flashing that fucker at me right now. It's been asking me for the last ten minutes if I'd like to run the final program. And if she's dead, I will just go ahead and do that."

A slow clap echoes off the walls of the room. "How. *Romantic.*"

"Believe me, or not. One way or another, we'll find out."

He stands up, walks over to the control panel on the screen, and sighs. "Very well. Protocol number two. Begin."

Immediately, every part of my body lights up with pain.

I hear myself screaming as the threads make their way deeper, and deeper into my tissues.

The world goes black.

But this is exactly how I need it to happen.

Because while Tyse Saarinen lies on the table, writhing in pain, I get up. Sit right up. And when I look down at myself, I'm empty again. Just an outline of blue glow.

A traveler. One who slips between worlds.

I see them all, all at once. Layers upon layers of worlds.

We're underground, so again, there are limits here. Some worlds are just rock. But there are plenty that aren't. That have trains or underground facilities. No monks, not like last time. No Spark Source. But there are men. Groups of them running some kind of heavy machinery in some unknown world.

I float down to one, and settle beside him inside the cab of the excavator. And then, with one touch, he unspools. All his little threads of spark float into me. Filling me back up.

I do this many times. Dozens. I take everyone's spark I can find.

And then, I float up, and up, and up.

Until I am back in Epsilon's Factory city, inside the lab where Clara is strapped to a wall with a harvesting cage pressed against her body, and I kiss her. Unspooling myself.

I give it all back.

Then I pull away, looking at her sweet face as the color comes back. Her glow returns. Her spark lights up inside her. And I give her my vow. "I will kill everything in this universe to save you Clara Birch. God or human, it won't matter. They will not take you from me."

And then, spent from the unspooling that happened here as well as the threading going on in the next room, I simply... disappear.

WHEN I WAKE UP, I'm still on the table, but the threads have been taken out and the cage is hovering above me.

A slow clapping fills the space. "Well done, Mr. Saarinen. Well, done."

I sit up, find Epsilon leaning against the far wall, and look down at myself. "What did you do to me?"

"Well, we need to find out, don't we?"

"No. Where's Clara?"

"She's fine. Filled herself right back up, just like she said.

I've given her the day off. It's a fight day, after all. I figured she'd want to watch."

"What?"

Epsilon snaps his fingers and suddenly, a group of mutant augments have me by the arms and legs. They lift me up, high above their heads, and carry me out of the lab.

That's when I hear it.

*Epsilon! Epsilon! Epsilon!*

The chanting.

"It's fight time!" Epsilon's words boom through the arena as I'm carried in and the crowd of mutant men goes wild, making the whole place shake.

We are on some kind of platform now. It ascends, taking us up, up, up. It stops with a jolt and all the hands release me, so my back slams hard onto the cold metal surface.

I'm naked, save for a pair of military-issue boxer shorts. And Epsilon's voice is once again booming through the speakers. But from this high up, it's distorted, so I can't actually understand what he's saying.

What I do hear is the screaming from above. And when I look up, here they come. A horde—dozens of mutant augments spill out of the ceiling. Clambering down ropes. Sliding off scaffolding. Dropping from poles.

And all of them are after me.

"*Finish him!*" Epsilon booms.

Filled with spark, though—and not just any spark, but Clara's spark—I am... much, *much* more than just another one of Epsilon's experiments.

They fall like dying stars, their light stolen before it can burn.

I take them apart, unmake them, return them to dust.

And all the while, I am walking. Hunting. Searching for spark.

Because when this is over, once again, she will be dying. And I will need more.

# CLARA

*everywhere*, there are fluttering blue butterflies. The spark radiates off them like heat.

"So… what do you think?" The haughty Little Sister—the arrogant one who rolled her eyes at me while she was having her first tour of the Maiden Tower—spins, twirling the skirt of her short dress.

"What is this fabric?" I ask, Reaching for the paper-thin silk that makes up her bell sleeves. It's not any silk I've ever worn. It's sheer, and shimmery, and soft.

"Don't you just adore it? It's called *organza*." Then Jasina laughs. One of those 'ha-ha' laughs that sometimes bursts out of people when they're in the middle of a moment of pure joy. "Can you believe this weave? I need to find a supplier— I'll make us dozens of dresses! But what about the length? Do you like the style?"

"I love it! Absolutely. Shows off your legs."

I blink. *What?*

Then, Tyse is whispering in my ear. "You're all right. You're OK, Clara. You're fine."

This is when I realize I've been dreaming, my whole body is covered in sweat, and I'm no longer strapped to a wall. "How…" But I feel too weak to think. My throat too dry to speak.

"Just be still now. Your reserves are buildin' back up. You'll feel better in a few hours."

And now I feel the warmth. His body pressed into mine.

His arms around me. He's so hot, he feels like a furnace. But I'm so cold, I push myself into him, trying to get warm.

"You're OK," he says again. "You're all right. You're gonna be fine."

I'm sleepy and his words echo in my head as I go back into the dream to see the Little Sister with the blue butterflies swarming around her like a cyclone. Jasina Bell. Then I'm being pulled back in time, to the afternoon when I first saw her inside the Maiden Tower when she was getting her tour.

It was the last day of my innocence.

The last day before the bells started ringing again.

The day when everything started to unravel like a loose thread of silk...

THE NEXT TIME *I wake up*, the world is shaking. Booming, thunderous vibrations echo through the walls. I know this sound, and it terrifies me. I try to take a deep breath, hoping to steel myself, but it comes out as a gasp and ends like a whimper.

"It's OK," Tyse says. "It's just the horde. Somethin's goin' on down there."

I open my eyes. Tyse is wearing nothing but a white towel around his waist. He's wet, like he just got out of the shower. And he's sitting in a chair across the room.

The *room?*

"Where are we?" My words come out throaty. Croaky.

"Our new quarters, darlin'—courtesy of Epsilon." When he says these words, he... *he lights up.* Patterns of lights, specks, and dots cover the length of his arms, his torso, his neck. Even his face.

Lights inside his skin. Not on him—*in him.*

I try and sit up, but the headache is so acute, I nearly double over and vomit. Only my extensive years of Spark Maiden training stop the act before it happens. I close my eyes again, propping myself up on one elbow, hoping the wave of nausea passes.

The lights go out. "Sorry," Tyse says. "I forgot about the headaches."

Feeling a little bit better in the near darkness, I open my eyes and find him standing up now, hand still on a light switch on the wall. He's lit up. Entirely lit up. Every part of his visible skin is glowing with lights. Some kind of tech that should be on the screen of a computer, but is now embedded into his body.

"What happened to you?"

His brow furrows, eyes narrowing. "What?"

"Your body, Tyse! What the hell happened to your body!"

"Oh." He blows out a breath, looking down at his arms where all his tattoos are now covered in orange and green glowing patterns. "This is just..." His eyes find mine. "An upgrade."

"Upgrade? You're glowing with lights!" I might be getting hysterical. "I don't understand. What happened to you? Because this doesn't look like an upgrade, Tyse. You look like one of those *things!*"

He sighs now, glancing away. Absently rubs his hand through his hair. A flicker of something clenches in his jaw.

I just compared him to a Delta Factory worker bot. It's an

insult. He's well aware of what has happened to him and he's not in the mood for my judgment.

He looks back at me. "It's just augments, Clara. Like the eyes." He points to his eyes, which are the least glow-y thing about him right now. "Nothin' to get upset about."

My mouth drops open. *Nothing to get upset about?*

He uses my dumbstruck silence as an opportunity to duck into another room. From the steam pouring out, I decide that this is the bathroom. When he returns a few moments later, he's wearing a pair of black tactical pants, a belt, and a piece of sleeveless chest armor that should dial back his bot factor, but instead only adds to it.

Because this armor looks like it grew out of him. It's so tight and sculpted to his muscles. Plus, it's got lights on it as well.

"Tyse," I breathe. "Where... what? I don't understand."

"It's all right. You'll be OK."

"You keep saying that, but I don't feel OK, Tyse. I feel like shit, actually. And I'm not even that worried about me. It's... you."

"You're just confused, that's all." He draws in a deep breath and lets it out as a tired sigh. "You were drained."

Drained. It takes... well, much longer than it should for me to connect the dots. To remember where I am. What we're doing.

What I agreed to.

Drained. Of spark, he's saying. Harvested.

Because I gave the god Epsilon permission to take everything I have and give it to Tyse so he can survive the experiments and the fights that come after.

And this is what I gave Epsilon permission to do to him.

He doesn't even look human.

"How long? How long have we been doing this?"

"Ten days."

"Ten—" I gasp. *"Ten?"*

He doesn't answer, just nods.

"And... how many times have I asked you these questions?"

"Seven. You recovered pretty quick the first several times —just a few hours. But it's takin' longer now."

"I've lost my memory?"

"Not exactly. You do remember. At least, you will. It just... takes time. And it's... gettin' worse."

"How long was I out this time?"

"Two days."

"Two *days?*"

"That's how long it took for you to make enough spark to fill your reserves."

My reserves. And then, I remember. All of it. The lie I told to keep the secret of Tyse and me. That he walks through worlds, killing people so he can steal their spark and fill me back up.

There is no lake of spark inside me.

Well, I guess there is now. But I don't make spark. He just fills me back up with the souls he stole.

"It's OK," Tyse says again, for the third time.

And in my experience, when people feel the need to convince you that things are OK, they are decidedly not OK.

So I drop it. And look around the room. It's not big, or luxurious, or even clean. But it's better than being strapped to a wall and surrounded by a cage of needle-thin harvest tubes.

There's a bed, which I'm in. A little table to the left of the bed with some knives scattered across the top.

On the other side of the room is a large screen built into the wall. It's black now, so that means it's off.

Under the screen is the chair where Tyse sits. And next to the screen is the open door with steam still pouring out—the bathroom.

Finally, just to my right, there's a countertop that acts like a little kitchen. There are dirty dishes all over the counter. Evidence of us living here that I simply don't remember.

"Do you want a shower?" Tyse asks.

What I want are answers. But I don't think it's safe to say that. I'm not sure why, I'm just picking up a vibe from Tyse. He's... distant. Different. "How many times?" I ask.

"Seven." He doesn't even ask for clarification. Which tells me, this is the only thing on his mind as well.

Seven times. "Seven fights?" I ask.

"Yeah. And seven... recoveries."

Which is referring to me. Which also matches up with the seven times I've questioned him. "When is the next one?" I ask.

"Tonight."

It's too much, that word. *Tonight.* "We don't even get a day off?"

"I've had two days off now, Clara. He's not a patient guy. I had to bargain pretty hard to get him to let you recover fully before... you know."

"Harvesting me?" I shake my head as these words come out. How the hell did we get here so fast? I feel like we were just leaving our quarters in Delta. And now... it's almost two weeks later. And while the memories are floating on the surface, I have to rescue them to make the timeline fit.

And I don't feel like rescuing them. So I don't even bother trying to understand.

This is my life now.

I am one of those women in Delta's factory.

My only purpose is to be harvested.

Suddenly, the bed dips down and Tyse is next to me. He slips an arm underneath my body and pulls me close as he lies back, allowing my head to rest on his chest.

I have so many questions. It's just... I don't want to ask them. Because I already know the answers. How many times can he do this? Maybe eleven more? Maybe only four.

But the most pressing question is how many times can *I* do this. Because right now, I feel like that number is zero.

"You're OK," Tyse says, for the fourth time.

"Are you sure?" I feel exhausted.

"Positive, darlin'. Absolutely certain. You're doin' great. And... I'm making a deal with Epsilon."

I was just getting sleepy again, but this wakes me right back up. "What kind of deal?" I say these words through clenched teeth. Not because I'm mad. I'm not mad. I'm *angry*. At that stupid god. For what he's taking from us. For what he's doing to us. Because we're *dying*.

"It's no big deal," Tyse says. "Just some mRNA injections."

"I don't know what that is." My voice sounds very weak now and I feel like I might start crying if I don't make an effort not to.

"It's just another way to augment. To change things inside me."

"Change *what things*?" The pitch of my voice is too high, the panic building inside me.

"Clara," he says, pushing some sweaty hair off my forehead, "I've been augmented with so much mRNA, it's not even trackable at this point."

"Is that supposed to make me feel better?"

"Yeah, it is. Because I've got this. I promise you, I've got this. All I need from you, is rest. I *need* you to recover."

"So he can harvest me."

"Nah. Well, that's one way to think about it, I guess. But the way I see it is that, I need you to recover so I can *fight*."

There's a pause here. Not long. Maybe a second. Possibly two. But in this pause an infinite number of explanations bloom in my mind.

*So I can fight.*

The literal meaning is so he can fight in that cage thing in that mutant arena.

But there's another way to interpret those words.

*So he can fight for us.*

I mean… I actually chuckle a little. Just a little, not really out loud. Because I feel that god's eyes on us. He's *so* present, it's uncomfortable. But the reason I chuckle isn't because any of this is funny.

It's because he's *Tyse fuckin' Saarinen.*

Failed augment, who wasn't.

Rescuer of baby gods and Spark Maidens alike.

A man who walks across the veils between worlds and steals spark to feed me.

So he can take my spark to power himself.

It's not a good vibe, but as far as hidden gifts go, this one is giving hero.

He's going to save us. That's what he's saying. He wants me to recover because he made a deal with Epsilon and whatever this deal is, he feels like it's worth it.

*That your life is worth it, Clara? That he's the hero of this story and therefor, you should just give him all your spark and let him save you?*

These questions pop into my head unsolicited. They're honest questions, I suppose. Does anyone really want to be the damsel in distress like in the fairy tales?

No. No one wants to be helpless.

But if one *is* helpless, having a hero to save you is the very best option.

And anyway, what are my choices here?

I'm being *harvested*.

I'd be dead by now if Tyse wasn't walking through worlds to steal spark.

*Steal spark, Clara? That's what you're going with?*

Fine. He's killing people to save me. To keep me alive long enough so we can escape.

I get it, it's gross.

But is it wrong to want to live?

Is it wrong to let him save me?

"I love you," Tyse says. Just out of nowhere. Just like that.

"I love you too." And I say it back, just as naturally.

But what we're really saying is... *I've got you.*

Because that's what our relationship is based on. Trust and loyalty.

*If I have your back, then you must have mine.*

We linger in the bed a little bit longer, but only a handful of minutes. Because I do want a shower. I want to clean myself up. Not so I can look good for the god as he harvests my spark, but just to show him I'm not done.

I'm still here.

I'm playing the game.

When I get out, Tyse is tucking those knives into little straps or holder things on his legs. He's going to take them into the arena, I guess.

I don't want to know what he's doing with those knives, so I don't ask. I simply pull on the least dirty set of clothes that Delta gave me, lace up my boots, take a deep breath, and then I follow Tyse out into the hallway.

The world is shaking beneath my feet. Booming,

thunderous vibrations that resonate with the chant of the horde.

*Epsilon! Epsilon! Epsilon!*

# JASINA

*he week goes by like a blur*, but I mark the days in two ways. First, by the new changes I see in Finn each morning when we wake. He always gets home late, tired, and in need of a shower. Either having eaten already or just not hungry, because we don't share meals together.

So mostly, he just falls into bed next to me. Usually, reaching for me as he falls asleep. There's no time for sex at night because his exhaustion is overwhelming, so this reaching that he does is the last thing I register each night.

Being in his arms and feeling safe and happy.

But the mornings are another matter. This is when he's rested—whatever augmentation he went through the day before, having processed overnight.

After day one, it was all the new muscles. But after day two, it was his touch. Whenever his fingertips touched me, they would leave a glowing blue spark imprint on my skin.

After day three, I woke with my head on his chest and noticed that his heart was beating in synch with mine and there was a faint purring sound coming from inside him.

After day four, I woke to him pressing his thumbs against my wrist. "It's a pressure point," he told me. "If I press right here—" and then I lit up blue. But what made it even more intense... I *felt* it.

I'd never felt my spark before. It wasn't something extra or something foreign, it was just such a part of me, it didn't trigger my senses.

But while he pressed on my wrist, his fingertips buzzed. Like we were making a new kind of connection through the spark.

The second way I marked time throughout the week was by the activities I did with the girls.

That second day, we powerwalked. Which is just fast walking, but Lilika said it gets the heart going and makes us fit. I guess I knew that. Obviously. But I had never thought about it in a sense of conditioning before. That's the word Elsha used. Conditioning is preparing our bodies for strenuous things.

Veyra said this conditioning was for sex, but Maelis disagreed and said it was for our husbands. To which, Elsha replied, "Same fucking thing," in a very snobbish tone that reminded me so much of Clara Birch, I almost took Maelis's side on the matter just out of spite.

After the powerwalking, we went to the beach and swam in the canal. All the girls had brought bathing suits in their tiny backpacks, but I didn't know about the swimming, so obviously, I hadn't.

Maelis had brought an extra with me in mind, but it was so plain and... well, ugly, I declined and just bought my own from one of the shops.

Only after I got home that night did I realize I hadn't told them about Finn. But I was sure I would the following day.

Which was painting. All four of my new friends had already started their paintings, so when we got to the studio their canvases were covered in sheets from their last session.

I got a brand-new canvas and spent most of the morning just staring at it, wondering what it might turn in to. Eventually, I just picked up a brush and got on with it and after the session was over, I realized it was turning into a picture of Finn and I embracing in a whirlwind kind of way.

Kind of like the butterflies that came to me the first day we met Xi.

At least, there were the beginnings of that image.

After painting, we had lunch in a movie theater. I was so enamored with the giant screen that played out a drama, I forgot to eat my nachos.

Again, when I got home that night, I realized I still hadn't mentioned Finn.

WHEN I WAKE **up on day five**, Finn is staring down at me with glowing blue eyes.

I gasp and sit up. "Finn! Your eyes!"

He just smiles at me, reaching for my wrist. The pressure point has gotten interesting over the past couple of days, because not only can he make me light up, but if he strokes it in just the right way all the spark begins to collect and throb between my legs.

Which is what it's doing right now, and it's enough to drive a girl crazy.

"Do you like them?" he asks me, winking to indicate he's asking about the eyes.

"They're... bright. Is that spark—" But I can't finish my sentence, because he's gently dragging his fingertips up and down my arms with the lightest, feathery touch, and the sensation that was only between my legs a moment ago fills my whole core.

I close my eyes, breathing deeply.

We have sex every morning, and every morning, he tries something new. That first time, it was the wall sex in the shower. On the second day, he bent me over the couch. Which took me back to that first night we met. When he was pretending I was Clara and I was trying not to like it.

Only this time, it was all about me. He dirty-talked me constantly. Fisting my long, red hair hard enough to pull my head back. That's how I came that morning, head all the way back, staring up into his eyes.

After the third augmentation, the sex was agonizingly slow. He was on top of me, inside me, his chest on mine. And our heartbeats synced up. That purring noise coming from inside his chest almost lulling me into a dream state as we made love.

I craved him that day. All the while I was painting, I was thinking of how perfect we are. How connected and united. That's probably why the picture I started painting that day was of us wrapped in a whirlwind of spark.

Now, here we are, the morning after the fourth augmentation, and his eyes are glowing, and once again, he's found a new way to turn me on. Because he's stroking me into oblivion, and I'm lighting up, ready to lose it at any moment.

I want to pinch myself, or make him stop so I can ask him if this is real—because it's so perfect.

My life went from a literal disaster to *this*, in the span of a week.

Not only did we hop into another dimension filled with real gods and worldly delights, but I'm pregnant. We're going to get married. We're going to have a family. And there's nothing that Clara Birch or that monster she's attached herself to, can do about it. Because Finn will fight for us, and he will win.

I know he will win. Each day he grows stronger, smarter, *better*.

"Come for me, Jasina," he whispers into my ear, his fingers now between my legs.

And I do. Immediately.

Before it's even over, Finn lifts me up off the bed and places me on top of him. He gently caresses my breast with one hand while the other grabs my hip, lifting me up a little so he can press himself against my opening.

I moan as I lower myself, letting him slip inside me. But I keep my eyes open, watching him. Watching those new glowing eyes of his as they light up blue with spark. I can see little patterns moving across the black of his pupils. Like one of those screens. And for a moment, my heart stops. But Finn squeezes my breast, pulling me down onto his chest, and then starts kissing me.

I get lost in these kisses. In the lovemaking. In the climax. In the sleep that comes after, as he dresses and kisses me goodbye, then leaves.

I get lost in happiness.

*I wake* **up to the sound of chirping**, then paw absently for my PPD on the bedside table until I find it and answer. "Yes," I mumble.

"Where *are* you?"

"Maelis?"

"Is… everything OK?"

"Yes, why?"

"You're an hour late!"

"Oh." I sigh, sitting up. "Sorry. I was…" But I stop. Because I realize I still haven't told them about Finn. "Tired," I finish. "But I'll be down soon. What are we doing today?"

"Book club and tea."

"Right. We're back to that. Meet you in the restaurant in ten minutes." Then I end the call and force myself to get up and shower.

Every day I've done a little bit of clothes shopping because one needs a new outfit for every day. Not to mention lingerie and random things like swim suits. I've even picked up a few things for Finn, mostly guessing his size because he's changing so much. But when I check the closet, I find that he put on one of the shirts this morning.

This makes me happy in a weird way that I can't really explain. It makes me feel… useful, or something.

"Stop daydreaming," I chastise myself. Then choose a short summer dress, put it on, and drag a comb through my hair until it's sleek and smooth.

When I arrive in the dining room, Maelis, Veyra, and Elsha have already finished their breakfast and are reading our book, The Season of Lilies.

I haven't read a single page yet. I didn't even bother to purchase a copy, even though we've all been to the bookstore browsing the shelves, every day this week.

Lowering myself into my chair, I notice that there are only four of us. "Where's Lilika?"

Veyra lifts up a glass of sparkling wine, then spits her words at me. "Every Spark Has Its Purpose."

"Um…" I blink. Confused. "OK. Well, listen. I'm really sorry for being late, OK?" I look at Maelis because she's the one who called looking for me, and now that I think back, she was worried. "Is… everything all right?" I ask, looking at her, and not Elsha and Veyra.

"Ask *them*," Maelis huffs. Not even looking me in the eyes.

"What?" I turn to Veyra and Elsha. "What is she talking about?"

"Like you would care," Elsha says. She *does* look me in the eyes. And she squints them too. "You don't have a husband, remember?"

"Stop it," Veyra hisses, kicking Elsha under the table, because she kinda kicks me too.

I blow out a breath. So that's what this is about. "Fine," I say, throwing up my hands. "I have a… well, he's not my husband. Yet." I smile. "But he will be because…"

Oh, my God, am I gonna tell them?

Yes. Yes, I am. Because my life is perfect and I have no friends to share it with. I need friends. I'm a social butterfly. And while Finn is definitely my best friend, a girl needs her crew.

Besides, these girls look like they could use a bit of good news.

"I'm pregnant!" I blurt, trying not to squeal. "My man's name is Finn and he's…" This is where I draw the line. I can't tell them I'm from another dimension, so I can't even tell them who he is. So I just say, "He's super important. I mean, back where we come from, he's like—"

"Super *strong*," Elsha deadpans, rolling her eyes. "Let me guess, Xi told you that he's the brightest spark in the cascade, didn't he?"

My mouth drops open.

"Cut the shit, Jasina," Veyra says. "Why are you acting like we don't know who you are and why you're here?"

"W-*what?*" I'm stunned.

"We all know, Jasina," Maelis says, her voice quiet and soft. A sharp contrast against the other two.

"You're nothing special," Elsha sneers. "You're not above us."

I place a hand over my heart. "I never said I was. I don't know what sparked this—"

"Sparked this," Elsha laughs, spitting out some wine. "Oh, that's so funny!"

"You're gonna end up just like *her*, you know," Veyra says. And then she points to the empty space where Lilika should be, but isn't.

I look at this space, blinking. Confused.

"One day," Maelis says, her voice still very soft, "it *will* be your turn. Every spark has its purpose, Jasina."

Then, as if they planned it this way, the three of them just get up and walk out.

Leaving me sitting at a table filled with dirty breakfast dishes.

LATER, **back in the room**, I replay this morning over and over in my head. The looks on their faces.

The sneering attitudes of Elsha.

Maelis and her almost pitying manner.

That stupid city motto—*Every spark has its purpose!*

Veyra's threat.

That's how I took it when she said I'm going to end up just like Lilika—which is missing, I guess.

I only sat at the table for a minute—probably less. But when I got up and tried to find them again in the lobby—I mean, we had tea scheduled, they can't just *leave*—they weren't there.

Maybe the days aren't structured like I assumed. Maybe book club and tea aren't always paired together. But I went to the beach, and the movies, and the art studio, and the shops, but I couldn't find them anywhere.

I even did the whole powerwalking route backwards, hoping I'd bump into them.

Nothing. They were gone. At this point, it was well into the afternoon and I figured I'd just go home. That's probably where they were the whole time.

I walk into an empty room, sit on the bed, and flop back, wondering how this day went so wrong. Bored, and so not in the mood to do anything but nap, I reach over to the bedside table and grab the remote for the big screen on the wall across from the bed.

They have these big screens all over the city, and I've been enough places now to understand that they're... well, stories, but in vids. Which is a new word I feel weird using in context, but there it is.

The point is, people watch these screens when they're bored because they tell stories. It's a way to pass time Maelis told me.

Since it's only two in the afternoon, Finn won't be home for many hours. Well, *well* past dark. So I might as well use the screen to pass time like everyone else. The girls and I will work things out tomorrow, so I put the weird morning aside and let out a breath, resigned to an afternoon of well-earned laziness.

I've used the remote before, and after pressing a few random switches—which are actually called buttons here, weird—the screen finally comes to life, and sound booms through the room.

Music over a black background. A slow, dramatic organ swell that reminds me of a wedding march. Then a woman's whispered voice: "Vows are forever…"

Violins—high and tense—screech, then go silent as a sparkling sound, like crystal wind chimes, fills the emptiness.

Then a boom, and a desert appears on the screen. Cracked and golden under a sunset sky. Something blows across the sand—a wedding veil? And then, an altar appears, glowing with spark. Three men stand behind it. Three women in front. Like they're about to get married.

A deep male voice cuts through the music—

"In a city ruled by gods… where power is sacred, and love is lethal…"

A montage of absurdly beautiful people flashes across the screen.

Then: a single woman standing on a balcony in a silk robe, makeup streaked down her face. The name Sophie Beaumont lights up just below her chin. She's sobbing when she says, "He didn't just cheat… he swore on Xi."

I blink. Sophie Beaumont? Why does that name sound familiar?

"One heart betrayed…"

A heartbeat sounds as the scene shifts. A shirtless man, slick with sweat, slams his hand down on a stone table. His glowing blue eyes stare straight at the screen. The name Dominic Castille flashes underneath him. His voice is low, almost a hiss. "You can't vow yourself to two gods, Delilah!"

Dominic? Who the hell is Delilah?

Right on cue, her name appears. She's running barefoot through a misty garden in a flowing white gown. Clearly panicked. She looks over her shoulder and gasps, "I don't remember who I am—but I know who I love!"

"What the actual—"

"And one vow..." the narrator booms, "that could destroy them all."

Back to the desert: a burning wedding veil. A masked man holding a ring. A god statue cracking down the middle.

Then it hits—ONE GOD, MANY VOWS appears in shimmering gold across the screen, the spark flickering across the O.

"One God, Many Vows," the voiceover says. "This season... betrayal has never burned so bright."

I sit on the bed, blinking in confusion. "What *is* this?"

The screen comes to life—beautiful people at a beautiful house. Or maybe it's a hotel? I'm not sure. They're having breakfast and a tense conversation about—

"Holy shit," I mutter. Because I suddenly remember where I heard all these names before.

The maids. Back in my room. In the lower dimension, helping me dress. Chatting like it was gossip. Casual. Real.

But now, after sitting through the full hour of this show, I know the truth.

They're not real.

None of them are real.

It's fake. The whole thing is fake.

It's like the movie I watched the other day, but... different.

Deeper.

More personal.

I don't know.

I feel... *stupid.*

But it's more than that. It's not just about feeling stupid for not realizing the maids were probably snickering behind my back as they fed me fake garbage—knowing I couldn't yet tell the difference between what was true and what wasn't.

It's about being played the *fool.*

And the double-dose of truth I got today.

Veyra, pointing to the empty space where Lilika should've been, but wasn't: *You're gonna end up just like her, you know.*

That's when it hits.

That creeping, sinking feeling.

That sense of...

It's too good to be true.

# FINN

*The hallway is gold and white.*

Ornate.

Quiet.

I hear everything.

Door click.

Vent hum.

Footfall pattern shift near corridor junction C4.

AUDITORY SYSTEM: range +210%.

Sympathetic vibration detection: functional.

Echo cancellation engaged.

VOICE RECOGNITION: ambient inputs muted.

Focused filter: Jasina.

HEARING: stable.

Step.

Step.

My body walks the path before I think about it.

My thoughts trail behind.

MUSCULOSKELETAL SYSTEM: restructuring 84% complete.

Myofibril density: +340%.

Tendon elasticity: increased.

Joint integrity: stable.

Fast-twitch ratio: optimized.

A breeze hits my cheek as the ventilation cycles.

DERMAL SENSORS: active.

Pore function: suppressed.

Temperature regulation: internal modulation active.

Hair follicle replication: paused.

Facial hair growth: suppressed at root.

I see a light flicker overhead.

My head tilts 7 degrees.

Instinct.

VISUAL FIELD: 360° mapping functional.

Luminance tolerance: maximum.

Color depth: expanded.

Motion prediction: enabled.

A woman speaks two doors down.

The words don't register.

Just the sound map.

COGNITIVE FILTERS: language parsing disabled.

Emotional tethering: suspended.

Response protocol: none.

The floor shifts beneath me.

Elevation ramp.

BALANCE SYSTEMS: gyroscopic alignment functional.

Spinal buffer: reinforced.

Knee torsion capacity: +70%.

Hip rotation mod: cleared.

I blink once.

OCULAR SYSTEMS: LED iris stabilized.

Retinal overlay: spark frequency mapping enabled.

Night vision: default ON.

Target lock: dormant.

The memory hits me in static.

The fight.

Joreth's eyes, just before I ended him.

NEURAL FLAG: First kill recorded.

Adrenaline spike: 0.6s delay. Dissipated.

Post-trauma response: absent.

Moral checksum: bypassed.

Memory log: visual only.

Subject: Joreth.

Status: deceased.

Source link: unknown.

I don't feel anything.

NEURAL ACTIVITY: dream-state suppression 100%.

REM cycles blocked.

Memory isolation: active.

Conscience loop: offline.

Moral inhibitors: dormant.

Aggression threshold: rising.

I hear the door to our suite unlock before I see it.

HEART RATE: steady.

Sync mode: pending.

CIRCULATORY ADAPTATIONS: pressure variance stabilized.

Oxygen saturation: 99.8%.

Blood volume: increased.

I place my hand on the door.

TACTILE UPGRADE: fine motor mapping at 98%.

Response latency: 0.0014s.

Spark contact threshold: neutral.

Emotional reflex: suppressed.

The display across my vision flashes a soft blue.

CURRENT STAGE: 6.

COMBAT SCENARIO EVALUATION: complete.

Joreth: neutralized.

Score: 94.7% efficiency.

RECOMMENDATION: push Stage 6 early.

I don't agree or disagree.

I don't think at all.

Just step inside the room.

The lights adjust.

I hear her voice.

I see her stand.

EMPATHY LOOP: quiet.

Bond reinforcement: queued.

Desire simulation: optional.

Partner protocol: active.

I walk past her, data scrolling down my field of vision like a glowing blue waterfall, step into the bathroom, and close the door.

The water is hot.

Too hot.

My skin adjusts before the sensation registers.

DERMAL RESPONSE: thermal adaptation engaged.

Skin integrity: stable.

Subdermal flex lines: reinforced.

Contaminant trace detected: foreign blood.

Location: fingernails, right hand.

Analysis: type mismatch. Non-self.

Biological origin: human.

Subject match: probable – Joreth.

Cleaning protocol: auto-initiate.

Sterile field: achieved.

I scrub without thinking.

Watch the water spiral down the drain.

A moment passes. Or maybe many.

My head is tilted under the stream.

No thoughts come.

No feelings follow.

The room is dark.

The sheets are cool.

She's there. I hear her breathing.

PARTNER LOCATION: confirmed.

Temperature sync: passive.

Pulse rhythm: logged.

Emotional frequency: unreadable.

INTERFACE PRIORITY: rest cycle.

I lie back.

No words.

No touch.

No thought.

SLEEP MODE: authorized.

REM bypass: engaged.

Augmentation stabilization: ongoing.

Stage 6 prep: queued.

Darkness folds in.

I disappear into it.

Whole.

Empty.

Waiting.

*I WAKE up reaching for Jasina.* Her warm body melds into mine perfectly as I slide an arm underneath her back and pull her close. "Are you awake?" I ask, hoping she is because I've got some serious morning wood.

"Mmmhmmm," she hums.

Which is a 'no' when it comes to Jasina. She's a lazy sleeper. But I like it. Waking her up with soft caresses is definitely my favorite part of the day. "I'll let you go back to sleep if you want," I tease, whispering these words right up against her ear.

She turns, pointing her face up at me, trying to open her eyes, but only marginally succeeding. "Hi."

"Hi," I say back.

"I've missed you."

"I've been here every morning."

"No," she says with a chuckle, turning her body so we're face to face. "I mean, at night. You're so... *tired*. What does he do to you all day that you get so tired?"

"Do to me?" I shrug. Mostly because I don't recall. "I'm asleep for the procedures."

She sits up a little. "You sleep all day and come home that tired? How's that work?"

Again, I shrug. "Well... I'm asleep, so..." Yeah, she's kinda right. Why *am* I so tired? "I only vaguely remember coming home each night. I guess it's the augmentation. And I don't think that being unconscious on a threading table counts as sleep.'"

She places a hand on my cheek, her eyes narrowing.

"What?" I ask.

"There's something on your pupils."

"What?" Then I understand. "Oh, that. That's just the data display Xi augmented me with."

"What's a data display?"

"It's like... a screen. Over my eyes. With lots of switches that I can control by..." I blow out a breath. I don't really know how to describe it. And no one described it to me, I just kinda... knew what to do when I woke up on the third day and found all this code splashed across my vision. "It's just internal mechanisms," I say. "Blinking, and a head nod here, an eye swipe there. Just gestures like that."

She looks concerned. "Not a single thing of what you just said makes sense to me."

"Well, then it's a good thing that you don't need it to make sense," I joke. And then, before she can ask any more questions, I slip my hand under her lingerie top, eager to drop the subject and have a little fun before I have to get up and go back down to the Factory.

She arches her back and moans my name when I enter her.

And for a second... I don't recognize it as mine.

# TYSE

*Epsilon! Epsilon! Epsilon!*

This is how the chant starts.

*Epsilon! Epsilon! Epsilon!*

They won't shut up until I kill. Then, and only then, will it change to *Rise a God.*

I've spent the last ten days trying to figure this shit out. In between killin' mutants, stealing spark from other dimensions, and spoolin' Clara back up, that is.

So, admittedly, these spare minutes haven't added up to a lot of thinkin' time. But I think I've worked it out now. The Epsilon chant is the swing. The frequency, in the analogy I told Clara all those years ago.

Weeks, Tyse.

It's only been two weeks.

The swing. The frequency. That's what the Epsilon chant is. A way to *hone* it.

But Rise a God is the push. That little push you give the swing when in that one moment between up and down. The *resonance.* A way to elevate it.

These mutants aren't chantin' for fun. They're not wound up like a bunch of drunken sportsball fans.

It's a process,

It's part of the *process.*

And by process, I mean what that melty-face fuckin' god is doing to me on the threadin' table.

Clara's boots thud on the concrete floor of the hallway

469

next to me. Her steps shorter, so her footfalls are like an echo of my own.

She has almost no idea what is happening right now. If we had more time, it would all come back. But our time is up. Either she trusts me, or she doesn't.

And since we're shoulder to shoulder, walkin' towards an almost certain death, I'm gonna go with she does.

Which is good. Because she's strong—very fuckin' strong. But if this keeps going much longer, it will reach its inevitable conclusion.

I can fight forever. There's no limit to me now. Not after what the Corrupted God has done to my body.

But we're gettin' close for Clara. I had to unspool seventy-four men that last time to fill myself back up. Every time, it takes more. More, more, *more*.

Just... *more*.

Like... I'm gettin' bigger—or possibly... emptier—each time I go there. Each time I walk the worlds I disrupt the natural order of things in ways I can't even imagine.

Well, that's not true. I've got a pretty fuckin' powerful imagination actually. I can imagine plenty. But it's not the point. The point is, we're done here. This is it. We can't live like this. And I'm not sayin' that as some romantic gesture towards Clara, meanin' I'll be checkin' out with her, if she goes.

I will, but that's not the point, either.

I mean, we just can't do this. And this understandin' I have about the state of the situation goes far, far beyond some romantic grand gesture.

It's about *everthin'*.

Not just all the worlds I'm trespassin' in, but the actual glue holdin' it all together.

Each time I defy the Grand Design and take what isn't mine, the foundation shakes a bit.

And these bits of shakin' are cumulative.

They add up and there isn't a way to even it out.

We're fallen.

Falling. *Falling*, Tyse. Not Fallen.

But it is Fallen.

This, what I'm doin', is the end of everythin'.

And it's all his fault.

*Epsilon! Epsilon! Epsilon!*

Clara and I stop at the junction between the rooms. Hers, to the left, mine, to the right.

She grabs my hand. Squeezes it. "I'll be OK."

I nod.

She won't be OK.

She's never gonna be OK again.

This shit is changin' us in ways I cannot imagine. And this time, when I say that, I mean it literally.

"You'll be OK," I echo her words. Then I lead her off to the left, to the open door of her lab.

*Don't look at it, Tyse. Don't look at it.*

But I do. I always do.

The harvester is on the right-hand wall. Luther prances around it—fists filled with needle-thread tubes as he inserts them into the machine. His movements jerky, uncoordinated, and seemingly without reason as he feeds the tubes into the ports.

He looks up, spies us, and starts babbling his incoherent sentences filled with unspooling metaphors that really, only make sense in his demented mind.

He drops the needle-threads and calls her Dolly. "Come here, Dolly!" Comin' at us with both arms outstretched, making grabby-hand gestures with his fingers.

I growl. Not an exaggeration.

He backs off. "Needles and thread! *Needles and thread!*"

I look down at Clara, take her face in my hands, look her in the eyes. "Be strong."

She presses her lips together, straightens her back, tilts her chin up. And with her most up-city, Spark Maiden voice, tells me, "Don't worry about me. I've got this. *You* just worry about *you*." Then she pokes me in the chest, smiling. Like this is no big deal.

*She gets drained of her lifeforce all the time, Tyse.*

*She's a pro.*

And she is.

But this is it. It ends tonight.

It took days for her to wake up last time. She hasn't even gotten her memories back. It's gonna kill her. You're gonna come back too late this time, and—

*Epsilon! Epsilon! Epsilon!*

I kiss her, she kisses me back, and this is when she loses it. It's a moment. A single moment when a soft, small, sob escapes her well-polished fortitude.

It kills me, this sob.

Fuckin' *kills me.*

"*Dolly!*" Luther screams. "Come here now, Dolly! I need to thread you with the needles!"

I want to kill that little monster. Drag his soul out through his throat and braid it into a leash. Lead him around like a dog beggin' for mercy.

*Just FYI, Luther—I don't grant mercy to anyone.*

"Later," I mutter.

"What?" Clara asks.

"Nothin'." I take her hand, squeezin' it one last time. "*You* take care of *you*, Clara." And this time it's me pokin' her in the chest. Then, and only with my eyes, I say, *Please.*

She nods like she heard me. Then she turns on her heel and walks into the lab.

Luther slams the heavy, metal door in my face.

And then I'm alone.

*You* take care of *you*.

I start prayin'...

*I am the executioner and the death.*

I walk over to my own lab, find the Corrupted God hovering in front of a panel of screens, cacklin' softly to himself.

He hears me, turns, smiles. Gestures to the threadin' table. "Welcome home, Tyse. Let's get started. I have big, big plans for you tonight."

Moments later I'm strapped in. Threaded. *Dyin'.*

And then the sweet, sweet spark enters me for the *tenth* time.

*I* WAKE **in the cage maze.**

*I am the dark soldier, standing in the blood of the fallen.*

Once again, at the bottom of the arena. Immediately, I'm on my feet. Unreal eyes scannin' the place. Thousands of lines of code are fallin' down my field of vision like rain. Every number, every letter, every symbol is decoded before I even see it.

*The spool of Source, the thread of Spark—I am the machine made flesh.*

This is what it means to be workin'.

My eyes are glowin' so bright, it lights the place up red.

*Red.*

*Red.*

Not blue.

*Red.*

*I walk the hush that follows ruin.*

*I utter no prayer—for I am the override.*

*A weapon of the sandy sea.*

What am I? What has he done to me?

*In the image, I am made and in the image, I will unmake.*

*For thine is the kingdom made in sand.*

No time to care. I move.

*And thy rule was made in wind.*

*And in the wind, as in the days of dark imprisonment, the new gods rose as tall as the hollow towers.*

The cage wires rattle under my grip. Steel twists, groans, gives. I don't climb—I *rise.*

*And in this rising, they conquered.*

*Swept the land of everything and left it clean like a bone.*

One hand. One boot. One pull. The metal's a blur beneath me.

*And on that bone, was born I.*

*The executioner and the death.*

Below, the mutants scream. But they don't matter. Not yet. They won't touch me.

I'm already gone.

The arena shifts around me—grids of rusted wire, warped scaffolds, spikes where the old walls caved in. My boots don't slip. My hands don't falter. The maze knows me now.

Above, the crowd pounds their feet in unison.

*Epsilon! Epsilon! Epsilon!*

The rhythm echoes down through the cage stacks, like blood in a throat.

Not cheering. Not chanting.

*Calling.*

My blood vibrates with the sound. My limbs sync to the rhythm.

*Epsilon! Epsilon! Epsilon!*

Each stomp is a pulse. Each pulse is a command.

I obey.

My breath is steady. My vision floods with targeting overlays, proximity heatmaps, exit vectors. But I ignore them. I'm not calculating. I'm ascending.

My hands tear through the last grid. I stand on the top of the cage maze—above the arena, above the pit, above the screams.

The crowd roars. The drums of their boots shake the world.

*Epsilon! Epsilon! Epsilon!*

I open my arms. Let them see me. Let them think I belong to him.

The first one reaches me and...

I'm somewhere else. Peace. Quiet. Dark.

The space between worlds.

*The silence so loud it roars like a memory.*

I want to stay. I want to grab Clara from that lab, bring her here, and let this peace be our 'good world'.

But I can't get to her. Not from here. Not empty.

I need to be able to fill her back up.

So I sift. Ignoring the peace. I sift. Scanning the frequencies, dippin' in, backin' out when I don't find what I'm lookin' for.

Because I can't use a cave filled with monks now. I need more than the diggers under the ground buildin' tunnels.

I sift. Again. Again. Through broken timelines and threadbare cities.

I need fodder.

The kind of sacrifice one only finds in war.

I find it.

Not a battlefield. A slaughterhouse.

Blown-out buildings in an underground city, fire in the streets, men fightin' with pipes and broken glass. Screamin' in three languages. Limbs twitchin' in the gutters.

It's beautiful.

I drop into the chaos. Land on a roof. Slide down a wire spine of twisted rebar.

The moment my boots touch dirt—

I feel them.

The dying.

The nearly-dead.

The afraid.

The spark curls off them like mist.

My fingers ache for it. My chest opens without tryin'.

The first one rushes me—blood in his teeth, gun in his hand.

I touch his throat.

Unspool.

It doesn't even take effort. He falls like cloth.

The spark floods into me. Sweet and sharp. Hot enough to melt the back of my teeth.

I breathe out—and somethin' inside me *purrs*.

I don't stop.

I move through the alleys. Through the trenches. Through the fire.

And with each one I touch—each body I strip of that glowin' thread—

I feel better.

Stronger.

Cleaner.

More.

I tell myself I'm doin' this for Clara. To refill what's lost.

But somewhere deep in the override, deeper than the mission, deeper than her—

I like it.

They beg.

*I take.*

They fight.

*I take.*

And when they scream?

That's when the spark flows fastest.

I lose track of time. Lose track of bodies.

The ground is slick with it.

The air's thick with it.

I think I laugh.

No. I know I laugh.

And the war keeps goin', and I keep unspoolin', and for the first time in a long time—

I don't feel like I'm dyin'.

*And on that bone, was born I.*

*The executioner and the death.*

I feel alive.

And *that*... is the problem.

I'm somewhere else. Peace. Quiet. Dark.

The space between worlds.

*The silence so loud it roars like a memory.*

I step out, back into the fray.

Then out again, into the void.

Into the emptiness.

I walk across the air like a Messiah.

The whole Grand Design bows to me now.

I own this place.

Clara is strapped to a wall, the needle-threading cage pressed up against her body. All the little tubes barely glowin' a dull-gray color.

I lean down and kiss her.

It pains me to unspool, and only my love for this woman gets me past the urge to keep it all for myself.

She takes it. Her color comin' back.

Alive.

Saved, once again.

I turn, forcing myself to go back to that body. To be his slave. To keep going—*for her.*

Half a step later I'm face to face with the Corrupted God.

"I knew it," he says. A smile of joy creeping up his face. "I *knew it!*" he laughs.

Somewhere, deep inside this factory, the crowd erupts—a distant roar.

*Rise a God! Rise a God! Rise a God!*

And this is when I understand the true meaning of losing.

# JASINA

*I*t was the disappearance of Lilika that triggered it. After thinking about this for three days, I'm absolutely sure of it now.

Finn was perfectly fine that morning.

*Was he, Jasina?*

*Was he really?*

He was attentive, affectionate—the sex was good.

*Wasn't the sex good that first time too? When he bent you over the couch, got you off with his fingers—then passed out?*

I hesitate, unsure once again.

I've been going through it in my head, over and over, deciding something new each time, only to talk myself out of it a moment later.

He was fine that morning. But. Just for the sake of argument—the argument I'm having with myself—let me think… his eyes were glowing, but it wasn't a bad glow.

*Do you hear yourself, Jasina?*

*Eyes don't glow!*

I understand this. But he's being augmented. It's part of the process.

*Is what he did last night part of the process too?*

That's it. I can't even bother to pretend to play devil's advocate anymore. The pretense is over. Because this nagging inner voice of mine is right.

None of this was good.

None of it. It was a set up.

JA HUSS

Deep down, I know this. I *know* this.

It's just... I don't know what to do with this information. What do I do? Finn is gone.

Gone!

He's not the same man I met back home. Which wasn't even a good man. Only marginally an acceptable one. But he got better. *We* got better together. And it was good before we came here to this city.

That's not even true. Because we didn't come to this city, we were brought. We don't even live in this dimension, we're visitors. This god is...

Say it.

Just... say it.

Evil.

There's something wrong with him. With this place. With all the people here, even. Because the girls—how could they not notice Lilika's gone?

It's ludicrous. Absolutely bonkers that we all meet up in the mornings and just pretend that we didn't lose a fifth friend just four days ago.

I tried to talk to them about her. The next day, after they left me in the tea room, book club unfinished, I went downstairs early. Maelis was waiting, but I tried to engage her about what happened the day before—when Elsha spit her words at me—*You're nothing special. You're not above us.*

And Maelis—quiet, frumpy Maelis—told me the same thing as she did the day before. *One day, it will be your turn. Every spark has its purpose, Jasina.*

That creepy motto.

Every time I asked her what she was talking about, that's all she said. "Every spark has its purpose."

When Elsha and Veyra showed up, I didn't even get one question out before they started doing it too.

That was power walking day.

What a disaster. The three of them all showed up in the lobby with little ear plug things that played music. Which I didn't have—because I didn't even know they existed. So they made a big production about putting them in and... whatever. I don't even know what they were doing. Listening to the same song, or something. Because all at once, their lips started moving like they were all silently singing the same words.

The next thing I knew, they were power walking out the damn door. And I don't know how long they've been power walking, but for me, this was day two. They were fast. Much faster than last time. I spent the entire session almost running alongside them to keep up.

By the time we made it to the beach, I was sweaty and exhausted, and had forgotten my little backpack with my bathing suit in it. They hadn't said a single word to me. Nothing. And that's how it stayed. They kept those little ear plugs in, the tinny sound of music leaking out of them, as I sat there in my walking clothes, ready to pass out.

Which, I did end up doing. Only to wake up and find they'd left me there! Alone! Didn't even bother to shake me awake! And it was late afternoon. The sun was sitting low on the horizon. I must've slept on that beach for hours.

Walking back to the Observation Tower, I was in a daze.

What was happening to me?

What was happening to my perfect new life?

Things were decidedly off that night when Finn came home. He didn't even look at me. It's like I wasn't there. And when I woke up in the morning, he was gone.

That was not normal.

Was that day seven? Or day six of his augmentation?

I can't tell anymore. I'm losing track of... well, everything.

Again, I went downstairs early to meet the girls for painting. And they were there, no ear plugs, either. They were chatty, laughing. So I was hopeful.

And it was OK for a little bit. On the walk over to the art studio, I listened to their casual conversation about their husbands. Veyra and Elsha, at least. Maelis didn't say much. But she was a little bit quiet, anyway.

But then, when we walked into the studio to work on our paintings, Lilika's painting was still there. So I walked over to it, pointing. "Should we take this to her? It's too pretty to just let it sit here."

Veyra snickered.

Elsha sneered.

Maelis said, "And where might we find Lilika, that we might return this painting to her?"

I shrugged. "She lives in the tower, right? We take it to her as a pretense to visit and make sure she's all right."

Veyra laughed out loud.

Elsha's eyes narrowed down into slits.

Maelis said, "Every spark has its purpose."

And that was the last thing any of them said to me that day. Because every time I spoke after that, they would all say, in unison, "Every spark has its purpose."

When it came time to cover our paintings and go to the movies, I didn't do it. I didn't move.

And they just left without me.

That was yesterday.

I went home, didn't even grab food—hoping against hope that once Finn came home, I could convince him to stay awake long enough to go out to eat. I have this coin card with my name on it. Enough coin to pay for anything I want, and Finn and I haven't even had a chance to use it for dinner.

But I was crying at this point.

Which makes me tired.

So I just fell asleep.

Today, is the next morning and the bed sheets next to me aren't even wrinkled.

Because Finn never came home last night.

I'm sitting on the floor of the room, backed up to a corner, staring at the door. Willing, with all my might, that he will come home.

He doesn't.

Eventually, I get up, dress, and make my way down to the lobby.

But it's like I'm walking through a nightmare. Because the entire place is empty. And the reason the entire place is empty is because this lobby is no longer attached to the upper dimension.

I'm back in the factory world. Standing inside a decrepit building with blown-out windows. Outside, there are workers pushing crates around.

And then, an elevator dings. And when I turn, Xi steps out. Looking just like he did when we first met him.

Which is funny, but not in a funny way.

Because he told Finn he wanted us to meet the real him.

But he never came to see us in the upper dimension.

This is when I understand the meaning of the words, 'too good to be true'.

He didn't bring us here to save us.

He brought us here to *use us*.

Xi opens his arms, wide smile on his face. "Every spark has its purpose."

# CLARA

*t is the day everything changed.* Before Finn's father, Aldo, died and the bells rang for Haryet. It is warm, and sunny, and perfect.

I had everything that day. A man who loved me, and who I loved back. Two best friends to share my Spark Maiden life with. An entire suite of rooms on the ninth floor of the Maiden Tower. Floor-to-ceiling windows with a view of the canal and the Extraction Tower across it. More coin in my accounts than I could ever hope to spend. A social order that catered to my every whim.

It was all a lie.

Not a single thing about that life was real.

I'm floating above my Tau City, but it's just an outline of cyan-blue spark against a black background. Appropriate, I think. Because it was hollow. But there's a current of spark up here in the wind. Flowing. Taking me past the city now and into the desert where everything turns into the night sky.

The stars are made of spark. They glow, twinkling in the dark.

But beyond all that emptiness, there are the women and girls. The ones I named. The ones that live inside me now. They make a long chain, connected to each other by holding hands, that leads back to the Source. The spark flows through them the same way it came out of my fingertips when I was a girl. A mini arc of lightning.

Haryet is the woman closest to me. Reaching for me. *Please*, she mouths. *Please!*

I don't take her hand because it feels like the end. "I can't," I tell her. "I can't join you, Haryet. I'm not done here."

She's begging now. *Please, please, please...*

I shake my head. "Not yet," I explain, more forcefully. "Tyse. I can't just leave him. We're partners now, Haryet. He's depending on me."

"Clara."

My name comes out of Haryet's mouth, but it's not her voice.

"You can wake up now."

The god's voice is low, and calm, and steady. And I suddenly have the urge to cry because it reminds me of that first time I woke up in Delta City and the god was trying to have a conversation.

I would go back to that moment. Not any moment in Tau City, but that one I would. Because Tyse and I were safe. Life was getting better.

But all these memories are nothing but a stupid fantasy. You can't go back in time. The real world doesn't have do-overs.

You get one shot. One chance. And that's it.

"Come now, Clara. I'm bored. I would like for us to have a conversation."

My eyes open. I'm strapped to a wall plate made of cold, hard metal. My eyes have rolled up into my head, so I find myself staring at a cement ceiling that has been sloppily painted white. For a moment, I mix up the timeline and I see the tower, and the banner, and the words, 'Sparktopia Was Here' splashed across it.

But I sigh. That's not where I am. I'm not in Tyse's room in the God's Tower.

I'm in some factory lab where a psychopathic machine, passing itself off as a living creature, is making mutant augments and using the man I love to test them in fights.

I lower my gaze and find myself staring straight at a harvesting cage on the opposite wall. "What is going on?" I whisper.

"Ahhhh, good. There you are."

I turn my head and find the melted-faced god staring back at me. He's so many kinds of wrong, I don't even know where to begin. "What do you want? What the hell do you want from us?"

The god laughs, his eyes shining red.

It's so wrong.

"I want to push the limits, obviously. It's not every day an authentic Sweep Augment gets dropped into my lap with his very own rechargeable power source."

So he knows.

"Oh, yes, Clara. I know. I caught him, you know. I caught him in between worlds. Right after he spooled you back up."

I barely understand what that means, but an image of Haryet making dresses out of spark comes to mind.

"That's why you're fine and he's dying." He juts his chin to the other side of the room, and when I turn my head, I see Tyse, also lying on a medical bed, wires coming out of him, a cage of needle-thread wires hanging from the ceiling above him. But he's naked—creepy, sculpted armor gone—and his skin, once golden and inked with tattoos, now pulses in strange places. Thin lines of orange and green leave glowing trails across his chest and arms, like veins of light under the surface.

He doesn't look broken.

He looks rebuilt.

On top of his chest is his weapon. The VersiStrike.

"Isn't it poetic?" Epsilon asks. "What a picture this paints. The great Tyse Saarinen. You know they get buried with those weapons, right? They're biological. I thought it be fitting to place it there. Since... he's dying."

My eyes linger on the weapon as Tyse continues to breathe erratically. Watching it shake a bit with each breath.

"Don't bother," Epsilon says.

"Don't bother what?"

"Coming up with a plan that involves that weapon. It's not loaded, nor is it charged."

"I can't even lift that weapon, let alone wield it."

"No, I suppose you can't. It's coded to him, anyway. No one can use that weapon except Tyse Saarinen."

Which isn't true. Because I did actually use that weapon once. But that was before Tyse came back online, so it might as well be true. There is no romantic scenario where I suddenly get the strength to grab it, load it, charge it, and shoot it to save us.

Never gonna happen. That weapon is dying, just like the man underneath it. "What are you doing to him?"

"Oh, I've done lots of things to him," Epsilon chuckles. "Pretty much everything I could think of."

I don't take my eyes off Tyse. "Why? I don't understand. Why are you doing this?"

"Because I *can*, you simple girl." He exhales. It's one of those satisfied exhales. "Is there any greater reward than unraveling the mysteries of the Grand Design? That's what I do, young lady. I unravel mysteries."

"No," I say, gasping a little. "You make monsters."

This answer elicits a full-on laugh from Epsilon. It comes out, "Ha, ha, ha, *haaaaaa*." Something you'd read in a book and not a sound people actually make. "Yes. *Monsters*. Isn't it fun?"

"Fun? No. It's... *gross*."

He doesn't say anything for a few seconds, so I turn my head. He's mad now, I can tell. He didn't like that answer. "Do you want to hear what I'm offering?"

"No."

"Come now, surely you're curious."

"You misunderstand," I say. "It's not that I don't want to know, it's that my *answer* is no."

"That's because we haven't negotiated yet. Stop posturing. I already know your commitment to him is as great as his commitment to you."

"And how would you know that?"

"*If I have your back, you must have mine.*"

His words—*Tyse's words*—cut me. Deeply. It feels like an attack on my soul. On my heart. I sneer at him. "Where did you hear those words?"

His reply comes with a grotesque smile. "Where do you think? I plucked them right out of his mind. It's the promise you made each other. It's why you let him drain you. Because you know he's got your back, doesn't he Clara? *If I have your back, you must have mine.* And he knows you will keep giving him everything to the very end." Epsilon shrugs, opening his arms wide. "And if he knows this, so do I."

"What. The hell. *Do you want.*" It's not even a question at this point.

"I want you to fill him back up, obviously."

"But... it's not up to me," I say. "He just... takes it."

"How romantic," Epsilon chuckles. "Well, that might've been the case before he got caught. But now it appears... he's refusing."

"Why would he do that?"

The god shrugs. "Perhaps he feels like you're not up to it?" I don't say anything back. Just remain still and silent, trying to figure out what is going on here. Tyse wouldn't refuse to take my spark without a reason.

What is the reason?

*Please.*

This word enters my mind like an echo.

Haryet. Floating in the emptiness. Made entirely of spark threads. The chain of Maidens behind her. Her hand, reaching for mine.

*Please.*

But this time, it's not the face of Haryet I see.

It's Tyse.

I look over at him. His body is shaking now, so badly, the VersiStrike is bouncing on his stomach. His wrists are bound to the table, as well as his legs, his chest, his head. If not for these bindings, the seizure might bounce him onto the floor, that's how strong it is.

"What's happening?" I say, feeling panicked. "What's wrong with him?"

"He wants to fight, dear girl! He needs your spark! Can't you hear him begging? *Please*, he's saying. *Please* fill me up!"

*But that's not how it works!* That's not what he's asking! I know this. I *feel* it. Yes, he does need my spark, that is true. But this is not what he's trying to tell me. If it was that easy, he would just *take it.*

This is something else.

Suddenly, his body goes still. A machine nearby sounds an alarm. I look over at a screen where a flat line travels across a black background.

"You better hurry," the ugly god says. "This is it. That's his heart, *stopping.*"

"Take it!" I yell. "Take it!"

"I've tried," the god says, gesturing at the wall across from me. "I've hooked you up to the harvester several times. It works, on your end. But his body is *not* accepting it."

*Why? Why Tyse! I'm not dying! You can see that! We can do this!*

I send these mental thoughts to him, knowing perfectly well he's not a mind reader.

But there *is* a response.

His body seizes up, the machine monitoring his heart begins beeping a steady rhythm again, and the shaking stops.

*What? What did he just tell me?*

"Hmmm," Epsilon muses. "Perhaps he's ready to play now. Let's give it a go, shall we?"

Before I can answer, the harvesting cage on the wall across from me comes to life. Quickly, it moves into place. A moment later, a thousand needle-threads are piercing my skin.

A moment after that, I'm empty.

# FINN

*S**tatic. Blinking. White noise***. Everything's blurry.
White-blue flash.

Data display online.

SYSTEM REBOOT: COMPLETE

COMBAT READINESS: 92%

SPARK FLOW: STABILIZED

RECEIVER NODE LINKED — VERTEBRAL PORT 2

I see. A room. A lab. Sterile. Bright. Still.

The room is circular, metallic, humming. My boots lock into the floor with a soft click.

Directly ahead, a thick pane of glass. Behind it, four girls —strapped upright in glowing rings. The rings aren't just rings. They're full-body restraints—vertical halos lined with silver-gold bracing, shaped to hold a girl in perfect presentation. Arms extended, ankles bound, spine arched just enough to be vulnerable.

The metal isn't cold, not visibly. It glows faintly at each point of contact, like it's reading her pulse through her skin. Straps cradle the curves of their bodies with unnerving precision—as if the frame was made for these girls, their shapes, this moment.

Small notches on the inner rim mark pressure points where needle-thin threads feed into the skin, designed to coax the spark out.

The rings don't just hold them—they drink from them. And each girl glows where she bleeds energy, faint veins of blue crawling along her throat, her wrists, her ribs, like vines.

All this information comes to me as naturally as if I built this apparatus myself. Chills run down my spine as I begin to understand what it is I'm looking at.

White-blue flash.

COMBAT ROOM: 7-A

AUGMENT ID: F-SCOTT-579-A

AUGMENTATION STAGE: 9B

AUGMENT STATUS: STABLE AND HOLDING

UNIT 4-ALPHA-PRIME COUPLER: J-BELL-579-B

STATUS: ENGAGED

SPARK OUTPUT: STABLE

A vision of Tau City comes to mind. I smile, the edges of my mouth barely move, but I feel this smile. Because that was the day I saved her.

Clara. My biggest failure.

Jasina. The only thing I ever did right.

White-blue flash.

OPPONENT 578-A

UNIT 3-ALPHA-PRIME COUPLER: 578-B

OPPONENT 577-A

UNIT 2-ALPHA-PRIME COUPLER: 577-B

OPPONENT 576-A

UNIT 1-ALPHA-PRIME COUPLER: 576-B

What the hell is this?

A speaker crackles overhead. Xi's voice fills the chamber like static poured into a throat. Smooth, but flat. Robotic. Like he's forgotten how to speak to people.

"Elsha, one misstep and you're out. Maelis. I expect you to fail, but feel free to challenge my assessment. I would love it. Veyra, you've been excellent. You always are."

"And Jasina..." There's a pause here. I have the sudden

urge to vomit. I can't see him, but I feel him like he's a part of me now. And he's smiling. At my woman. He's smiling at her. "Don't disappoint me."

White-blue flash.

SPARK FEED: STABILIZED

HEART RATE: ABERRANT

EMOTIONAL NOISE DETECTED. FILTERING…

On the other side of the thick glass, the girls are screaming. I can't hear them, but their mouths are open, wailing.

But not Jasina.

She's looking right at me with those royal-blue eyes. Spark dances around her bindings, curling up into the air in the shape of… I lean in, squinting. Are those—

"I expect your best," Xi is talking again. My attention snaps back to him. "Failure to keep your partner alive will result in relocation to the Epsilon Factory for a complete harvest."

I take a step, stumbling forward, unable to breathe. Because I know what this is.

I whirl around, falling over.

BALANCE COMPROMISED

Autocorrecting posture…

WARNING: SYSTEM UNSTABLE

SPARK INTAKE: IRREGULAR

NEURAL FEEDBACK LOOP DETECTED

EMOTIONAL SPIKE: 87% ABOVE NORMAL LIMITS

RECOMMENDATION: Initiate sedation protocol.

USER RESPONSE: BLOCKED

USER RESPONSE: BLOCKED

USER RESPONSE: BLOCKED

Override request denied.

Operator remains conscious.

"Override failed." These words come over the speaker like tin crackling in a fire. "So... the dog bites back, does he?" A chuckle. "Good. I love rebels."

*Rebels.*

A flash of memory...

*"I thought that's what you wanted? For the Rebellion to succeed?"*

*Jasina is looking at me like I'm the worst. "Well, in the beginning, I did."*

*"The beginning of what, Jasina? We've known each other three days. This is the beginning."*

*"The beginning of three days ago, then. I'm mad at my auntie. She's not the person I thought she was. In fact, I'm not sure this whole Rebellion is what I thought it was."*

The *Rebellion.*

That's what this room is about.

*No, Finn. You're gone. That place is gone! You blew it up!*

"Do you have any idea who I am," Xi says. The room hums louder. His voice deepens—not in volume, in gravity. "You are standing in the heart of RhoXi, Finn Scott. *My* city. I carved it from scrap and spark. I built its towers, its tunnels, its systems—every breath taken inside these walls is a breath I allow. I don't rule by force. I rule by architecture."

He chuckles. Low and distorted, but all the more godlike.

"You were never chosen. You were configured. Your loyalty is a line of code. Your love? A useful glitch. You don't *protect* Jasina. You don't *love* her. You *power* her. It's not you, I want, my boy. It's *her.*"

I ignore him. Because I *did* protect her. I *did* save her. I *did* it all right!

The speaker crackles, just once. Then stillness as another memory comes to mind. Small, it is. Like a drop of water on a parched tongue in the mid-day sun.

*"I want to know things, Jasina. I want to understand what's happening to us. I'm tired of the lies and I want the truth. I think it's up there in that room. And if you want the truth as well, then I would like you to join me so we can find it together."*

"Do you understand what she is, Finn? She is the closest I've come to perfection. A maiden who glows without death. A spark that recharges. Do you realize what that means?" A silence here so I can contemplate what it means.

And I know what it means. It means... we lose.

"It means I win the Game of Gods."

A static pulse rolls through the floor, like the Factory is listening too. "The others talk of freedom, of revolution, of faith. But I play for reality. I am the architect of the Grand Design. And this girl of yours will be the spark that gets me my final tower between worlds, where every system, every soul, will realign to me.

Now the voice lowers—soft, intimate, cruel.

"So stand up, Augment. You were made for this moment. Your fight is the matchstick I strike against her skin. Let's see how brightly she burns."

Something buzzes in my head. I fall to the ground, hands over my ears, trying to make the high-pitched screeching go away.

But it's not external, it's *inside* me.

White-blue flash.

CRADLE ARRAY: ACTIVE

SPARK INTERFACE: STABLE

FEMALE CONDUITS – ONLINE

This is when I see them. I'm on my feet again, not even aware how that happened. I scan the three men standing before me. Tags pop up as my eyes sweep across the room.

OPPONENT 578-A-DAINRIK

UNIT 3-ALPHA-PRIME COUPLER: 578-B-VEYRA

OPPONENT 577-A-ZAYLEN
UNIT 2-ALPHA-PRIME COUPLER: 577-B-MAELIS
OPPONENT 576-A-UNKNOWN
UNIT 1-ALPHA-PRIME COUPLER: 576-B- ELSHA

Each man's eyes glow blue. Spark comes out of the back of their necks as a flickering wave of blue static—arcing high up into the air, flowing through the thick pane of glass that separates us, the combatants, from them, the Maidens.

But it connects us too. This is what Xi was talking about. Jasina is powering me. I can feel her. The other women are powering my opponents.

This is a death match.

We fight until we die.

Last man standing saves the girl.

I almost laugh.

White-blue flash.

SPARK FEED RAMPING — LEVEL 3

TARGETS LOCKED

BEGIN COMBAT IN 3... 2...

I strike. Swinging before I even lock on my target. My fist lands, flesh cracks, bones fold. Someone screams—it might be me.

I blink. Dainrik's already down. Neck wrong. Blood everywhere.

White-blue flash.

Zaylen lunges. I don't feel it when he hits me, I only feel it when he stops moving. His arm's still twitching on the ground.

White-blue flash.

The last one moves differently—calm, brutal, practiced. No fear, no fire. Just precision.

Power surges through like I've been hit with lightning. We collide in the center of the room, and for a second, it's like watching someone else wear my body. I stab my fingers through his throat—his spark explodes across my face in a flash of blue light. In the same moment, his fist slams against the side of my head with the force of thunder, cracking bone, snapping me to the side.

He drops fast.

I drop slower. My knees hit first, then my shoulder, then my cheek hits the floor, slick with blood—his and mine.

I roll over on my back, looking up at the ceiling.

This is when I see her.

But it's not her.

It's her spark.

Tiny wings flicker in the air above me. A shimmering, like a perfect summer night. Swirling like a tidal pool along the Tau City canal. Soft and pulsing, like a heartbeat.

Her voice in my head...

*"You settled for me."*

*"I didn't settle for you, Jasina. You're the only damn thing I've ever done right. I didn't save Clara. I saved you."*

"And now," her fluttering blue butterflies land on my cheek and whisper in my ear, "it's my turn to save *you*."

# TYSE

*The minute my eyes open* inside the arena, I know one thing.

It's not enough.

Whatever spark Clara gave me, it's not enough.

Because I'm in a makeshift cage, hangin' high above the mutants, and they are comin' for me. And it's not like the cage bars were put there to keep me in—or keep them out. Because there's too much space between them. Even a guy as big as me can slip through.

This isn't a prison, it's a trap.

And the predators below are comin' for me.

They're climbin'. Hand over hand, claw over claw, swarmin' up the metal beams like ants after meat. Half of them aren't even whole—missin' eyes, draggin' limbs, sparks sputterin' from half-dead augments. One lets out a shriek as it slips, falls, and another one climbs right over its body like it didn't even happen.

I brace, breath caught in my throat—then stop.

Wait.

I look past the ones comin' now.

The arena floor below isn't packed anymore.

It used to be a tide. A sea.

But now… there's a darkness down there. Emptiness.

How many of them have I already killed?

And why am I still standin'?

I blink, hard. My fingers twitch against the rail as I

picture the augmentation room. And then, a memory...

*I am fourteen.*

*The bright lights above me.*

*The straps, tight around my body.*

*Skin buzzin' like static electricity before a sand storm.*

*I am strong, and willin', and ready.*

*I am not afraid.*

*I'm not.*

And I wasn't. Not then. I didn't understand enough about what was happenin' to be properly afraid. Nanothreads, replicate body systems, data displays—they were just *words* to me back then.

Today, they're consequences.

*Not enough.*

The mutant to reach me first is a fast climber with long limbs, spindly fingers, and no eyes—just a slick metal plate where the eyes should be, etched with a glowin' blood-red triangle. It hisses when it sees me. Not a scream. Just a hiss, like it's breathing outrage. Then it lunges, shoulder first, shoving through the cage bars like they aren't even there.

I twist, catch it mid-leap, and slam it into the railin' with a grunt, making the whole cage shudder. Bone cracks. My knuckles tear open. But this thing doesn't care. It keeps writhin', bitin', clawin'.

It's never gonna stop.

Not until I make it stop.

Fingers twitchin', I turn it around, shove it into the cage bar, snap its neck, and throw it over the side—taking out three mutants as they climb up.

Then I spin—too late—to face the one that just came up behind me.

This one's big. No armor, just skin stretched tight over metal bones. Its jaw hangs wide open. Too wide, like it was taken apart and never quite put back together. There's no spark in its eyes. Just hunger. Rage. Programming.

It strikes—and everythin' that comes next is just instinct.

Seventeen years of killin', and death, and loss, and lessons.

Seventeen years of mods, and upgrades, and glitches, and patches.

I'm not even an animal at this point. Nothin' but a machine.

This isn't my fight—*it's his.*

Let the protocol run.

Because my mind is somewhere else now. Floatin'. Watchin'. High above the arena. Detached. Unaffected by what Tyse down below does.

*I am back in Tau City, just inside the boundary of the Tower District. Kissin' Clara Birch to tame her spark. Lettin' it spill into me. Lettin' it fill me up. Taking it all, as much as I can, to save us from the spyin' eyes of Stayn.*

Where am I?

*Epsilon! Epsilon! Epsilon!*

For the first time, this chant is only in my head. It's not real.

I look down again—further down. Scannin' the scaffolding of the cage and the arena below. Countin' bodies. Not dead ones—there's too many. Livin'. And there's so few.

I've torn through his horde—his mistakes.

But on the big screen, Epsilon's laughin'. That twisted, burned face is laughin' as he pumps his fist in the air screamin', "That's the spirit!"

And then, just when I think I'm about done here, wall panels open up in the side of the arena and they pour out. Hundreds of mutant augments.

Only these ones can *fly.*

Not enough.

I knew it. The moment I got here, I knew it.

*Clara!*

I had a plan. I did. I *do*. But I can't do it, not fightin' on fumes. And now, that plan is the least of my worries because now, when I beg for her help, it's not about a plan.

It's about survivin'.

*Clara!*

This plea for help is inside me. Down there, in the fight, I don't even have time to think, let alone scream.

*Clara!*

Down below the first flying mutant arrives at the cage, makin' it swing wildly in mid-air. I watch myself drop to a knee, duck a swipe, punch up into its gut. It folds, wheezes, then I rip a wing off and kick it through the bars.

Another lands behind me, claws raking my back. I turn, grab its head, slam it into the rail until it stops moving. Blood sprays. I wipe it off my eyes, fists already rocking the face of the next one.

Back up here, things go quiet and a blue mist slowly begins to undulate its way towards me. For a moment, I suspect poison. That mad god is gonna kill us all with poison.

But it's not poison. It's... *spark*.

Clara?

No. Not Clara. Somethin' else. Somethin' I've never seen before appears in the mist all around me. Women. Girls. Even babies. All of them empty and dark, made up only of an outline of spark.

This spark manifests as a glowing, cracklin' line of light. Arcing off in many directions at once, like I'm in the middle of a sweep storm, born from the minds of ancient gods.

Flickerin' and hangin' in the misty air.

Then, it silently splits the air, no wind, just a high, stingin' hiss as it branches off into a million little fingers, like it's reachin' for retribution itself.

Suddenly, the air becomes buoyant, liftin' me up. Makin' me float. I can no longer right myself. I spin, helpless, in a sea of spark.

Then—the first one hits me. The jolt of electric current penetrates my soul, jerking my body through the mist, like a toy boat floatin' on a ragin' sea.

*Clara!* I call again—but it's still silent, because there's no air left in my lungs.

But she's not here. And I want to panic about that, but there's no time because the arcs of spark keep hittin' me. One, after the other, after the other.

Everythin' burns.

I'm screamin'.

Clueless as to what the actual fuck is happenin'.

Helpless to stop it.

I... surrender.

But still, I beg.

*Clara...*

Because I have a plan, just get me out of here! *Give me a chance to save us!*

A great sonic boom pulls my body into millions of parts. Splits my mind into billions of pieces. Renders me nothin' but darkness.

But still, I float.

Everythin' silent now.

Mist, all around me.

And the women.

Maidens, I realize.

Like them, I am empty. Only here, only manifest, by an outline of glowing, blue spark. Inside me, there is nothing but black.

*What do you want!*

I scream it, but it comes out as silence.

*What do you want!* I try again. Because that's all I can do. It's either keep goin' or give up. And I will not give up. Not without Clara by my side.

This time, I hear a voice…

A woman floats out in front of the rest. And for some reason, I think I know her.

She smiles at me, reaching for me.

I pull away, but it does no good. I'm floatin', so all this movement does is make me spin.

An arc of lightning stops me. Stills me. Rights me. And then we're face to face.

Me, and her.

She's reaching out for me, offering a hand. And when I look past her, I see that there's a woman behind her, reaching for her. And behind her, reaching as well.

My eyes follow the long line of Spark Maidens, all holding hands to form a chain. And at the end of the chain, when I look past this realm, this place—I see through the worlds and find… the *Source*.

The crystals we found in that cave.

I blink. Look down at myself. Fightin' like crazy—but still losin'. I can already see how it ends.

"There's something really wrong with me now," I tell the woman who's reaching for me.

She smiles, and for the first time, she speaks. "Clara…"

I want to stop this now. I want to stop the ride and get off. Because this name comin' from this Spark Spirit's mouth, *kills me.*

"I need her," I say. "Or we're both gonna die."

The woman just shakes her head, then she lifts up a

finger, spark flashin' out of it like glowin' blue static, and touches me on the arm.

Burning pain sears my skin. I want to scream, but I have no breath to do it. When she withdraws her finger, the pain lingers, but slowly, as this pain dissipates, a mark appears.

A symbol.

One that looks very familiar because I've seen it, burned into the body of my love when she lights up for me at night.

I look up at the women. "What is—"

But that's as far as I get, because they're all around me now. Millions of them. Billions of them. All tryin' to touch me.

All tryin' to leave their marks burned into my skin

The pain is so intense, I just blink out.

Floatin', floatin', floatin'.

But... also... pretty fuckin' full too.

My eyes snap open and I'm me again. There's one small moment between mutant attacks, and I use this moment to look up, trying to find the mist. Trying to validate the spark.

I'm stronger, I can keep going now, I know it was real.

I also know something else—something they didn't explain, but implied.

This is not mine.

This spark belongs to *them*.

It's a debt I accept. I can deal with paybacks later.

Right now, I just need to live.

After that, I need to win.

And I do not have enough.

It's just not enough.

"*Clara,*" I beg, lookin' down at my right hand—trying, trying, *trying* to make it work. "*Please, please, please...*"

And then the next attack hits, stealing my happy ending.

# JASINA

*And now... it's my turn to save you.*
I wake with words on my lips.

Blue butterflies swirl around me, gently brushing powder against my skin with their flutter wings.

The God's Tower Stage is to my left, the Maiden Tower to my right, and directly in front of me is the God's Tower Waterfall. This is the source of the canal. I am eight years old and it has been months since Imogen Gibson walked through the God's Tower Doors. Long enough for people to forget about her.

There is a special gala tonight and Auntie invited me so I could mingle with the up-city children. "If you could manage to fit in," she'd said, "you could be one of them. I could bring you up here, educate you in the ways of the rich, and you could mount the Rebellion from a place of privilege."

It never happened, obviously.

I became Jasina Bell, the down-city whore.

Auntie didn't like my dress that afternoon. Being eight, I couldn't afford fabric. So I picked a tattered dress from the trash bins behind a Shipping District whorehouse, ripped the seams, and turned it into something new.

The look on Auntie's face when I got off the boat at the Maiden District made my insides quiver with fear.

Long story short, I didn't go to the gala. I was sent away, chased by nasty words and condemnation. I went to the waterfall so I could dream of a day when no one was in charge of me, and no one could judge me, and all I wanted that day was to go home without having to ask for help.

If I had wings, I could fly. If I had gills, I could swim.

But I was helpless and I had nothing but a dress made from second-rate silk picked out of the trash.

I hated that feeling.

The helplessness.

It's why I stayed in the Rebellion, odd as that is, since it was Auntie who injected this futility into me. I hated the way we were treated down-city. I hated the lack of... well, everything. We had nothing. And the people up-city had it all.

This is what I see when I wake with words on my lips.

Finn Scott. The absolute poster-boy for up-city fucks.

I am face down on a large piece of circular glass. If this feels familiar, it's because it is. My lot in life. To be strapped to a spark harvester to feed a god or power an augment.

Luckily, there's no Donal here.

Just Finn. Directly below me, standing on a black-glass stage that pulses with lines of light, holding a fighting stance like he's been put on 'pause', and looking more like one of those workers in the Factory Dimension than the man I met a couple of months ago.

His body looks like it's been chiseled from stone. Glowing eyes, blond hair now white, and two streams of crackling cyan-blue spark come out of his shoulders and attach to my plate.

Aside from Finn, there are three other men being held hostage on the circular platform below, as well as three other girls strapped to plates of glass above them. The air is wet with the spark that's being harvested from us. It hisses and crackles around the plates like little bits of static holding the power of lightning.

"Gentlemen!" A voice roars from below the mist. It's Xi. My first look at the real him. Which is jarring because he looks nothing like the hologram he presented to me in the Factory. His style is lead singer in a spinecore band that plays the down-city docks back home.

A young, muscular man stuck in his clash-boy era, Xi is tall, and lean, and wears no shirt. His eyes glow cyan-blue, his face etched with light. Hair sticks straight up, white and spiky, like it's been electrocuted. At first, I think his chest is inked up with tattoos, but then, I realize that he's not covered in skin, but black glass. And those designs aren't tattoos, they're *switches*.

Glowing with blue-gold spark and orange-green swirls, the switches wind around his torso and arms like snakes. Bright against his glassy skin, they flicker on and off, making captivating patterns that I find hard to look away from.

He wears pants that look like they were stitched from the hides of ancient animals and his shirtless upper body jingles and clanks with chains. They are every width—thin and thick—hanging from his neck and dropping from his belt. Gold, and silver, and heavy with charms—they must number in the hundreds.

He makes quite a picture, I'll give him that.

But now, at least, it makes sense. Because this narcissistic god remade Finn in his own image. He turned Finn into one of *them*.

"May I present to you," Xi opens his arms in a wide gesture, motioning to Finn. "The answers to all our prayers. My fellow Medians, please indulge me as I list the full capabilities of my latest—and best to date—success!"

This is when I notice the other gods. Placed around the massive circle like a clock with only nine hours in the day, Xi stands at midnight. "First, and foremost," he bellows! "The final solution to our greatest problem—the Cognitive Port Interface! This is a direct link to the augment's brain stem that allows for total mind-body control. Divine spark signatures are converted into neural patterns readable by the augment's cortex. But it gets better—because this model comes with bidirectional syncing, allowing the god to receive real-time feedback from the host augment. Which allows for a more natural response in combat, speaking, and decision making."

He's got his claws in Finn's brain stem. I don't actually know what that is, but I can take a good guess. Rage fills me. Who gave him the right? Why does this thing assume that humans are his pet projects?

How many young men has he done this to? How many young women has he drained to power these mad experiments?

I am not a victim. I refuse to be a victim.

But this thing has turned me into one.

And that... I cannot stand.

My rage builds, the spark all around me begins to crackle violently. Hissing and sputtering, it travels down the cord of light to Finn's shoulder, making him spasm for a moment.

Something chimes in my head and suddenly, spread out before me is...

Well, I have no idea what it is. Some kind of... table. Like the one in the Looking Glass rooms, only it's not attached to a desk, it's floating in the air in front of me like a screen on the PPD I've been using all week.

"Second!" Xi's voice is booming, echoing off the dark metal walls all around us. His voice is so loud, it overpowers the sound of the spark and makes the golden lights embedded into the walls flicker with excitement. "Dimension Stability Core!"

Right in front of my face, glowing like a hologram, the PPD screen lights up with words in blue. COGNITIVE PORT INTERFACE: ACTIVE.

What the hell am I looking at?

"This reworked Dimension Stability Core is embedded in the chest of the augment to prevent dimensional rejection syndrome when a god enters. This ensures the human body remains anchored across multiple planes, allowing for cross-dimension piloting. It also auto-tunes to the god's home dimension, preventing degradation of the vessel."

Cross-dimension piloting?

Just as I think these words, a new line appears on the holographic PPD screen: DIMENSION STABILITY CORE: ACTIVE.

My mouth drops open.

"Third!" Xi is still going on and on about how he's ruined the father of my child. "A Multi-Threaded Cognition Matrix that allows parallel processing of two minds in one body."

Again, a new line of words appears in the air in front of me: MULTI-THREADED COGNITION MATRIX: ACTIVE.

"Your augment will remain aware while being piloted— no memory loss, no dissociation. This enables tag-team combat and decision stacking, where both the augment and the god can act independently or in tandem."

That's great, that's just great. How long has that god been inside Finn's head? The whole time we've been in the Upper Dimension? Was he inside Finn while we were... oh, my god. I can't even finish that thought, it's so gross. *Was I having sex with that thing?*

"Fourth!" Xi must add a flourish of spark to this bullet point, because a wave of it hits me, taking my breath away as it pierces my throat and enters my lungs. "The Phase-

Reinforced Neural Sheath will prevent the human brain from melting under divine presence. It reinforces key neuraaal... pathwaaays..." His voice slows into a purring warble that makes the words feel left behind. "And with conductive spaaaaaark-threaded myeliiiiiin—"

Then—everything stops.

Everything down below on the floor, at least.

Just not the mist of spark all around me. This turns into something thicker, wetter—like actual water. And for a moment, I'm that little girl again, wishing the canal of spark-water would take me home.

But it's no longer a direct route down-city.

I don't even know what dimension I'm in.

*That's not true, Jasina. You're in the Upper still. Because Xi can't be a clashboy lead singer in a down-city spinecore band in the Factory dimension.*

*Because he's not real. He can only exist there as a lie.*

And this, I realize, is a good thing.

Because while Xi-Factory was a hot mess of a place, devoid of spark—RhoXi *is certainly not.*

The air is wet with it. It's all around me, like a sea.

I swim in the spark the same way I swim in water.

It's not even a plan, that's how inevitable what comes next is.

Because I've been here before.

I've been strapped to a plate in a weird Looking Glass room three times now and they all end the same way.

Me spooling up power to break shit or win a fight.

But this time, I'm gonna kill a god.

Because I'm no longer Jasina Bell, down-city whore.

I'm piloting the answer to all Xi's prayers.

I've got one card.

Master's Bargain. And his name is Finn Scott.

A voice wails out over some kind of system speaker, forcing Xi to shut the hell up about his new Bio-Synch Halo upgrade as the PPD interface in front of me—the mind of Finn Scott himself, flashes bright green.

COGNITIVE PORT INTERFACE: *ONLINE*
DIMENSION STABILITY CORE: *ONLINE*
MULTI-THREADED COGNITION MATRIX: *ONLINE*
PHASE-REINFORCED NEURAL SHEATH: *ONLINE*

And then, a very simple question.

INITIATE COMBAT MODE? Y/N?

*Let's fucking go.*

I smash 'yes' with my mind and Finn Scott breaks free of his holding pattern—moving before I even know what 'yes' feels like.

One breath, and he's gone—vanished from the center of the stage and reappearing like a blur. A crash to my left. A body to my right. The first man doesn't even scream before his chest caves in. The second folds backwards, spine in the wrong direction. The third tries to run but gets pulled back by something I can't see—Finn's hand? A spark leash?—and he crumples like wet paper.

A shrieking sound—glass under pressure, warping—and I realize it's not coming from me. It's the other girls. The circular harvesters they're strapped to are cracking. The spark cords are still draining them, even though their augments are dead. No outlet. No balance. The spark is boiling. The glass is spiderwebbing out beneath them like ice under a heavy foot.

My own harvester plate hums louder. The spark running through me is scorching now, flooding into Finn like water from a faucet. I feel him draw more—pull harder—like he's chasing the next threat, but there isn't one.

I scream, but it comes out silent. A whip of pain lashes

through my legs. My vision goes spotty. I hear myself gasping, but it's far away, like I'm underwater. Every time Finn strikes, my spark drains. The cord connecting us isn't a line—it's a siphon. My power flows into him in big gulps, faster than I expected. Too fast.

One plate of glass shatters, a girl's body falls like meat. Then the second and the third.

Gods are shouting, cheering, laughing.

Finn turns to them.

I see through his eyes.

I feel his helplessness. His hate.

And I make it my own.

Xi is our target. The object of all this loathing. And Xi knows it. He's not in control. He's not cheering, or shouting, or laughing like the others.

Finn takes a step.

Xi raises his glowing blue eyes, they land right on mine. Locked. "You want a fight, girl? You think you're in control here? You're nothing but a baby."

The other gods have noticed Xi's confusion now. They're not afraid though. They snicker, taunt him, laughing louder. I see the rage build inside Xi as he takes a step forward, outside the glowing circle at the edge of the stage that marks his place at midnight. "Shut down," he says. Calmly, almost a whisper.

Fear spikes through me like a wave of sickness. Then the pain as his command becomes law inside Finn's augmented brain. My heart stutters. My limbs seize. Spark drains out of me so fast I feel hollow.

"*No!*" Finn screams.

Xi turns, rage pasted all over his face. The other gods are relentless with their mocking insults, igniting his fury and turning it into wrath. "SHUT DOWN!" he commands again.

Finn pulls the spark out of me in a rushing stream as he attacks. But Xi is not his target—it's the god to his right. He spins, covers the distance between himself and the god in two strides, slams his palm into the god's shirtless, glowing chest, and a wave of lightning ignites his fake skin. The spark drain spikes inside me, burning down my spine as something hot, sharp, and unstoppable. All the lit-up switches on this god's body flicker and go dark. He jerks, staggers—eyes dull and filled with confusion.

Then he folds backward over the stage edge like a broken hinge.

The other gods have caught on now—something is very, very wrong here. They are moving out of their positions on the clock, rushing at Finn.

I close my eyes, feel the force of spark inside me, *pull on it* —desperate to wring every last drop out of myself. Because this is it.

It's over.

Either we play the Sweep card and wipe out this tower of gods, or we die.

Finn reacts down below. Himself again?

No. Never again. But in control?

As close as it gets, I guess.

While he fights, I pull, and pull, and *pull* on the spark. I've got a little left—Finn takes it all.

They drop, these gods. These stupid, petulant princes. They burn with the gift I hold inside me like a treasure. This power only I have now, this power they want so badly they will grow girls like pigs and harvest them like meat.

Carnage below me. Spark flying around the room like wild lightning.

Finn pauses, breathing so hard—so weak now, he stumbles to the side, barely keeping his balance. He drops to one knee, bodies of broken gods scattered all around him.

I'm exhausted and spent. The glass below me is cracked, but somehow, still holding.

Are they dead?

I'm just beginning to hope, desperate for this to be over because I've got nothing left to give—when a shape steps out of the shadows.

"Well done, my boy," Xi says, as a slow clap echoes through the large room. "You've exceeded my highest expectations."

A sob leaks out of me as a sizzle of spark. The last of my power gone as the jaws of defeat clamp down with sharp teeth. He's still here. The others are all dead, and he's still here. The only god who really needed to die, alive.

Finn, still on one knee, does not rise. He doesn't even turn his head to acknowledge the god. Just presses one hand into the black-glass floor, bracing himself as he attempts to recover.

"I didn't expect you to be so willful," Xi says.

At first, I think he's talking to Finn. But when he raises his head so his eyes can meet mine, it's pretty clear he's not. He's talking to me.

"Just a baby, you are. But so, *so* desperate to break free. I almost had you, didn't I? You liked it, didn't you? All the girls I bring up here are the same, and you are no different, Jasina Bell. You're all a bunch of little down-city whores who grew up with nothing but big dreams of pretty dresses, and accounts filled with coin, and lazy days where your every whim is satisfied."

Finn gets to his feet, but he doesn't look the least bit recovered. He's gasping for breath, hunched over, barely able to stand. And he's pulling on me.

Looking for spark that isn't there.

"The offer stands," Xi says. Then he pans a hand at the bodies all around him. "This is the Game of Gods, after all. Players gonna play." Then he laughs. "You and Finn just took out all my rivals. I will rule the Medians like a tyrant from now on, thanks to the two of you."

I am gathering my strength, just about to respond, when Finn says, "I'm not done yet."

Xi laughs.

And I'm thinking the same thing. *Yes, Finn. You are. Because I've got nothing left to power you.*

But Finn raises his head, looks Xi in the eyes, and spits blood onto the now less-shiny black-glass platform. "I still see one last piece of shit standing."

He pulls on me again, looking for power. I can feel his desperation. Hear his thoughts. *Just a little more, Jasina. Just a little bit more—I got this.*

I try, I really do, but there's truly nothing left but drops.

Finn takes them, just as he takes a step towards Xi.

"SHUT DOWN," Xi commands.

Finn takes another step, spitting out more blood. "User response blocked," he whispers. "Override request denied. Operator remains conscious."

"Jasina!" Xi yells. "Listen to me now. This was a very good demonstration of power, but the test protocol is over! I will disable him," he threatens. "I will turn him off, and put him away, and you will be all alone in this world."

Finn takes another step. Growls, "No, she won't," and takes one more. Still pulling on me. It hurts now. Bad. I feel like I'm unraveling from the inside out. Like I'm literally about to come apart.

Xi backs up two steps. "You, and that baby of yours, will live penniless, lonely, and painful lives in the Factory

Dimension. Forever regretting the day you crossed the great god, Xi."

And the moment I hear that word, 'baby', things shift.

A light inside me. A tiny glimmer of life. Something... *created*.

Something... *female*.

Someone who, even at this tender age of less than zero, has *spark* inside her.

I will burn in Hell for what I do next. Burn for all eternity.

But I will do it anyway.

Because there can be no baby if there is no mother.

And I will not—*will not*—live as a factory slave to a god in *any* tower, let alone one I don't even have loyalty to.

I'd rather die trying than be that.

So I do the unthinkable.

I steal her spark.

Push it to Finn.

And Hell answers back with open arms.

# CLARA

*I* come out of the emptiness to chanting.

*Please. Please. Please.*

It's a prayer in my head.

Begging.

Then, I open my eyes.

Haryet stands before me. Floating in a mist of cyan-blue spark. Made entirely of spark threads, the chain of Maidens behind her. Her hand, reaching for mine.

*Please.*

I am empty. But I don't have to be.

This is the message that Haryet delivers. She points to my arm, floating up next to me until she can touch it. Immediately, a symbol appears. The same symbols that first showed up on my hands when I was nothing but a Little Sister.

First, my palms. Then the backs of my hands. Then my wrists, and finally, on Imogen's Extraction night, before any of this madness ever started, the spark inside me leaked out as light all the way up to my elbows.

Once I met Tyse, this went further. Sometimes, they cover my whole body.

When she pulls her finger off my skin, the mark disappears.

"What are they?" I ask Haryet. "Do you know?"

She smiles, nodding. Then points to herself. I'm shaking my head, not understanding. Then she holds up this same finger and spark spools out of her like thread.

I hate that word now. *Needles and thread!*

But I shake that feeling of dread off, and try to concentrate on what she's telling me. She's got a message. That's why she's here.

Her thread hovers in the air, weightless. Then begins to come towards me. As soon as the thread touches the skin on the top of my wrist, there's a hissing sound. Then intense burning as Haryet sears a mark into me.

The same mark she just showed me a minute ago.

The same mark that tagged the Factory women.

A mark that has always been there—under the right circumstances.

"They're names," I say. "I get it now."

I'm desperate to finish whatever is happening here and get back to my real body because ever so slowly, over the course of this interaction, the sound of chanting has come back. And it's not just the begging, either.

It's the horde.

*Epsilon! Epsilon! Epsilon!*

The fight! It's happening right now!

And that's what the begging is!

It's... *Tyse.* Calling for me!

*Clara!*

He's dying.

He's losing. "*He needs me!*" I yell. Aiming my frustration at Haryet.

"*No.*" For the first time since that night she walked through the tower doors, Haryet speaks to me. "He doesn't need *you*, Clara. *He needs this.*" She steps aside, allowing me to see the chain of Spark Maidens behind her. They hold hands. Millions of them. Billions of them. All dead from harvest.

"I don't understand."

"You will. When you take it."

I stare at her, blinking. Trying my best to sort this out. "Take... the source?" My gaze lifts past her, looking at the chain. Maidens connected through touch. Haryet, the end. Delivering a thread of spark.

I can take as much as I want.

I can save us!

"Look again, Little Sister," Haryet coos—only she's not pointing to the Source, she's pointing to my body. All over it are the names of the Factory women. Dull and lifeless, save for one, which is glowing. The symbol Haryet touched. The one that has a tiny bit of spark to make it glow.

"There is a price," she says. "And you will have to pay it."

"I don't care, how do I do it! Tell me what to do! I want to give all the spark to Tyse, *right now!*"

She tilts her head at me. Almost asks me if I'm sure.

But I am, and she knows this.

Suddenly, that tiny bit of spark thread grows thicker. Becomes a stream of blue-white static. Turns into a wave of lightning.

And then, I'm in the arena. Hovering over a fighting Tyse. Winged mutants are throwing themselves at him. One, after the other, after the other.

He's losing.

But he's trying.

"Give it to him!" I order Haryet. "I don't care what the price is, I will pay it!"

"Done."

Every symbol on my body lights up in unison as lightning cracks through the arena like a writhing serpent. Raw spark hits Tyse in the back. He folds forward, falling to the ground. The spark stream coming from Haryet is as thick as an ancient tree trunk. As volatile as a blazing sun. It pours into him.

But it's not saving him! Because while he's on the ground, the flying mutants are still attacking!

"*NO!*" I scream, pushing both my hands forward into the air.

Spark pours out of me now too, and I hold them off.

Three things happen at once now.

First, Haryet and the factory maidens have emptied all their spark into Tyse, so she retreats. Floating backwards like she's being pulled by a string. Before I can even comprehend what this means, she's gone. And the chain of Factory Maidens go with her.

Second, one by one all the glowing symbols on my body begin to extinguish.

*It's not enough!*

Having bought him a chance, Tyse is back on his feet, "Clara," he begs, looking down at his right hand. "*Please, please, please...*"

"How could it not be enough!" I scream back. "I gave you *everything!*"

Then, I'm gone. Done. Empty.

My eyes open. I'm strapped to a wall plate made of cold, hard metal. I can't think. I can't move.

I can't do anything because *IT'S NOT ENOUGH!*

And I don't know what more he wants from me! I don't have anything left.

But then, something.

A noise. Clattering.

My head is still strapped down, but my eyes shift just enough to see the cause of this clanking.

His weapon is on the floor, shaking like it's alive.

Or, more accurately, like it wants to *come* alive.

*Not enough!*

*Please, please, please.*

Tyse looking down at his right hand.

The hand that holds that weapon.

A memory hits me.

*Tyse, Anneeta, and me. Escaping from Tau City. He's holding the Versi. Lasers are targeting eighteen men in a wide arc, at the same time.*

He warned them.

*"One more step, Stayn. I'm not fuckin' around." Tyse is in front of us, that weapon of his pointed at the men who are blocking our way out.*

He warned them, not because he wanted to make a threat —but because the Versi *acts on its own.*

Epsilon, just a little while ago, saying, *You know they get buried with those weapons, right? They're biological.*

*Not enough!*

*Please, please, please.*

*Clara!*

Tyse looking down at his right hand.

A revelation. A terrible, gut-wrenching revelation.

It's not *Tyse* that needs more spark.

*It's his weapon.*

Panic. Pure panic hits me so hard, my heart thumps in my chest. Because I fucked up! I fucked it all up! I gave all the spark to *Tyse*, not the weapon! And now I have nothing left!

I can't breathe. I'm dying. Literally dying. Gasping, horrified and heartbroken. I let him down. He was counting on me to understand—to think and act. To have his back.

And I let him down.

*Shhhhhhhh*, a little voice hushes me. Soothing. Calming. Rational. *It's not over yet, Clara. Quiet now. You've got more. You know you do. You feel it. There's more, you just have to—*

I look down and there it is.

My heart shard.

My eyes roll up. And there's another little bit. The cherry spark. The final little bits of *me*. Mine. To use, or give away. Not much, but maybe enough if I combine them together.

It's not even a conscious decision. My heart shard sputters, goes out.

The clinking and clanking turns into a loud bang. And just before my little cherry spark extinguishes, the VersiStrike hovers up into the air, hits the wall, pulls backwards, and leaves through the fucking door!

# TYSE

*I'm the last man standing* on a stage made for monsters. Down below me, several dozen dead mutants are splayed out on the floor. Some didn't even make it that far, their bodies catching the scaffolding of the maze so they're hangin' off railings and platforms like discarded life-size dolls. There's blood everywhere and the whole arena reeks like death.

The winged mutants keep comin' at me. They don't seem sentient. They're all teeth, claws, and instinct. But there are a lot of them.

I'm full of spark now, though. So it's not much of a problem. It's just… this isn't how we win. I don't know how many more of these things Epsilon's got, but surely he does have more.

It's a time waster. He sent his best guys up first, they're already rottin' down below.

These mutants here, they're a holdin' pattern, and nothin' more.

Because that fucker knows he's lost. And now he's tryin' to get away while I'm up here, busy workin' my way through a horde of mistakes.

But there's no point in runnin', tryin' to catch him. Because as long as he's got one minion left, they're gonna stand between him and my revenge.

And now, when you add in the fact that the stands are

empty—and I didn't kill all those men—it means they're hidin'. Waitin' for an ambush.

Maybe, if it were just me, I could find a way out. It wouldn't be easy, but I could pull that off. But it's not just me anymore—*it's us*. And there's no way—not even as small way —that I get away from these semi-sentient battle bats with Clara in tow.

I need to finish them, and then I need to finish the hundreds of men who weren't yet augmented into battle monsters, and then I need to finish Epsilon.

And this blessin' of spark—deluge as it is—isn't enough.

*It's just not enough.*

I look down at my right hand. Trying to lock in. My palm seizes, every nerve in my hand firin' off like a system glitch. Tendons burn as an ice-cold wave of pressure climbs up my arm, only to be shut off at the elbow.

Data display flashes at me: *RETURNCALL FAILURE.*

*Please, please, please.*

*Clara!*

All this takes but half a second, that's all the time I have before more of the battle bats come at me. They are pathetically slow. Which is why Epsilon waited to use them.

It's a last-stand kind of moment for him.

But again, they don't have to be boss-level murderers to be effective—they just need to waste my time.

I kill a few, rip off some wings and throw 'em over the railing, punch one in the throat and let it choke on the metal platform while I try again.

But this time, I pray—and I pray hard.

*I am the executioner and the death...*

My heart thumps.

I can't breathe. I'm dyin', gaspin'. A feeling of horrific guilt washes over me—*her heart is breakin'.*

Because this is *Clara* I'm feelin'.

And it's a good thing, *because she heard me!*

She understands.

Immediately, my data display lights up. Commands flowing down like a cyan-blue waterfall. A snap, a click in the tendons of my palm. *RETURNCALL ACTIVATED.*

*Yes!* I laugh. *Yes!*

My forearm pulses. A low-frequency rumbles through my chest as my hand locks up, then bolts open like a trigger.

I hear it before I see it. Metal clankin' against metal. The pressure in the arena drops. The air folds around somethin' incoming—resists it for a split-second, then surrenders. A gale of wind passes me by, slammin' into the battle bats. They scatter like debris, wings shredded, bodies flung against the far wall.

And then—a whizzin' sound. Half a second later, the Versi snaps into my hand with enough force to knock me back a step.

*RETURNCALL ONLINE.*

A split-second later, my data display detonates in a flood of cascadin' light—

*PULSEMATCH: ONLINE.*

*AUTOSELECT: ACTIVE.*

*MINDLINK: ENGAGED.*

*SOULBIND: LOCKED.*

*PHASETETHER: LOADING...*

*VERSIPATH OVERRIDE: SEARCHING...*

*GHOSTMARK: CHARGING...*

The air around me distorts—heat, static, pressure.

The Versi isn't just a weapon anymore.

It's a system.

It's a goddamn event.

Now the game's fair.

VERSIPATH OVERRIDE: TARGETS LOCKED
GHOSTMARK: DEPLOYED.

I raise the Versi, no aiming necessary. The weapon hums low, then screams when I activate it.

GHOSTMARK FIRING: BIOMETRIC SWEEP INITIATED.

The world bends as everything not tagged as 'friendly' gets ripped from the arena like a tempest sweepin' dust across the desert in a storm.

Because the only 'friendly' in this place, *is me*.

The world bends back. A few moments of inhuman screamin'. Bodies thumpin' to the ground far below. Then... silence.

NON-SIGNAL ENTITIES: PURGED.

I breathe out. Relaxin'. Smilin'. Workin'.

I've missed it.

So what comes next, is kind of a bonus. With no holster for the Versi, I grab the platform railing with one hand and swing down a level. The scaffolding's not much—just a janky weave of rebar and rusted plating, the kind of patchwork shit you'd find in a halfway-collapsed mining rig back in the Outlands. Gaps everywhere. Welding marks like scars. Parts of it groan when I land, flexin' under my weight, like they weren't built to hold a Sweep-class anything.

But that's fine. I'm not here to ask permission.

I drop again. One level, then two. I grip a support pipe, slide down fast, boots sparkin' off the friction. Metal shudders. My shoulder clips a crossbeam, rattles my teeth. I land hard on a grated walkway—knee bent, Versi still hummin' in my hand like it's buzzin' for round two.

From here I can see the ground—just a few more levels down.

Dead mutants below. Twisted bodies. Wings torn, limbs bent at angles no god ever intended.

But somewhere deeper in this place... Epsilon's runnin'.

Good.

Let him.

Chasin's the part I like.

Blood squelches under my boots when I drop to the arena floor. It's everywhere—slick, congealed, steamin'. Mutant limbs twitch in piles, wings still flutterin' like they don't know they're dead. I keep the Versi at high-ready, barrel smokin', nerves buzzin' from overload, ears ringin' from the last scream that hasn't quite faded yet.

This is cleanup, not victory.

I breathe out, a low growl in my throat. Confidence isn't peace—it's pressure, coiled tight. I scan the bodies one last time. Then turn, find the nearest tunnel mouth—black, gapin', stinkin' of metal and meat.

And I walk in without lookin' back.

It's cold in here. Damp, too. Metal pipes above are drippin' and hissin'. The whole place stinks of rot and stale coolant. I pause at the first corner, shoulder to the wall, eyes scanning the dark. Nothing moves.

OK. They ran. That's fine. I'm gonna clean them up no matter where they try and hide. Then I'm gonna hunt down Epsilon and we're out.

Easy.

Blinkin', I trigger the PhaseTether on my data display so the plan I've been concoctin' in my head the last few days can play out.

Time to end this shit.

But instead of the usual data flash tellin' me it's online, I get a flicker and a message...

UPDATE REQUIRED: *It has been 2972 days since your last update.*

UPDATING MOD...

STAND BY.

I lower my Versi—lookin' at it. "Really? You're gonna do this to me *now*?"

*1%...*

"This is not cool."

PREPARING PROMOTIONAL PACKAGE...

Oh no.

No no no—

As if to mock me, the speaker on the Versi comes to life, emulating a carnival-barker-like pitch, tryin' to sell me a newer version.

"Step right up, step right up! Feast your eyes on the crown jewel of forbidden warfare, the myth, the menace, the *PhaseTether 7.77*!"

"For fuck's sake!" I shake the weapon, hopin' the gyro might kick in and knock the update offline.

Doesn't work.

"Not your daddy's bullet, no sir—this little beauty doesn't *kill* the enemy, it unhooks 'em from reality!"

*5%...*

Why me?

"*Pull the trigger—watch 'em vanish!* One twitch and your target's shakin' in limbo, slippin' sideways into a dimension so unstable, even death won't follow."

*9%...*

"Contain 'em! Banish 'em! *Torment* 'em, if that's your fancy! We don't ask questions—we just displace."

"Yeah, yeah, torment 'em, got it—just fuckin' load already."

*12%...*

"PhaseTether: Because dead is too easy. *WARNING! Highly unstable! Side effects may include spontaneous howling, spatial screaming, and cosmic regret!*"

15%...

Of course there's muzak. I hum along like a jackass, because of course I know the tune. Everyone who's ever bled in the Outlands does.

Fuckin' Myra. She was the one who loved the mods.

*Don't think about that shit now, Tyse. Focus. You don't need to wait for the update! You're a goddamned Sweep Augment!*

Right.

Let's go. No more sales pitch. No more spark miracles. Just me, my hands, and the shit left over.

I move through the tunnels like I was built for it—low light, close quarters, blood in the air. My boots splash through standing water and streaks of something thicker. Every few steps, a mutant lunges from the dark.

One gets a blade through the throat—flesh parts like wet paper.

Another drops from the ceiling—I grab its jaw mid-roar and snap it sideways.

Crack. Toss. Step.

I don't breathe hard. Don't break rhythm. This is muscle memory.

This is *me*.

Shoulderin' a corner, I spot him before he sees me. He's hunched over, limp in his gait, hauling a couple of packs like they weigh more than he does.

My fuckin' rucks.

Every instinct goes quiet. No rage, no nerves, just target lock.

*Luther.*

That wired-up psychopath *lived*. And not just lived—he's draggin' both of my Versi ammo rucks like they're trophies.

He stumbles forward, muttering to himself, "We unspooled her, didn't we? We did, we did..."

Heat rises up inside me, burning rage.

*Unspooled her.*

*Calm down, Tyse. Breathe. She's fine. She gave you spark less than ten minutes ago. Whatever they did, it didn't work.*

OK. I'm good. I'm calm. But this one here, he's not gettin' away. Even if he didn't have my gear, he's got seconds left in this life.

I step out in to the dim light of the tunnel, purposefully letting my boots scuff on the ground so he hears me.

With a whimper, he turns.

"Hello, puppet. Whatcha got there?" The Versi—still updating— sits in my thigh pocket. I'm gonna get my hands on this one. After what he's done, he deserves a more personal exit from this world.

His face warps into something meant to be a smile, but comes off more like a partial paralysis. "You're the puppet!" He screams, words echoing down the dark, wet tunnels. "You! Not Luther! You're a monster! All monsters, 'cept for Luther!"

I blow out a breath, kinda speechless. It's sad, really.

"*Don't look at me,*" he snarls. "Nothing to see! Luther is nothing to look at!"

I don't bother taunting him. It's not worth it. "I'm gonna kill you now and take my gear. Would you like to... run? Or something? Or should I just get on with it?"

Luther doesn't run. Doesn't scream. Just tilts his head and gives me a crooked, yellow-toothed smile like this is all some inside joke only he understands. "We unspooled her good, didn't we?" he hisses. "Cracked her open like a cherry. All that spark, drip-drip-dripping out—"

I move. No hesitation. My hand closes around his throat mid-sentence, slamming him into the tunnel wall so hard the wet pipes above rattle.

He claws at me. Gasps. Eyes bulging.

I squeeze harder.

No words. No mercy.

Just pressure until his eyes go glassy and blood vessels burst.

Then I let him drop. Like trash.

I pull out the Versi—78%—shoulder my rucks, and move deeper in to the tunnels.

Fuck the augments, I've got a laser-focus on Epsilon now.

One more kill, then we're out.

The further in I go, the quieter it gets. No more claws on steel. No ragged breathing in the dark. Just silence—tight, coiled, waiting. When the tunnels widen, pipework gives way to polished walls, flickering with low emergency light. Factory core. Lab zone. I know the stink of it—burned metal, chemicals, blood that's gone stale in the vents.

He's close.

Not hiding. Waiting.

Good.

Let him wait.

I check the Versi. 93%.

Not enough to relax. More than enough to kill a god.

I keep moving.

A four-way intersection ahead. I've just barely processed this when the air shifts. I don't see him—I feel him. Static behind my eyes. Stench of rot all around me.

Then—*movement*.

From the side. Fast. Too fast.

I twist, raise the Versi—but I'm not fast enough. Something *stabs* into my side. It doesn't feel like a blade. It feels... *wet*. A fleshy *puncture*. Like a wasp the size of a man has jabbed me with a syringe full of fire. My ribs explode in pain. Nerve endings ignite. And then comes the *injection*.

Oh fuck.

Whatever's inside me—*it's moving*. Twisting. Unfurling like a *living thread*, crawling beneath my skin. I can feel it *burrowing*—trying to hook into something. To find a home. Rewire my threads. Rewrite my DNA. Like it wants to *take me over*.

My data display *flickers*. Glitches. A stream of corrupted characters floods the screen like infected code trying to worm its way into my neural pathways.

Myra. Jast. Stepan and Kirt. Infected. Writhing in pain. Screaming—beggin' me to kill them!

Epsilon steps out of the shadows, *smiling*. Burned and melted, skin sloughing off like wax, eyes gleaming red. "You're not special," he rasps. "You're a container. Let's see what happens when we fill you with *me*."

A beep. A flash on the data display. The corrupted stream halts. One word pops up in clean, glowing cyan-blue:

PHASETETHER: ONLINE.

Let's fuckin' go.

Most people, when presented with a problem set such as this one, would panic. It's normal. Natural. But I'm not even people at this point. I don't really believe in panic. Not since I had to shoot my team in the head to save their souls.

So... yeah. I blow out a breath—lookin' Epsilon straight into those demon-red eyes—and smile. Then I raise the fully-updated Versi and blow him into another dimension.

PhaseTether: Because dead is too easy. *WARNING! Highly unstable! Side effects may include spontaneous howling, spatial screaming, and cosmic regret!"*

The warped air smooths over, like the Corrupted God was never here.

I glance down at my wound, fingers pressing into my skin—which is lighting up green and orange in the surrounding area. It's not a deep wound. Barely bleeding. And that wriggling I felt a few seconds ago is subsiding now. The pain fading. It's a psyop—that's what this is. A war-stunt. Make the soldier question his own body long enough to break the mission.

My inner voice scoffs. *You're insane. You're Luther-level crazy if you think this injection was meant to scare, not scar.*

Maybe. But there's nothin' I can do about it now.

Nothin' I can do about it *here*.

I took care of business, it's time to leave.

Sucking in a breath, I grit my teeth and head for the lab.

It takes several minutes for me to find the right door, but when I do, it's open. Like Luther and Epsilon left it this way on purpose. Imaginin' this moment—me, walkin' in, gettin' my first look at Clara since all this shit went down.

It's... almost poetic. Tragically romantic, maybe.

Because from where I stand in the doorway, she looks dead.

My data display goes haywire—panic triggers firing across my field of vision. Cortisol spike. Adrenaline dump. EMOTIONAL OVERRIDE: STABILIZE.

My heart rate jumps, tries to sprint—

REGULATING...

It slows down against my will. My breathing evens out. I hate it.

The Versi system thinks I'm gonna lose control.

It's probably right.

But I don't move. Not yet. Just stare. Focused concentration as I take it all in.

Blood's seepin' out of her eyes and drippin' down her cheeks like yesterday's makeup. It's comin' out her nose, her ears, her mouth. Like something exploded inside her.

*Maybe somethin' did, Tyse?*

*Maybe it was you.*

HEALTH SCAN: SCANNING...

HEALTH SCAN: SUBJECT HEALTH CRITICAL.

I breathe.

Critical isn't dead. It's the best I could hope for.

Dropping to one knee, my rucks thud against the concrete floor.

Opening the first pack, I search for what I need. Find two of one, then two of the other, and snap them into the quad chamber.

I breathe.

Both cartridges locked in, I stand. Then turn to the door, walk out and aim the Versi down the long hallway to the right. I empty two chambers—one with VersiPath OverRide, the other with GhostMark.

Then I turn to the left and repeat the action.

That takes care of anything that got out of my way. Because VersiPath will hunt down an unsanctioned VerisStrike and kill the operator, no questions asked, and GhostMark'll mow down a horde without hesitation.

The Sweep of Epsilon Factory, Dimension 702, is now complete.

I breathe.

Find a spare holster in the ruck, strap it on my hip. Slip the Versi in. Then calmly—ever so calmly—walk over to Clara and extract her from the cage.

It takes nearly an hour to get the needles out, manually push the cage back into its restin' cradle on the opposite wall, and unstrap her.

She falls forward like dead weight the moment I unhook the chest belt. Then I pick her up in my arms, and walk out.

# EPILOGUE

*Though no god walks with me, I go where I must.*

*Though no heaven waits for me, I walk forward without fear.*

*Built in fire, tested in ruin—I carry the code that cannot break.*

*I do not serve, nor submit, nor bow.*

*I stand with those who stand beside me.*

*Their names are my armor; their memory is my shield.*

*In their silence, I move on.*

*In their absence, I find strength.*

*In their wisdom, I survive.*

**FROM THE FIELD OPERATIONS MANUAL: Sweep-Class Augments (declassified fragment, p. 17)**

"WHERE THE CREED ends in confession, the Prayer begins in consequence. These are not marching orders, nor is it liturgy. This is the final protocol of something that once was human.

'I do not serve, nor submit, nor bow.' It is a refusal. A rejection of gods, chains, and the illusion of purpose. But buried within its defiance is grief. Memory. Loyalty. I do not believe this was ever meant to be recited aloud. Only remembered."

—*MASTER FINNEGAN SCOTT, Lectures on the Line So Bright,
Final Chapter Addendum: "Prayer in the Wake of Code"*

# TYSE

*Though no god walks with me, I go where I must.*

It was a hot morning, the final day of our pre-deployment R&R, and I was sweatin' out last night's drink on the floor of our hotel room—which was nothing but a fuckin' tent. That's all there is in Psi City, just tents.

*Though no heaven waits for me, I walk forward without fear.*

Myra woke me up early, shakin' me. "Come on, Tyse. We're gonna miss all the good shit."

I pushed my hand into her face, then turned over, groanin'. Was up 'till three partyin' last night and the Sanddji comes with a wicked hallucinatory hangover, so I was not in any mood to get up at six-thirty am just so Myra could drag me around the Psi City mod-market.

She's kind of a prepper.

She *was*, Tyse. *Was*.

*I do not serve, nor submit, nor bow.*

But I did get up, and I did go with her.

Myra was always thinkin' up the stupidest scenarios where she'd pull through because she was a hoarder of the most bizarre aftermarket Versi mods you could think of. Even in the here and now—with my eyes closed, so fuckin' tired from stealin' spark from other dimensions to keep Clara alive, feelin' like death—I smile at this memory.

"It's not hoarding, Tyse. Not if it comes in handy later."

"Since when are three cases of spark cartridges gonna come in handy *later*?" I flicked her in the head. "They're the

551

first fuckin' thing you use when things go sideways. No one's savin' 'em for *later*, Myra."

*Built in fire, tested in ruin—I carry the code that cannot break.*

"How much for the PhaseTether?" she asked the coder selling mods in the next tent over.

"What the hell am I gonna do with PhaseTether?" I nearly guffawed. "Myra, it only works on *gods*. Where in the holy hell are we gonna taze a god with PhaseTether in the hell-fucked Outlands?" Then I eyed the coder. Givin' him a look. "Probably doesn't even work. Prolly gonna hit me with a fuckin' mandatory update the moment I need it, isn't it?"

The coder scoffed. "Maybe the better question is, what kind of augment doesn't update his mods before deployment? There's no updates in the Outlands, *augment*." He threw that word around like an insult. "Because there's no functional datanet."

Myra was frustrated by this time. Absolutely done with me. Because this was my general attitude about everythin' we'd bought that day. "For fuck's sake, how unimaginative do you have to be *not* to picture a scenario where PhaseTether saves your ass? Ya know what? Forget it. I'll take one, he's a hard pass."

I rolled my eyes. Sighed. Slouched a little. Gave in. "Fine. Hook me up too." Then I slid him my Versi-mod cartridge across the makeshift counter and turned my back while Myra took care of the credit exchange.

*I stand with those who stand beside me.*

I didn't know it at the time, but that would be the last aftermarket Versi mod Myra would ever talk me in to.

Because two weeks later I shot her in the head.

*Their names are my armor; their memory is my shield.*

I'm sittin' on the floor of the train, cradlin' a limp Clara in my left arm while I hold the Versi at high-ready with my right, when it rolls to a stop.

The doors hiss as they slide apart. I'm aimin' for the head.

I got sick of the fuckin' worker bots eight factories back when we pulled into Zeta. Started shootin' 'em as they tried to board my train. So this train is empty, save for Clara and me.

*In their silence, I move on.*

But this time, at the Xi Factory—it's not a worker who appears in my doorway. It's Lover Boy. Holdin' a limp red-haired woman in his arms. I don't actually recognize him. He looks nothin' like the man I saw fleeing Tau City with this same fuckin' woman lookin' the same fuckin' way.

But it's him.

Lookin' so much like me, my heart thumps.

He's even got the same regret all over his face. I don't know what he wants to take back, but for me, it's that moment on the tracks when I had my Versi in hand and I didn't fight, I ran.

It was seventeen against one in that tunnel. A losing bet when it's nothing but Sweep sanctioned augments.

But those mutants weren't sweep sanctioned. That's why I could use the Versipath OverRide and the GhostMark to clear out the entire factory before I left.

I should've fired. If I hadn't jumped us into all that hectic world-hoppin', and just fuckin' stood my ground and fought, we'd have won. The whole battle would've been over in seconds.

We'd have been on our way to find that good world.

We would still be whole right now, instead of broken.

Lover Boy registers Clara, his newly augmented eyes flaring up cyan-blue as he takes in the blood still drippin' out her ears, eyes, nose, and mouth.

"She's fine," I say quickly. Which is a lie. "She *will be* fine."

He looks confused for a moment, which gives me time to log the changes. He's shirtless, wearin' nothin' but a pair of black tactical pants. No shoes. Everythin' about him has been augmented. Muscles chiseled from stone, eyes flashing blue, then yellow, then back to blue. Blond hair now white, sides shaved like a proper Sweep recruit. And under his skin I can see the lights. Not functional yet, but there.

"Who did this to you?" I ask.

He looks down at the dyin' woman in his arms, then back up at me. "I didn't know."

That's not what I asked, but I don't ask again.

Because it's a lie.

He *did* know.

Whatever happened to this girl, he's the reason she's dyin'. He took her spark, the same way I took Clara's.

We're both guilty as fuck.

So I've got nothin' to say to him, but a lie in return.

"Join the fuckin' club." I nod at the floor and he slumps down, back against the bulkhead, whisperin' something in his girl's ear.

I look away.

Neither of us says anythin' as the doors close and we pull out of the station.

*In their absence, I find strength.*

"One day, Tyse," Myra says, pullin' me back to my tragic past, "you're gonna need these mods. And then you'll thank me."

*In their wisdom, I survive.*

Thank you, Myra.

# END OF BOOK SHIT

*Welcome to the End of Book Shit*. This is the part of the book where I get to vomit up all my feeling about what you just read or listened to. It's never edited so excuse any typos. I always write it last minute and this time is no different. So get ready, here we go...

*FIRST OF ALL*... it feels like I wrote this book forever ago, but I actually only started it the first week of January 2025 and finished April first. It was a solid three-month effort and I think it came out exactly the way I pictured it.

When I first start imagining a new world and a new story, the image in my mind is more of a gut feeling than anything tangible. And when I first came up with the idea of Game of Gods it was always Game of Gods. That idea of Gods in towers making power moves was there from the very beginning. I wanted to put all that stuff in book one because it's easy to imagine a world. It's all very big picture with grand ideas. But using words to explain things is a whole other matter.

I did my best to shoehorn the Game into Sparktopia, but it was never going to work. There was so much backstory, I couldn't even explain what the gods were doing without giving them a point of view, and that wasn't how I envisioned book one.

While I do write a damn good plot—and people can have all kinds of opinions about that, it's their prerogative—but if anyone says I *don't* know how to plot a book, they're just a fuckin' liar.

BUT... my books are never about the PLOT.

And the Gods in Game of Gods aren't my characters.

So no, there was no way to introduce the game in Sparktopia until the final chapter when Delta mostly spells it out. The Game firmly starts in book 2, Godslayer.

All along I had planned on doing a duology. It was gonna be two books. But as I started writing Godslayer, I realized it's at least three, and more likely to be four. Because I realized that the Omega Outlands were a whole separate matter that needed to be dealt with before I could properly end the series and there was almost no room for it in Godslayer.

But there's a very good reason why I spent so much time on Tyse's friend, Myra in this book.

I gave you some hints about the kind of Alpha City she came from—which is Alpha. About the myths and legends. About the train line itself. About what the Outlands might be.

But that's it. You've gotten hints, but the whole story is something else altogether and it's gonna take an entire book just to set that up. lol.

It was a very ambitious move on my part to have four main characters, each with their own story. And let me tell you, it became clear pretty early on in writing Sparktopia that this could very easily turn into a logistical nightmare if I didn't pay close attention.

It took me a very long time to write the first 50,000 words in Sparktopia for this reason alone. Three months to write a book might not seem like a long time to people, but it's an eternity for me. And Sparktopia really took more like four.

Matching up timelines for two different couples traveling in two different worlds, while still making sure they ended up in the exact same place at the exact right time, was hard. But the payoff was pretty fuckin' cool.

At least on my end. I saw that last chapter in Godslayer very early on. I had it all mapped out. It doesn't always come to me like this—I've written many, at least several dozen books, where I had no idea at all where it was gonna end.

That has not been the case with this series. While I didn't predict the ending of Sparktopia in chapter one, I did set it up and did not have to edit the book to make that ending happen.

Godslayer was different. I knew the last chapter and I wrote toward it from page one. I SAW that scene with Finn entering Tyse's train carrying a dying Jasina. I SAW that scene with Myra and Tyse in the Psi City mod market. I had that last line—*Thank you, Myra*—way before it came with the heavy emotional overload on the page.

It's a very rare thing as an author to have a story like this in your head. And I'm gonna say it for like the hundredth time in the EOBS—I do not do this for money. Money cannot buy the feeling at the end when I wrote the words, *"Thank you, Myra."*

Three fuckin' words. It's kinda dumb. But in those three words lies everything. It is the moment when we see Tyse as something real. Who he was before he killed his team to save them. Who he was before Sparktopia.

And the reason it's so fucking awesome is because he's given up every bit of his humanity for this moment to happen. It's raw, and real, and tragic.

If you buy the paperback, all the unique images for the chapter headings were created very carefully with this transformation in mind. Every character is transformed in images in the paperback as the story progresses. I did this in Sparktopia too, but the changes were much less dramatic.

And while Finn's transformation is quite spectacular, it's not emotional the way Tyse's is. In part one of the Godslayer paperback, the image of Tyse is somewhat innocent. Which is kind of funny since he's guilty as fuck of so much shit. But it conveys his *contentment* with his life. He's come to terms with it. The journey was long, but it was worth it. Having Clara, being back online as an augment, it was worth it.

It's only when you contrast who he is at the end of Godslayer with who he was at the beginning that you realize it wasn't. Not really. And this Game he's playing is going to ruin everything.

Playing the game isn't a choice. He can't *not* play. He's a piece on the board. So it's not even like he has to take responsibility for what's coming up in the last two books, but all the same, it's tragic.

Anyway, my point is this... I write books for the journey of my characters. And this series right here might not sell the most, might not get the best reviews, might not land the way some of my others have. But it doesn't matter.

I don't do this for the money. I certainly don't do it for the reviews. And while it was a very nice surprise that Audible chose Sparktopia as Best of the Year for 2024, it wasn't necessary.

The only thing that matters is how I felt when I wrote those words, *Thank you, Myra*. When all of the more three-hundred-thousand words previously written all lined up to paint one single picture of a man who lost everything before he was even born.

That's why I write books.

This whole EOBS is about Tyse and there's a lot to say about everyone else too. Especially Finn. As I said in the EOBS for Sparktopia, I have always believed in Finn. Yeah, he was somewhat of a jerk in the first book, but I don't blame him for that. He didn't control who he was at birth any more than Tyse did. And now... now we get to meet the REAL Finn Scott.

As far as Clara and Jasina go, they are only just beginning to understand who and what they are. And how special it was that they lived their whole lives in Low Tau City.

Jasina's story is very tragic. And what you think happened at the end, but are probably hoping it didn't, DID happen. This is life. It's nothing but a series of complex moral choices. You make decisions, and then you live with them.

Clara is the same. Tyse will keep her alive as well, but what will she be when she wakes up?

This was a true *'stand by your man'* moment for these ladies. And they did it. *If I have your back, then you must have mine.* Loyalty. That's the whole fucking point of *Love*.

I look at what 'dating' has devolved into in this 'new modern world' filled with AI, and apps, and technology that's so godlike, it's sick. And I feel sorry for these kids. They have no idea (most of them) what that word 'loyalty' even means.

But these two couples are very, *very* clear about the definition of loyalty. *If you will die for me, I will die for you.* It's more than a moral code, it's a covenant—a sacred bond that transcends convenience and circumstance, binding two souls in unbreakable trust.

And this, in my opinion, is the *definition* of romance.

Thank you for reading, thank you for reviewing, and I'll see you in the next book.

Julie
JA Huss
June 22, 2025

# ABOUT THE AUTHOR

JA Huss is a *New York Times* Bestselling author and has been on the *USA Today* Bestseller's list 21 times. She writes characters with heart, plots with twists, and perfect endings.

Her books have sold millions of copies all over the world. Her book, Eighteen, was nominated for a Voice Arts Award and an Audie Award in 2016 and 2017 respectively. Her audiobook, Mr. Perfect, was nominated for a Voice Arts Award in 2017. Her audiobook, Taking Turns, was nominated for an Audie Award in 2018. Her book, Total Exposure, was nominated for a RITA Award in 2019.

AND... Sparkopia was awarded Best of the year from Audible Editors for 2024 in Romantasy!

www.ingramcontent.com/pod-product-compliance
Lightning Source LLC
Chambersburg PA
CBHW021725190726
48289CB00008B/2694